Special Agent Mike C[illegible] stood unmoving, surrounded by three werewolves, his gun hanging lifelessly at his side. It did not cross Mike's mind to resist, he knew he was already dead.

"Please don't kill me," Mike pleaded. "I won't tell anyone you killed the other agents. Let me go, please." The fear within him was so great, that Butch whined with ecstasy. The man lost control of his bladder and a wet flow of urine ran down his right leg.

Butch said, "Cherrie, kill him for what they did to your parents."

FUR BEARER

By

John L. Fort

ISBN 978-1-60145-763-9

Printed in the United States of America.

Booklocker.com, Inc.
2009

Acknowledgements

I would like to thank Bonnie Fort, Nancy Blair and Jerry Walker for the help they provided in editing and making constructive suggestions for improving my book. I would be remiss if I did not include my three youngest grandchildren, Alexah, Evan and Juliah for listening to me read parts of the novel to them. They provided a good sounding board for me. A special thanks to my wife, ViAnn who put up with me on the computer all the time.

Table of Contents

Chapter 1
Hospitalized

Tear-shaped raindrops shattered into miniature droplets, as they pelted the black pavement. The micro-droplets bounced into the air and then dropped back to the pavement to add its minute volume to the sheet of water. The wind gusted in a syncopated thrust driving the rain horizontal for a few moments and then allowing the raindrops to fall vertically.

On the street, the rain coalesced into sheets of moving amoeba-like creatures, which fused into torrents of water swirling along the gutters. The water pooled at the end of the block and disappeared down the storm drains.

Across the street, neon lights from Denny's, Jim's Coffee House, Wilma's Tattoo Shop, a couple of beer joints, Anderson's Dry Cleaner shop, Lorraine's Specialty Clothing Store and Nick's Pawn Shop reflected from the pavement in a kaleidoscope of colors soon dispersed in the darkness. Angry, dark clouds rolled overhead pushed westward by gusting winds.

Red lights flashed down Valley Creek Road accompanied by the shrill sound of a siren. The emergency vehicle stirred the darkness sending a row of cars to the curb.

A boxy, white, Ford ambulance screamed in the night, throwing red lights out as a protest of the cold, wet night. Two cars shot through the intersection, as the stop light turned red. The ambulance swerved around the second car and continued north on Valley Creek Road toward Woodwinds Hospital on the north side of Freeway 494. A pedestrian splashed by the passing ambulance shook his fist at the retreating vehicle.

In the back of the ambulance, two paramedics worked to stanch the flow of blood from two bullet holes in the chest of a brown haired teenager. A police officer sat in the passenger seat, muttering to himself on the stupidity of kids today.

Five minutes later, the vehicle swerved down a ramp lined with bright lights on both sides of the ramp. At the bottom of the ramp loomed the emergency entrance. The ambulance turned away from the dock, stopped and then backed two feet from the waist high ramp before skidding to a stop. Floodlights high on the brick wall illuminated the scarred, rain soaked cement pad. Black trails from previous emergency vehicle tires snaked across the pad.

The driver jumped out, pushed his glasses up off the tip of his nose and hurried to the back of the ambulance. He jerked open the dual rear doors, while shielding his eyes from the pelting rain with his left hand. The right rear door banged the wooden bumper rail on the ramp and bounced back hitting his elbow. He cursed.

The police officer rolled out of the passenger's seat, pulling his plastic covered, billed cap down over his eyes. He sauntered to the back corner of the ambulance, frowning at the cursing driver.

"No need to hurry," the officer said, "this one's not going to make it." The police officer pulled his plastic raincoat over his bulging stomach and held it bunched with a pudgy fist. Instead of stopping the ambulance door from swinging, the officer stepped out of its way and watched the paramedics do their job.

The tall, blond paramedic grabbed the ambulance door as it swung back and pushed it open as he jumped out. Together the paramedics pulled the stretcher out of the ambulance. They slid the stretcher onto the ramp and then jumped up. They lifted the stretcher and the aluminum tubular frame, with wheels attached dropped to the cement, as metal sleeves slid into place, locking the frame in its upright position. Each paramedic grabbed an end of the stretcher and propelled it towards the glass entrance doors. The doors opened, spewing forth odors of alcohol, disinfectant and sickness.

The chubby police officer followed the paramedics through the doors, raincoat flapping behind him. His dark blue coat showed coffee stains and traces of powdered sugar, watered down by the rain.

A doctor in a white lab coat, accompanied by a nurse and two orderlies jogged down the hallway toward the incoming stretcher. The quartet swung around as the stretcher went by them. The orderlies took control of the stretcher relieving the paramedics of their patient.

Tension went out of the tall, blond paramedic as he dropped back to join his sandy-haired partner. Both of them trailed along behind.

The doctor leaned over the patient and forced his eyelid open. He flashed a pen light across the eyes. “What happened here?” he said.

The tall paramedic looked at the clipboard he was carrying and said, “The patient is Butch Guhl. Twice the liquor store clerk shot him. We tried to stabilize him, without much success. He is losing blood internally.”

The other paramedic said, “He is going downhill fast.”

The doctor shook his head. Concern etched his face. He gave orders to his nurse, “He is unconscious. Get a saline IV running. Type him for blood and get two pints into him fast.”

Turning to look at the paramedics, the doctor said. “What was his last blood pressure?”

The sandy-haired paramedic skipped a step to keep up and said, “89 over 54,”

“Get me x-rays of the chest and abdominal area. Let’s put him in---.” The doctor looked at the nurse with a puzzled expression.

“OP two is open,” the nurse finished.

“Okay and prep him for surgery fast.”

“Yes, Doctor,” the nurse said.

The doctor lifted the white, blood-spattered sheet covering Butch’s chest. He noted the bright red circle of blood on the two bandages. “Jesus, we might lose this one,” the doctor continued, shaking his head. When the doctor lifted the bandage, red, frothy bubbles welled from the chest wound. “It looks like his lung is penetrated,” he said.

The policeman, panting from trying to keep up with the fast moving stretcher, shook his head and said to nobody in particular, “It’ll save the county a lot of money if the bastard dies.” He raised his voice at the doctor and said, "They shot a liquor store clerk during the holdup. He’ll go to prison if he lives.”

Chapter 2
Blood Conversion

A dark-haired man with furrows etching the corners of his eyes sat on an orange, vinyl, padded chair in the emergency waiting room of Woodwinds Hospital. He picked absently at a torn piece of vinyl on the chair.

Rod Guhl thought about all the trouble his son caused him for the past several years. With a shake of his head, he thought, "and now he's in the operating room fighting for his life."

Rod was six feet two inches tall, with a narrow waist and broad shoulders. He had a runner's body. Exhaustion and worry distorted his normally handsome face.

Absentmindedly Rod picked at a loose piece of vinyl on the edge of his chair. His eyes glazed over without seeing, as he stared at the floor.

Doctor Roberts stepped into the waiting room and looked at the half dozen people inside. He walked up to Rod and said, "Hi, I'm Dr. Roberts. Are you Mr. Guhl, Butch's father?"

Rod blinked and looked up with cold, steel-colored eyes. "Yes, I am." He pulled his hand away from the broken vinyl pieces on the chair and with a coloring of red on his neck, brushed the pieces to the floor. "How's my son? Did the surgery go well?" Rod said. Wrinkles of sadness puffed out around the edges of his red eyes.

The doctor's face sagged. "He's still alive and stable. We stopped most of the bleeding, but he suffered a lot of internal damage."

In a clinical voice, the doctor went on to explain. "He lost part of the posterior lobe of his right lung. One of the bullets shattered two of his ribs and sent bone fragments slicing down through his intestines. The chance of peritoneal infection is high in these cases. We are pumping him full of antibiotics, which should control any infections. We were not able to cauterize all the damaged blood vessels, but have given him several pints of blood, which should make up for the ones we missed. They will clot on their own." The doctor shrugged, "That's all we can do for now."

Tightness grew in Rod's chest, followed by a tingling moving down his left arm, if felt like someone hit his funny bone. The tingling fanned across his chest and he felt short of breath. "What are his chances?" Rod said. His stomach churned.

The surgeon shook his head. "He had a ten percent chance to survive the next twenty-four hours. If he makes it that long, then I would say he has a fifty percent chance of pulling through."

Rod glanced at the doctor, his mouth opened with another question, but before he could speak, the doctor reached with a shaky hand and patted Rod's shoulder, and said, "I'm sorry. We did our best. His fate is in God's hands now."

"Thank you doctor, but that is not good enough," Rod said. He extended his hand and shook the Doctor's hand. Rod stood, turned from the doctor and walked toward the courtesy phone sitting on a table in the corner of the waiting room. He was going to make sure Butch survived.

The phone rang twice, followed by silence. Rod knew someone listened on the other end.

With a shaky voice Rod said, "Father, this is Rod. I'm at Woodwind Hospital."

"What's the problem?" His father said in a stern, reserved voice.

"Butch was involved in a liquor store robbery tonight. He was shot and is in the hospital I think he is going to die," Rod sobbed. "Can you come?"

A long silence followed.

"For my grandson I will come."

"Thank you."

The phone went dead.

Rod looked at the dead phone and then replaced it on the cradle. He walked back to his orange chair and sat down with a weary sigh. It took a lot of courage for Rod to call his father.

It was ten years ago that he and his father last spoke to each other. A dark family secret created the schism between them. Rod refused to let his family take part in the Guhl family's activities. Breaking from his father ostracized him, his wife and Butch, from the rest of the family. None of Rod's brothers, sisters or their children would speak to them.

Rod walked to the coffee server in the corner of the room. He stood lost in thought. After a few moments, he shook his head, dispelling the thoughts of his past that occupied his mind. He poured himself a cup of dark, bitter coffee and made his way back to the orange padded chair. He plopped down to wait the arrival of his father.

He dreaded facing his father, but it was the only way to save Butch's life. Asking his father to save Butch would force him to become involved in family affairs again. Rod shrugged his shoulders. He would wait and see what demands his father made on him. A tear welled up in his eye and slid down the edge of his nose. Would it be worth it? Was Butch's life worth it?

Twenty-five minutes later, Rod's father pushed through the glass doors of the emergency waiting room. He still looked very distinguished; six feet four inches tall, with a broad chest and steel-gray eyes. He looked the same as Rod remembered him from ten years ago. His hair was thick, gray and curly. He wore a double-breasted gray suit with a freshly ironed white shirt, fronted by a dark blue tie.

Rod's father glanced around the room until his eyes fell on Rod. He walked with brisk, quick steps across the carpet and stopped before Rod.

"Rod, what is Butch's condition now?" Jerrold Guhl said, without any formality or friendly greeting. Jerrold sat down on the twin to the orange chair Rod sat on and looked him in the eye. He straightened his suit jacket and flicked a piece of lint from his sleeve. Then his eyes locked on Rod's face.

Rod flinched, "Not good. The doctor gives him a ten percent chance to survive the next twenty-four hours." Rod rung his hands and then said, "They removed part of his right lung and stopped most of the bleeding. The second bullet shattered two of his ribs. Some of the pieces of bone tore up his intestines. The doctor said he was afraid the intestines leaked and spread infection into his abdominal cavity."

Rod stared at his father. Jerrold's eyes were shadowed and unreadable. A feeling of dread spread through Rod.

"You understand what it means if I save Butch's life?" Jerrold said, returning Rod's stare.

"Yes," Rod said, tearing his gaze from the hypnotic stare of his father.

"You are still asking me to save him?" Jerrold said.

"Yes," Rod said, holding his folded hands out toward his father, in a pose that looked as though he was begging. "I have no other choice. I love my son and I don't want him to die."

Jerrold nodded. "Okay, bring the doctor to me," he said. He leaned back in the orange chair, crossed his legs and waited for Rod to carry out his command.

A red color sprouted on both sides of Rod's throat. Ordered around as if he were a servant angered him. As usual, there was no discussion; it was his father's way or nothing. Rod rose and stormed from the waiting room to carry out his father's wishes.

Jerrold moved his shoulders away from the back of the chair and sat erect. He looked like a Bald Eagle preparing to dive on a rabbit. In his regal pose, Jerrold looked lean and feral, a formidable predator. His stance and look often instilled instant fear in other men. Crow's feet at the corner of his eyes, plus dark bushy eyebrows perched over steel-gray irises were the focal point of his face. He exhibited an untamed intensity. A vibrant magnetism surrounded him with such strength that most people encountering him felt afraid and intimidated.

Across the waiting room, a middle-aged man sat next to his wife. The man was six feet tall with oversized hands. Muscles rippled in shoulder, arms and back. He made the mistake of looking in Jerrold's direction with a smirk on his face. The man got up to get a cup of coffee and started to walk by Jerrold.

Jerrold stared at the man; letting a low growl escaped his lips.

The man's eyes swiveled and locked on Jerrold's eyes. His knees buckled and his face paled. He pivoted on weak knees and retreated to his wife. With shaking fingers, he grabbed her hand and pulled her to her feet. She protested, but he ignored what she said and led her out of the emergency waiting room.

Jerrold smiled, squared his shoulders and sat up even straighter. He knew he had won. The orange chair groaned with most of his weight on the front two legs. He intimidated the man. Jerrold was a dangerous man and enjoyed the fear he instilled in others.

Meanwhile, Rod walked down the abandoned corridor searching for the doctor. The dire circumstances that brought his father to the hospital were just what his father was looking for. Jerrold did not like his family separated. He wanted to reunite the family, to bring Rod back into the fold. Rod had fought to keep his family free of the curse, free of killing, but now that was no longer possible. Asking his father to intervene and save Butch forced him back into the evil group.

Doctor Roberts, wearing a white coat with a stethoscope draped around his neck, walked through the emergency room doors, accompanied by Rod. They hurried to where Jerrold sat. The doctor was a thin, balding man and walked with small quick steps.

Rod said, "Doctor Roberts, this is my father."

"Hello Mr. Guhl," the doctor said, offering his hand. "Rod tells me you want to talk to me regarding your grandson," The doctor looked at his watch. "What can I do for you?"

"I need absolute privacy with my grandson while I . . . ah . . . pray for him," Jerrold said.

Rod said, "The head nurse said I'd need your permission before my father could do that."

The Doctor just stared at Jerrold.

"He has my permission," Rod said, "But during the prayer session he mustn't be disturbed." His face flushed and he hoped the doctor did not notice. "Can you arrange for the necessary privacy, Doctor?"

Jerrold sprung from his chair to stand before the doctor. The doctor's eyes widened, as he involuntarily took a step backwards.

Jerrold said, "No one must interrupt my prayers. Do you understand, Doctor?" It was a command, not a request.

The doctor swayed. "Well, your request is somewhat irregular, but prayer cannot hurt anything." Doctor Roberts nodded, his Adams apple bobbed up and down with small jerks. "I will clear your request with the head nurse right away."

"Thank you, Dr. Roberts," Jerrold said. The corner of his lips curled upward.

Rod watched the exchange between his father and the doctor, afraid what his father might do. Rod sighed with relief when the doctor departed.

Now he knew Butch would survive, but he was already worried about what would happen to him after he recovered. He knew what his father was going to do. There was no doubt it would be more than enough to save Butch's life. Rod's eyes followed his father as he left the waiting room.

Jerrold stood just inside Butch's hospital room door. He stared at his grandson. He watched Butch's chest rise, followed by a slight wheezing sound at the end of the exhalation. Jerrold walked to the bedside and studied his grandson's face. The skin around Butch's lips and neck was the color of bread dough. A wave of concern ran through Jerrold's mind. The last time he saw this face was ten years ago. Butch had his grandfather's nose, eyes and ears. Jerrold's face softened as he thought how senseless the loss of those ten years was.

Jerrold paced around the glass-enclosed room, pulling the drapes shut to keep anyone from seeing what he was going to do. He slid a green, fabric-covered chair from the wall next to Butch's bed. Clear plastic tubes dripped blood, saline solution and antibiotics through a stainless steel IV needle strapped to his grandson's arm. Opening a drawer in the bedside cabinet, he found a length of rubber tubing and a packet of IV needles. He pulled two of the needles from the sterile package and attached one to each end of the rubber tubing.

Jerrold removed his jacket, flicked a couple of hairs from it, folded it and laid it on the foot of the bed. He rolled up the shirtsleeve on his left arm, tightened his fist and watched the veins of his arm pop out.

With the touch of a professional, he inserted the needle from the tube into the puffed out vessel in the bend of his elbow. His blood filled the tube and squirted out the needle at the other end. Jerrold pinched the tube to stop the flow of blood and then stuck the needle into the IV tube leading from the blood and saline solution bags to Butch's arm. Jerrold mounted the chair and sat on the back of it, elevating himself over his grandson's body.

Jerrold's blood flowed into the IV tube mingling with the antibiotics, saline solution and blood. The mixture flowed into Butch's arm and spread throughout his body.

Butch convulsed several times and then lay still. After a few minutes, Jerrold removed the needle from his arm and from the IV tube. He pulled the needles from both ends of the tube, wrapped them in a Kleenex and put them in his jacket pocket. He coiled the short rubber tube and put it in the same pocket.

An hour later, Doctor Roberts knocked lightly on the door of Butch's room. Receiving no response, he pushed his way into the room and froze. The doctor's lower jaw dropped and a shocked expression spread across his face. "What the hell is going on," the doctor stammered.

Butch was sitting up in bed talking with his grandfather. Butch turned with a puzzled look and smiled at the bewildered doctor.

The doctor rushed to Butch's bedside and with shaking hands glanced at the bank of monitors. He put a hand on Butch's forehead, while his mouth continued to sputter incomplete words. Color washed out of the doctor's face. His mind could not comprehend the fact a patient, he believed was going to die was sitting up in bed, and for all appearances, acting like a normal healthy person. There was no way his patient could have recovered that fast, maybe in three or four days, but not in a few hours. "What the hell happened? What did you do? This cannot be," the doctor sputtered.

Grandfather Jerrold laid his hand on the Doctor's shoulder. "Take it easy," he said. "We don't want you to have a heart attack."

The doctor ignored Jerrold as he began to remove the bandages covering Butch's chest. He became even more unsettled when he could not find the stitches or scars from where he cut open Butch's chest two hours ago. "This is impossible. This cannot happen." The doctor looked at Jerrold. "Prayer can't do this . . . can it?" the doctor sputtered. The strength went out of the doctor's legs and he dropped down on the green hospital chair next to the bed. He shook his head back and forth. "Tell me what you did." His arms flew in circles, as though he was trying to draw a picture of his confusion. "I do not accept this. I have never seen … My God, this is a miracle."

Jerrold glanced at Butch. "It looks like we won't be allowed to finish our visit after all. Not with all this noise." Jerrold stood up, grabbed his suit jacket from the foot of the bed, swung it over his shoulders and slipped his arms into the sleeves all in one smooth motion. "Butch, I will see you tomorrow," he said, as he walked out of the room, leaving a bug-eyed doctor staring after him.

Jerrold walked down the corridor to the emergency waiting room. Inside, he found Rod with his eyes closed, reclined on the orange vinyl sofa. As Jerrold's shadow blocked the light from the overhead fluorescent lights, Rod opened his eyes and sat up. A look of concern etched on his face.

"Relax Rod. Everything is fine," Jerrold said, with a wink and a smile. Then a serious look stole across his face. "You do understand that you are now obligated to the family? I expect you and Butch to be at the next family gathering, for his sake. You do understand why?"

"Yes father, I understand. We will be there. Just let me know when." Sadness smothered his heart, for he knew that he lost his son to the 'family'.

The next morning two police detectives walked into Butch's hospital room. Butch looked up from his breakfast.

"Hi Butch," one of the detectives said. "I'm Captain Bill Kollecki representing the Bureau of Criminal Apprehension out of St. Paul. " He pointed to the other officer and said, "This is Detective Brubaker. We'd like to ask you some questions."

Do I have to talk with you?"

"At some point in time you will. We know you did not shoot the clerk. We have a good idea who did and he is the one we really want. If you cooperate with us, we will see that you get a break. If you do not want to work with us, you have the right to have your attorney present before we ask you any questions. Is that what you want?

"No, an attorney isn't necessary."

"You realize that anything you say can be used against you in court?"

"Yes."

"You still willing to set aside your legal rights and talk with us?" Brubaker said.

"Sure."

"Okay, explain your role in the robbery?" Captain Kollecki said.

"It is simple, I let myself get shamed into taking part," Butch said, as he pushed his tray table away from his bed.

"What do you mean shamed?"

"Ben called me a chicken. He said I did not have the guts to rob a store. I could not lose face, so I said I would do it." Butch's face colored, "I guess that was stupid, huh?"

"That's too bad, because the clerk was seriously injured and that means you are just as responsible as Ben," Captain Kollecki said.

"Is Ben's last name Johnson," Brubaker asked, holding a pad up before his eyes with a pencil poised to take down Butch's answer or note his refusal.

"Yes. He lives in an apartment in Newport, just behind the Super America station."

"Address?"

I do not know the address, look for a two story building with yellow vinyl siding. There is a staircase on the side of the house leading upstairs to his apartment."

Captain Kollecki sat back on his chair and said, "Thanks for being up front with us. You realize you are in a whole lot of trouble?"

"Yes, I know. I did try to stop Ben from shooting the clerk." Butch hung his head.

"Because you cooperated and agree to testify agains Ben Johnson, we'll try to help you," Captain Kollecki said.

Butch looked up, "I'm sorry that old man was hurt. No one was supposed to get shot."

"You should have thought about that before getting involved."

"Yeah, I know that now."

Kollecki raised an eyebrow and said, "By the way, how do you explain being alive? According to the doctor, the bullets caused extensive damage to some of your organs. He expected you to die."

"I don't know," Butch said shaking his head. "All I know is that I woke up in my hospital bed with my Grandfather in the room."

"What was he doing there?"

"I, I don't know. Praying, I guess. All I remember is he was mumbling something about blood would tell and when I asked him what he meant, he said he would tell me later."

"Hmm," Bill Kollecki said pinching the point of his chin with the fingers of his left hand. "I wonder what he meant by blood will tell? With a shake of his head he added, "Beats me."

"What's going to happen to me", Butch said.

Bill Kollecki stood up followed by Brubaker. "I don't know kid. It doesn't look good." From the doorway, he turned and said, "Thanks for being honest. We'll see what the District Attorney can do for you."

An hour later, Jerrold Guhl called the St. Paul Police Headquarters and asked for Captain Bill Kollecki. The desk sergeant said Bill Kollecki was on special assignment and gave Jerrold Guhl a number to call. Jerrold tried the number. A female answered the phone and buzzed Captain Bill Kollecki.

"Good afternoon Mr. Guhl," Bill Kollecki said. "What can I do for you?"

"I understand you interrogated my grandson, at the hospital this morning. Is that correct?" Jerrold Guhl said, with firmness in his voice.

"That is correct. He admitted being involved in the robbery and the shooting of the clerk in the Woodbury Liquor Store robbery," Bill Kollecki said. "He was very cooperative."

"I don't want you or anyone else interrogating him without my attorney being present. Do you understand?"

"Don't give me that crap, Butch is an adult and consented to answer our questions. He was read his rights and everything we did was legal," Bill Kollecki said.

A cold silence hung over the open phone line and then Jerrold Guhl said in very controlled choppy words, "I don't make empty threats Captain. I produce results and if you don't follow my instructions regarding my grandson you will find out just what I mean."

"Let me ask you a question Mr. Guhl," Captain Kollecki said. "How is it your grandson survived two bullet wounds that should have killed him? What did blood have to do with his survival?"

A loud click over the phone was all Bill Kollecki got for an answer.

Chapter 3
Frustration And Confusion

Rod leaned over the drafting table in his office and put the final touches on his design for a new twenty-eight story office building. A thick stack of blueprints and drawings highlighted the last of his recommended changes. After months of effort bringing the project to this point, he was now ready to move on to the construction phase. This project above all others was his pride and joy.

He was apprehensive, thinking he was done, but feeling he forgot something important. He was experiencing the emotional high that always came him when the designing phase was completed and the construction phase was about to begin.

Next week, was his presentation of the final design to his backers. If they approved, construction would begin. He was confident approval was a mere formality. There was not another building like it in the United States. He was confident he would receive national acclaim for his architectural wizardry once the building was completed.

The phone rang, Rod jumped. He did not want to answer. He suspected who would be on the other end of the line and it filled him with dread. The phone rang again and then a third time. He stared at the phone. After six rings, he shrugged his shoulders and answered. There was no way to postpone the inevitable. Rod held the phone to his ear and waited.

After a few seconds, a voice broke the silence. "Hello, Rod, this is your father."

"Yes, I thought it might be you," Rod said without enthusiasm. His forehead wrinkled.

"The family meeting is set for two weeks from this Friday. We will meet at the hunting shack. Be there with Butch. Do you remember how to get there?"

"Yes, father, I remember. We will both be there. Goodbye." Rod hung up. His mind raced, trying to come up with some way he could break his promise. Maybe we could leave the country. What could my father do then? Butch and I could to Cancun, no, Europe. Rod's shoulders sagged he knew it was useless. Whether in Cancun or Europe, it would not make any difference.

What was going to happen to Butch would happen, whether he was at the shack, Cancun or in Europe. What Butch was going to experience needed the presence of his Grandfather and those that could help him. When he decided to involve his father, there was no way to prevent the inevitable.

On Wednesday morning, Rod, Butch, and his attorney met with the Washington County Attorney in Stillwater. The County Attorney agreed to probation for Butch in exchange for his testimony against Ben Johnson. Ben was a hardened criminal and the DA was anxious to put him in prison for good.

Something happened to him in the hospital and whatever it was changed the way he thought about everything. Butch felt guilty for testifying against Ben. His moral code said he should not rat on a friend, but then Ben was not his friend. There was another reason for giving Ben up; he lied to Butch. Ben's fingerprints were on the cash register, the glass counter top and the shotgun found in his apartment. The evidence proved Ben was the one who shot the clerk. He was a three-time loser and a jerk.

Butch gave his deposition to the County Attorney and received instructions when to appear in court to testify against Ben. Following Butch's deposition, the trial proceeded. Butch testified against Ben. Ben received a sentence of twenty-five years to life in prison.

That night after the trial ended, Butch was in his bedroom trying to sleep. His thoughts turned to the robbery and the role he played in it. He was not proud of what he did. The shooting of the store clerk still bothered him. The biggest confusion came from trying to understand how he survived. He was supposed to die, but he did not. The thought of nearly dying scared him. Something happened to him in the hospital, but his mind would not let him remember what.

Many questions plagued him. How did he heal that fast after the surgery? Why was his grandfather in his room when he woke up? He remembered being very surprised when he opened his eyes and saw his grandfather standing next to his bed. Why did he come to see me? He could not understand why after all those years he picked that night to show an interest in him.

Butch did not accept his father's explanation that he was not hurt as bad as the doctors said he was. The doctor showed him the x-rays of his wounds and they looked bad to him. What happened to the scars that should have been present from the wounds? The doctor said the wounds he worked on would leave scars and could not explain their absence.

In his mind, Butch knew he was different, some how changed. Before the robbery, he was an ass, always negative, often depressed, a loudmouth and cocksure of himself. Now those feelings were gone, he was quiet, thoughtful and reserved. He held his rebellious nature in check. The hostile feelings he exhibited toward his father changed to appreciation and respect. He could not explain the change in his personality and it bothered him.

He knew the answers were buried somewhere in his mind, but when he probed that dark spot in his memory, he could not bring them to the surface. No matter how hard he tried anything that happened after the robbery was a blank. Somewhere in all this, his Grandfather was involved, but he could not put his finger on the role he played.

His drug using, heavy drinking friends no longer came around and what surprised him the most, he did not care. Butch no longer desired to associate with them. In fact, after the first few phone calls from them, they gave up trying to get him back into the gang. He sensed something was pulling him in a new direction, but again he could not explain what it was or where it pulled him. He could not identify the forces at work and it drove him crazy.

Butch suspected his father was hiding something from him. It was almost as if his father was afraid for him. Butch was sure it was nothing to do with the robbery, but in some way involved his grandfather. Every time he asked his father what happened in the hospital, he received a frightened stare and silence.

His parents were pleased with the change in him. Butch was surprised he and his father could have a calm, intelligent conversation without yelling and screaming at each other. Hell, Butch even listened to his fathers ideals without becoming angry and running out of the house, as he used to do.

Butch sat on the edge of his bed trying to sort through everything that plagued him. He happened to look out the window and saw the full moon sitting in the sky. Yellow bolts of lightening shot through his mind. He lost consciousness and fell back on the bed.

Chapter 4
Northward To Destiny

Butch woke the next morning wondering why he was lying on top of his bed with his clothes on. There was so much happening to him he did not understand. He put the problem out of his mind.

Today was Friday, the day his dad and him were heading north for the Guhl family gathering. Butch took two sleeping bags from his closet, carried them out to the garage and threw them in the back of the Jeep Cherokee. Later, he set a bag of candy, a bag of chips, and a six-pack of Pepsi on the floor of the back seat.

Butch was excited about the trip. The last time he attended one of the family gatherings was when he was nine years old. He remembered playing with all of his cousins and all the fun times he had with them and his uncles and aunts. He remembered riding a bumpy road for a long time before they got to a big brick building that looked like a castle tucked back in the woods. He recalled being mad at his father for making him go to bed and missing the bonfire. That was the last time he saw any of his relatives.

He sensed his father was not thrilled they were going to the gathering. For the last two weeks, he complained about the three-hour trip "up north".

Many years ago, his grandfather bought six hundred and forty acres of wooded hunting land south of Crosby, Minnesota. He enclosed the entire area with a ten-foot high chain link fence topped with four rows of razor wire. The land around the enclosure was mostly state and county tax-forfeited land, used by a few grouse and deer hunters in the fall.

Butch heard the kitchen door open and his father waked into the garage carrying a cup of coffee and a sandwich.

Butch said, "Did we forget anything?"

Rod shrugged his shoulders, "No, we got everything." He set his coffee cup in the holder on the dash and laid the sandwich next to it. Rod walked out of the garage to the deck, grabbed a black suitcase, and carried it to the back of the Jeep. A frown creased his forehead, as he slid the suitcase through the back window of the Jeep. He turned to Butch and said, "Butch, Crosby's only eight miles from the shack, if we forget anything it'll give us an excuse to run into town. Then he added, "Unless your grandfather has changed, he'll have a spare of anything we forgot at the shack."

Elizabeth stuck her head through the window of the Jeep and gave Rod a peck on the cheek. Rod turned to her, gave her a kiss, and said, "Are you sure you don't want to come with?"

Butch chimed in, "Yeah, mom why don't you come?"

A pained look spread across her face. "No thanks, you know how I feel about your family. You do what you have to. I'll see both of you when you return."

Rod started the motor. Butch jumped in the front seat. Rod backed out of the garage and down the driveway. As the Jeep moved down the street Rod's thoughts were on the dreaded family gathering. With a shake of his head, he admitted to himself that it would be nice to see his brothers and sister again. Ten years was a long time.

Rod had five brothers, a sister, eight nephews and two nieces. They would all be at the shack this weekend.

The sun peeked out from behind a dark cloud. A smile broke across Rod's strained face. "Yeah, everything will be okay," he told himself.

As they passed Forest Lake on Interstate 35, Butch turned to Rod with a puzzled expression on his face. Questions raced through his mind. He still did not understand the reasons Rod gave him for getting back together with the family. He could not hold the questions back any longer, "Dad, Why are we going to the family gathering? We haven't gone for ten years."

Rod did not answer.

Butch said, "Come on Dad, the last time we were with the family I was nine years old. Why now?" Butch watched his dad pucker up his lips, as a worried look swept across his face.

Rod shrugged and said, "All I can tell you is my father and I talked that night he came to the hospital to see you. I made him a promise that if you lived, we would forget the past and take part in the family activities again."

Butch stared at his father's face searching for some clue to the hidden meaning of what he was not saying.

When Rod was a young boy, the family was close knit. When he reached the age of consent, he chose not to participate in any more of the family gatherings. He did not want that kind of life for him or his own family. What the family did was wrong and he wanted no part of it. His face sagged.

"Dad, what did Grandpa do to me in the hospital?" Butch probed a suspicious look on his face. "Dad, I know he did something. The doctors were shocked I survived." Butch's voice took on a pleading tone. "I would like to know."

Rob shook his head. "I cannot tell you son, your grandfather is the one to tell you what happened."

"Ha, then something did happen to me?"

Rod glanced over at Butch, a pleading look on his face. "Wait until tonight, will you? Then you will have all your questions answered. I promise."

Butch could tell from the look on his father's face he would not tell him anymore. He shrugged his shoulders and said, "Okay, I'll wait, but I don't know what the big deal is."

Butch crawled over the front seat and plopped down on the back seat. He pulled himself up over the back seat and grabbed a sleeping bag. He laid his head on the bag, punched it a few times until his head fit better and relaxed.

As Butch lay in the back seat, he felt a tightening around his temples. He closed his eyes tightly. Bright yellow lightening bolts flashed across his vision. He opened his eyes and saw the same golden yellow bolts zig zag across his eyes, virtually blinding him. He closed his eyes tight trying to make the flashes and pain go away. He brought his fists up to his eyes and pushed his knuckles into the sockets. The area around his temples throbbed and ached.

Every time he experienced one of those headaches, weird thoughts spun through his mind. Often the thoughts were frightening and at other times exhilarating. He kept his eyes closed and waited for the pain to subside; it never lasted too long. In a few minutes, the pain relented and he fell asleep.

When they passed through the small town of Deerwood, Rod reached into the back seat and shook Butch. "Butch, its 7:30, time to wake up, we are in Deerwood and will be at the shack soon."

Butch grumbled and rolled over.

When he did not hear any additional movement coming from the back seat Rod said, "Butch, wake up."

Butch stirred, stretched his arms over his head and pushed his hands against the roof of the jeep. "Ohhh," he said. "I could sleep for six more hours."

Rod said under his breath, "It wouldn't do you any good."

"Huh?"

"Nothing."

Gray clouds raced up from the South, as though in a hurry to cover the setting sun. The sun's rays shimmered, trying to postpone their disappearance. Red rays shot upward around the edges of the clouds, forming a golden-red corona.

Rod turned on the headlights. When he came to County Road 112, he turned south, leaving the Deerwood shortcut behind. He drove past the McMillan Truss Plant. The buildings at the plant housed machinery for converting poplar logs into wood chips. The process glued the chips together and formed roof trusses and 4 x 8 sheets of pressed wood. Yellow light shined from the windows, like eyes watching them pass.

Two miles farther down the road, Rod guided the Jeep east onto a bumpy, narrow gravel road. Another mile brought them to the forest road cutoff that took them through a thick growth of Oak, Aspen and Birch leading toward the shack.

Rod flipped the 4-wheel drive switch on as they entered the rut-filled cutoff. Fifty yards ahead, a metal gate stood open, inviting them in. Rod stared ahead into a dark foreboding tunnel of overhanging tree branches.

Thoughts of turning back raced through his mind, and then he remembered the promise he made to his father. Rod started the Jeep forward, down the dark uninviting tunnel. Destiny awaited his son.

The darkness wrapped itself around the vehicle and propelled it forward. To go on was to bring his son closer to a legacy Rod had worked hard to avoid. What his father did to Butch in the hospital meant that hard work was lost and there was no turning back.

Rod sighed and yielded to the overwhelming forces at work in his life. “SHIT,” he said, pounding his fist on the steering wheel and then he let out a big sigh. “Well, we passed the point of no return and I gave him my word.”

Butch leaned forward and hung his arms over the front seat. “What did you mean by, ‘the point of no return’, Dad?”

The corners of Rod's mouth drooped, as he said, "Nothing son, Nothing at all."

Butch pulled his face into a scowl. “You also said something about, no going back”

“I was just expressing my thoughts out-loud. Forget it, son.”

Butch shrugged and looked through the trees ahead. In a minute, he saw the lights from the shack shining from its hilltop perch. The Jeep turned up the hill. Off to the right side of the trail was a clearing.

The Jeep bounced over roots and potholes in the grassy trail, sending the headlights playing on the Hazel bushes. Butch saw black shadowy monsters rise out of the mix of light and shadows. The shadows wavered for a moment and then disappeared into the blackness. The Jeep’s headlights bounced on to new monsters in the bushes.

The clearing sloped down to a pond nestled among a grove of Spruce trees. Butch recalled a trail, which led from the shack down to the pond. He remembered walking on that path when he was ten.

“Butch,” Rod said, “do you see the pond down there?”

“Yah, I was just looking at it. The clearing and the pond sure make a nice picture,” Butch said.

“I helped Dad build benches around the pond. I bet they are still there. Do you see the field off to the side of the pond? When I was a kid, we used to play softball there and then at night we would start a roaring bonfire and roast marshmallows and wieners. My brothers, sisters and I used to have a lot of fun playing together.

Butch smiled as he pictured the scene his dad painted.

A few moments later, Butch jumped and his heart pounded in his chest. A spooky face appeared next to the car window. He recognized the face. It belonged to his Grandfather. Butch glanced at the speedometer. The Jeep was traveling twelve miles per hour and his Grandfather was running alongside the vehicle with little effort. A smile spread across his face.

"Hi Butch," Grandfather's reflection said through the window.

Butch rolled the window down, "Hi Grandpa."

Rod parked the Jeep alongside a dozen other vehicles resting in the night air, engines already cool.

Jerrold stared into the interior of the Jeep, "We've been waiting for you to arrive. The family is anxious to begin the festivities." As an afterthought, Jerrold glanced at Rod and said, "Hi son. I am glad to have you here with us again."

Butch noted the sour look on his dad's face.

"Don't worry," Jerrold said, "everything will be okay,"

Butch jumped out of the Jeep and gave his grandfather a hug. Rod walked around the Jeep and shook his father's extended hand. They walked to the back of the Jeep, grabbed their sleeping bags and other gear and followed Jerrold toward the shack.

Butch looked at the shack. Some shack. A four-story brick fortress with ten bedrooms stood before him. It looks more like an old castle.

Jerrold put his arm around Butch's shoulder and pulled him close in another hug. Together they stepped onto the wooden bridge, which took them over a small creek. The creek meandered in front of the shack and then disappeared into the darkness beneath overhanging branches of oak trees at the side of the yard.

Standing just inside the door of the shack, Butch saw two of his uncles, Richard and Bruce, behind them stood three of his cousins.

"Gosh, I have not seen them since I was nine years old. They sure have grown", he thought.

Everyone started yelling greetings at the same time. The words melded into a blur of noise. Once Butch stepped inside the shack, he felt like he belonged. It was as though the shack in all its brightness was inviting him home. There was no doubt, he missed many years of being with his family, but there was still time to make up for lost time.

When everyone quieted down, Butch was able to move around the family room and greet everyone.

"Hey, Butch, I am glad to see you," cousin Tom blurted out.

"I am happy you could come," Uncle Ben said waving from the bar.

"I haven't seen you in years. About time you came back to the family." Brad, another of his cousins said. He was Butch's favorite cousin ten years ago.

Butch felt warmth spread through him. Being part of an extended, caring family was nice. I have missed my relatives, more than I thought I would.

Butch watched his dad walk around the room greeting everyone. He looked happy to see his brothers and sisters.

Brad grabbed Butch's duffel bag and sleeping bag sitting next to the front door. He threw the sleeping bag to Butch. "Come on," he said, "I will help you get settled upstairs."

Brad led Butch up the stairs and into one of the bedrooms on the third floor. Together they laid out his sleeping bag next to Brads. Butch threw his duffel bag in a corner. They both lay down on the sleeping bags.

Brad's face broke into a wide smile. "So, you're one of us, huh, Butch?" Brad said, with a weird look covering his face.

Butch's forehead wrinkled as he looked at Brad with a questioning scowl. "What do you mean one of us?"

Brad looked at Butch with a sheepish gaze, alarm showing on his crimson face. "Oh, no, you don't know?" he blurted out.

Before Butch could pursue the mystery, someone downstairs yelled. "Come and get it."

Brad jumped up and raced for the head of the stairs. Butch lurched to his feet and followed him down the stairs, two at a time. Spread on the kitchen table was a late supper of hamburgers, hot dogs, chips, pickles, potato salad and liters of pop.

Butch followed Brad's lead and grabbed a paper plate. He heaped the plate full of food and then followed Brad out to the porch.

The rest of the teenagers soon joined them. Some sat around a long table while others seated themselves in patio chairs or sat on the floor. Everyone stuffed food into their mouths and listened as Brad brought Butch up to date on family gossip.

After they finished eating, the teenagers threw their garbage into a trashcan sitting in the corner of the porch. They ran out of the shack, across the bridge and followed a gravel path toward a bonfire that flashed in the distant clearing. They crossed an open field and followed the path around the pond.

Butch's eyes grew sensitive to the moonlight. He saw well enough to note belt loops and patterns in the clothes others were wearing. He followed his noisy cousins as they galloped through the field around him.

The whooping teenagers burst into the second clearing where the bonfire blazed high in the night air. Butch recognized two of his cousins, Jake and George, standing next to a brick fire ring filled with burning logs. He slid to a stop in the circle of light and greeted them.

After the usual arguments about the existence of ghosts and goblins, Cherrie suggested they play a game of Hooper Rye. The cousins selected Butch as the first 'catcher' and then they fled into the surrounding woods while Butch counted to the traditional one hundred. When he finished, Butch walked away from the fire, to alleviate the night blindness he was experiencing. It took a few moments for his vision to adjust to the dark. He walked along the edge of the field away from the bonfire and stared into the trees.

The flickering light from the bonfire projected between the tree trunks and illuminated leafy plants. The firelight cast shadows, which made it hard to distinguish what he was looking at. Butch squinted and strained to see beyond the shadows, looking for one of his cousins lying on the ground. He felt his cousins watching him from the darkness, waiting for him to venture into the woods after them.

Butch slipped in among the dark tree trunks and shadows. He crawled fifty feet from the edge of the clearing, until he was well beyond the lighted area. He rose to a crouch next to an oak tree. He cocked his head and listened for any movement coming from the surrounding bushes.

Butch looked up at the full moon hanging in a cloudless sky. The stars twinkled with bright flashes behind and around the yellow moon. He followed moonbeams down through the leafy canopy, where the light splattered across the forest floor, creating wavering shadows among the shrubs.

At a noise from his left, Butch's head turned in that direction. He listened and heard another noise. It sounded like cloth scraping on a bush. In a moment, his eye caught a movement in the mix of shadows and moonbeams. The motion came from where he heard the noise.

His eyesight sharpened and he recognized the silhouette of Brad. Brad stopped next to a tree with rough, scaled bark. Butch remained motionless. Brad moved with slow steps in Butch's direction. If he stuck to the direction he now moved, he would pass close to Butch.

Butch waited, controlling his breathing and movement. When Brad was a few feet from him, Butch bunched his muscles and launched himself through the air. His knees hit Brad and slipped around his waist and his arms draped around his shoulders. Brad screamed. Their tangled bodies flew through the air, arms and feet flailing around each other. The two boys landed in a heap among the ferns and grass.

Butch laughed at the thrashing bundle he held in his arms. "I guess you cannot say I didn't catch you," Butch said, as Brad continued to struggle in his arms.

Brad relaxed. "Jesus, you scared the shit out of me," he said. He shrugged Butch's arms from around him.

"Come on, you have to help me catch the others." Butch said, as he stood up and pulled Brad to his feet.

"I will let the others know I caught you," Butch said, as he cupped his mouth and yelled, "HOOPER RYE, BRAD IS CAUGHT."

Butch and Brad huddled together discussing their strategy for going after the others. They agreed to split up and walk parallel to each other, staying fifty feet apart. That way one might flush someone hiding toward the other person.

As Butch moved through the trees, he heard Brad stepping on twigs and sliding his feet through the leaves.

"Boy, with all the noise Brad is making, he's sure easy to keep tabs on," Butch said to himself. He closed his eyes and formed a mental picture of Brad stumbling along in the dark. The picture he created was so clear it surprised him.

Something was happening to him. He never saw pictures that clear in his mind before, or heard noises so far away. It amazed him how well he could see in the dark. It was not normal.

Butch's skin tingled. He felt alive. He was experiencing things he never noticed before. All of his senses were more acute. He focused his hearing and was able to detect the rustle of grass from the movement of a mouse beneath an oak tree twenty feet away.

He even saw the mouse. The blades of grass stood out individually, but in an off-green color. Butch sniffed and then turned his head into the gentle breeze, which blew from the northwest.

The wind brought the scent of a 'new victim' to him. He sniffed the air again, detecting a weak skunk-like odor. "Who the hell could that be," Butch wondered. He recalled smelling that same odor earlier tonight. Then it dawned on him. The smell came from the body odor of his cousin, Carey. He smelled that same mixture of Right Guard and sweat earlier tonight when Carey hugged him. "Wow, I'm a regular detective," Butch thought.

Butch dropped to his knees and crawled toward the scent. His unsuspecting victim would not know what hit him. Five feet in front of Butch a shadow separated from the trunk of a tree and moved in his direction. Butch froze and adjusted his vision until he was able to see Carey's outline against the backdrop of dark vegetation.

Butch covered his mouth and suppressed a giggle that tried to escape from his throat, but could not prevent a low growl from escaping from deep in his chest. "I will scare the shit out of him."

He watched Carey's head rivet back and forth looking to pinpoint where the growl came from.

"Hey, you guys," Carey whispered. "We are not supposed to do that, not until Grandpa starts the ceremony."

"GRRRRRRSSSSsss," Butch said in a louder voice this time. The growl echoed from the trees. Butch covered his mouth to stop from laughing.

“If you do it again, I’m going to change and come after you,” Carey threatened.

"Change, what did he mean? Change what?" Butch thought. “What did Carey mean?”

He decided to capture Carey before he lost track of him or he ‘changed’. Butch crawled closer to Carey and then rose up into a crouch. He launched himself through the air. Butch’s clothing brushed against some branches. Carey started to turn, but was too late. Butch’s body slammed into Carey’s chest. Together the two boys staggered and tumbled into a stand of Ironwood saplings. The boys bounced off the saplings on their way to the ground.

“Ohhh,” Carey moaned, holding the back of his head.

Butch sat up in the dark massaging his right shoulder. He felt wetness run down his arm. As he fell, a sharp stick cut his arm, drawing blood.

Carey turned toward Butch with a snarl, “Christ, Butch all you needed to do was tag me, not kill me.” Air hissed out of his lungs as he relaxed, still rubbing his head.

“Sorry, Carey,” Butch apologized. “I guess I got carried away with the game.” Butch turned to face Carey’s silhouette, resting his chin on his arms. “Say, what did you mean with that talk of changing?”

“What do you mean?” Carey said, his voice shaking. He stood and brushed debris from his shirt and pants.

“You know, when I growled at you, you said you would change and come after me. What did you mean?”

“Oh, I can’t tell you. You’ll have to wait until Grandpa explains that to you tonight during the ceremony.” Carey said, and then he walked away from Butch into the shadows.

Chapter 5
Initiation

Around midnight, members of the Guhl family meandered down to the pond area and gathered around the bonfire. The kids stopped their game and joined the adults around the fire.

The full moon was poised just above the feathery branches at the top of the surrounding trees. A thin layer of cirrus clouds moved across the lower corner of the golden orb. Moonbeams penetrated into the surrounding forest, splashing everything with a blue-white coating; witch's light. A gentle breeze stirred the vegetation, producing shadows, which moved among the trees, giving life to the darkness. The odor of pine and cherry blossoms filled the field with their presence.

Jerrold Guhl glided up to stand before the bonfire. He gazed out over the seated family members. Butch heard a rumbling growl come from deep within his Grandfather's chest and a quiet fell over the family. Butch sat next to his father on a log, just behind Uncle Richard and Brad.

Jerrold raised both of his arms with palms extended toward the moon. "Tonight we welcome back Rod and Butch, who is a new member to our pack," he said in a low haunting voice.

Butch stared at his Grandfather and then jerked back on the log when he saw his Grandfather's eyes glow with a bright metallic, red color. A trickle of fear shot through Butch's body. Goose bumps rose on the back of his arms and neck.

Butch tried to explain what he just witnessed; "It was the reflection of the red flames from the bonfire," but in his heart, he knew he lied to himself.

Jerrold lowered his arms. "Butch, when I came to you in the hospital you were dying. I saved you by giving you some of my blood. My blood saved your life and now you are one with the pack."

Butch straightened his back and leaned toward his father, "Dad, what does he mean by a member of the pack?"

"Shhh, Butch," Rod said. "Listen, everything will be explained to you soon enough."

Jerrold put up a hand to still Butch and said, "Butch, look at the moon. Does the light hurt your eyes?"

Butch stared at the full moon. The bright light held his eyes even as tears filled them and spilled down his cheeks. Butch moaned, "Oh, yes it hurts." His breath came in short gasps. His muscles contracted and relaxed like squirming worms. His mind swirled with prehistoric scenes of animals running from him in horror. With an effort, Butch tore his eyes from the moon. He leaned over to his father, and said, "Dad, what's happening to me? I feel funny, and weird thoughts are shooting through my mind."

"Butch," Jerrold's voice echoed in his mind, "You are experiencing the change. Do not fight it. As a pack member, you have to learn to control the change."

"Yes, yes, we control the change," echoed from several of the family members around the campfire.

Jerrold said, "No one is allowed to hunt alone."

A chorus responded, "We hunt as a pack."

Jerrold pushed his arms toward the moon. "If any pack member hunts without permission of the pack, they are an enemy of the pack, no longer part of the family and will be hunted down and killed. The pack must be protected and never exposed."

The chorus said. "We cannot afford exposure. We must protect the pack."

Butch felt like he was on drugs. He stared at the moving shadows outlined by the flames of the bonfire. His mouth dropped open when he caught a glimpse of several, hairy animals moving among the family members. "God, they look like wolves. No, like werewolves," his mind screamed.

Butch started to shake. Goose bumps made the hair on the back of his neck stand up. Cold shivers ran down his spine. He tried to convince himself Grandfather was just telling a scary story, but his mind would not accept that explanation.

Butch knew werewolves were fictitious beings, science fiction and makes believe. There is no way a human can change into an animal.

Butch turned to stare at the moving shadows, listening to his cousins, uncles and aunts chanting in unison, "The pack must be protected. We control the change."

Butch was not so sure anymore that werewolves were make believe. How else could he explain the furry animals moving around him?

Chapter 6
Welcome To The Pack

"I must be going crazy," Butch thought. Confusion twirled through his mind. He could not comprehend what he was seeing. He did not have enough background on which to base what was happening. He tried to convince himself that he was coming down from a high and was hallucinating. Frightened, he grabbed for his father's arm.

A thick, cloudbank rolled over the moon, thrusting the dimly lit, grassy area around the dying bonfire into darkness. Someone slammed into Butch and he lost his grip on his father's arm. Butch's eyes dilated. His head jerked around trying to locate his father. Some of his cousins and shaggy, fur-coated creatures swirled around him. He could not see well enough to recognize anyone. All he saw was moving shadows. Large hairy creatures bumped into him. He tried to move to the outside of the swirling group. He kept kicking soft mounds with his feet and tripping. He bent down and touched one of the soft mounds; it was a pile of clothing. Another creature bumped into Butch and he fell. He looked up and heard growls and snarls.

Someone added logs to the fire and flames shot into the air, lighting up the surrounding treetops. Butch's eyes flared wide, as he recognized Uncle Richard standing before him as a large werewolf. Then he identified Uncle Thomas and Cousin Brad, both fur covered beasts.

Butch's heart slammed against his chest. He jumped up and tried to back away, but his legs would not move. Yellow bolts of lightening flashed across his vision. He sagged to his knees. Dizziness swirled through his mind, he moaned, "Oh, God."

Butch closed his eyes, hoping the wolf-beings prancing around him would be gone when he opened them again, but when he opened his eyes the beasts were still there. Some of the creatures sat on their rear haunches, staring at him. Others stood upright on two padded feet. Shaggy fur covered their bodies.

The clouds drifted away from the moon and moonbeams brightened the scene around him. "My God," Butch screamed, "You are all werewolves."

He swayed from the dizziness that exploded in his head. He twisted around wanting to run and at the same time looking for his father. "I have got to get out of here," he cried.

When his vision cleared, Butch rose to his feet and started to back away from the encircling werewolves. They were not paying attention to him. He thought he was free and was poised to make a run for it, when two of the creatures grabbed his arms. Butch looked at the two of the beasts holding him. He screamed. Carey in his wolf form held his left arm in a vice grip. Brad held his right arm and growled when Butch tried to pull free.

His fur bearing cousins held him fast. Butch glanced at Carey, who growled in his face. He stared into deep yellow eyes, which shriveled his very soul. Butch thrashed and squirmed to escape, but could not free himself.

"No, No," Butch screamed. "You cannot do this to me. I will not be a part of this. Let me go. You are all crazy. Dad, Dad, Help me," he cried, struggling harder to break loose. "Dad, they are going to kill me."

Rod pushed through the circle of giant wolves. He reached his son's side and threw his arms around him. Tears rolled down his face. He stepped back and shook Butch by the shoulders. "Son, listen to me, decisions were made when you were in the hospital dying and there is no going back. You are one of them. The change is already in your blood."

Butch looked up at his father through tear-filled eyes. "No, No, I am not one of those things."

Rod sobbed and shook Butch again. "Listen to me. I needed to make a decision. You would have died in the hospital if I had not ask Grandfather to save you. He transfused his blood into you, that saved your life, but it also made you one of them.

Butch collapsed, sobbing in Rod's arms. "No, No," he moaned.

Rod held Butch. "I'm sorry, I wanted you to live. I'm sorry, it was selfish of me, but I loved you too much to let you die."

Jerrold pranced forward on pawed hind feet. Butch saw him and pushed away from his father. Jerrold shouldered Rod out of the way. Butch looked into his Grandfather's blood red eyes and knew it was true. His grandfather stood in front of him, a big, red-haired werewolf, with elongated snout and long, sharp fangs. The werewolf placed his furry arms on Butch's shoulder and then raised his head to the moon and let out a blood-curdling howl.

Butch convulsed, as electric shocks rocked through his body.

Jerrold gave Butch a shake, and in a soothing voice said, "Butch, you must not fight the change. You cannot. The change will come over you no matter what you do." He moved his hair covered paws up both sides of Butch's head and squeezed. "The pack is here to guide you and help you," he said. "You are one with the pack and we will let no harm come to you. Now, listen to me and be calm--calm--calm," he chanted.

The words filled Butch's head with a ringing echo. Calmness came over him, soothing frayed nerve endings. Calmness flooded through his body. He opened his eyes and stared into his grandfather's blood-red eyes. Something in those eyes brought comfort to him.

He glanced over his grandfather's shoulder and saw the milling group of werewolves. They were growling and snapping at the moon; possessed. The presence of all of these werewolves no longer bothered Butch. It felt natural that they should be there. Jerrold dropped his hairy paws from Butch's head and turned to the others.

Butch shook his head, as though he was waking up from a bad dream. A turbulent whirlpool of new violent feelings boiled through his mind, rising toward the surface of his consciousness. Butch threw back his head trying to blot out the wicked thoughts. He overpowered the thoughts and pushed them into a hidden recess of his mind. Relief surged through him, until he turned his head upward.

Moonlight flooded his eyes blinding him. Wicked thoughts resurfaced. He closed his eyes and screamed in pain. The moonlight penetrated his eyelids and the pain increased.

It was like looking into the sun. Flashes of light exploded on the back of his retinas, sending fireworks bursting out along neural pathways to all parts of his brain. Madness spiraled upward, growing and flooding his consciousness. An uncontrollable rage was set free within him. He wanted to kill, something, anything.

Butch struggled to break free. An overpowering will to run and kill became stronger and brought on a frantic attempt to escape those holding him. When he found he could not pull loose, a piece of rationality returned. He looked for what was holding him back and saw two of his cousins holding his arms. He screamed, "Let me go."

They were both much larger and stronger than Butch. Again, the madness welled up in him. He whipped his arms back and forth until the cousins lost their grips.

Brad and Carey glanced for help. Butch could no longer contain the inner primitive forces. The juices of change flowed without restriction.

A scream of primordial ferocity exploded from Butch's lungs. He released a howl from his contorted mouth, into the clearing. "NOOOOOOOOOooooowwwwww." His body raced through its transformation. No longer restrained by his werewolf cousins, he ripped off his clothing and dropped to his hands and knees. Coarse reddish-brown fur grew from his follicles, covering his entire body with a dense mat. The shape of his bones altered, shifting and remolding into new shapes.

His face caved in and then grew. Butch's nose protruded from his face, broad and flat, pointed fangs jutted from both upper and lower jaws. Butch's feet changed until they were round paws. Curved claws replaced the normal toenails and fingernails. Butch no longer resembled a human nor a wolf, but something in between. His front shoulders were higher than his hindquarters, so that his body sloped backwards.

Rabid thoughts flashed through Butch's mind. It was difficult to stop the madness that welled up inside of him. He wanted to kill, to rip flesh with his claws. Insatiable cravings for human blood and flesh blotted out all other thoughts.

The family of werewolves received Butch's telepathic thoughts and experienced heightened wildness. The group absorbed Butch's ungovernable rage. Fear and anger emanated from Butch in distorted waves. The other werewolves gasped and trembled, as they drank in those waves, which carried them to a higher level of excitement. Experiencing Butch's strong emotional sending encouraged a growing need to kill.

The strength of the sending by Butch shocked Jerrold. A frown creased his hairy brow and his lips peeled back in a snarl. He had never witnessed another werewolf elicit such total empathy in others. Jerrold concentrated on Butch's mental emanations and felt the animal side of his change smash into his mind with unleashed fury. He never experienced such savagery before. Jerrold flinched when he realized how this affected the others.

Jerrold grew very concerned. He needed to do something soon, before Butch would be too strong for him to control. If he did not do something quickly, he would lose control of the pack. Visions of his pack on an uncontrolled killing spree flooded his mind. Exposure of the pack would result from any unplanned killing of humans. He could not allow that to happen. He was the pack leader and responsible for keeping the pack safe. Jerrold jumped to the center of the swirling pack, knocking several werewolves aside and released a loud howl. "AAARRRROOOOOOOOOO."

Members of the pack pushed and jostled one another. Heads swiveled toward the pack leader. The leader always led the hunt and they were more than ready. Jerrold smiled at the ease with which he regained control.

He noticed a disturbance at the edge of the pack. Thomas was circling away from the pack in an agitated gait. "Oh, no," Jerrold said to himself, "He's out of control." Hard knots twisted and turned in Jerrold's stomach. A wave of nausea passed through his body as he rushed toward Thomas.

Thomas ran among the fringe of gathered werewolves, nipping at their necks, trying to entice them to follow him on a killing spree. Two of the younger werewolves turned and circled Thomas.

Jerrold overtook Thomas in two powerful leaps and rammed his shoulder into Thomas's side, sending him flying. Thomas rolled over several times and came to rest against the legs of his brother, Richard. Stunned by the blow, Thomas blinked his eyes several times. He did not remember what happened or how he ended up on the ground. Thomas's lips peeled back with fear at the rapid approach of the angry pack leader.

Jerrold leapt through the air and landed with his front legs on Thomas's stomach. The air whooshed from his lungs, like the air from a blown tire. Jerrold's muzzle flashed towards Thomas exposed throat and clamped down on fur and skin.

Thomas squeaked, but was smart enough not to offer any resistance. He froze, his earlier madness overshadowed by the fear of his eminent death. His madness was gone. Thomas knew he was one bite from death. His body went limp. In a moment, the white fangs of Jerrold relaxed. Thomas whined, as sanity seeped back into his mind. The thought of dying sobered him quickly and he no longer though of running off and killing humans.

Jerrold growled and backed away from Thomas. Jerrold turned toward the rest of the pack and sent out the mental command, "Don't let the wild side control you."

The strength of those words sent electric shocks through Butch's whole body and he dropped to the ground on all four legs like the others. Sanity flooded into his thoughts. He waited for the pack leader to issue instructions. Even though the pack needed to hunt and kill, intelligence regained dominance over the wild animal instincts.

Thomas stood and shook dust and leaf litter from his fur. Embarrassed by his loss of control, he lowered his head submissively before the others.

Jerrold shook his head in relief and thought, "I am getting to old for this. I need to step down. I averted a breakout this time, but will I be able to stop the next one?"

Butch walked on shaky feet to where his Grandfather stood. He was aroused and impatient to make his first kill. He whined.

Butch heard his Grandfather's thoughts enter his mind. "Butch, you no longer have control of your own destiny. It lies with the pack. You must never allow the animal part of you to gain the upper hand. If you cross too far to the animal side, crossing back to the human side is difficult. If you cannot control yourself, you will put the pack in great danger. Do you realize what would happen if one of us were seen as a werewolf by the humans? They would hunt us down. All of us would perish. You must remember the safety of the pack always comes first, never forget this."

"Yes, Grandfather. I hear you," Butch said.

"Good," Jerrold turned and stood erect. He released a menacing growl, "Now all of you listen to me."

The entire pack grew silent.

"Our hunt tonight will be for deer. Do not kill any other animals. No human will be harmed." Jerrold peered at Butch through red-slitted eyes. "Butch, as the newest member of our pack, you will have the honor of making your first kill with me."

Jerrold swept his gaze over the rest of the pack and said. "The rest of you control your hunt and keep your howling to a minimum. We do not want the surrounding humans to get alarmed and call the sheriff. Remember; kill one deer per team."

He looked at Butch, a proud smile on his muzzle. Jerrold turned to the rest of the pack. "Everyone should return to the campfire in three hours. Does everyone understand?"

The pack members growled their understanding of the pack leader's instructions. Small groups of werewolves broke away from the campfire and loped into the surrounding forest to begin their hunt.

Butch followed his grandfather around the edge of the pond, loping with awkward jumps, not yet used to running on four legs. He was clumsy for a few minutes, but soon adjusted and caught up to Jerrold. They followed the edge of a swamp, which took them towards Ward Lake, two miles away. Butch was amazed how easy it was to run through the woods. The trees flashed by the edge of his vision in a blur.

"Grandfather I must be running fifteen miles an hour and I'm not even breathing hard," Butch projected from his mind.

Jerrold said. "We're traveling closer to seventeen miles per hour, Butch," Jerrold corrected. "Your physiological make-up has been altered quite a bit from what you are in human form. Werewolves can run at this speed for hours without tiring."

Butch felt giddy and leapt with abandon over a fallen log, without breaking stride. A feeling of joy and true freedom flooded through his mind. Consumed with the desire to kill made him more alive than he ever felt before. Butch bunched his muscles and sprang high into the air, celebrating his newfound freedom. Butch blinked his eyes, which were still sensitive to the light from the full moon. His vision was more acute in the moonlight than it was in human form on a cloudy day.

An exhilarating feeling permeated his body and mind. It was as though the physical exertion of each step pumped euphoric compounds through his body. He never felt this free and in tune with his surroundings before. Butch could not contain the pent up feelings any longer and let slip from his muzzle, a howl of intoxication. “AAHHWhooooooooo.”

Jerrold glanced at Butch from ten feet away and allowed a snarl of understanding crease his muzzle.

Butch’s mind returned to attention, as the smell of deer musk entered his nostrils. Immediately a picture of a doe flashed into his mind. The deer was a hundred yards ahead of them, standing at the base of a fir tree, poised to run away. The deer's nose wrinkled as it sniffed the air. Butch marveled at his ability to know what the deer was experiencing.

The deer was not physically aware of any danger, but in its simple mind a tinge of anxiety over something it could not see bothered it.

Butch was amazed. The deer felt his presence, the presence of a predator even though it could not see or smell him. Butch tasted the fear emanating from the deer and it excited him, he found it hard to concentrate on what he was doing.

Butch sensed his grandfather veer to the left.

Again, it amazed him, because he could not see Jerrold; it was more a feeling that was the correct action to take. Butch responded by jumping off the trail to his right. He wondered how he knew that was what he was supposed to do. Instinct came into play and he just automatically responded.

The desire to kill grew in his mind, driving him faster and faster toward the deer; his first kill. Butch accelerated to twenty-five miles an hour.

Jerrold came in toward the deer from the left side. When Jerrold was fifty feet from the deer, he made a slight noise. The deer swiveled its head toward him. Butch was less than twenty feet from the deer, coming in from the right side. The deer bunched its muscles in preparation to flee from the noise Grandfather made.

By the time the deer made its second jump, a large, fur covered beast flew through the air over its back. The deer blinked, not comprehending a noise from its right side, when it saw the wolf being coming at it from the left. The deer was sure it was escaping from Grandfather, and bunched its massive muscles for another jump. The jump never happened.

Butch reached down, as though in slow motion, and raked the claws of his right front leg across the deer's throat. Razor sharp claws passed through the carotid artery and trachea of the animal, sending a spray of blood squirting into the night air. The stream of blood looked black in the moonlight. The deer jumped into the air and leapt two more times before dropping to the ground.

Butch hit the ground ten feet beyond the deer. He sprang back toward the deer and landed near the carcass. The deer's hind legs gave a final reflexive kick, its eyes dimmed.

Butch stood with four legs spread on both side of the deer. He reached down with his muzzle and used his canine teeth to rip a strip of flesh from the deer's throat. He threw his head back, flipping the slab of quivering meat into the air. He reared up on his hind feet and caught the descending flesh in his mouth. Warm juices and blood flowed down his throat causing him to squirm with ecstasy.

Not able to control his emotions, Butch reared back and let a howl of victory spring from his throat," AHHHHHHOOOOOO."

Butch's lips curled back with deep satisfaction when he heard the answering cries of the pack acknowledge his first kill.

Jerrold approached the kill and stopped a few feet away. Butch looked up from the bloody throat of the deer and said mentally, "Grandfather, why are you just standing there?"

Jerrold's lips curled, "Custom dictates one needs an invitation to feed by the one who makes the kill."

Butch stepped back in deference to the leader of the pack, the Alpha male. "You are my grandfather," he said. "Come feed, I cannot eat this deer by myself."

Jerrold was happy to see Butch demonstrate the proper respect by inviting him to join the feast. Butch ripped fur and flesh from the deer's hindquarters, gulping down chunks of venison. In short, order, the choice pieces of venison disappeared from the carcass as the two werewolves gorged on the deer. The two werewolves stepped back and used their long tongues to lick the blood from each other's faces.

Jerrold looked at Butch with a satisfactory expression. "Well done Butch. You made an efficient kill." Jerrold looked at the skyline. "But, the time is late, we need to return to the bonfire," he said.

Jerrold took the lead as the two ran back in the direction of the shack. Jerrold and Butch were satiated and happy with the night's hunt.

Butch broke out of the woods in the field near the pond. The glowing coals from the bonfire mesmerized and drew his eyes in an unfocused stare. He stopped well back in the shadows to check things out before continuing in to the opening. He saw his father slumped against a log near the fire. A wave of disappointed swept over him. "He couldn't even wait up to see how everything went for me."

Jerrold changed back to his human form with apparent ease and approached the fire, where he gathered up his clothes. Butch watched him throw logs on the dying embers, sending sparks twirling skyward. The area around the fire brightened and pushed back the gray of pre-dawn. Butch settled down on his rear haunches in front of the rekindled fire to await the return of the rest of the pack.

In a short time, the rest of the pack began to return. Each member approached the fire circle, walked up to Butch and licked his muzzle, congratulating him for his first successful kill. His chest pushed out, as he accepted the accolades from the pack. He hoped this was just the beginning of his adventures as a werewolf.

In the meantime, Rod woke and pulled himself up on the log in front of the fire. He watched the pack congratulating Butch. Seeing the look of excitement on Butch's muzzle brought a feeling of heaviness to Rod's heart. He knew there was nothing he could do to reverse what happened.

Butch saw his father walking toward him. He looked into his father's eyes, trying to read his thoughts.

"Dad, I made my first kill tonight," he sent from his mind.

"I know, son," Rod said, with a sad expression spreading across his face. "You are a member of the pack now and even though you have turned in to what I feared you would become, I am still happy you are alive."

Butch was disappointed. He wondered why his father showed so little excitement for him. He did not tell me he was proud I made a kill. He is unhappy I am a werewolf. At least he is happy I am alive, that is something. Butch shrugged and walked back into the trees, feeling a little depressed. The hell with it, he thought. He remembered how all of the werewolves accepted him and his dejected feeling lifted.

All of a sudden, a buzzing raced through his nerves. Butch dropped to the grass and curled up like a sleeping dog. The buzzing increased. Bolts of electricity exploded in his muscles. Feelings ran through his mind alternating between agitation and elation. Agitated because, he felt something unpleasant was going to happen to him, and yet, elated because of his accomplishments last night. The buzzing grew stronger and his body started to jerk and spasm. He staggered to his feet and moved farther into the trees where he collapsed.

"What's happening to me," he moaned. Like echoes, he heard the crunching and cracking of his bones. He was changing. Pain coursed through his muscles. Fright welled in his mind. He realized he was changing back to his human form. He whimpered. The transition took him from the height of pain, down into a valley of fear and back again. His body convulsed as the changes continued. Bones melted and then reformed into their human shapes. The pain diminished as the change reached completion. Perspiration soaked his body. He lay exhausted on the grass and leaves, but was happy the buzzing and pain were gone.

Cold seeped into his body as perspiration evaporated from his bare skin. Images of last nights activities replayed in his mind. The chase and the kill brought forth exhilarating feelings. Other emotions he experienced pushed their way to the forefront of his mind. When he realized all that really happened, his heart thumped and banged in his chest. The deer was there once again and he felt the elation of flying over its back.

Experiencing the feelings brought on an intoxicating euphoria. He wondered if killing a human being would be more exciting than killing a deer. A twinge of guilt flooded his mind, but the pleasurable thoughts from killing the deer quickly washed away the guilt. "I cannot wait for the next hunt, he thought."

Jerrold stood behind some trees and shrubs and watched Butch go through his change back to his human form. When Butch was finished, Jerrold approached him.

The hair at the base of Butch's head sprang erect as he sensed his grandfather's presence. Butch rolled over and his eyes riveted on his grandfather's eyes.

Jerrold was surprised Butch became aware of his presence that fast. Jerrold had never seen another werewolf adapt that quickly. Butch was on his way to becoming an exceptional werewolf. A big smile widened across Jerrold's face at Butch's nakedness. Jerrold removed his jacket, draped it over Butch's shoulder, and smiled again when Butch blushed.

"Grandpa, I didn't realize I was naked. Where are my clothes?" he said, trying to cover his genital area. He slid the jacket down around his waist and tied the arms together.

"You shredded them when you changed," Jerrold said. "You will learn to remove your clothing before making the change then you will have them when you change back. Don't worry now, you can get dressed when we go back to the shack."

Jerrold put his arm around Butch's shoulder and guided him toward a bench overlooking the pond. Grandfather sat down, leaned back, extended his feet in front of him and crossed them at his ankles. With a contented look, Jerrold gazed out over the pond, watching the cattails sway before a light breeze. Lily pads, yellow-blue in the gray of predawn, danced at the pleasure of miniature waves. Jerrold patted the spot next to him. Butch sat on the edge of the bench.

Jerrold stared at Butch for a moment and then said, "Butch, I know a lot has happened to you in a short time. I am sure you have a lot of questions, you'd like answered."

Butch leaned forward and his mouth dropped open.

Jerrold raised a hand. "Let me finish and then I will answer any questions you have. Right now, I need to make sure you understand some important things that come with being a part of a werewolf pack. What I'm going to tell you will answer some of your questions."

Butch nodded toward Jerrold. "Yes, I have a lot of questions, but I will wait."

Jerrold uncrossed his legs and sat up straight. "Among humans, there exist many superstitions about werewolves."

Butch shook his head, but said nothing.

"You've perhaps heard that vampires and werewolves can be killed by silver bullets," Jerrold said. "That's a bunch of nonsense. The truth is any weapon can kill us just as it kills any other being. The real difference is that we heal much faster than humans do. Our tissues possess special properties that repairs damaged cells and flesh usually within minutes."

"Another misunderstanding that has been around for hundreds of years is the idea that werewolves must change every time a full moon lights the sky. That is pure hogwash," Jerrold said. "We normally have full control over the change, when and where the change takes place." Jerrold said, "We do need to eat human flesh but can go without it for five years. We have found if we wait longer than that, we start to lose control of our change. When that happens, we can be lost to the wild side for good. Human flesh and our bodies need for it is by far the biggest factor forcing our transformation."

Butch could not hold back any longer. "But, tonight as soon as I felt the moonlight, it hurt my eyes and I started to change," Butch, blurted out.

Jerrold smiled, "Remember this was your first time. When you are not prepared or are in a weakened condition, the full moon can be influential in causing a change. If you are in control, you cannot change unless you choose to. Moonlight does have an effect on us, it still excites me after all these years, but it is a minor factor in bringing on the change."

Jerrold reached over and grabbed Butch by the shoulder and in a serious voice said, "But, the main thing I want to emphasize is the importance of maintaining a tight reign on your control. Once you lose control of the change, the madness makes you careless and you end up doing something crazy. For example, you may kill a human in front of witnesses." A shudder vibrated through the bench as Jerrold shivered. His voice became louder. "Under no circumstances can you ever be seen in your werewolf form. If humans learn we exist, they'll hunt us down and exterminate us."

Butch absorbed the fear permeating from his grandfather and turned toward him, a concerned look on his face. "Grandpa, Butch said, "I did not control my change tonight, it just happened. How do I learn to control it?"

Jerrold leaned forward a smile creasing his face. "Don't worry Butch," he said in a comforting tone, as he dropped a hand off Butch's shoulder. "We'll guide you until you have full control of your change. Once you gain full control, you can exist in either form. Seriousness crept back into Jerrold's voice, "The safety of the pack must be your first consideration." Jerrold cleared his throat. "To avoid anyone hunting on their own, the family plans a controlled human hunt every five years. This has worked well for us. No one has gone over to the wild side since I became pack leader.

"But, Thomas lost control tonight," Butch reminded him.

"Yes, he did," Jerrold said, lowering his head. "I stopped Thomas from going all the way over. If I couldn't have stopped him, I would have been forced to kill him," Jerrold said, looking up into Butch's eyes. "Do you know what sent him over the edge?"

Butch shrugged his shoulders and said, "No."

Jerrold said, "Last night you were the cause of Thomas's wildness."

"Me?"

"Yes, you, when you were going through your change, your emotions were unchecked. Those emotions transmitted to all of the pack. Thomas did not hold his emotions in check and balanced on the edge of the wild side. I hope you see how important maintaining self-control is?"

Butch gulped before responding, "Gosh, grandfather I did not know. I will control myself in the future."

"I know you will."

Curious, Butch said, “Have you ever seen anyone go all the way over to the wild side?”

Jerrold hesitated for a moment and then said, “Yes, before my father became a werewolf, a whole pack lost control and stayed on the wild side. He and the townsmen hunted the werewolves down and killed them. That pack was out of control and because of it the humans hunted them down and destroyed them.”

“That must have happened before your time,” Butch said.

“Yes, it was. There was one other instance of someone going over to the wild side,” Jerrold shook his head remembering the incident. “When I was a young man, I was involved in tracking him down. It was a very sad time for my family. One of my uncles’ lost control. My father and I hunted him down. We caught up to him in an isolated rural area and killed him.” Jerrold stopped talking with a choked sob. After a moment, he said, “We ripped him to shreds.”

“That is what would happen to me if I lost control?” Butch said, hoping he was the exception.

“Yes, the pack would hunt you down and kill you,” Jerrold said. “Remember once you have gone over to the wild side, getting back is next to impossible, at least it is questionable you would ever make your way back to sanity,” Grandfather said.

Butch shivered as a picture formed in his mind of his own family ripping him apart. “Don’t worry Grandfather, I won’t ever forget.” Butch leaned forward on the park bench, his eyes widened. “Are all of my relatives werewolves?” he said.

“Not your parents. Rod decided not to become a werewolf, and you wouldn’t have been one either, except he called on me to save your life.”

"But, I don't understand. Why isn't dad one?"

"All family members have a choice of becoming a werewolf or remaining a human. Some chose not to become werewolves, but they still serve the family in other ways. Except for your father, the rest of the non-werewolf members were involved in family hunts and activities. The fact I saved your life obligates your dad to become involved in the packs activities once again."

"Why didn't dad work with the family?" Butch said, trying to understand.

"He was ashamed of us. He wanted nothing to do with the pack from the time he was a child. He preferred to isolate himself and his own family from us."

"Oh, I see, he does not accept the werewolf way of life," Butch said.

"You are right," Jerrold, said. "But, when he asked me to save your life, he knew the cost. Only an active pack member can ask a favor of the Alpha. When he asked me to save your life, he knew you would become one of us. Even though he is not a werewolf, he is now obligated to take part in family matters from now on."

A lump grew in Butch's throat. He reached over and placed his hand on the back of his Grandfathers. "I'm glad you saved me. I have never felt as alive as I did tonight when we were hunting that deer. I am glad dad is a part of the family. He'll be here when I need him."

Jerrold gazed over the pond and watched a pink bubble grow on the horizon. He took Butch's hand in his own. "Listen to what I'm going to tell you," Jerrold said, as he gazed into Butch's eyes. "To kill a human is a privilege requiring permission from the pack leader. In the second place, every member must preserve the secrecy of the pack. If humans learn of our existence, they will hunt us down and destroy us. The extinction of the pack is my greatest fear."

Butch pulled his hand free from his Grandfather. "I know, Grandpa, you already told me that," Butch grew annoyed; he did not like childish treatment.

Jerrold noted the irritation in Butch and said. "Well, here's something you don't know. You will live much longer than a human."

A puzzled look appeared on Butch's face, "How much longer?"

"At least three to four hundred years."

"What? That is unbelievable. You mean I won't die when I'm seventy or eighty?"

"No, you will live a long time, unless someone kills you."

Butch slapped his leg. "Hell, that's wonderful."

"Yes, but it will also create some problems for you."

Butch's eyebrows furrowed. He could not think of any disadvantages of living four hundred years. "How can living that long be a bad thing," Butch said. I will be immortal, flashed through his mind.

"For instance, do you plan on ever getting married?" Jerrold said.

"Well, sure I do."

"What happens when your wife grows old and dies long before you do?"

Butch thought about losing someone he loved and understood what Grandfather was trying to tell him.

Jerrold hesitated and then said, "Of course, you could always make her a werewolf."

Butch's face brightened, as the problem appeared solved. "Yeah, I could do that."

"I have married three times," Grandfather said. "Each time my wife chose to remain a human. I have outlived each of these women I loved." Grandfather looked down.

Butch watched sadness sweep over his grandfather's face.

"It hurts to lose someone you've loved for forty years or longer."

Butch leaned back as understanding flooded his face. "I see what you mean," he said.

"The sun will be up soon," Jerrold said. "Let's get back to the shack and get you some clothes and a few hours sleep."

Butch extended his hand and stopped Jerrold from getting up. "Grandfather, before we go, explain to me how you control the change?"

Jerrold could see from Butch's expression that he was concerned.

"Last night, the change just happened. I did not control it," A tear coursed down his cheek. "What if it happens when I don't want it to?"

Jerrold patted Butch's hand, "Don't worry, to change takes effort on your part. Like learning anything new, you will find a way that works best for you and then perfect it. Some of us use anger to work the change. Others recall previous experiences or feelings to bring on the change."

Butch's eyes grew bigger. "You mean, like when I saw that all of you were werewolves, the fear I felt caused me to change?"

"Yes, fear brought on your change last night," Jerrold said. "It may not be the way you do it in the future. Just make sure you find a method you can control," Jerrold said, as he pinched his lips into a pout and then said. "Anger isn't the best way to bring on the change; most of us cannot control our anger well enough. It often results in things getting out of hand. With anger, you might find yourself changing too fast. If that happens, you have to regain control of your thoughts and reverse the process."

"But, how do I control my anger or whatever method I choose?"

"Balance is the key," Jerrold said. "Remember, as a werewolf, you still retain your intelligence. You have to learn at what point to stop the transition. If you let it go too far, you will cross to the animal side and experience total madness."

"How far did Uncle Thomas go?" Butch said. "He lost control didn't he?"

Jerrold felt goose bumps rise on his arms, as he remembered the earlier incident. "He was about half way. He was going to lose control. If I didn't stop him, he would've crossed over."

"What would he have done?"

"When you are on the wild side, only human flesh will satisfy the madness. Thomas would have run off in search of the nearest humans and killed them." Jerrold grabbed Butch's arm. "Can you see what that would have done to the rest of us? We would likely have been exposed through his madness." Jerrold's voice caught. "I would have killed him tonight rather than let that happen to the pack."

Knowing that his Grandfather would have killed his uncle for losing control, he knew he would not hesitate to kill Butch if he lost control.

Butch stared at the ground and then looked up and changed the subject. “You know, Grandfather, I have thought about killing another human being. I don’t know if I can do it.” A pained expression covered Butch’s face. “What if I can’t?”

Jerrold smiled. “That should be the least of your concerns. Take my word for it; you will be able to dispatch a human when the time comes, my son. The desire for human flesh will increase in you, until your entire mind can think of nothing else. You will have to kill and eat human flesh to drive the incessant thoughts from your mind. If you do not, the animal within you will rise up and take control.”

Butch did not understand everything his grandfather told him. “Why is human flesh special? I was satisfied after killing and eating the deer last night,” he said.

Jerrold said, “You became a werewolf for the first time last night. The need for human flesh has not developed in you yet, but it will. We do not know what makes human flesh able to satisfy our craving, but it does. There may be some chemical present in human flesh that helps us keep the animal side in submission.” Jerrold said. “Maybe the frenzy that goes along with killing a human satisfies the need to kill again or maybe the excitement of the hunt, the chase and the kill. Hunting and killing deer is nothing compared to hunting and killing humans.” Grandfather shook his head. “Whatever the reason, all I know is that every five years I have to kill and eat human flesh or risk madness.”

Butch gave serious thought to what his Grandfather shared with him. He nodded, “I hope I’m ready when the time comes. You know,” he blinked. “I got a lot of pleasure from hunting and killing that deer tonight, but killing a human will take some getting used to,” Butch said.

Jerrold faded from Butch’s eyesight, as thoughts of the night's hunt raced through his mind; his heart started thumping in his chest. The picture of the deer in his mind brought back the wonderful feelings he experienced during the chase and the kill. Maybe I can use these thoughts to start my change.

He blinked and Jerrold was still standing before him. A few seconds must have elapsed.

“I know what you’re saying Butch, but when the time comes, you will kill humans and enjoy doing it.”

Butch gave his grandfather’s words some more thought. He was shocked when his subconscious mind considered the idea of killing humans, of eating another human being. The excitement that grew in his mind was euphoric. The desire to taste human flesh welled up in his mind. He shook his buzzing head and realized that when the time came to kill a human being he would not hesitate. His human side tried to tell him it was wrong to kill a human, but the stronger animal side rationalized the necessity for doing it.

“When will I be able to hunt humans?” Butch said.

“I have scheduled a hunt for this coming October. We’ll do it the night of the harvest moon.” Grandfather said.

Butch straightened his shoulders. “Grandfather, I think I will be ready. Should I feel guilty?”

“No, my son, we are what we are. Being a werewolf is what we are. We do not have to apologize for what we have inherited. We have no more control over our needs than any of our other drives, such as thirst, hunger, sex or survival.”

Grandfather put his arms around Butch and hugged him. Butch knew that a special bond had formed between them with that hug. They turned without speaking and walked up the path toward the shack, Grandfather’s arm around Butch’s shoulder.

The sunshine of a new dawn broke over the treetops signaling the beginning of not just a new day, but also maybe a new era.

"Hmm, this one has a special power," Jerrold thought to himself. "I’m going to have to keep an eye on him. Before I know it, he’ll be challenging me for leadership of the pack," Jerrold smiled.

Chapter 7
Let's Plan The Feast

The first Saturday in July started out as a dark and dreary day. Black cumulonimbus clouds rolled overhead threatening the peace and tranquility of what should have been a memorable day. Accompanying the menacing weather was a cold wind blowing out of the north. For once, the weatherman forecast the correct weather. Raindrops splattered against the basement window. The rat-tat-tat noise of pieces of ice hitting the window caught Butch's attention.

Butch poked Brad and pointed to the windows. Brad made a face, hit Carey on the arm, and pointed to the ice droplets on the window.

Carey pounded the arm of the couch. "Shit, that's all we need, an ice storm in July."

The entire Guhl pack gathered in the basement of Grandpa Jerrold's mansion. The meeting room was more than adequate to hold all the family members. They waited for Jerrold to start the meeting. Older family members sat around a large, oval, mahogany table occupying the center of the room. The non-werewolf members made up the second circle, sitting on chairs and sofas.

The walls of the meeting room were ten feet high. Ornate decorations and expensive family portraits covered the walls. The house served as the headquarters for the Guhl werewolf pack. Who would expect a werewolf to live in the prestigious and expensive Wedgwood development in Woodbury, Minnesota? The back of the mansion faced an eighteen hole golf course. Mansion-sized homes occupied the land around Colby Lake and extended to the south and east.

Logs blazed in the massive brick fireplace at the end of the room, creating a cozy atmosphere for an unusual meeting. Brad complained the basement felt like a sauna. Avoiding the heat was one of the reasons Butch, Carey and Brad sat on the floor against the wall, where it was cooler.

This was a very important meeting. The Guhl pack was here to plan for their human hunt and feast in October. Butch jumped when Jerrold banged his hands on the table. “Okay everyone,” he said from the head of the great table. “Let’s get down to business.”

Butch pushed Carey over and sat up with a determined look on his face. He did not want to miss anything to do with his first hunt.

Jerrold turned the slide projector on. An enlarged map of Minnesota flashed onto a beady, white screen, suspended over the fireplace.

“The summer is coming to an end and we need to begin preparations for our Autumn Hunt. I know many of you have been traveling and searching for a suitable target. Let’s hear what you have found for the group to consider?” Jerrold said, as he panned the room waiting for a response.

Brad started to whisper something to Butch.

“Brad, be quiet,” Butch said. “I don’t want to miss anything.”

Brad leaned back against the wall with a sullen look on his face.

Uncle Bruce with his jet-black hair and smooth olive skin pushed his chair back from the table and stood up. “Yes, father,” he said, “I have scouted the town of McGregor, it‘s located on Highway 210.”

Jerrold slapped a pointer on the screen and looked with a quizzical expression pasted on his face at Bruce, waiting for additional directions.

“Farther to the right.”

The pointer moved across the screen.

“East of Aitkin,” Bruce said. “Yes, right there. The town has a population of 450 people.”

Jerrold studied the spot on the map and the surrounding area for a minute and then said, “Okay, any comments?”

Uncle Thomas raised his hand, like a school kid.

Jerrold smiled. “Thomas, what have you got?”

“I have found the perfect spot. This town is smaller than McGregor, two hundred and forty people. It is located in the western part of the state, just east of Fergus Falls.”

Jerrold moved the pointer to the western boundary of Minnesota.

"Right there, father, by the lake, ah, Ottertail." Thomas waited until his father moved the pointer to the right spot before continuing. "The area is a quiet farming community located on Highway 108. We would have to block traffic on the east and west sides of town. I found three possible escape routes; one being across the lake, another through farm land and the third, on one of three roads leading out of town."

Jerrold studied Thomas's selection and then turned back to the group. "Good job boys," Jerrold said, "both spots look like they have potential."

Butch watched Jerrold, suspecting he did not like either of the spots mentioned.

Jerrold looked around the room before saying, "Any other targets?"

Butch watched Uncle Steve lean back with a fanatical pose, studying the map, deep furrows creased his forehead. "I don't like McGregor," he said more to himself, but loud enough for everyone to hear. "The population is too large for our family to handle without losing control of the situation. With that many people, the chance someone would escape and summon help is too great. We cannot afford exposure or the chance of not being able to make a safe withdrawal. It might be a problem to interrupt traffic on Highway 210, because of the large amount of traffic. All that heavy traffic might get in the way of our project and lead to someone seeing something they should not see."

"Good point Steve," chimed in Barbara. She flipped the bottom of her curls and then without being aware of what she was doing, wrapped hair around her fingers. "I was thinking the same thing, regarding both McGregor and Ottertail." She banged her pencil twice on the table to emphasize her point. "In the past, we've always concentrated on towns having less than two hundred people."

Diana interrupted in a high-pitched voice. "Well, Barbara, if you don't like those targets, let me tell you the perfect city for this year's feeding."

Even though Diana was not a werewolf member of the family, like others at the table, she was still involved in pack activities. In working with her, Butch found her thoughtful and levelheaded.

"Andy, the kids and I spent a week in June vacationing near a small town called Longville located in North Central Minnesota."

Jerrold moved the pointer across the map and looked at her for directions.

"Farther to the right, Grandfather, No, East of Walker on Highway 200," she directed. "Now, go south on Highway 84. Okay, there you got it. The population is 195. We would have to block Highway 84, both north and south of town. The two small county roads, Highway 5 from the east and Highway 7 from the west should not be a problem and we could use either of them as escape routes. If those roads were not an option, the surrounding wooded areas offer many escape routes. For example, Land O Lakes State Forest is just southeast of Longville. The whole area is a wilderness in which we could disappear without a trace. Swamp land to the east of town would make a nice place to dispose of our kills."

Butch smiled when Diana sucked in a big volume of air and continued talking.

"Longville looks like a better city than the one we ravaged five years ago." She pumped her hand in the air trying to remember the name of it. "What was the name of that town?"

"It was, ah, Littlefork," Francis said. He was Jerrold's sixth son, the only blond child in the Guhl family.

"Yeah, that's right," Diana said, shaking her head. "Well, Dad. How does Longville look to you?"

Jerrold studied the map, looking back and forth between the three suggested sites. A few heads began to nod. Smiles broke out on faces of several of the older pack members seated around the table.

Butch felt a rise of excitement in the room. He suspected his first hunt for humans would take place in Longville.

Grandfather looked around the room and noted the nodding heads, "Okay, it looks like we've picked the town, let's get down to assignments." He clicked to the next slide and a list of names and assignments jumped on the screen.

Coordination of project--Jerrold
Street and house attack assignments--Richard, Amy, Aerial
Road isolation--Bruce, Barbara, George, Butch & young Tom
Communications disruption--Francis, Steve, Xianth, Fred & Aerial
Escape routes and safe houses--Thomas, Brad, Jake, Elliot & Carey
Community scouts--Diana, Andy, young George, Coreen & Cherrie

Jerrold gave everyone ample time to study the assignments and then said, "If you have any objections to your assignments and would prefer a different one, talk to me," he said.

Thomas scratched his head. "How many hideouts should we plan on?"

Richard turned toward his younger brother, "Last time we set up two, but did not use either of them. That doesn't mean we won't need them this time." He looked at his father. "Dad, this looks good to me. Do we need more than two?"

"You'd better plan on a minimum of two places again. Just make sure to plan for every possible contingency."

"Our fund balance is sufficient, so money's no problem," Richard said. "Don't be concerned with expenses, but make sure you turn in expense vouchers.

Butch caught his grandfather looking at him and flinched at the intensity of his gaze.

Then Jerrold said. "The full moon occurs on the third Wednesday in October. I have set our attack for that night. The pack will meet in one month, which should give everyone time to work out the details of their assignments and arrange vacation time. Until then, report any useful information or finalized parts of your assignments to me. I will add your information to our database.

Remember, we kill only one person for each werewolf. As in the past, it will raise a big stink, but should not lead to an intensive investigation, as long as we make sure we carefully dispose of the remains of our kills. Plans must be completed a week before the full moon or we will have to postpone the attack until November.

"Okay remember, we need to do it right, so we don't put ourselves at risk for another five years. If anything goes wrong during the attack and we do not complete our quota, we will set up a secondary attack site for November. The worst thing that could possibly happen is exposure."

Butch felt the emotional excitement emanating from others in the room. Like an aphrodisiac, a growing excitement pulsed through his body. Pictures of his deer kill earlier in the summer rolled like a film through his mind. For him, the deer kill was a memorable time for him, where he lived on the edge. It was hard to imagine killing humans could be that much better than killing a deer. He did understand there was much more at stake in an operation involving so many werewolves and the killing of humans.

Fear shot through his mind when he considered that humans would hunt them down if they screwed up. He realized the need to plan carefully, as they were doing.

He returned to the moment and heard his grandfather say, "If there are no other comments or concerns, let's go to work. Happy Hunting."

The next day, Diana called Woman Lake Lodge and arranged to stay with them again. She wanted the same cabin her family used in June and was surprised when the owner said it was available. Andy placed their dry cleaning business in the hands of Walter Jacobson, their office manager, for the rest of July and August. The following Monday they left on a month's vacation.

As second in command, Richard insisted that before the pack carried out the invasion of Longville, everyone must visit and become familiar with the town. It was important they see the houses they were going to attack and where they would dispose of their kills. Once the safe sites were set up, each pack member would travel the various escape routes. Andy worked out a schedule of when each of the pack members would visit the Longville area and stay with Diana and

Andy on Woman Lake. This would be the packs base of operations while in the Longville area.

Butch, Carey and Brad started referring to the expedition in October as 'Moonlight Madness' soon everyone was using the title.

Bruce, Barbara and Tom drove up to Longville two days after Diana and Andy settled in the resort. They met with the Hansen Real Estate agency. They let the realtor know they were looking for two parcels of land to buy along Highway 84. The real estate agent took them to look at two twenty sites, one on the north side and the other south of town. The cost of the wooded parcels was inflated, but they did not haggle over a few dollars and purchased both of them.

Water covered part of the property closest to the highway. Culverts under the highway would drain the wet spots and a road into the property would make the parcels acceptable to build on. Putting in culverts was the perfect reason for digging up Highway 84 and stopping traffic the night of the attack.

Thomas, Jake and Elliot hired a four-passenger Cessna to fly them to Longville during the second week of July. The reason given was to scout out a good deer hunting spot for November's hunting season. They spent the whole week flying over the area. Using aerial maps, they located three different trails leading to safe sites at two nearby resorts. They entertained the pilot in the evenings by hitting all of the local dance spots and bars.

Brad and Carey arrived in Longville toward the end of the second week of July and grumbled as they hiked the trails. The mosquitoes and black flies were tenacious, especially when hiking in human form through the swamps. Once they confirmed the usability of the trails, they reserved six cabins at both resorts for the whole month of October. A number of the spouses, who were not werewolves, would occupy the cabins and have everything set up in case an emergency came up.

George and Butch drove to Walker, the county seat for Cass County. At the courthouse, they arranged for the necessary permits needed to dig up Highway 84. After getting the go ahead, they hired an excavation company from Walker to install the culverts under

Highway 84, at sites, north and south of Longville. They insisted the digging take place on the day of the attack, Wednesday.

When Francis and Xianth visited Woman Lake Lodge the last week in July, they spent time locating telephone, electrical relay stations and cell phone towers. It took them several days to select the best spots to disrupt communications to the town. By the time their vacation was finished, they had mapped the best approach to the structures where they would put them out of commission.

Three days later, Fred, Aerial and Steve joined Francis and Xianth in Longville. They spent a few days water skiing and fishing on Woman Lake. In the evenings, they enjoyed the nightclubs in the area. They spent the last day before they were to return to the Twin Cities locating the exact address of every ham operator with battery backup in Longville. Finding the ham operators were easy, just look for their antennas. It took a little deeper digging to determine which ones possessed battery back up. They would be the first people in Longville to die.

September arrived. School reopened and everything was proceeding as planned toward 'Moonlight Madness'. Every few days, information poured in from the various teams. When Butch was in the Twin Cities, he helped load the information into grandfather's computers. The files were full of valuable information; including each members name and assignment, a time line of when persons would journey to Longville and with whom, what they were to accomplish and once the job was completed a write up of their findings.

Jerrold insisted the plan be in such detail that he would know where everyone was at any given minute during the actual attack.

October started out as a dry, warm month. Jerrold sat in the library studying the computer screen. Closing the Venetian blinds covering the wide expanse of windows on the south wall of the room kept out the bright sunlight. The dimmed room made it easier to see the computer screens. Jerrold stared at the information on the screen, reading the material over for the third time. He smiled with pride at the efficiency of his children and grandchildren. He was confident the details of the plan to attack Longville were fine-tuned. There should be no problems.

Across the Library from his grandfather, Butch rested in a leather recliner. He was analyzing printouts from the accumulated information coming in for the 'Moonlight Madness' project. He read page after page, running a red pen through changes and writing in the margin how he would modify the plan.

Butch's eyes watered and itched from staring and not blinking. He pushed his knuckles against his eyelids and moved them back and forth, relieving the itch. He looked up from the printout and gazed at his grandfather. Since Butch, began working on the Longville raid, his every thought focused on each facet of the plan. Being involved made him feel needed and an important part of the pack. He wondered if it was all the detailed work, he did on the plan or was it the prize at the end of all the planning that made him feel extremely alive.

Butch's thoughts flashed back several months, to his former life, as a stupid, lost kid. It seemed like that life was a long time ago, ancient history now. He understood why his father had been so disappointed in him. He was a liar, a cheat and high on drugs most of the time. In his new life, everything changed, he was responsible and dedicated, and he belonged to the family. Others depended on him to do his job, and he worked hard to do it to the best of his ability. He felt belonged.

Butch's imagination took him off into one of his daydreams. He told himself, "Someday I will lead the pack." He understood that in order for him to do that he would have to challenge his Grandfather for leadership. He would have to fight him and force him to step down. He could picture the two of them standing nose to nose ready to do battle. After he was victorious, he would change the way things operated in the pack. He pictured himself speaking to the pack at a future five year planning session. He would be the one that everyone looked to for leadership.

Butch jumped to a new scene that appeared in his head. He saw himself breaking down the front door of a home, attacking and killing the people inside. The scene was real in his mind. His heart started to pump and bang in his chest. He moaned at the realism of the daydream. He could almost taste the human flesh. The vision looked so real, saliva squirted into his mouth at the thought of eating human flesh. His stomach growled in protest, it wanted the real thing. Sweat beaded on his skin, coalesced and ran down his forehead. A loud buzzing grew in his mind. He moaned aloud, losing his daydream.

His heart still slammed against his ribs. He gasped for breath. His hands tingled. He held them up to his face and recoiled. A dense mass of tangled fur covered the misshapen bony structure of his former hands, fingernails curled into claws. With a frightened inhalation, he brushed his face with his hand and felt a knobby, elongated jawbone. He moved his hand down the length of the jaw and felt the sharp fangs protruding from his mouth. "Oh God, I'm changing. I have got to stop it."

The springs of Jerrold's chair squeaked as he turned and watched Butch fight the transformation.

Butch focused on what was happening to him. He was not aware of Jerrold or the squeaking chair. Butch said, "Shit." He trembled and slipped to the edge of his chair. "I won't lose control. I can't," he said. He bit down on his tongue, pain shot through his mind. Blood leaked from the edge of his mouth.

Anxiety and fear over the change caused it to accelerate. His spine cracked, reshaping itself to better accommodate the contour of the werewolf form. Butch was afraid if he did not stop the emotional high he was experiencing; he would lose control and end up locked on the wild side.

Butch took in a deep breath of air and let it out with a hiss. He forced himself to visualize white, cottony clouds, floating in a bright, blue sky. He focused on relaxing his muscles, as he floated on one of the soft clouds. Butch crunched his eyes closed and saw yellow stars exploding on a black background. He pictured his racing heart and then clamping down on this thought tried to slow his heart rate by one beat and then another. After a few anxious seconds, the beat of his heart slowed.

He felt there might be a chance to regain control of his runaway emotions. He breathed in and then let the air escape from his lungs.

He concentrated on calm thoughts and pictured himself in human form. In seconds, the crunching of bones stopped. The room was quiet for what seemed like an eternity and then Butch felt his bones begin to bend and melt, as the reversal began. The change back to a human picked up speed.

After a while, Butch opened his eyes and glanced at his hands. A wave of relief swept through his stomach. His hands were human again. He sighed with relief. His body began to shake. Perspiration beads dotted his forehead and then coalesced to run down the side of his face.

Butch jumped when he heard his Grandfather‘s voice, “Well done, my boy.”

Butch turned with a snarl to see Jerrold examining him from across the room.

Grandfather stood next to his computer, a big smile on his face. “I have never seen another werewolf reverse the change as fast or as easily as you did my boy.” he exclaimed.

“Easy,” Butch cried. “I was frightened. I did not even know the change started until it was too late.”

Jerrold tapped the computer table with his knuckle emphasizing each word of what he was saying, “Well, you’ve learned something, haven’t you?”

Butch breathed a sigh of relief. “Yeah, I learned that to change is easy and that I have got to keep better control of my thoughts,” he said.

Jerrold shook his head in agreement. “Butch, you will be a leader of the family some day. Work hard and learn all you can. Remember, being stronger than others is only one requirement of being a good leader. You must also be intelligent and able to see the big picture. You just proved you were able to control your thoughts. Not everyone in the pack could have stopped the change so quickly.”

Butch’s face broke out into a wide smile. Was he happy for the praise his grandfather bestowed on him or because he now knew where his destiny lay, as leader of the pack?

Chapter 8
Regrets And Acceptance

Butch switched on the lamp on his father's desk. It was not late, but the clouds outside made the room darker and more dreary than normal. Butch plopped down in Rod's padded swivel chair and threw his feet up on the desk. He squinted, as he sat back and peeled a banana.

Rod walked into his office and saw Butch sitting in his chair. He changed direction and sat on the stuffed leather sofa. "Son, I need talk with you."

"Sure Dad, what's up?"

"I knew there was no turning back once you received the tainted blood from my father," Rod said, exhibiting a degree of nervousness.

"Hey, Pops, I don't consider my blood tainted," Butch said.

Rod nodded. "Okay, that is a matter of opinion," Rod countered, and then said before Butch could continue his defense. "Your grandfather told me you experienced an incident with an unforeseen change yesterday."

"Boy did I ever," Butch said. He looked at his father and a frown crept across his forehead. "Don't worry. I handled it. I just let my thoughts get away from me. It won't happen again."

"Good," Rod said with a smile and then his face grew serious. "Butch I'd like you to make me a promise."

"Yeah," Butch said gazing at his Dad with a suspicious look.

"For my sake, will you promise not to kill more humans than the one you have to kill every five years?"

"Grandfather says we cannot kill at any other time."

Rod bounced his hands on his knees and said, "That's what he says, but a number of humans are killed by werewolves at times other than the scheduled feasts."

Butch stood up with a surprised look on his face, "What do you mean?"

"Some of your relatives don't or can't always control their changes. Some kill more frequently. They choose not to or could not wait five years between feedings. I suspect a few of them enjoy killing too much."

Butch stepped closer to his father and interrupted him. "Grandfather said he would hunt down and kill anyone that goes off and kills on their own."

"The ones doing the killings are not out of control. Your grandfather would discipline them if he knew when it happened and who was doing it. The kills are made on homeless people, who are seldom missed."

Butch stumbled, ashen faced, back to the desk chair and plopped down. "Jesus, I don't know if I can make that promise. I do not know enough about my needs. I don't want to lie to you dad, but if I can control this force that has me, I will try to do what you ask."

"Thank you for that much. I guess that's all I can hope for."

Butch sat up and looked into his father's eyes. "Dad, is that why you never became a werewolf, because you'd have to kill a human?"

"That is the main reason." Rod's eyes drooped. "When I was very young, nine or ten, I witnessed the killing of a human child by my older brother, Richard. I could not condone something like that. It sickened me. After that, I wanted nothing to do with being a werewolf." Rod looked at Butch. "Do you understand, son?"

"Yeah, Dad, I do. Remember, there was no choice for me in becoming a werewolf. I do not blame you, but for me, getting the werewolf blood was the best thing that happened to me. The way my life was heading, I would have ended up in prison or killed in some holdup. As much as you detest the werewolf way, I owe my life to it." Excitement beamed from his face.

Rod sat up straight and slapped his knees with open hands. "You are right," he said.

Butch's eyes dilated in surprise. He did not expect his father to agree. "You know, dad, today I learned two things," Butch said. "I learned I could lose control and the need to clamp down on my emotions. If I can do that, someday I will take Grandfather's place. Some day I will be the pack leader."

Rod's eyebrows rose.

Butch read his father's skepticism in his face. "I mean it, Dad; I have found something that interests me, something I can put all of my energy into."

Rod lifted his hands palm up in front of him. "I hope you can fulfill your dream and yet, at the same time I'm filled with sadness, sad for humanity."

"Dad, I understand, but the world has to take care of itself, just like I'm going to take care of myself."

Chapter 9
The Night Of The Harvest Moon

Quaking Aspen trees stood like sentinels around Colby Lake. The crisp, cool, autumn air turned the leaves yellow. In a gentle breeze, the leaves trembled, weakening the petioles hold to the twig. Along the west shore of the lake a cluster of Red Pine trees huddled, preparing for the colder days that lay ahead. Wind whistled through the needles, breaking free the dead, reddish-brown ones. They floated to the ground to join others already there forming a spongy cushion. October marked the end of the growing season.

Butch trembled, empathizing with the shaking leaves overhead. Philosophically, he thought all things must look forward to the same fate; death. He sat on a park bench looking out over the lake and listened to the wind whistling high in the pines. The smell of decaying leaves and fresh mown grass came to him on the wind. In front of him, several milkweed plants, with pods hanging broken, open and dry, glistened in the sun. The wind aided the escape of silken parachutes from the pods and carried them away, spreading hope for the next generation.

Butch felt agitated. Maybe the agitation grew in him because his job of planning for "Moonlight Madness" was completed and now all he could do was wait impatiently for the event to arrive. He was anxious for the human hunt to take place. All of the pack was showing signs of agitation. It was becoming difficult to control his feelings. He had to force himself to complete his daily mundane tasks.

To lay his anxiety aside, he busied himself in several projects at once, hoping the increased workload would divert his thoughts from the promise of ultimate ecstasy. By working hard, the date for 'Moonlight Madness' would soon arrive that much quicker. He was not sure if any of these tactics would work, but he knew the killing of his first human lay just ahead. As far as he was concerned, all the preparations for the invasion of Longville were in place, waiting implementation. He was more than ready.

The non-werewolf members of the pack, Sharrie, Big George, Marsha and Carol, left on Sunday for the cabin hideout on Inguadona Lake. Several others would open up the cabins in the woods near Land O Lakes State Forest. Two safe sites would be occupied and available if necessary.

Monday, the Isolation Committee left for Longville. Their primary task was to make sure the road excavation took place on schedule. There could be no delays. The road equipment must begin digging Wednesday morning, no sooner, no later.

According to the plan, the excavation crew would close the roads Wednesday and begin digging. Thursday morning the culverts would be set and covered and the highway patched with new tarmac. By the end of the day, the highway would be back to normal and open to traffic.

Grandfather, Richard, Amy and Aerial planned to arrive in Longville Monday afternoon. They would stay with Diana and Andy's family at Woman Lake Resort.

The group to disrupt communications arrived Wednesday afternoon in Longville and took the necessary steps to shut down phone lines, cell phone towers and electrical lines later that evening.

Late Wednesday morning the digging started on Highway 84 on both sides of town. The backhoe tore up the tarmac just south of where Hardy lane intersected the highway north of town. On the south end of town, a bulldozer dug up the road on School Lane. Traffic soon backed up behind the gap in the road and diverted onto a single lane.

By 6:00 p. m., Highway 84 into town from the north and south was completely blocked. Townspeople coming home late from work would have to leave their cars at the excavation site and walked around the deep trench and high piles of gravel to get home. Either that or drive miles out of their way to come into town by one of the two side roads.

At 7:00 p.m., the phone service died and at 7:30, all of the lights in Longville went out. At 7:45, cell phone towers lines ceased to function. The Ham operators with battery backup would be the only link to the outside world and the first to die. Then isolation would be complete. The feeding frenzy would begin.

The harvest moon, large and golden rose above the eastern horizon, an hour before sunset. Butch watched the sun disappear over the horizon, as the golden moon rose in the east. Moonlight penetrated his eyes touching his soul and incapacitated any mercy that remained within. In spite of what Grandfather said regarding moonlight not being a strong determining factor in bringing on the change, it affected Butch a great deal.

This was his first ‘hunt’ therefore; he was to accompany Grandfather and Andy. For efficiency and safety, other members of the Guhl family hunted in groups of two or three. Before the night was over, twenty-four Longville residents would die and disappear, if everything went according to plan.

Grandfather stood with Andy and Butch behind a screen of trees near their first target. As soon as darkness was complete, the long awaited feeding would begin.

Butch paced, glancing skyward each time he turned. As the darkness increased, the moon changed from a pale gold to a bright golden color. The moon appeared suspended in the sky by a spider web of fine branches at the top of a dozen trees. Moonbeams wrapped around the branches and tethered the moon in place. The moon looked like an alien spotlight, poised to witness the horror that would begin very soon. Butch cringed at the thought of something watching him.

Twenty-one additional werewolves were in their assigned positions around Longville. Grandfather and Andy stirred in the bushes nearby. Jerrold uncurled from his reclining position and looked at the others. “Time to change,” he said.

A tremor of fear shot through Butch’s body. He was nervous, anxious and frightened, but he was ready. He sighed with relief. The waiting was over. What he looked forward to all summer was finally here. He hunched his shoulders and concentrated on images of his first kill, the deer. He felt the change begin. Butch’s head turned back and his eyes became glued on the moon. “The light’s so bright,” he cried out. He rubbed his eyes with hair-covered hands. “I cannot see.”

"Shhh, Butch, t will pass," Grandfather's assurance rang in his mind.

Butch twisted in pain, as bones crunched and reconfigured themselves to fit the altered DNA of his cells. Growth hormones poured forth from his endocrine glands, stimulating the flow of calcium deposits from bones into his blood stream and back into the bone cells again. Bones reformed into their new shapes. Muscle elongated to accommodate the modified bones. Butch grimaced with more pain as a new series of changes swept over him. He welcomed the pain, for what it promised, the pleasures to come. The pain intensified and he squirmed. Muscles bulged and hair shot out from follicles.

Feelings of anger, hate and madness led the onslaught of emotions racing through Butch's mind. Craving for human flesh multiplied with every breath and fueled the growing desire to kill and rip apart a human with his fangs. Gastric juices flooded into his empty, growling stomach.

"Careful," Butch thought, "I cannot let the animal side overpower me and gain control." The warning did nothing to slow his change, if anything; it raced through him faster than he could monitor it. Primitive animal thoughts erupted in his mind. "Oh Lord, I have to maintain control. I must," he moaned. His body twisted, as he reacted to the internal fight. A fight he was losing.

The strong feelings bursting from his neurons were pushing him beyond reason. The animal side surged to the forefront, becoming dominant, sublimating rationale thought and any semblance of control.

Jerrold heard Butch moan and glanced at him. "Oh no," Grandfather said, as he watched Butch battle for control. Jerrold raced through his change and launched himself through the air at Butch. He crashed into him and sent him tumbling.

Butch rolled up against a tree trunk and lay stunned for a few moments. Uncontrollable anger flooded through his brain, like a glowing red ball. The red ball exploded and Butch growled and jumped back to his feet.

Grandfather bared his fangs and growled a warning. "Listen to me, Butch," he thought.

Butch's mind heard the warning, but his mind was unfocused and echoed, like an empty chamber.

"Maintain self control," Jerrold said, walking stiff legged toward Butch.

Slobber ran from the corners of Butch's mouth. Madness ruled his changed body and mind. He stared at his Grandfather without recognition. In his mind, he saw an enemy, someone attacking him. Butch pranced away from his attacker. The beast in him wanted to feed.

Grandfather recognized the signs. He feared Butch was ready to bolt, and if he ran, he was not sure he could stop him. "Control yourself or I will have to stop you." Jerrold lowered his body and projected from his mind as loud as he could, "I am the pack leader. You must obey me."

Butch growled a challenge. Right now, his rational side gave way to his animal desires. Hostile, evil thoughts flipped through his mind, relegating the clear message Grandfather sent him to some hidden recess in the back of his mind.

"I don't have to listen to anyone," Butch said, directing his rage back at the pack leader. "I don't have to obey anyone."

Butch's muscles bunched in preparation to attack the creature trying to stop him. Before he could spring into action, Jerrold uncoiled like a spring and slammed into Butch's chest, bowling him over again. Jerrold's right paw slashed Butch across the neck, the claws biting deep. Even though Butch was out of control, he felt the pain through his growing wildness and a white tinge of fear exploded in his mind. The fear returned a bit of reason to his mind and he teetered back to the side of reason. Jerrold stood growling over Butch, fangs inches from his exposed throat, ready to execute the killing bite, if necessary.

With a submissive growl, Butch relaxed and worked his way to a four-legged stance, his tail curled between his legs. He hung his head, embarrassed at having lost control. "Thank you, Grandfather, for saving me," Butch said. "I did not, could not realize I'd lost control. It won't happen again," Butch was repentant; he dropped to his belly and crawled forward, until he lay exposed under his grandfather's bared fangs. Blood flowed from the wound on his neck and shoulder, matting his fur. Butch ignored the wounds, even as the damaged tissues began to close and the bleeding stop.

Jerrold relaxed, he was glad to have his grandson under control again. He knew how easy it was to lose the battle. The important thing was he averted another breakout. "I warned you to control the wild side," Jerrold said. "Next time I will have to hurt you. Now get up, you are forgiven."

Butch raised his muzzle and licked his Grandfather's face.

Andy remained mesmerized during the conflict between the Alpha and Butch. He was shaking as he stepped toward Butch. "Shit, Butch," he said, "You scared me."

"Not half as scared as I'm feeling now," Butch said. He looked at the ground, not able to meet his Uncle's eyes.

"Finish your change Andy," Grandfather said. "We've got work to do."

Their target was one of three ham operators on their list. It was imperative to eliminate those with battery backup. This was the most critical assignment. If they did not put the ham radios out of commission, calls for help could flood the airwaves and bring help from the surrounding towns. The ham operators were the only link between Longville and the outside world.

Jerrold led Andy and Butch toward the house with a tall aluminum antenna disappearing upward into the dark night sky. Quiet growls emanated from their chests, like rumbling motors. The three werewolves walked erect on their hind feet with a rocking motion. They reached the side of the house. Their hind legs consisted of muscular thighs tapered to narrow lower limbs with padded and clawed feet. Standing, they were over seven feet tall. Jerrold peered through a darkened window. Andy and Butch stepped to the other side of the window and gazed through the glass.

Butch saw a woman, man and boy sitting around a kitchen table. They were talking to each other, unaware of what stood outside their window. A candle's flickering flame illuminated their concerned faces.

The parents were attempting to comfort the boy, who was frightened and talked loudly. The boy could not understand why the lights went out. Butch felt fear emanate from the boy through the walls of the house. The fear excited him and he trembled. A growl of ecstasy escaped between his fangs. Butch inhaled, trying to take in more of the fear with his breath. It did not work that way.

Grandfather dropped to the ground and twirled on all fours. He ran back a few steps, and then turned and raced toward the window. He launched himself into the air and smashed through the glass.

Shards of glass flew into the kitchen, tinkling on the linoleum floor. Screams erupted from inside the house. Jerrold landed amid the glass and slid against the wall before stopping.

The air around Butch reverberated with screams. Butch heard the humans inside scream again, but this time the screams were much higher in pitch. Fear radiated from the house sending euphoric impulses racing through Butch's mind.

Jerrold struggled to right himself, but kept slipping on pieces of broken glass. Finally getting control, he walked on four feet toward the darker shadows of the kitchen. Jerrold released a low growl and that set the people screaming again.

Butch grew lightheaded from the pleasurable waves of fear filling his mind. He was not sure he could stand the waves emanating from their fear. He became intoxicated with the feelings flooding his mind and leaned back against the side of the house.

Another chorus of screams escaped from the house, as the family members saw the wolf-like animal standing just outside the ring of candlelight.

Butch broke free, moved back from the house and then jumped through the broken window. Andy followed close behind. They both landed a few feet from Grandfather. Butch noticed the boy sitting at the table. The humans were frightened; their eyes bulged out in disbelief, mouths molded in the shape of Cheerios.

The father made sweeping motions with his hands at the three werewolves and yelled with a shaking voice, "Shoo, get out of here. Go on, get, you damn dogs."

The mother, a tendril of brown sweaty hair hanging over her right eye, rose and grabbed a broom from the between the stove and refrigerator. Deep maternal instincts prompted her to defend her family. "Gill, do something," she screamed. "There are three of them in here, now."

Grandfather growled and launched himself through the air. He hit Gill's chest. The man's arms flailed, as he flew through the air. His back hit the refrigerator and he slumped to the floor. Grandfather thrust his fanged mouth forward, grabbing the man's throat. He bit down, crushing the windpipe and severing the carotid arteries on both sides of his neck. Jerrold snarled and jerked his head to the side, ripping a mouthful of flesh free. In the candlelight, black blood squirted from severed arteries, flying several feet through the air to splash against the kitchen wall. The man convulsed arms and legs tapping on the floor. His eyes clouded, but his body did not accept the fact right away that he was dead and kept up its dance of death.

Butch's growl sounded gleeful, as he leapt to the top of the table. He was in a total state of frenzy. He whirled around and curled his body toward the boy. He slashed out with his right paw and then froze. His nose wrinkled as he sniffed the air. A smell of urine permeated the air. He shook his head in disgust as his nose pointed toward the boy. The boy had wet his pants.

Butch's bloodshot eyes locked onto the boy's glistening, half-crazed eyes. The boy kicked back, as he tried to escape the crazed animal in front of him. His chair slid across the floor and banged into the wall behind him. Butch leapt from the tabletop to the boy's lap, snapping his fangs around the top of his head. Sharp, white, glistening fangs pierced the boy's skull a fraction of an inch.

The boy stiffened, rocking his chair to the side until it tipped over. He reached up and tore Butch's teeth from his head. He screamed and then jumped up trying to escape. He turned to flee, but Butch jumped on his back driving him to the floor. The boy spun around, grabbed thick fur on Butch's neck and pushed his muzzle away from his face. Butch yelped as his skin separated from the underlying muscles. He released his grip and pulled free. Butch whirled and bit the boy just above the knee. He clamped down hard and felt the separation of the femur from the knee joint.

Butch grew dizzy from the burst of fear spilling from the boy. The fear came in pulses, with whirlpool intensity that made Butch wobble, as a feeling of weakness spread through his muscles. Butch's jaw muscles relaxed and the boy scrambled across the kitchen floor, screaming.

Afraid the boy was going to escape; Butch shook the dizziness from his head and leapt over the squirming body. Angry with himself for his mental lapse, Butch clamped his fangs over the boy's head again. The boy shrieked. The crazed, fear from the boy coursed through Butch's mind like an orgasm. Butch whipped his head back and forth in time with the waves of pleasure assaulting his mind. The boy flew through the air, like a rag doll. Butch heard the skull crack and he reduced jaw pressure. He wanted to delay killing the boy in order to milk as much fear as possible from him. He wanted the exhilaration to continue.

Jerrold stood to the side of the kitchen. "Butch, end it," Grandfather said. "You are finished for the night. We've got to get moving."

Butch returned a growl of defiance, but relented when he saw the stern look on his Grandfather's face. Butch released the ecstasy he was experiencing. He brought his upper and lower fangs together. They met in the middle of the boy's cerebrum. The boy stiffened, convulsed once and grew limp. Butch released the dead body, which no longer provided him any pleasure. The discarded body slumped to the floor.

Butch glanced around for another victim. He lowered his head and swiveled it back and forth. His nerves stretched to the breaking point. He was coming down from his high and needed more of the exhilarating feeling. That was not quite right. He realized he needed the fear and sheer panic that came from frightened, dying humans, to fuel his emotional high.

He saw Andy was still toying with the mother. Butch's euphoric feelings were subsiding and the promise of reestablishing them waited for him in the woman. Butch stood and moved toward her.

"No, Butch," reverberated in Butch's mind. "I told you, you were finished. You have already killed. This is Andy's victim," his grandfather's dominating voice said. "Now consume your victim, so we can go."

Butch growled with frustration, but stopped moving in the woman's direction.

The woman swung an old, worn broom at Andy and screamed. Butch shuddered experiencing the ecstasy; at least he could wallow in her fear. In the candle lit scene, the mother witnessed her husband and son's death. Her mind overloaded, sending her over the edge into insanity. A chuckle slipped from Andy's throat, as he pranced toward her.

Jerrold stood over the body of the husband feeding. With a mouthful of flesh, he said, "Andy, finish it. "We have to go." He ripped another piece of flesh from the body in front of him.

Butch turned away from Andy and the mother. He began to feed on the cooling flesh of the boy.

Andy growled and swept aside the broom with a paw. He swung the other paw and ripped open the woman's stomach. Her intestines snaked to the floor in front of her eyes, like undulating giant worms. The broom dropped from her lifeless hands, as she stared at the squirming mass sliding to the floor. She slipped into shock and was not aware when Andy's fangs ripped into her stomach cavity, to reach upward and rip out her heart. Andy chewed on the still pulsing organ, as a huge sigh of satisfaction escaped from deep in his throat.

Butch glanced out the broken kitchen window and flinched. The golden moon suspended in the ink black sky was watching him. A tendril of fear raced through his mind, as he recalled his earlier thoughts, of the moon, rising to watch and record his actions tonight. Butch shrugged his shaggy shoulders and turned back to feed on the cooling body.

After the three finished feeding, Jerrold said, "Andy, bag the remains and dispose of them in the swamp. Make sure they will not be found."

On the other side of town, Gretchen Fletcher was walking home from the grocery store. She did not get to finish shopping before the lights went out. Henry, the store's owner told her to take the groceries and pay him tomorrow. He could not open the cash register anyway.

It was after nine o'clock and pitch dark. Everyone in town considered Gretchen a pain in the ass. She wore a dark, brown, wool coat that reached down to her ankles. A purple scarf with swirling red lines crisscrossing the fabric, in a haphazard pattern, covered her head.

Without streetlights, she blended with the darkness, except when the moonlight reflected from her shiny scarf. Just because the electricity was out all over town and the streets were dark, that did not scare her. She walked to the store and home many times, she could do it in the dark and tonight she got her chance.

She grumbled, still angry with her oldest son, Arnie for not getting home in time to run to the store for her. She carried a grocery bag filled with a half-gallon of milk, a loaf of bread, five pound of potatoes, and a six-pack of Coke. She hurried homeward, with the grocery bag in her right arm. She swung her left arm in cadence with her rapid pace.

A feeling of guilt swept through her mind. She had left her one-year-old baby home alone. She rationalized; he was sleeping in the crib when she left. She did not want to wake him and take him to the store with her. He would have been a grouchy crab.

"Damn that Arnie," she said aloud. "He should've come right home after football practice. I will whip his ass for making me go to the store." She shifted blame to her oldest boy, when forethought and planning on her part would have alleviated leaving the baby home alone and going to the store.

She followed Bell Street, walking along the edge of the sidewalk. The cement slabs were crooked from years of frost heaves and neglect. She moved forward shuffling her feet in the dark, until she tripped on the jutting edge of slab. She caught herself, then stepped over the uneven cement and shuffled on her way again.

She thought, "Boy, it is really dark without the streetlights on." She came to Highway 84 and followed the edge of the road southward. She felt some comfort hearing the click-click of her shoes echoing back from the surrounding trees.

The rundown Fletcher house was on the south side of town, just beyond a grove of Black Spruce trees that bordered Highway 84. She started into the tunnel of overhanging Spruce, which towered over the highway from both sides. The tunnel ran for two hundred feet. She sighed. She was almost home.

Waiting in the Spruce trees was Big George, Xianth and Thomas.

Thirty feet into the dark tunnel, Gretchen heard a soft growl ahead of her. She turned her head from side to side, like a bat using radar to locate an insect. She could not pinpoint where the noise came from.

"Damn dogs," she said under her breath. "Why don't the dam dog lovers keep them tied up?" She stooped and picked up a broken branch lying alongside the road. She shifted the grocery bag into her left arm and held the stick with her right hand. Feeling more confident with a weapon, she shuffled ahead once more, seeing her moonlighted home just down the road.

When she approached the spot where she thought the growl came from, she heard another growl from farther ahead. Then another growl hissed from across the road. "Damn dogs," she said. "Come out here and I will beat your growling asses."

Gretchen stopped and wet her lips. She took a few more steps and then froze when she heard a shuffling noise behind her. She whirled around, raising the branch over her head. She squinted, finding it hard to make out the shape of Big George in 'were-form' standing at the edge of the spruce trees. All she saw was a dark shadow and could not distinguish what it was. She knew it was not a dog it was too big.

"Shit, it looks like a bear," she cursed under her breath. She walked backwards a few steps, trying to put more distance between herself and the animal.

She stuck the branch under her arm, as she rifled through the grocery bag. "I will throw it a few slices of bread," she said, "that should distract it long enough for me to get the hell out of here."

Until a few moments ago, Gretchen was not frightened, but quite angry; now terror welled up in her breast and her knees sagged. A couple of cowering dogs were one thing, but a bear, that was something else. The thought of screaming for help did not even enter her mind.

With shaking hands, she ripped open the package of Wonder Bread and pulled out several slices. She threw them toward the 'bear'.

The three werewolves took in the waves of fear emanating from Gretchen, like drinking a glass of vintage wine.

Gretchen turned and hurried down the lane, back toward town. She wanted to get out of the darkened area under the trees and into the moonlight, as fast as she could.

Thomas in 'were-form' jumped on to the road and advanced toward the woman.

Gretchen heard Thomas moving behind her and turned her head around. Thomas was three feet behind her. All Gretchen could see was something that looked like a man wearing a shaggy, fur coat. A breeze blew aside a branch allowing moonlight to shine on Thomas. She squinted and saw more of the creature's distinguishable features.

"No," she screamed in her mind, "that is not a human. It has a face like a wolf." It was standing on two feet. The words 'Bigfoot' raced through her mind.

"God, could this be one of those 'Bigfoot' creatures? Or whatever the hell they call that prehistoric human-like thing," Gretchen asked herself. Fear burst from the deep recesses of her brain, releasing quantities of adrenaline into her blood stream. Her primitive brain knew she needed to escape, but she was beginning to understand that might not be an option.

Another beast appeared at her side and advanced. Turning towards the third beast, she saw two hair-covered breasts protruding from its chest.

"The creature looks like a human, but why isn't she wearing any clothes?" Gretchen asked herself.

Xianth growled, low in her throat, "Grrrr."

Taking small side steps Gretchen moved away from the she creature. She still carried the stick and held it out in front of her, as if trying to ward off the animal. "Go on, get," she screamed. "Leave me alone."

Xianth advanced; saliva drooled from the corners of her mouth. She kept pace with Gretchen, closing the distance between them because of her longer stride. Xianth thrust her arms high into the air and emitted a blood-curdling scream. "AAiiiiiieOOOOOOOOOO."

Gretchen knew for sure the 'thing' was not human. No human could scream like that and neither could a bear. She squinted, watching the animal. It surprised her when Xianth, the werewolf, leapt high into the air, somersaulted over her head, and landed behind her.

She spun around to face the beast. Town buildings and the moonlit streets were no longer open for her escape. The beast moved toward her, forcing her to move back, deeper into the dark tunnel of trees. Step for step Xianth followed, until Gretchen backed into the darkest region of the overhanging spruce boughs.

Over the growls of the 'thing' in front of her, Gretchen heard another growl behind her. She started to swing her head, but before she could turn, she felt an excruciating pain in her neck. Thomas in 'were-form' drove his fangs through her cervical vertebrae dislocating Gretchen's head from her body.

Gretchen died in an instant, unaware as the raking claws of Thomas, ripped open her chest and exposed her quivering heart. Xianth leaned over the headless body, extended her muzzle into the opened cavity, and grabbed Gretchen's throbbing heart in her fangs. She twisted her head, tearing the heart from her chest. Blood sprayed through the air, landing several feet from the body.

Similar gruesome attacks were occurring on other streets and in homes throughout the besieged city of Longville. Barking dogs mixed their voices with the howls of the werewolves, extending far beyond the city limits.

From the forests, surrounding the town, answering howls from several local wolf packs answered. The wolves were moving toward town, coming to investigate who was invading their territory.

Grandfather and Butch left the ham operators house behind and were moving along the street toward town center to check on the other teams. Suddenly, gunshots reverberated through the air and brought them to a stop. They sniffed the air, smelling ‘were-danger’. A forced hush drifted over the city. Butch looked to the west. He knew where the shots came from.

Jerrold listened for another moment and then said, with a trembling voice. “Come on.” He ran toward the west part of Longville. He said to Butch, “Hurry, members of our pack are in trouble.”

Butch followed Jerrold across Randall Street, running at fifty miles per hour. As they approached the short main street, two more shots filled the night air from two blocks ahead.

Butch swerved to the right side of the street, while Grandfather continued running down the middle. They covered the two blocks in a few seconds.

As they approached the corner of Randall and Main Street, Butch saw a flash and then heard another blast from a shotgun. The foot long stream of fire reflected in the window of the white house on the corner of the intersection. Butch saw a werewolf crumple to the ground and lay unmoving on the lawn in front of the house. He stopped behind a big oak tree growing in the boulevard. He looked at the wounded werewolf and recognized Fred. He lay a short distance from an oak tree. Fred’s father, Steve huddled behind the oak tree avoiding the gunfire spraying the area.

Jerrold using the same tree as a shield ran up behind Steve. Steve gave his father a mournful glance.

“What happened?” Jerrold projected from his mind to Steve.

"Be careful, Dad," Steve sobbed. "Fred is dead."

"Steve, control yourself," Jerrold said.

"Steve calmed down and answered from his mind, "We attacked several humans inside the white house. They must have been expecting us. There are still two humans inside the house, with guns. They've killed Fred and wounded Barbara."

"Where is she?"

"She is around the corner of that building. Francis is with her," Steve said, nodding toward a brick bakery on the corner.

Jerrold glanced at the building just as Francis stuck his 'were-head' around the corner.

"Francis, stay with Barbara, "Jerrold telegraphed.

"Yes, father."

Jerrold clapped Steve on the shoulder, "Steve, stay here."

Jerrold peeked around the tree and then raced toward the white house. Thirty feet from the house, a shotgun blast from the first floor window hit him in his left shoulder. Butch saw Jerrold's left front leg collapse and watched him tumble through the air and roll to a grinding stop. Jerrold howled. It sounded like he was more frustrated than hurt. The Alpha was down and the hunt was falling apart.

Flashes of blinding light burned across Butch's eyes. Without thinking, he scraped bark from the trunk of the tree as he hurled himself toward the white house. He moved at such a rapid speed, he was a blur to the two men inside the building. In two seconds, he reached the house and leapt through the window where the shotgun blast originated. He burst through the remaining splinters of glass and sent them showering in all directions. As he flew through the window frame, Butch sensed a man crouched to his left.

With lightening reactions, Butch thrust out his left paw and sliced through the man's throat. Butch hit the floor and slid through an archway all the way into the next room. He heard the man cough on his own blood and watched him fall to the floor, where he laid kicking and gurgling. In his dying throes, the man jerked the trigger of the Twelve-gauge shotgun. The first blast tore through the top frame of the window and the second slammed into the ceiling of the room.

Butch rolled to his feet and bound without stopping through another archway leading into the next room. A shotgun blast sizzled above his back. Butch was operating on animal instinct alone.

He used the wall to change direction and landed at the feet of the second man. Flickering candlelight illuminated the man's surprised open mouth, when he saw Butch in werewolf form standing in front of him.

Butch shoved his head forward. A muzzle full of fangs and grinding teeth clamped onto the man's testicles. Butch jerked his head to the side ripping the testicles from their sacks. The man dropped his gun and let out a pitiful squeak from between clenched teeth. On tiptoe, the man began a delicate dance as he pounded on Butch's forehead with both of his hands.

Butch released his hold and sat back on his rear haunches. The man grabbed his bleeding groin and sagged to his knees. Butch with a vicious swipe of his right paw ripped the man's head from his body. With a second swing, he opened the man's chest and with snapping fangs, ripped out his heart.

Butch's attention shifted from the dead man when Grandfather's mind-scream forced him to his knees.

Grandfather broadcasted to all the werewolves, "Come to me."

Butch could not believe the intensity of the call that assaulted the chambers of his brain. There was no way he or any of the others could not obey the demanding cry of their pack leader.

Every member of the family, even though some were on the other side of town heard the Alpha's cry. Butch backtracked through the rooms and jumped out the same window he used to enter the house. He ran across the lawn and joined the other arriving werewolves around the pack leader. Butch felt panicky. He did not know what to do. Grandfather stood over the dead body of Fred. Whimpering sounds escaped from his nostrils. Jerrold dropped down on his rear haunches. With tender movements, he lifted Fred with his forepaws. In spite of his wounded arm, Jerrold cradled Fred in his hairy arms and rocked him back and forth. He lifted his head to the sky, heart-wrenching howls floated from his muzzle, "AHHHOOooooooo. AHHHHOOoooooo. AHHHHHOOoooooo."

The loud cries reverberated back and forth between the surrounding hills, sending a mournful lament to the skies and the all-seeing harvest moon. His cry seemed to say, "We have lost one of our own."

Two wild wolf packs nearing town howled in reply, "ARRRRROoooo. ARRRROoooo. AAARRRROOOOOooo."

Butch understood what their howls meant, "We understand. We have also lost many of our kind to the humans, but that is no reason for you being in our territory."

Grandfather released Fred and stood up on three legs, favoring his wounded leg. He sent mind thoughts to the pack. "Steve, we are all sorry for your loss. Take your son's body and leave. Thomas, you and Jake help Barbara. The rest of us will join you at the cabin on Lake Inguadona. Leave no trail. Now the rest of you, if you have not made your kill do it now and be quick about it. Be sure to dispose of the remains. We leave town in thirty minutes. Go now."

In twos and threes, the werewolves scattered in all directions. Butch and Andy, who had returned from the swamp, hesitated, not knowing what to do. Grandfather looked at them. "I want the two of you to seek vengeance. Leave no witnesses. Go now and kill."

The two glanced at each other and then loped off to find more prey.

In spite of the havoc the Guhl werewolf pack already caused, most townsfolk were not aware of what was taking place or that werewolves were the cause of it. Several families heard the gunshots and came out of their homes. They gravitated toward the shooting.

Five werewolves descended upon three people standing in the middle of Randall Street, a block from Main Street. The werewolves charged through the group at top speed, slashing and tearing. Not one of the humans saw the werewolves; all they felt was the breeze of their passing. In those few moments, all of them lay on the ground dying from wounds inflicted by the werewolves. As each person toppled over, none realized what caused them to fall. Not a single scream of fear or awareness escaped their lips, until the shock of their wounds wore off. Then the fear was so great, their nerves went into overload.

The five werewolves slowed to a stop and stood around the thrashing humans; then the screaming started. The werewolves went orgasmic from the peals of fear radiating from the dying humans and could only stand frozen in an ecstatic stupor.

On the north edge of town, Walt Peterson, old and cancerous, lay in shock. His left arm was severed and pumping blood in spurts out the main brachial artery. He turned his head until his eyes locked with Butch's red-rimmed eyes. The fury in Butch's eyes and his open-mouthed gape made Walt think the Devil had returned to punish him for raping his daughter twenty-two years ago. Walt knew he was dying and didn't object. He was ready to accept his punishment. In fact, he felt it was long overdue. He waited. Walt put up no resistance when Butch leapt on him and ripped open his throat. The last thought that washed through the deep hidden recesses of Walt's mind actually brought him fulfillment.

Suddenly, the promise he made to his father popped into Butch's mind. "I promised I would not kill more humans than I needed to. Shit, dad does not understand what being a werewolf entails. No way could I have resisted killing tonight or in seeking revenge."

A trickle of madness resurfaced. He knew he did what he needed to do tonight. Well, maybe that was oversimplifying the event, but Butch knew that without eating human flesh, he would have been lost to the animal side. The side of Butch's mouth pulled back into a smile, as he bent to pull Walt's heart free. He swallowed the quivering organ in two bites.

Other werewolves hunted down and killed another twelve citizens of Longville in the next ten minutes. Each victim died with no clue as to what was going on. The werewolves traveled fast, people did not see what hit them.

Four citizens of Longville would see the specters of death and live. Traumatized by their encounters; two of them would escape into their own minds and never find their way out. Another became a babbling idiot.

The fourth was a five-year-old child, who hid beneath the front porch of his home. From his vantage point, he witnessed a 'wolf' kill his mother and sister on the front lawn, only feet from where he hid.

"TO ME," Jerrold's mind thought-blared. "WE LEAVE-NOW."

Butch and Andy gulped one last piece of flesh and then raced at sixty miles per hour toward the stand of trees on the east edge of town. In a matter of a couple of minutes, the rest of the pack joined them.

Jerrold limped among the returning pack members. "Is there anyone that hasn't satisfied their need to kill?" he said.

Butch noticed the scabbed over wound on Jerrold's left leg, he still favored his leg as he moved.

All of the gathered werewolves answered in the affirmative. Each werewolf fed and would not need to feed again for another five years.

"Okay, it is time to leave. Butch, lead out," Grandfather said.

"But, Andy and I have not disposed of the extra kills you sent us out to do."

"Never mind, we leave now," Jerrold said.

Butch shrugged his front shoulders and headed for the swamp with his grandfather limping behind him. Butch entered the swamp grass followed by the rest of the pack and loped off at a fast run. He led the group through a stand of small Aspen trees at the edge of the swamp and then followed a meandering trail through bigger Birch trees. In a short time, they entered the main part of the swamp. He followed the same deer trail he traveled on back in July through the swamp grass and water.

After a half hour the deer trail came up out of the swamp onto a Birch-covered ridge. In another four miles, the trail would come out on Lake Inguadona where their 'safe cabins' were located. Richard and his team were responsible for choosing the cabins on Lake Inguadona as one of the safe havens.

The owners of the resort knew the 'family' was having a reunion and that others would be arriving late into the night. Several non-werewolf members arrived during the night with vans to carry the rest of the family.

The pack would be in the Twin Cities by Sunday afternoon, once again safely hidden among thousands of people.

Chapter 10
The Whole World Knows

Minnesota radio and TV broadcast the first reports of the 'Longville Massacre' Thursday morning. By Thursday afternoon, the massacre made the front pages of every national newspaper. The news media moved with amazing quickness. There were personal interviews with residents of Longville, included in the evening newspaper, radio and TV reports.

NBC News reported, Thursday on the six o'clock news.

"Fifty-four residents from a small city in north central Minnesota are missing or dead.

The carnage, the wanton destruction of human life was unprecedented. On Wednesday evening, two packs of wild wolves attacked the citizens of Longville. The slaughter of twenty men, women and children took place; other people are missing and presumed dead. No clues have shown up to indicate where the missing be. Only in a wartime setting would something this gruesome happen. Earlier this morning, authorities found footprints of wolves entering and leaving Longville. The blame for the killings, the carnage points to wolves. It is unusual for wolves to attack humans, but apparently, times are changing.

Longville is a small resort community located between Grand Rapids, Brainerd and Aitkin."

Butch got up from the sofa, with a worried look on his face. He walked to the table and leaned over supporting himself on closed fists.

Bruce moaned, from the other side of the sofa. "That's the third national TV network to broadcast information of the attack."

"Let's face it," Richard said, "We were supposed to kill only twenty-four people. We screwed up and killed many more than we needed to. Killing that many humans was bound to draw unwanted attention. We have brought national attention down upon ourselves."

Tom jumped up from the sofa. "You darn right we screwed up," he said. We killed more than two people for every werewolf."

"How did we let things get that out of hand," Richard said, looking at his father. "One human would have satisfied our individual needs. Instead, some of us went overboard and killed an excessive number of humans."

Butch looked accusingly at Jerrold. "Grandfather ordered us to kill the others."

Jerrold rose from the leather recliner and walked to the fireplace. He leaned against the mantle with the arm that was injured and winced. The wound was scabbed over and nearly healed, but still bothered him. "What were we suppose to do," he said. Jerrold leaned forward with a snarl on his face; his neck blushed red, as veins popped out on his forehead. "Don't forget they killed one of my pack members and injured two of us."

Richard saw the anger displayed by his father and responded carefully. "But, father," he pleaded, his voice just above a whisper. "We shouldn't have killed that many humans."

"We were a pack out of control," Butch said.

Jerrold slammed his fist down on the fireplace mantle. "My pack was not out of control," he screamed, "You were doing what I ordered you to do." Grandfather stepped forward, his breath coming in gasps. "What difference does it make, whether we killed twenty-four or fifty-four, the publicity and panic would have been the same?"

"But, would a wild wolf pack have slaughtered that many people?" Brad questioned, in a meek voice.

"No, they wouldn't have," Jerrold spit out, "but don't jump to conclusions just yet, they have only found twenty bodies." Jerrold admonished Brad with a sideways glance and then relaxed. A big smile grew across his face. "Just remember, no one has blamed werewolves for the attack." Jerrold returned to lean against the mantle and said, "When they come knocking at our door, that's the time to panic."

Either Butch was not aware Jerrold was perturbed, or he did not care as he said, "Grandfather, that's not right. We screwed up by killing that many humans. I admit that I am to blame for six of those deaths and responsible for putting the pack at risk. The time to correct that mistake has passed, but we sure in hell shouldn't wait until the authorities come after us to take precautions."

Tom feeling a confrontation coming on tried to diffuse the situation. "Butch, the pack leaders has the job of controlling the hunt. Father did not want things to get out of hand, did he?"

"He sent some of us back to kill more people," Butch said. "Only the ones who needed to feed should have been sent. What happened should have been anticipated and a plan worked out to prevent panic," Butch said, turning from the table to face Tom.

Jerrold turned from the fireplace with a growl and dropped into a crouch. "Are you challenging my leadership, Butch?" Jerrold did not even wait for an answer; hair started growing from his face, as he started his change.

Tom blanched. He knew Butch had gone too far. "Father, Butch did not mean anything," he said.

Butch felt the hair on the back of his neck stand erect, as he responded by implementing his change.

Richard stumbled to the center of the room between the two glaring combatants and extended his hands toward Jerrold. "Dad, you're right," Richard shrugged, hoping he could head off this one-sided challenge. "Up to now, werewolves have not been blamed."

Jerrold was satisfied with Richard's response and seeing no challenge from Butch to his leadership, reversed his change.

Diana stood in the kitchen with hands planted on her hips. "It was in poor taste for the TV stations to show pictures of human victims. They even showed some of the bodies with chunks of flesh missing and their necks ripped open," Diana complained and sputtered as she said. "They even showed bodies with arms, heads and legs missing.
That sucks."

Butch smiled at the irony of Diana's comment. "We can kill humans, but the media should not show the dead bodies on TV?"

Richard defended Diana. "I guess that's what she means."

Bruce pushed his chair back a few inches and raised his hand in the air, like school kids do. When no one paid any attention to him, he blurted out, “The media is getting closer to what happened. CBS News said it was hard to believe unintelligent animals, like wolves, could have carried off a coordinated mass slaughter.”

“I hope no one agrees with them,” Richard sighed, “or we might be in the spotlight sooner than we’d like.”

Grandfather turned white. “We cannot let that happen.”

“Now he is concerned,” Butch thought. “He should admit he made an error

Chapter 11
Public Speculation

Friday morning, Butch and Carey volunteered to go into Remer to buy some groceries and see what kind of talk was going around town. Remer was close to Longville and people there would know what the stories were coming out of Longville.

Carey grabbed the keys off the table for the Ford Explorer. "Come on Butch, I get to drive," he said shaking the keys in front of Butch's face.

Amy, their sixteen-year-old cousin came out of the bathroom with toothpaste on the corner of her mouth. "Hey guys can I go with you," she asked.

Carey frowned and a pout grew on Amy's lips.

Butch smiled and said, "Sure Amy, you can come with us."

Carey gave Butch a dirty look, but nodded his okay.

The three headed out the door of the two-story chalet. Amy stumbled on the bottom step and Butch reached out and grabbed her arm. "Careful girl," he chided, "we cannot afford to have you get injured."

Carey jumped behind the wheel of the Explorer, started it up and accelerated down the gravel road. Reaching the end of the half mile driveway, he spun the wheel at the tar road and turned east onto County Road 7. The road curved through a wooded, hilly, deciduous forest toward Highway 6 and Rice Lake. In a short while, they reached Highway 6 and turned north, for Remer.

Butch sat with his knees on the seat. His head was half-way out the open window on the passengers' side of the car. He stared with watery eyes at Big Rice Lake, on his right. A ring of golden-leafed aspen surrounded the lake. Close to shore, thick patches of wild rice stems hung broken from the recent harvest. Butch eyed a flock of mallards splashing in the water a short distance from shore. A feral growl escaped his lips.

Carey slowed to the speed limit, as they passed the lumber store on the edge of town.

Butch turned in his seat and slapped the backrest of the driver's seat, "Say, when we get into town you and Amy pick up the groceries. Diana sent a list of things needed at the cabin." He dug in his shirt pocket, pulled out a quarter sheet of paper, and handed it to Amy. "While you are getting the groceries, I will see if I can pick up any information on the street."

Butch ambled down the street, stopping at a rusty newspaper dispenser. He dropped fifty cents in the slot and yanked out a copy of the Minneapolis Star & Tribune. The headlines caught his attention.

LONGVILLE CITIZENS KILLED BY WOLVES

Sheriff McCarthy of Walker reported Thursday that at least two pack of wolves entered the city of Longville and attacked
its citizens Wednesday night. Twenty men, women and children are dead and thirty four are missing from this Northern Minnesota resort Community.

According to Sheriff McCarthy, It is the most devastating thing that has ever happened in Cass County. The sheriff with the cooperation of a National Guard unit from Grand Rapids are sweeping the wooded areas around Longville, hunting the wolf packs responsible for this atrocious attack on the residents of Longville.

National guard helicopters are being used to locate and shoot the wolves. John Regan, Animal Biologist from

> the Minnesota Zoo said, "It's the first documented instance of wild wolves attacking humans on this scale anywhere in the world. I still cannot believe that wolves are responsible for killing those People. There must be another explanation."
>
> Relatives are still pouring into Longville to help arrange for the burial of family members and to console the living.

Butch turned to the inside pages of the newspaper where vivid color photos graphically depicted the savagery of the slaughter. He glanced up, concern showing on his face, as Amy and Carey came out of the grocery store. Butch leaned back against the Explorer and waited for them. Carey opened the back door and sat the groceries on the seat. Amy saw the startled look on Butch's face. She did not say anything, as she started to get in the back seat.

"Wait, Amy," Butch said, looking up the short main street. "We came to town to find out what the people are saying about what happened in Longville. Let's go in Kral's Drug Store and see if we can learn anything."

The drug store was in a dark red brick building in the middle of the block. Without waiting to see if they agreed, Butch headed for the drug store. Carey and Amy jogged to catch up. Butch pushed through the heavy, glass front door. Along the far wall toward the rear of the building, was an old-fashioned counter with real swivel stools. They sat down at the counter. A tall, hairless clerk, with a dirt-stained apron tied around his waist moved in front of them and asked what they would like. Butch ordered a Pepsi, Carey a Coke and Amy settled for a strawberry malt. Butch twirled his stool around and glanced at the aisles of merchandise. Towards the back of the store, several men sat around a glass-topped table.

Butch leaned toward Amy and Carey and said. "Hey, those guys are talking about Longville, listen."

Butch watched a grizzled old man, with dirty, ragged, bib overalls bulging over his fat stomach. He turned up his hearing and heard, "We need to organize a posse and hunt down every son-of-a-bitching wolf in the county."

A second man with faded red hair, long overdue for a haircut, said, "I don't think wolves done it, do you Hank?"

Butch glanced at Amy and Carey; his eyes bulged. He mind-spoke to them, "Oh, Oh, Here it comes."

A third old man in a red flannel shirt, with a hole in the toe of his right boot, injected, "You know, it was some kind of military attack. The damn army was trying out some new weapons. They don't give a shit for us civilians, you know."

"Bull shit," interrupted the fourth man at the table. He was short, just over four feet tall. His hair cropped short except for long sideburns that stopped at his chin. A deerskin vest covered a dirty white shirt and there were holes in the knees of his worn blue jeans. He sucked in a big breath of air and said, "It was werewolves that done it."

Butch choked on his Pepsi.

"Ah shit, Will," the bib overalls said, with a laugh, "there ain't no such thing as werewolves."

From that point, the conversation among the men degenerated into mindless talk. Butch sipped the last of his Pepsi and waited for the other two to finish up. Together they rose and walked out of the drug store.

On the drive back to the cabin, they listened to WCCO radio's Eric Eskala, "The Minnesota Legislature was called into special session this morning by Governor Anderson. The seriousness of the killings in Longville prompted the Governor to take action. The legislature met in a joint session called for the express purpose of dealing with the killings in Longville. They passed a proclamation demanding the Federal Government appoint a special investigator to look into the cause of these deaths."

Within two days, President Thompson appointed Federal Marshall, Ralph Morsching to head up the investigation of the 'Longville massacre'. Headquarters for Marshall Morsching was in Madison, Wisconsin. He is a decorated officer and respected throughout the law enforcement community. Unknown to anyone, Ralph called in a few favors in order to receive the appointment.

Ralph Morsching and his team flew to St. Paul on Monday for an appointment with Minnesota's Governor Anderson. The yellow cab dropped him off at the steps of the State Capitol. A security guard escorted him into the Governor's waiting room. In a couple of minutes, a young, dark haired man approached him. "Mr. Morsching?"

Ralph nodded.

"Please come with me, the Governor is ready to meet with you." The aide escorted him into the Governor's office.

Governor Anderson sat with his back to the door looking out a picture window, which provided a scenic view of the city. To the south, pieces of the Mississippi River, like a blue ribbon sparkled and flashed between two buildings. The Governor's office was immaculate. A polished oak desk was bare, except for one sheet of paper. On the walls hung two pictures, one of President George Washington, the other of Governor Anderson's wife.

Ralph looked at the gray-haired, overweight man behind the desk. He fought the dominant, superior attitude that was a major part of his personality. "Governor," Ralph said, and waited for the Governor to swing his chair.

"Ah, Mr. Morsching," the Governor said, "I'm glad you have arrived."

Ralph nodded.

The Governor crossed his legs and smoothed out his tie. "I see that President Thompson has appointed you to investigate the slaughter of those folks in Longville." "Yes, sir, it was such a ridiculous, senseless slaughter. If you will give me a month to conduct my investigation, I will give you a complete and accurate report of my findings."

The Governor looked at Ralph over the top of his glasses. A hard look grew on his face. "You've got fourteen days to lay your report on my desk," the Governor snarled and then his face softened and a smile broke the corner of his mouth. "The citizens of Minnesota want immediate action. They're screaming for my scalp, as though the wolf attack was my fault." His face took on a persecuted look.

Inside Ralph seethed, but his face was a mask hiding his true emotions as he stared back at the Governor. "I guarantee you one thing Governor; the investigation will proceed quickly and efficiently. I'll have my report on your desk within your time frame." Ralph was not happy with the short time permitted, but apparently, there were no other options.

"Then, get to it," the Governor said, jumping up, "my constituents want the answers yesterday."

Chapter 12
Investigation Northward

Ralph sent the rest of the team to the parking lot to bring the rental cars around to the front. He and Tom paid their hotel bills and headed for the street.

Inspector Morsching and his brother-in-law, Tom Jarvis waited on the sidewalk in front of the Radisson Hotel, in downtown St. Paul. Tom was Ralph's chief deputy. He was tall, skinny and possessed a big curved nose. He served in Vietnam in Special Forces, as an assassin.

"You know, Tom," Ralph said, staring across the street. "Something is funny with this whole deal in Longville."

"What do you mean?" Tom said, taking a step forward and swiveling to face Ralph.

Ralph brushed his hair back before answering, "If you go back in history there are only two documented accounts of wolves attacking people. One attack occurred in Russia in 1784. A group of trappers was traveling through a forested area, when a pack of wolves attacked them. One of the trappers died from wounds inflicted by the wolves. The trappers were able to drive the wolves off, killing seven of them. Later they attributed the attack to the fact the men were all wearing animal skins and carrying the pelts of animals they trapped.

"A second incident occurred in 1877 in the Colorado Territory. Wolves attacked a group of mountain men. In both cases, the wolves probably thought they were attacking other animals. Never have wolves come into a city and attacked humans."

Tom looked impressed, "Where did you learn all of that?"

"From an encyclopedia."

"I guess I better start reading again."

A puzzled expression covered Ralph's face. His eyes grew smaller, as tiny wrinkles appeared at their corners. "What I can't understand is what would cause two packs of wolves to join together in an attack? Why didn't they attack each other?"

"Maybe they were related," Tom said.

Ralph smiled, "Naw, something is weird. Something we aren't seeing."

Just then, the cars came around the corner and pulled to a stop in front of Ralph. He and Tom jumped in the lead car. The caravan headed for freeway 35E as their first leg of the journey to Longville.

Ralph's team consisted of ten hand picked professional law enforcement officers. Each deputy was a specialist in several different fields of investigation. Ralph worked with all of them before and was aware of each man's capabilities.

Ralph leaned his head back on the headrest and closed his eyes. Before he fell asleep, he promised himself that his team would uncover what happened in Longville.

Chapter 13
Testimony

Several hours later, the three-car caravan pulled into Longville. Mayor Stimpson met Ralph on the sidewalk in front of the bank and led him to a vacant building that was a former hardware store. This was to be their base of operations. The building stood on Main Street. Faded, green, wood siding showed splinters of roughness from years of neglect. The big picture window in the front of the building was dust covered, Ralph did not know if the lights were on inside until someone cleared an opening in the center left side of the window and peeked out.

Ralph walked in the front door of the building and saw a group of volunteers cleaning and arranging several old school desks and other furniture in front of a long oak counter. Ralph heard a vacuum cleaner humming from a hallway to the left. Down a second hallway on the right, a flurry of pounding created a deafening racket. From the back of the store, the sound of a saw tearing through wood added to the chaos.

A man with a shirt reading Johnson Telephone Company pulled a cable up the left hallway to a counter in the main store area. He threaded the cable through a hole in the side of the counter, pulled it along the middle shelf, and then up through a hole in the top of the counter.

Mayor Stimpson pulled on Ralph's sleeve and said over the din. "We're having them install phone jacks in the back rooms, along with high speed internet hookups in most of the rooms." He cupped his mouth, leaned closer to Ralph, and said. "We assumed you would want some offices. Am I right?"

Ralph glared at the Mayor and then remembered himself and smiled. "That's right Mayor, we'll need offices. Thanks. Now if you will excuse me I need to get my team settled."

Morsching's team marched in carrying boxes of equipment they brought with them. Each member scattered down the two hallways, as if they knew where they were going. They each claimed one of the vacant rooms.

Tom followed the crew down one of the halls shouting orders over the noise. He stuck his head in one of the larger rooms and said, "Bubba, I want this room for interrogation. You gotta move."

Bubba nodded, picked up his box and hurried farther down the hall to another empty room.

Tom followed. He peeked in the next room. "George, let's leave this room for Ralph. Okay?"

"You bet, boss," George said, picking up the box he set on the desk and hurried down the hall to claim another room.

The team wasted no time moving in and setting up their base of operations.

By late afternoon, Ralph sat in his office, thinking of what the team would do first. Tom Jarvis walked in and sat on a wooden chair across from Ralph. Tom's hawkish nose dominated his round face and his protruding ears added to his comical appearance. Despite his looks, Tom was intelligent and an efficient peace officer. A few people would have added the word ruthless to the description.

Ralph leaned back and rubbed the crew cut bristles on his head, as he looked at Tom and said, "I still can't believe this happened. Tom, as I told you outside of the hotel this morning wolves do not normally attack humans. Now, all of a sudden we have possibly fifty-four people killed in one evening by wolves." A look of disbelief grew on Ralph's face as he said, "The way it sounds, it was a coordinated attack involving at least two different wolf packs. It just doesn't make any sense."

Tom stood up and moved to the one small window letting in light from outside. He peered through the smeared glass and spotted two boys playing with small metal cars in the dirt between the sidewalk and the street. Tom turned back to Ralph. He glanced out the open office door, to see if anyone was within hearing range. He walked over to Ralph's desk, leaned down and whispered with a serious look on his face, "If I did not know better, I would say our pack carried out the attack."

Ralph's mouth dropped open until it looked like a big Cheerio. Blood drained from his head and he slouched back in his armchair. "Christ, you might be right." Ralph jumped forward in his chair and slapped his forehead. "This must have been a feeding. I should have thought of that myself?"

Tom beamed; proud he came up with the idea that excited Ralph. "Maybe because you did not want to accept it," he said.

"Oh, shit," Ralph said, squeezing the edge of the desk with his hands. Ridges of wrinkles covered his forehead. "If that's true, it means there is another pack of werewolves in the United States. That is not possible?"

Tom's face turned white. "It must be."

Ralph cupped his chin, and then looked into Tom's eyes. "If there is another pack, we can't allow them to survive," he said, matter-of-factly.

"I agree," Tom's lips curled in a wicked smile. "They've already endangered our pack, by their wanton slaughter of that many people. It's lucky we are in charge of this investigation, otherwise the findings could end up exposing their pack and in the long run, ours as well."

Ralph slapped both of his palms down on the top of his desk with a frightened look on his face. "We cannot let that happen."

The next morning, Ralph checked the schedule of activities for the day. He saw that his inspectors scheduled an interview with the two surviving witnesses from the massacre. A note at the bottom of the page suggested that one of them was still suffering with mental issues. Ralph's eyebrow rose as he wondered what they would have to tell. He decided to sit in on the sessions. He walked down the hall and entered the interrogation room.

Joe Petrie, the team leader, pulled open the door leading into the hall. He looked out and saw a woman in a white uniform holding the hand of a small, nervous looking boy. The woman turned toward the creaking noise from the door's hinges. "Ma'am, will you please bring the boy in?" Joe said.

"Let's go Jimmy." The nurse stood and pulled five-year-old Jimmy by the hand. Jimmy held back for a moment and then slid off the chair and let the nurse lead him into the room. Jimmy wore faded jeans and a short, sleeved shirt with alternating red and white horizontal stripes. His dark, wavy hair hung over one robin's egg, blue eye, which looked around the room, alert and intelligent.

Ralph read the report of the boy's story; how he survived the attack on his family by crawling under the front porch of his home. From under the porch, he witnessed the 'wolves' attack and kill his sister and mother, as they ran out of the house.

Ralph Morsching sat next to Roger Stringley behind a long, chewed-up, oak table. The nurse and Jimmy settled on two mismatched, folding chairs in front of the table. Joe Petrie stood beside the table closest to Jimmy. He leaned against the corner of the table and said, "Hi, Jimmy," as cheerfully as he could, trying to put the boy at ease. "My name is Joe and that big guy over there is Ralph and the man sitting next to him is Roger. They want to hear your story again, of what you saw the other night."

Jimmy looked with a shy glance at the two men and then dropped his eyes back to his folded hands on his lap.

Joe frowned and said. "We've been directed by Governor Anderson. He wants me to find out what happened in your town and tell all the people in the United States the truth." Joe walked over to where Jimmy sat on the edge of his folding chair. He knelt down with his head at the same level as Jimmy's eyes. "Now, to do the job your Governor wants us to do, we need your help Jimmy. Four people saw what happened a week ago on Wednesday night, when all those people were hurt. Four people in your town saw the wolves. Of those four Jimmy, you're the most important witness."

Jimmy's head bobbed up and his face showed a slight smile on his lips, as he said, "I am?"

"Yes you are. Two of those people are sick and cannot talk. You saw the wolves and you can talk." Joe hesitated. "Jimmy, can you tell me what you saw?"

Jimmy stared at his folded hands. Ralph watched the boy's face contort, as tears began to flow down his cheeks. Jimmy started to shake, as remembrance flooded back into his mind.

"Jimmy," the nurse said, "tell these nice men what you told the doctor and me about the wolves. If you don't they cannot help us get rid of them."

Roger glanced at Joe, caught his eye, and then said, "Maybe Jimmy did not see anything."

Jimmy sat up in his chair and glared at Roger. "I did too see something," Jimmy said. "I, I saw great big wolves kill and eat my mommy and sister, Becky."

The nurse pulled him back on the chair and patted his leg. Tears continued to cascade down his round cheeks.

Joe patted Jimmy on the back, "Will you tell us the first thing you saw?" Joe said.

Jimmy sniffed a couple of times and the nurse handed him a Kleenex. He wiped his eyes and face, blew his nose and then handed the wrinkled Kleenex back to the nurse.

"My daddy made me go outside and sit on the porch," he stated.

"Why did he do that?" Ralph said.

Jimmy squirmed, "Because I was naughty, I made too much noise when he was watching TV. That was before the lights went out."

"Okay," Joe said and looked with sympathy at the nurse, "then what happened?"

"It was dark out, but I saw one of those big wolfs run from behind our garage to the side of my house. At first, I thought it was Cracker."

"Who is Cracker," Joe said.

"It is our neighbor's dog. But, I knew it was not Cracker. The thing I saw was too big. Then the first wolf went behind my house."

Joe interrupted Jimmy. "You mean you saw more than one wolf?"

"Yeah," Jimmy said, "I saw another one run after the first one. They were real big."

"How big Jimmy?" Ralph said.

Jimmy slipped off the chair and raised his hands over his head.

Ralph nodded, "Four feet tall. Did they run on two feet or four feet?"

The nurse looked at Ralph her eyes squinted together.

Wolves can't run on two feet," Jimmy said, looking at Ralph as if he was a dummy. "They ran on four feet, you know, like a dog," Jimmy said, his voice cracking with excitement now.

"Good, Jimmy," Joe said. "You're being a big help, telling us just what we need to hear. Go on, what else?"

"Then I heard a window break. I know what that sounds like, cuz I threw a ball through our garage window last week," he smiled and then said. "I looked in through the screen door and saw one of the wolves bite my daddy on his head and make him bleed. My daddy started to scream and that is when I ran and hid under the porch. My sister Becky started screaming and then she ran out the screen door. I looked between the steps and I could see her and mommy running across the grass," Jimmy stopped and wiped his nose on his hand.

Joe leaned forward, "And?"

"Then I saw two big wolfs run after them," Jimmy said. "He caught Becky and mommy and it. . . ." Tears flowed down his cheeks in tiny rivulets, as wracking sobs shook his body.

The nurse pulled Jimmy's head down on her lap. Jimmy's shoulders shook as he cried into the nurse's white skirt.

Ralph shook his head. He was now sure that werewolves were responsible for killing the people of Longville. What Jimmy described fit the werewolf size and mode of attack.

As Jimmy sobbed, the men discussed what Jimmy told them.

Ralph caught Joe's eye and then communicated with him via a mental broadcast. "Son of a bitch, this confirms it; there is another werewolf pack in the United States."

"That's what it looks like," Joe broadcast from his mind. "Tom warned me there might be."

Roger was not a member of Ralph's werewolf pack, therefore Ralph and the other pack members were careful what they said around him.

Ralph stood up and moved toward the door. "Well Roger, Joe, it looks like the reports are correct," he said, "Wolves were responsible for killing all those people."

Roger nodded and looked at Ralph with a question on his face, "Yeah, I guess, the only question I have is, do wolves get that big; four feet tall?"

Ralph chuckled and said loud enough for the nurse to hear. "Maybe they weren't quite four feet tall." He winked at the nurse and smiled. She smiled back at Ralph and then helped Jimmy from the room.

Based on reports, the other witness's account of what happened was of no value. However, his ramblings did support the theory of wolves being responsible for the killings.

The other two witnesses were under a doctor's care and were still in a state of shock. They were unable to give any kind of coherent statement. One of them babbled repeatedly of a "big . . . big wolf." The other witness said, "stand up . . . head flew through the air . . . eat mama."

According to the doctors caring for the two patients, it would be months before they might regain their sanity, if ever.

The next afternoon Ralph left the interrogation room where Tom was talking to one of the hunters. He walked down the hallway on warped, wooden floorboards to where another interrogation was taking place. Ralph opened the door and saw Sergeant Michel talking to a man that fit the description of Sheriff McCarthy.

Sergeant Michel looked at Ralph peeking through the doorway and motioned for him to come in. "Sheriff, I'd like you to meet Inspector Morsching. He is in charge of the investigation. He was appointed by President Thompson," the Sergeant said.

Ralph offered his hand to the Sheriff, who placed his other hand over their shaking hands.

"Hi, Mr. Morsching, sir," the Sheriff said, with a nervous tick causing his eye to quiver, "I was just telling the Sergeant here what we've found out so far."

"Go on, don't let me interrupt you," Ralph said, taking the Sheriff by the elbow and escorting him back to his chair. "If you don't mind, I'd like to sit in and listen," Ralph said.

The Sheriff nodded with a nervous twist of his head, exposing his awe of the Federal Inspector. Ralph smiled and sat down on an old cushioned living room chair on the other side of the table.

"Well," the Sheriff said, "we found thousands of wolf tracks all over town; in gardens, alleys, and in muddy areas at the edge of town. We found some weird shaped wolf prints inside several homes. You know, where the animals stepped in the blood of their victims."

Ralph nodded.

The Sheriff said, "The prints in the houses were like those of a wolf, but much larger, with longer claws. Some of the trappers in the area said the prints were those of wolves, the same number of toes and everything. Man, I tell you, some were gigantic, eight to ten inches across. A couple of experts from the Minnesota Zoo came in a couple of days ago and even they were hesitant to identify the real big ones as wolves, but couldn't suggest what else they might be."

Ralph leaned forward and rested his head on his two fists. "Did they say what they might be, if they weren't wolves?"

The Sheriff swallowed and then said, "Naw, they were not sure. They suggested the tracks could have been from some larger crossbred form of a wolf. I will tell you, the trappers around here have never seen prints that big . . . Ever, but they all agreed they were wolf tracks." The Sheriff glanced down at the paper in his hand and then said. "Twenty residents are dead, but what confounds me is that we have not found any evidence of what happened to the other thirty-four. I'm sure you have seen pictures on TV and in the newspapers. Some of the victims were dismembered and all of them were partially eaten."

"Are conditions in the forests that bad?" Sergeant Michels said. "What I mean is, could the wolves have been that hungry to have attacked people in a town?"

"No," the Sheriff said. "The trappers tell me there are an abundance of deer in the woods, along with rabbits and mice. No, the wolves were not lacking for their normal food sources." The Sheriff glanced down at his list and went on, "We have four National Guard helicopters carrying sharpshooters, flying over the area. As of this morning, they have shot twenty-eight wolves. The wolves were concentrated in three separate areas, suggesting they were three different packs, not two like the TV said. The shooters said they have annihilated the two wolf packs closest to town."

"How many wolves do they figure are left," Ralph said.

"They tell me there might be ten, maybe fifteen, still running around."

"Sheriff, if we kill off those wolves, do you think it will eliminate the same thing from ever happening again?" Sergeant Michels said.

"I have no doubt in my mind," the Sheriff said. "These wolves must have gone off the deep end to come into town and attack people."

"Your assessment of the situation should satisfy the people of Minnesota," Ralph said.

"It has to, what else can we do? Once we kill off all of the wolves, we have eliminated the problem," the Sheriff said, shrugging his shoulders.

A week later, the special investigation was over. The team compiled their final report and Ralph called a public meeting. He would inform the people of Longville what most of them knew and already believed. The mayor arranged for them to use the VFW Club, reserving most of the seats for residents and saving a few spots for members of the press and TV.

Inspector Ralph Morsching stood behind the podium mounted with a forest of microphones, waiting for his cue.

The Channel 4 news director pointed to him, counting down with his fingers, three, two, one. "Ladies and Gentlemen," Ralph said, to get everyone's attention. The room hushed. Ralph waited a few moments and then said. "Our investigation into the killing of twenty residents of Longville is complete. Thirty-four other residents are missing and presumed dead. What we have found can in no way make up for the loss to Longville for the deaths of their friends and neighbors."

"I hope what my team has learned from the evidence will satisfy the living. With the expert assistance of the Cass County Sheriff's department and Sheriff McCarthy, the Minnesota National Guard, the Minnesota Highway Patrol and the Longville Police Department, our team has gathered all of the available facts in this case. The evidence we have is in the form of footprints, medical evidence and the testimony of experts."

"All of our information supports the conclusion that the attack on the residents of Longville and the subsequent deaths of its residents was caused by three separate wild packs of wolves. We cannot explain how or why three separate wolf packs happened to attack Longville at the same time. All of the wolves we hunted down and killed, we found human tissue in their digestive systems. This was true of wolves from all three of the packs.

"Wolf behaviorists suggested to my team the possibility there was a territorial fight between the three wolf packs and that the people of Longville ended up in the middle of that fight. In addition to the fight between the packs, I have found another contributing factor which may explain the savagery of the attack," Ralph hesitated and then said. "Sharpshooters from the Longville area, with the help of the National Guard and their helicopters, have eliminated the three wolf packs. Veterinarians performed autopsies on all of the wolves shot. They found some of the wolves with an unusual brain infection, similar to, but not the same as rabies. They think this infection may have brought on the attack."

The reporters in the crowd leaned forward. Here was something newsworthy, something to explain why the wolves attacked that many people.

Ralph noted the heightened interest and said, "The Veterinarians suggest these infections may have something to do with the attack on the people of Longville, but cannot say it definitely brought on the attack.

"Because all of the infected wolves have been killed, nothing like this will ever happen in Minnesota again." Ralph stepped back and then said. "This is what I will report to Governor Anderson and the Legislature of Minnesota tomorrow. Thank you all for coming."

Several reporters pushed and shoved in their rush for the exit and the nearest available phone. Ralph did not mind. They would help spread his version of the cause for the 'Longville Massacre', just what he wanted.

"Hey, Mr. Morsching," a reporter from the side of the room said. "Are you sure you killed all the wolves?"

Ralph smiled, "Major Hendrickson of the National Guard assures me they killed all of them. To make sure, I will recommend in my report to the Governor and the Minnesota Legislature, that they hire a core of special hunters and trappers, who will continue scouring the woods for any wolves we might have missed."

Ralph gathered his papers from the podium and started to leave when another reporter said, "Inspector, Will you be providing a written report for us?"

Ralph turned back, "Our team will provide written copies of our full findings of the investigation to the news media following our presentation to the Minnesota Legislature on Wednesday, which is three weeks to the day the atrocity occurred. I might add I am within the time frame Governor Anderson insisted on."

The eyes of Chief Inspector Ralph Morsching and Captain Tom Jarvis locked. A secret message flashed between them. They nodded their mutual understanding. They knew what, or better yet, who was responsible for the 'Longville Massacre', and it was not wild wolves.

Sergeant Michels, one of Ralph's top inspectors, left the VFW and started back to the motel. He walked along the sidewalk, watching for irregular pieces of concrete sticking up. He heard the clicking of footsteps coming up behind him. A cold, icy chill raced down his spine. His werewolf senses flew to the front of his mind.

The word, "Werewolf" raced through his mind. He started in motion the steps that would bring on his own change. Hair started to sprout on the back of his hands, when he heard a female voice, "Excuse me, Sergeant Michels could I ask you a couple of questions?"

Michels stopped his transformation and whirled around, a frightened mask covering his face. He saw a woman with a press badge hanging from her jacket pocket standing silhouetted in the light from the VFW. She wore a gray sports jacket, with her long, blond hair splashing down around her collar. He gulped and tried to speed his return to normal. His hair reabsorbed and the follicles tightened.

A whoosh of air escaped from Sergeant Michel's mouth. He tried to assume a relaxed pose by placing his hands on his hips. It did not work, but he felt better. "Sure, why not?" he said in a deeper than normal voice.

The female reporter advanced. "I have been talking to some of the townspeople," she began, "and a few of them wondered about a link between the wolf attack and the digging up of the main roads leading into Longville. They told me the main road into Longville from the north and south prevented the flow of traffic. How convenient it was that the telephone, cell phone and electric services went dead at the same time? Would you care to comment on this?" She pulled a notebook from her pocket.

Sergeant Michels smiled. He thought to himself, just like a noisy reporter. "We heard that cock-eyed idea before. Let me lay it to rest for the last time. The digging of the roads was in no way related to the wolf attack. To believe that would suggest a coordinated, planned, intelligent maneuver between humans and wolves. Let me assure you wolves are not that intelligent or cooperative. How in hell, could any human control three wild wolf packs in the first place? What benefit would any humans have, assuming they could control the wolves? Nothing was stolen, just innocent people killed.

"The attack and the digging up of the roadway were coincidental. The buyers of the land on either side of town petitioned the County Board two months ago to allow them to insert culverts under the road, so they could build on the sites."

"Why did they have to dig up the road," the reporter asked.

"The group that bought the property is planning to construct some office buildings. The culverts will drain the water on the upper side of the highway. The work on the culverts and roads just happened at the same time the wolves attacked the town. The road work was repaired on Thursday, the day after the attack."

"Care to explain another unusual feature I dug up," the reporter asked.

"And that is?"

Every single ham operators in town was killed," she exclaimed.

Sgt. Michels grabbed his chin with his right hand and said, "Hmmm, I have not heard that one yet. I guess I do not have an answer for you. It must be another coincidence."

"It seems like a lot of coincidence in this whole mess, if you ask me," the reporter huffed.

"Come on Ms.," Sgt. Michels said. "To accept that would mean just what I said earlier; humans and wolves would have been working in concert. Do you believe that?"

The reporter nodded. "No, I guess not. The idea that humans could be working with or controlling wild wolves is kind of absurd," the reporter said, and then she flipped the page of her notebook and said. "That brings up another question I have."

Sgt. Michels huffed, "I must be going."

"Oh, oh," the reporter said. "Just one more question, please?"

"Okay."

"If three wolf packs were fighting each other over territory, why weren't any dead wolves found in town?"

Sergeant Michels face paled. "Well, Ah, Ah, I suppose because none were killed in town. The wounded ones must have been able to make it to the woods," he said.

"Yeah, sure," the reporter said, "According to the release from the Sheriff's Department, all the wolves brought in died from bullet wounds, none from other causes." The reporter grunted, "Something in this whole story just doesn't add up." She turned and walked back towards the VFW Club.

Michels wondered why no one on the Investigation team thought of some of the reporters concerns. He decided he would talk to Ralph tomorrow.

His mind forgot the dead wolves, as he admired the swing of the reporter's hips, as she disappeared down the sidewalk and into the crowd of people still leaving the VFW.

Ralph sat alone in his makeshift office in the old hardware store. A single light bulb made an effort to illuminate the room, but was not having much success. The shadows still controlled the perimeter of the room and the area behind the file cabinets. In a matter of a few hours, the town of Longville would lose half of its population when the press, National Guard, and police officials left. The invaders would all go home and soon forget the sinister events that happened in Longville. The people of Longville could finish grieving.

Ralph sat up and rested his hands on the old school desk. “We will go home and then soon I will be starting my own hunt,” he promised aloud.

Chapter 14
The Pre-Hunt

Ralph swiveled his chair around and gazed out the window of his office on the tenth floor. His eyes followed a Northwest jet, as it floated across the sky from right to left. He always felt at peace when he looked at the skyline of Madison. This was his home.

Tom Jarvis burst into Ralph's office.

Ralph jumped, frightened by Tom's abrupt entrance and tried to hide his reaction from him. Ralph admonished himself, "Jesus I wasn't very alert. I did not hear him coming down the hall." He turned slowly from the window and glanced calmly at Tom, who stood, puffing in front of his desk.

Tom always the military man, stood with his legs apart and hands locked behind his back, he said, "Ralph, what in the hell are we gonna do?"

"That's simple, we are going to find the other werewolf pack and exterminate them," Ralph said, pounding the top of his desk. "They bungled that Longville raid. If it wasn't for us conducting the investigation, there is a good chance they would have been exposed." His face turned ashen. "Chances are our pack would have been exposed too."

Tom said, "Doesn't that blow your mind?"

"What do you mean?

Tom's eyes grew round, "Ralph, weren't you surprised to find out another pack exists? Where did they come from?"

Ralph rotated the chair toward Tom. Ralph's nostrils flared and the artery in his forehead pulsed, "Surprised, I was flabbergasted. I have no idea where they could have originated from and that bothers me, but where they come does not worry me. Our main problem is our survival." He shook his head. "We cannot afford to let them repeat the killings. They were stupid," Ralph said, as he swung his chair back to his desk and slammed his elbows down. "Can you imagine what would happen to our pack if humans found proof werewolves existed?"

Tom moved to the couch and sat down. He picked at his fingernails with a small pocketknife. "Jeez, I suppose we'd have to run for it." His face took on a quizzical look. "But, Ralph, I'd still like to know where they came from. I thought our family was the only werewolves left in the world." Tom said.

Ralph spread his finger out on the desk. He did not want to worry about where the werewolves came from. They were here and that was enough. He knew Tom would keep bugging him until he knew where they came from.

"Okay Tom. It might be possible someone survived the Belgrade massacre. Great grandfather figured he was the only one to escape alive, but he always thought it possible one of the other werewolves passed on the curse to one of the hunters. In all the years following the massacre, he never ran across any evidence of the presence of another werewolf in the Belgrade area. Of course, he finally left Belgrade and immigrated to America."

Ralph's eyes took on a far away look, as his mind wandered, taking him back into the past. He saw the inside of his grandparent's old homestead. Without trying, he pictured his Great grandmother Rachel standing at the sink, peeling potatoes and humming to herself. Ralph's mind focused on that time, a long time ago when he sat on Great Grandpapa Adolph's lap. His father and grandfather were still out working in the fields, but should be home for supper at any time.

He could still hear the hoarse, rasping voice of his great grandfather, as he retold the story of the killing of the pack.

"Listen, Ralphie," Great grandpa said, "I'm going to tell you a story about our pack."

Ralph felt a shiver of warmth similar to the one that radiated from his great grandfather's body those many years ago. Every time he pictured his great grandfather holding him, he felt safe and secure.

"Back in 1480 our pack was well established," great grandfather continued his story in Ralph's mind. "Pack members owned a number of farms near Belgrade, Czechoslovakia. When our pack discovered a drug that held back the madness, the desire to kill and devour human flesh for long periods, we were ecstatic. In spite of the drug, at regular intervals, the desire for human flesh still becomes overwhelming and then we have to satisfy our needs or experience the madness. On those occasions, the pack would venture into Belgrade at night to hunt.

"Ralphie, we needed to satisfy the craving. Do you understand? We would hunt as a pack, and all members participated in the killing. The important thing was that each individual did not need to kill their own victim; one victim satisfied all of our needs. We always chose our victim from the streets, someone single, with no attachments. We would go down along the river, where the homeless people lived and choose a victim from one of them."

"On one occasion, the pack entered the city hunting for a derelict to feed on, when three members of my pack lost control. They became crazed, uncontrollable. They slipped over to the wild side. They ran off down the street toward the populated part of the city. We chased after them to stop them, but were too late.

"On a corner outside a tavern, the crazed ones came upon a group of people. They attacked and killed several of them. One of the humans escaped and ran into the tavern screaming for help.

"We were a short distance away when we heard the screaming. We raced toward the noise, fearful of what we would find. Even though we expected the worst, we were shocked to see what the three had accomplished in such a short time.

"Dead humans lay scattered on the cobblestone, blood splashed everywhere. The three out of control werewolves were feeding on the dead. They were engrossed in feeding; they did not even know we came up behind them. We attacked the renegade werewolves and killed them. Freed from their madness, their wolfish features changed back to their human forms. We raced off into the night, before anyone saw us and from a dark alley a block away we watched a crowd of people pour out of the tavern. The screams carried to where we hid as the humans circled the dead. Our three relatives lay among the dead humans and drew no special attention. They were just one more of the many torn and mangled bodies.

“The next day a group of angry townspeople using hunting dogs followed our trail back to your Great Uncle Frederick’s farm. The armed group of people attacked the farm. They killed Frederick, Alicia, and the rest of their children. Grappli was the only one to escape.

The lad fled through the corn fields to Uncle Herman’s farm located on the other side of the valley. The mob set fire to Frederick’s farm and then followed Grappli’s trail across the valley. By mid afternoon, the armed mob reached Uncle Herman’s farm. During the attack, two of Herman’s older sons changed into werewolves. They fought the city mob and killed several of them before dying themselves. In the end, they killed all of Uncle Herman’s family and decapitated the bodies. The mob incensed by finding out werewolves existed, continued down the valley attacking and killing anyone with the name of Morsching.”

Tears ran down Ralph’s cheeks. He blinked flushing more tears from his eyes. The daydream was clear, the burning buildings, and the maddened mob attacking and beheading his ancestors. He saw it all. His wounded great grandfather escaped into the forest. Every single one of his relatives died in the Belgrade Massacre. His Great grandfather left Czechoslovakia and later settled in Bavaria, Germany.

Ralph’s head shook with empathy, as he wiped the tears from his face. The picture of his sobbing great grandfather faded and his daydream ended. The memories left him saddened and feeling drained.

Ralph thought of his daydream, hoping to learn from the memories, “Tom, see if my reasoning is correct,” he said. “First, we know this new pack does not use the drug or they would not have killed so many humans.”

“Do you think they have fifty-four pack members?” Tom said.

Ralph said. “Jeez, I didn't consider that. It is still unbelievable any pack leader would allow the pack to get that big."

Tom replied, "Don't forget they are not us. Anything is possible."

"You are right. They can't be related to us or they would be using Aldropamine."

“True,” Tom folded the blade of his pocketknife and slipped it into his pocket. He stood up, walked over to the desk, and sat on a corner. He placed his hand on Ralph’s shoulder.

“You know,” Ralph said, still finding it hard to believe his pack was not aware of other werewolves. “It is even more amazing, we have not run across the other werewolves. We have been in Minnesota many times.”

"What makes you think they live in Minnesota?"

Ralph looked up with a startled look. "I just assumed that is where they live.

"Why not North or South Dakota or for that matter, they could have come from just about anywhere," Tom said.

Ralph shook his head and stared out the window. After a minute, he swiveled his chair back toward Tom. "You are right Tom, but we have to start somewhere."

“I agree,” Tom said. “We’ve got to stop them before they have to feed again. The next time they might be exposed and that would eventually pull us into the mix.” He walked over to the sofa and dropped like a lead weight.

Ralph made up his mind. “Here is what we are going to do. We will start with Minnesota, which in my mind is the logical place for them to be. Next Monday,” he said, with finality, shaking his head to emphasis his words, “I’m going to take a team to the Twin Cities. We will hunt for them and if we find them, we will destroy them. We have to be careful not to attract any attention to ourselves or to the fact werewolves are involved in the killings.” He turned to the window again and placed his elbows on the arms of the chair. He formed his fingers into a pyramid in front of his chin and looked out the window, formulating the details of the hunt in his mind.

A few moments later, he murmured, “Tom, I want you to stay in Madison and run the office.” Ralph hesitated and then said, “I have got some vacation time coming. I will handle the away team.”

Chapter 15
Back To Minnesota

Ralph watched the gusting north wind lift several shingles on the garage roof across the street. The shingles tapped out a cadence of a long forgotten death march that played in the back of Ralph's mind.

Black clouds rolled out of the northeast and bounced across the sky, producing a dark, foreboding feeling in Ralph's mind. Ralph rolled his eyes across the horizon looking for the sun, which was nowhere in sight. He wondered if the sun would show up and chase the ominous looking clouds away. He suspected that would lift the momentary depression he was feeling. Ralph shook his head and thought; "No matter, we need to get started for Minnesota."

Ralph became excited when he thought about embarking on this mission to Minnesota. The werewolf pack might be located elsewhere, but he felt their home base was somewhere in Minnesota and the Twin Cities was a good place to begin his search. The thrill of the hunt flowed through his body. He hoped this dismal weather was not an omen of what lay ahead. A touch of fear plagued him and rode the edge of his consciousness. Was nature trying to tell him something?

Ralph did not take starting a war between werewolves lightly. He knew some of his pack members would be injured or killed in the next several weeks. Nevertheless, today would mark the beginning of his search for the werewolves in Minnesota.

Looking out the kitchen window, Ralph watched five of his handpicked team members standing next to the Chevy Suburban. Alice with her pitch-black hair and dark complexion leaned against the front fender. She was Tom Jarvis's daughter, forty-seven years old and the most vicious killer in Ralph's pack. All of the others left her alone.

Pete stood near the rear door of the vehicle, avoiding the blustery wind. He was Ralph's second oldest son and slated to take over command of the pack if anything happened to him. Pete was intelligent and built like a bull.

Selected because of her role in the last feeding, Pete's seventeen-year-old daughter, Gretchen was part of the team. On her own, she prevented Bernie from losing control and going over to the wild side. Six months ago, Bernie started to go crazy and Gretchen jumped him, biting him on the back. She did not let go until Ralph came to her aid.

Ralph chose Joseph, also seventeen, because of his special ability to see into the future. With a little more experience, Ralph felt Joseph's unusual talents would be a tremendous asset to the pack.

The last member of the away team was Will Franzen. He was eighteen and another of Ralph's grandsons. Will showed the greatest promise of any member in the pack. He was intelligent and possessed excellent leadership skills. Will played a major role in planning the last two human feedings by the pack. He provided logistics and timing for both events.

Excitement radiated from their faces. Ralph knew they were thrilled at being included in this different kind of hunt, a hunt for their own kind. Ralph put on a light jacket and exited the house through the kitchen door. He walked toward the Suburban. "Okay, Pete, let's get going," he said, pounding him on the back.

The rest of the group heard and scrambled for a seat. Pete jumped behind the wheel. He turned the key and the vehicle coughed to life. Pete pointed the vehicle toward Interstate 94. A few minutes later, the Suburban crawled up the ramp onto the freeway and headed west for Minnesota.

"Wake me when we hit St. Paul," Ralph said with a yawn. He slouched down in the passenger seat and closed his eyes.

A moment later Ralph opened his eyes and slid, erect in his seat. He pivoted to look back over his shoulder. "Will, where did you arrange for us to stay?"

"Will stretched and shoved a pillow behind his head before he answered, "I booked us in the Hilton Hotel."

Pete glanced at Will in the rear view mirror. "Where's it located?" he said with a smile.

"South of the International Airport, ah, just off of Freeway 494," Will said sounding annoyed at the second degree.

"Will," Pete grumbled. "I don't like the Hilton."

Will bounced up off his pillow. "Well, tough shit. If you don't like it then you should have made the reservations." Will's face was red and his jaw muscles moved back and forth.

"Hey, kid, take it easy. I was just kidding," Pete said faking fright. He enjoyed the rise he got out of Will.

Ralph said, "Okay, you guys that is enough. Will, why not take a minute and explain to my bone-headed son why you chose the Hilton."

Will calmed down and said, "The biggest reason is the hotel is located close to both Minneapolis and St. Paul."

"Do you see now the wisdom of trusting Will to do the right thing rather than you?" Ralph smiled and slid back in his seat. Ralph knew everything was set. He closed his eyes and soon fell asleep.

Late in the afternoon, they crossed the bridge over the St. Croix River at Hudson, Wisconsin and followed 94 into the East side of St. Paul. When 94 hit 494, they turned south. It was not long before they spotted the Hilton Hotel, south of the highway from a bunch of planes and hangars on the north side of the road.

They checked in and rode the elevator to the tenth floor. Will had reserved three adjoining suites. Ralph and Pete chose the middle room. Their windows looked south, out over the Minnesota River bottoms that meandered behind the strip of hotels and business places. The river ran through Fort Snelling State Park and eventually emptied into the Mississippi River. Looking to the left Ralph saw airplanes landing at the Minneapolis-St. Paul International Airport.

Everyone unpacked and then gravitated to Ralph's room. Will was the first one through the door. He walked over to Pete's bed and sat down. He looked at Ralph and said, "Well, what do we do now?"

Ralph shrugged his shoulders. "The first thing we need to do is take a ride and get acquainted with the Twin Cities."

Ralph called the desk and arranged for the rental of two automobiles. He then explained everyone's assignments.

Ralph and Pete took the Suburban and headed for Minneapolis.

Will and Pete's daughter, Gretchen grabbed the red Chrysler convertible and headed east on 494. They exited on Highway 5, which brought them in to St. Paul on west 7th Street.

Alice, Tom Jarvis' daughter and Ralph's grandson, Joseph piled into the more conservative forest green, Escort and followed 494 east to 35E and then swung south toward Mendota and Inver Grove Heights. The three teams spent the next few days exploring different areas of the Twin Cities.

Monday night arrived with a loud declaration. Lightening raced across the sky from cloud to cloud. Other brilliant bolts followed a jagged path to the ground. The hotel windows rattled with each booming crash of thunder. Rain came down in sheets and pounded against the windows.

Ralph hurried in from the balcony and slammed the door to the rain. He left wet footprints on his way to the bathroom. He removed his wet robe and wiped his body dry. After putting on a dry robe, he walked out into the main room and plopped down on the sofa with a loud sigh. "Well," he said, "tomorrow we begin the search for werewolves. It looks like we will have to search each city and suburb to find their lairs."

Will slouched on the other end of the sofa. His face brightened. "Good, I'm tired of all this aimless wandering."

A familiar theme jumped into Ralph's thoughts, what would happen to the pack if he and Pete died? That concern occupied his thoughts lately. Ralph decided it was time to begin grooming someone else to take over the pack. He was fast concluding that Will would be the logical werewolf to assume leadership of the pack. Ralph studied Will. He was proud of his seventeen-year-old grandson. Several times, Will demonstrated exceptional leadership during pack activities. That was why Ralph went out of his way to give Will as much responsibility and experience as possible. The 'Minnesota excursion' would be a good chance for him to learn what it takes to lead. He turned to Will and said, "Will this has not been a waste of time. It gave us a chance to learn the layout of the Twin Cities."

Will blushed as he said, “I know Grandpa. I guess I’m just getting anxious to find the reckless werewolves and put an end to them.”

Ralph smiled. “I know how you feel.” Then he turned to the rest of his team. Any questions regarding your assignments for tomorrow?” he said.

Pete said, “Naw, we’ve gone over them enough.”

“Okay, then let’s get a good nights sleep,” Ralph said clapping his hands together. “Tomorrow the search begins for real.”

Joseph and Will went to the room they shared. Will finished using the bathroom and changed into his pajamas. He crawled under the sheets and stared at the ceiling. Joseph headed for the bathroom. Will wiped the sleep from his eyes and said,” Joseph, if the werewolves are here their days are numbered.”

Joseph looked over his shoulder. “I hope you are right, but aren‘t you worried some of us might be killed?”

“Not at all, they will ever know what hit them. I look forward to hunting and killing them.”

Chapter 16
Hanging Out at University & Rice

Across from where Will stood, was a street sign for University Avenue. To his right was another sign identifying Rice Street, which ran north and south. Will's gaze followed University Avenue to the east until his eyes locked on a white domed building, topped by golden horses and a chariot. From his studies of the area, he knew it was the Minnesota State Capitol.

Will rubbed his eyes and squinted, attempting to read the small letters on the harness of one of the horses. The November sky was overcast and hazy and he couldn‘t quite read what it said. A cool breeze blew up from the Mississippi River, and sending a shiver through his body. He should have worn a heavier jacket.

Will leaned against the brown brick wall of the building behind him and felt coolness penetrate his jacket. He studied every person passing by. Some of the people caught him staring, diverted their eyes, and hurried by.

He ignored the peculiar grimaces on their faces and wondered if he looked different to them. Maybe that was why they looked at him with weird side-glances. He caught himself sniffing like a dog; that would account for the strange looks he was getting. I must make them nervous.

A tall man dressed in a dark blue suit walked by carrying a leather briefcase. He stared at Will with a disgusted look before shaking his head and looking away. Will heard him murmur something like, "the crazies you see on the streets now days".

Will smiled and thought, "If only you knew."

Will spent the morning glued to the corner of University and Rice. The weatherman's prediction proved accurate. By late afternoon, the climate changed, turning colder and windy. Traffic increased, as people began to head home from work. Car exhaust polluted the air and made it difficult for Will to filter out and identify different human smells. Of course, he was searching for one specific scent.

A middle-aged woman shuffled toward him from up wind. She was a block to the east. He smelled the scent of blood, but it did not excite him. Will looked away, trying to disguise his disgust.

A few minutes later, a man driving an old, brown, rusted-out, Chevy, passed Will, traveling west on University Avenue. The exhaust smoke swirled on the breeze toward Will and he could smell alcohol coming from the vehicle. Will gagged and swiveled his head to focus on another man in a gray suit standing on the corner of University Avenue and Rice Street.

The man waited for the lights to change. Will smelled the strong scent of urine and knew the man wet his pants earlier in the day. From the strength of the ammonia, he guessed it happened close to nine o'clock in the morning. It would take that long for the bacterial decomposition of urea to produce such a strong smell of ammonia.

Smells of yeast and bread wafted on the currents and eddies of the easterly breeze. He knew the odors were coming from the Tastee Bread-Day Old Shop a few blocks away. His stomach growled. Wrapped up in his search for some sign of the other werewolves, Will forgot to eat anything all day.

Will grinned and leaned back against the building housing AAA Vacuum Cleaner. The store was two buildings from the intersection. He closed his eyes, as a scowl grew on his face. "This is a waste of time, standing around, waiting for a werewolf to walk by. Chances are one in a million that is gonna happen," Will said. "Waiting for an odor to awaken my primordial senses," he said talking to himself. "Hey, that's kind of poetic, but to locate the other werewolf pack will take more than my primordial senses."

He felt better after complaining and pushed away from the wall. He strolled toward the corner, hoping his patient efforts would bring results.

All of a sudden, instincts kicked in and Will's head moved erect. He could not prevent the growl that escaped from his throat or the sniffing sounds his nose made. Like a hunting dog, his head swiveled back and forth, directing his nose into the wind.

He honed in on a faint, but distinct smell. It was werewolf. His nose pointed eastward. Mixed in with the exhaust-laden currents, urine, baking bread odors and a hundred other scents, swirled a few molecules of werewolf musk. Although masked, there was no mistaking the distinctive smell.

Will jogged down the sidewalk toward the State Capitol, his nose leading him. He did not notice the deliveryman until he bumped into him. Two boxes of drugs tumbled from the man's arms. He did a funny dance to keep the other three boxes from dropping. Will ignored the string of curses that followed him as he ran east on University Avenue.

Will was no longer in charge of his actions, his nose was. He did not even know he crossed Rice Street against a red light, until he heard brakes screeching. Out of the corner of his eye, he saw a fat woman bounce back from the steering wheel of her Thunderbird. The Ford stalled in the middle of the crosswalk. In a daze, the women reached over and pulled a bleeding child up from the floor. Will saw the passenger side windshield was shattered.

Will said as he mounted the curb on the other side of the street. "Way to go Lady. It's your fault for not making your kid wear a seat belt."

Frightened people parted on the curb to let Will through. Half way down the block toward Park Street, Will stopped and sniffed the air. "Shit I've lost the scent," he said, turning to look in different directions.

His mind sought a solution; they could have passed me on the other side of the street or driven by me in a car. If they are west of me, Will thought, that means they can probably smell me by now.

A chill caused the hair on the back of his neck to stand erect. They could have gone north or south. What do I do? He shrugged his shoulders and without hesitation turned south on Park Street.

Will jogged down the street to where the street curved in front of the State Capitol, called Martin Luther King Jr. Blvd. Will stopped, the 'were odor' once again assaulted his nasal passages. He looked upwind and saw fifty people walking in all directions. Most of them were heading for Robert Street. Will raced down the Blvd. and lost the scent again.

He stood at the Robert Street intersection wondering if he should follow it to the northwest or southeast. He threw up his arms and then turned to the southeast. He passed over Freeway 94, toward downtown St. Paul.

A block ahead of him, three men walked on the other side of the street. Will saw their lips moving and one of them was using his hands to emphasize a point as he talked.

Will ran down the street, until he was across the street from them. The werewolf scent hit his nostrils and almost overpowered him. He stumbled, surprised at the strength of the werewolf odor. He regained his footing, hoping they did not notice him. Will slowed to a walk and took several deep breaths. He shivered at the speed of emotional drain on him.

He was afraid to glance across the street for fear that they would notice him. He felt their eyes boring into him. He steeled himself and stole a furtive glance across the street. The men were walking and talking as before. They were paying no attention to him.

Will looked at the men out of the corner of his eyes. Two of the men were dressed in dark blue business suits, one man was gray haired, while the other man was around thirty-five years old. The third person was a young man dressed in a Twins' team jacket and baseball cap.

To Will, they looked like two ordinary executives walking from one business meeting to another. He did not understand why the younger man was with them. The distinctive smell of the wolf identified them as being very different from ordinary humans. To avoid drawing attention to himself, Will dropped further behind and continued to follow them at a more leisure pace.

Across the street, oblivious of the presence of another werewolf, Grandfather Jerrold, his son Richard, and grandson Butch walked along discussing the meeting they'd just come from with Senator Bob Johnson. They met with the Senator in his office to discuss issuance of the new state highway contracts. The Senator assured Jerrold the contracts would be forthcoming for the Guhl Construction Company.

Will became alarmed when the three men stopped at the corner of Robert and 10th. They checked traffic and crossed to his side of the street.

"God," he screamed to himself. "They're coming after me." He began to shake. He wanted to run away, but his muscles would not respond.

The three men turned toward downtown in front of Will and continued walking. A half a block later, they turned into a three-story cement-parking ramp. Will relaxed, feeling his heart drop back under control.

Cracks and fissures covered the cement surface of the ramp, looking like it could collapse at any time. Will walked to the corner and peered down the side of the ramp. He looked for another exit. Seeing none, he walked back to Robert Street and watched the single exit. From his vantage point behind a garbage dumpster, he would see any vehicle leaving the ramp.

Will heard a vehicle coming down the ramp, then bounced his fist off his forehead. "Just great," he said aloud, then turned to the building behind him, and hit the wall with his fist. "How in the hell am I going to follow them?" he said to himself, kicking the wall with his foot.

Will recognized the three men in the red sports car when it poked its nose out of the ramp exit. The driver waited until three cars cleared the lane and then pulled out to follow them toward downtown St. Paul. Will memorized the license plate number, 385 ERW.

"That's all I can do for now," Will said, clenching his fists at his side. He walked across the street to the ramp, went inside and found a pay phone.

Chapter 17
'Were' Scent Reported

Ralph sat at the table in his hotel room, leaning over maps of the Twin Cities. He marked with a stubby yellow pencil the areas they had already searched. Closed windows and patio doors trapped the smell of old sweat in the room. In the corner, the twin beds were unmade and half-filled glasses of wine sat on a bedside stand. He glanced down at the maps and circled areas that still required searching by his team.

The phone rang. Ralph jumped. Wiping beads of sweat from his forehead, he picked up the receiver and cradled it between his head and shoulder. "Yeah?" he said. Ralph listened; a broad smile creased his face. "Good job, Will. This is the break we've been waiting for." He was quiet for a moment and then said, "Why didn't you follow them?"

Will said, "My car was blocks away and rather than get it and try to follow them, I chose to follow them on foot. When I first smelled them, I felt I needed to follow the scent right away or risk losing it. I managed to get their license number," he said.

"Will, you did good," Ralph said. "At least we know they are in Minnesota. If you were here, I would kiss you. Come on in. We have plans to make." Ralph slammed the receiver down, as he jumped up from the table. He raced to the door leading out to the balcony and threw it open. He screamed to the winds, "We got them now."

Pigeons sitting on the roof scattered as a frightening howl echoed back from the Minnesota River bottoms a mile to the south.

Chapter 18
Who's The Owner

Ralph wore a pair of gray shorts with a green paint streak on the left leg. A faded green T-shirt, with a Green Bay Packers logo on the front completed his wardrobe. He drummed his fingers on the table, picked up the phone, and placed a call to Madison.

In a few moments, a woman's voice said. "Good morning. This is the U. S. Federal Marshall's office. How may I direct your call?"

"Hey, Marge, this is Ralph."

"How are you, Inspector? How is your vacation?"

"I'm enjoying Minnesota," Ralph lied. "Did you know this is the fifth time I have been here?"

"No, is that right?"

"Yeah," Ralph said. "Say Marge, get me Tom will you? Ralph heard Marge ring into Tom's office. Someone picked up. "Tom, Tom is that you?"

Tom sounded surprised. "Ah, Yeah," he said.

Ralph interrupted him. "Good, Listen, I want you to check a vehicle license number for me. You will have to call the Minnesota Motor Vehicle Department."

"Hold on, let me grab a pen," Tom said, excitement shaking his voice. "Okay, go ahead."

"385-EWR."

"It sounds like you might have something?" Tom said.

Ralph knew Tom was dying to hear what they found, but Marge sometimes listened in on conversations, so he needed to watch what he said. "Yeah," Ralph said. "This is a definite link to the case we've been working on. Will's the hero, he eyeballed the lawbreaker."

Excitement overtook Tom and he jumped up and down in his chair. "Should I bring the rest of the rest of the marshals to Minnesota?"

"Not yet," Ralph cautioned. "Give me time to check everything out and get surveillance set up. I will call you in a day or two if we need backup. Get on that license number and call me back as soon as you get a name and address to go with it."

"Okay, talk to you later." Tom said.

Ralph felt Tom's excitement over the telephone line, but he could not tell him anymore of the details and hung up. A big smile cracked his face. It was years since Ralph felt this much excitement. A challenging hunt was ready to begin. He was exhilarated over the prospect of a fight to the death between his pack and the out of control Minnesota werewolves. Nothing was more stimulating than the hunt, especially for his own kind.

A half hour later, Will walked into Ralph's hotel room. Ralph jumped up with a big smile on his face and threw his arms around him. He hugged him tight and Will started to cough. Ralph loosened his grip a little, but the excitement was contagious. They both jumped up and down, with arms around each other, like a couple of football players who had just scored a touchdown.

"We got them now Will," Ralph said in his ear. "Those sons-of-bitches are gonna die soon.

Chapter 19
Into The Enemies Lair

"Take a right, just ahead, there on Lake Road," Pete directed, pointing to a side street that came up just after the sales office for the Wedgwood Development on County road 19.

Will signaled and slowed for the turn. The Suburban leaned around the corner. They passed between ponds on both sides of the street, where homes circled the pond on the left.

"Take a left at the next intersection," Pete said.

To the right was a small park, with some basketball hoops, tennis court and playground equipment. A small pavilion overlooked the south end of Colby Lake. Will turned at the corner and raced down the street.

"Good, now look for 9297 Wedgwood Lane," Pete said, checking house numbers and then glancing down at the map on his lap. "The house should be a six or seven blocks ahead."

They passed by impressive homes, laid out on spacious lots. Some were three story mansions. All of the homes possessed healthy green lawns, well manicured and landscaped, the right shrubs in the right places.

"I see it Will," Ralph said, tapping him on his shoulder and pointing.

Will slowed. On the left side of the road, stood a massive three-story brick mansion, with a four-car attached garage. A paved drive circled in front of a pillared entrance. The drive looped back to complete the circle just before the street. A bean shaped pool with a magnificent bronze statue occupied the center of the drive circle. Water sprayed out of flower baskets the statue held and splashed down on the heads of several bronze fish pointing upward, with their mouths wide open.

Ralph peered between the neighboring houses and saw several groups of people, off in the distance, golfing. Large homes ringed the Wedgwood Golf Course and Ralph leaned back impressed. "Keep going, Will," Ralph commanded. "We'll turn around up ahead and come back to take a look at the house again on our way out."

Will looked at Ralph with a puzzled expression.

Ralph noticed the bewildered look on Will's face and said, in a gruff voice, "We don't want to leave our scent. Do we?"

Will shook his head, not understanding. "But Grandpa, the wind is blowing from the south, and we're north of the house. They cannot smell us."

"Not now, Will," Ralph said. He was busy looking at everything he could see and paid no attention to what Will said.

In the passenger's seat, Pete was busy video taping the mansion and surrounding homes. Will sat behind the wheel, and believed that if he moved he would draw attention to himself from the werewolves inside the house.

Pete focused the camcorder on the security emblem sticking out of the ground beside the front door entrance; it reminded him of a limp, yellow flower. He panned the camera to show the curved metal bars decorating the windows on the first and second floors. It would be one tough house to break into, he thought.

The shadows created by the afternoon sun, cast a black and foreboding picture of the house from the street. The scene sent shivers down Ralph's spine. The mansion was heavily fortified; it would be too dangerous to attack. We will not make this our primary objective, he decided.

Ralph reached over the front seat and touched Will on the shoulder, "Let's go up a little farther and turn around. We'll come back for another look."

Chapter 20
I Spy

Unseen by the three men in the car, Jerrold, sons Richard and Bruce and grandson, Butch sat on the deck at the back of the house. A half hour ago, they finished nine holes of golf and now sat on the deck cooling off. They were enjoying a beer and watching the golfers still on the course.

Richard winked at his father. “Too bad Bruce bogeyed the ninth hole or I would be paying for dinner tonight.”

Jerrold noticed what Richard was trying to do and pushed it home. “Being the pack leader,” he bragged. “I have the power to control the ball.”

“Oh, shit, Dad, you can’t do that, can you?” Bruce whined. A disbelieving look spread across his face.

Jerrold said. “Of course not son, if I could, I would not have let Butch embarrass all three of us? Were beings cannot. . . .”

Richard listened to what his father was saying, but in the back of his mind, he heard the sound of car wheels squealing and he tuned out his father. A second later, Richard growled, interrupting the playful banter between Jerrold and Bruce.

Jerrold stopped talking and Bruce and Butch froze. Richard lifted his head high, sniffing the tendrils of a breeze that gusted and swirled around the house. The hair on the back of his neck bristled and then stood erect. “I smell ‘were-scent’ and not from us,” he said.

Butch, Bruce and Jerrold thrust their flaring nostrils into the air. Butch and Jerrold snorted when they caught a few molecules of foreign ‘were-scent’. Bruce sniffed, but did not smell anything unusual. In unison Richard, Jerrold and Butch vaulted over the railing of the deck, followed by a bewildered looking Bruce. They raced around the corner of the house.

Jerrold skidded to a halt when he saw the black suburban stopped on the street in front of his house. His eyes locked on Ralph Morsching sitting in the back of the Suburban. Even though separated by a distance of a hundred feet, it was close enough for Jerrold to see Ralph's dark blue eyes. Jerrold snarled, shocked at the brazen invasion of his home territory by another 'were being'. Who were they? Jerrold and Ralph growled at each other, like two German Shepherd dogs ready to fight.

Coming into another werewolf's territory was an invasion of privacy, a direct challenge. Jerrold acknowledged the threat with a low bark. From this moment on one of them would have to die before this affront ended.

Jerrold snarled his readiness to meet Ralph in a battle to the death, right now.

Ralph snarled his acceptance, but realized this was neither the time nor place and bowed his head. They would meet again.

The Suburban accelerated away from the house.

When the vehicle was a half, block away, Ralph said, "Shit." He hit the back of the front seat with open hands. Will's head bounced forward. "I wasn't ready for this. I didn't want them to know we were hunting them; not yet." He shrugged, accepting the deal fate handed him. "Well, nothing we can do about it now. They'll be on guard from now on and hunting us, just like we will be hunting them."

Pete snarled and dropped the camcorder on the seat between him and Will. "That's okay Ralph, it will make the fight and the outcome that much more exciting."

Ralph shrugged his shoulders, "Let's get out of here, Will. We don't want to make it too easy for them to follow us back to our hotel, do we?"

Will gripped the steering wheel with white knuckles. He accelerated and the Suburban roared like a charging lion down Wedgwood Lane. The tires threw pebbles into the air. He sped through the stop sign and turned right onto Lake Street.

Meanwhile, Jerrold called back over his shoulder, as he ran toward the Corvette sitting in front of the garage. "Richard, warn the rest of the family, while we see if we can follow them. Bruce you and Butch come with me," He pulled Bruce along behind him by the arm. Jerrold tore open the door of the Corvette. Bruce jumped behind the wheel and buckled up. Butch vaulted into the back seat. The Corvette growled and Bruce squealed out in pursuit of the black Suburban. Jerrold glanced at his watch, "Shit, they have a big head start on us."

The Suburban raced along Lake until it reached County Road 19, then Will turned left and headed north toward Freeway 94. On 94, he headed west to Freeway 494, which he followed south, back toward the Hilton Hotel, across from the airport maintenance facility.

The Red Corvette flew north on County Road 19 and then turned left on Valley Creek Road, heading toward Woodbury City Center. They circled through the streets of Woodbury attempting to pick up the were-scent. Fifteen minutes later, Jerrold shook his head and said, "We lost them. Let's go home, Bruce."

Chapter 21
Victory Anticipated

Later in the evening, the six members of the Morsching pack crowded into Ralph's hotel room. Will and Pete sat on the sofa, finishing the last two pieces of a Domino's Pepperoni Pizza. The carton sat open on the coffee table. Pieces of cooled cheese had dribbled over the edge of the carton and stuck to the glass tabletop. Ralph sat at the table with Gretchen, Alice and Joseph, eating the last of the sausage and cheese pizza.

Ralph wiped the oily, tomato mixture covering his fingers on a wad of paper towels and then ran the soiled bundle across his lips. "Okay, my family," Ralph said. "We did a stupid thing this afternoon, but were able to locate one of their hideouts. It took longer than I planned to find them, but now that we have, we can begin eliminating them."

He got up from his chair and walked over to stand in front of the French doors leading out to the balcony. He opened the door and walked into the darkness. He looked out over the Minnesota River bottoms and then swung with a dramatic flare around and reentered the room. "Remember, as we eliminate them, all of the killings must look normal, like an accident. You can rob or rape them, just as long as you kill them in human form." Ralph said. "In no way, will any of the killings be in werewolf form." He walked back to the table and banged his fist down. "Am I understood on this point?" Ralph scanned the room and gathered the nods and grunts of acceptance from his pack members.

Ralph picked up his whiskey & Sour mixed drink from the table and raised it toward the five pack members. They in turn raised their plastic glasses, joining in the toast. An air of confidence permeated the room, as Ralph said, "I propose a toast to the success of the Morsching pack and to a victorious hunt." Will and Pete raised their glasses and touched them together.

A giggle escaped Will's lips, betraying his nervousness. His body shook with excitement at the thought of killing another werewolf. A trickle of red wine spilled over the side of his glass and ran down his fingers. "Shit," he said to himself. "I am going to hunt werewolves. I can't believe it." He blanched when he remembered they would be hunting him as well and would be just as dangerous.

Pete swayed as he made his way up from the sofa and said, "A toast to successful elimination of the damned." He raised his glass into the air, spilling a third of it over the rim unto the carpet.

"Daddy," Gretchen said, with a disgusted frown. She moved over next to Pete. "Sit down before you fall down." She grabbed him by the arm and lofted it around her shoulder. She laughed when he poked her ribs.

"To the hunt," Will said. He was still feeling embarrassed for letting the childish giggle escape his mouth a few moments ago. His hand shook and a few more drops of wine dribbled down the side of his glass onto his pants this time.

"To victory," Alice Shoewinski quietly saluted.

Will looked at Alice and shivered. He feared her. She was one of the deadliest female killers in the pack, mostly because she lacked a conscious. Will witnessed her in action and knew how tough and evil she was.

"To a successful hunt," Joseph Morsching said.

Ralph with a broad smile spread across his face, raised his glass to his lips, tipped his head back and draining the glass, then he said, "To the Morsching pack."

"To the High Wolf," Will screamed in a high squeaky voice.

The others became as feverish as Will and chimed in chanting, "Ralph--Ralph--Ralph--Ralph--Ralph."

Subdued groaning, snapping and crunching sounds filled the room. Then the room went silent, except for the heavy breathing of six hairy werewolves. Five sat on their haunches within a circle of shredded clothing, around Ralph, the leader of the pack. Ralph stood before them with his hairy chest pushed forward. He in turn stared at the ceiling, eyes gleaming with excitement.

Chapter 22
The First Kill

Streetlights highlighted the sides of the six story parking ramp. Every hundred feet cement pillars rose on either side of rectangular openings, which admitted light into each floor of the parking ramp. Between faint blocks of light from the streetlights, shadows of tree limbs scratched against the cement walls. Near the elevator shaft, green-domed security lights illuminated the area. Every fifty feet along each level of the ramp, a light hung from the ceiling, dispelling some of the darkness.

On the fifth floor, a misshapen shadow moved among the cars. "Pop." One of the security lights sputtered and its circle of light disappeared. As each light extinguished, closer to the elevator, broken glass tinkled to the cement floor. Shadows were no longer visible, only uniform darkness was there to greet anyone trying to reach their automobiles.

Something at home in the darkness moved freely down the center of the isle, no longer inhibited by the light. The entire fifth floor was dark, except for a small bit of light from the streetlights. A black shadow moved in the eerie darkness, as though it belonged. A presence waited.

Three blocks away, on the eighth floor of the Cancer Institute, evening classes were ending. Students dribbled out of the lecture hall in twos and threes, going off in various directions. Soon the Cancer Institute would lack the bustle of students scurrying to and from classes. In an hour, the hallways would be abandoned and quiet.

Marsha Guhl, daughter of Jerrold's second son, Bruce, was a tall, blonde-haired woman. She was twenty-two years old and possessed a bubbly personality to go with her large breasts and narrow waist. She was attractive, but not beautiful.

Stuffing her book and notes into her backpack, she exited the lecture hall. Following a group of young people, she walked down the hallway and entered the elevator with three of them. She rode it to the ground floor.

Marsha walked through the revolving door at the exit into misty darkness. She hurried down the five steps to the sidewalk. The streetlights peeked at her through a fog, guiding her down the gray sidewalk. A chill trickled down her back causing her to shiver. She walked from streetlight to streetlight, not afraid, but feeling something was out of place.

Marsha heard a group of students walking ahead of her and then saw them appear out of the mist. Feeling alone and vulnerable, she hurried to close the distance between herself and the group, thinking, there was safety in number. A premonition that something evil was out traveling the darkness tonight, sat in a corner of her mind. Even so, she was not afraid; after all, she came from a family of werewolves. She was not one, but being around them gave her a different slant on fearful things.

Looking up through a layer of fog, she saw dark clouds swirling overhead, moving to the southeast, pushed by a cool northwest wind. Humidity hung heavy in the November air, sending another chill racing through her body. She pulled her jacket tighter around her neck appreciating the warmth of the down lining.

The warning her grandfather issued last week popped into her mind. Jerrold told the family a foreign werewolf pack was in the Twin Cities area and everyone should be careful until the Guhl pack found out what their intentions were. She wondered why she thought of the warning just now and shivered again, but this time not from the cold and humidity. She walked faster.

At Union Street, Marsha crossed ahead of two cars that raced toward her from half a block away. She jumped up on the curb just as the two cars zoomed by. She followed the sidewalk south toward the parking ramp. Through the fog, the open dark mouths of the parking ramp yawned before her. Over the entrance, a quartz light illuminated a circle around the door.

The brightly lit elevator room promised a safe haven. As she opened the door and walked into the small elevator waiting room, a cold, eerie feeling raised goose bumps on her arms and the short hairs at the back of her neck stood erect. She thought the response was from the cold. She pushed the call button for the elevator and the door opened, giving her a start. Feeling a little jittery, Marsha peeked into the lighted elevator.

"No one," she sighed, relieved. "Quit being such a chicken," she admonished herself. She stepped through the open elevator door and pushed the button for the fifth floor.

In the well-lighted elevator, her jittery feeling dissipated and her thoughts turned to her newest boyfriend, Frank Williams. He was handsome and sexy. She met Frank a week ago at the Gold Rush in Cottage Grove, a hangout for college kids and young adults. Sex occurred on their second date and she was anxious to see him tonight for more.

The elevator jerked to a stop at the fifth floor ramp and the door slid open. The light from the elevator illuminated the first three cars. The rest of the ramp was dark, except for the small amount of diffused light from the streetlights below. Marsha stared into the darkness and saw bits and pieces of other cars parked along the sides of the ramp. For a moment, she considered turning around and taking the elevator back down to the first floor. From there she could call for an escort. However, that would take time and she was in a hurry to see Frank.

Marsha stepped out on the rough cement of the ramp in front of the elevator. The elevator doors slid shut behind her, committing her to the darkness that faced her all the way to her car. Her Pontiac convertible stood at the far end of the ramp.

She wondered, "Why in the hell did I park so far from the elevator? Oh, shit, I have to stop being such a coward." She took a deep breath and took a tentative step away from the safety of the elevator. She lifted her backpack to her breast, folded both arms around it and started to walk rapidly down the dark wide aisle between the two rows of parked cars. She walked toward her car and the consuming darkness.

Marsha recognized the outline of her Pontiac, two cars from where the up ramp curved coming around the corner from the lower level. Marsha fumbled in her jacket pocket for her car keys. She did not want any delay in getting into her car. As Marsha rounded the back fender of her car, she heard something crash behind her.

With a scream, she turned toward the threat. Marsha could not see anything. The same crashing noise occurred again. The noise came from the street below and trapped air whooshed from her lungs. There was nothing for her to be afraid of, but her heart fluttered in her chest anyway. She turned back to her car; an audible sigh escaped her lips marking an end to this nonsense.

The moment Marsha turned she felt rather than saw a dark shadow rise up in front of her. She gasped, unable to move, as a presence darted toward her. Shadowy arms grabbed her by the hair. A fist smashed into Marsha's face. She screamed from the pain and sagged. The fist pounded her until the hurt went away and the ensuing unconsciousness welcomed her. Her body slumped to the concrete floor.

Will Franzen, stood over Marsha's unconscious body. He glanced around listening for the presence of anyone, but no one was there. They were all alone.

As though he didn‘t have a worry in the world, he pulled a pair of latex gloves from an inside jacket pocket and slipped them on his thin, delicate hands, the hands of a pianist or a surgeon. He dropped down, his knees on either side of Marsha's body and began to rip her clothes off. When Marsha lay naked before him, he unbuckled his pants dropped his shorts and slipped a condom on his erect penis. He spread Marsha's legs and savagely raped her unconscious body.

Will, nothing more than a shadow on a black background, rose up from Marsha's limp body. He removed the condom from his limp penis and stuffed it into a plastic sandwich bag. He pulled his underwear and pants up, taking his time buckling his belt. He slipped the plastic bag into his jacket pocket and brushed off his clothes. He picked up Marsha's purse and stuffed it in a pocket on the inside of his jacket. He said in a high-pitched nervous voice. "I dedicate number one to Grandfather Ralph and the pack."

Will bent down over Marsha's unconscious body and wrapped his gloved hands around her throat. He squeezed until he heard the cartilage rings crack and felt her trachea collapse. Marsha convulsed, as her lungs tried to take in air. Will felt her spasm again and then she was quiet. No more tremors came from her dead, cooling body.

Will's shoulders moved up and down, as he laughed under his breath, proud of what he had just done. He struck the first blow for his pack. Will peeled the plastic gloves from his hands and stuffed them into the bag with the condom, and then he turned and walked up the ramp to the elevator and pushed the down button.

The police wrote off Marsha's death, as a robbery-rape; suspect unknown, but she really was the first victim in the "Werewolf War."

Chapter 23
Dig' Em Out

Butch guided the green, Cadillac convertible down the off ramp from Highway 694 unto Long Lake Road. The sign for the Park and Ride Lot glowed white on green, a block ahead. He signaled and turned into the lot. Five cars were scattered throughout the lot. He headed for a dark corner, coasted in and killed the engine. Butch released his seat belt, got out of the car and walked around to the trunk. He glanced back as Brad got out and slammed his door.

"Brad," Butch said, "be quiet."

Brad shrugged his shoulders, "I'm sorry."

Butch turned and headed down a slight embankment behind the car. He waited behind some bushes for Brad to join him.

For several nights in a row, angry Guhl teams searched different suburbs for some sign of the other werewolf pack. The Guhl family knew the rival pack was somewhere in the Twin City area. They sent out teams night and day trying to locate them. Tonight, Butch and Brad were to search the New Brighton area, a suburb in north Minneapolis.

Butch punched Brad in the shoulder. "Well," he said, "let's do it."

They undressed, folded their clothes and hid them under the bushes. They were quite proficient at making the transition from one form to the other. They grunted and moaned, as their bodies went through the changes from human form to werewolf.

In a minute, two hairy werewolves trotted away from the shrubs. Butch melted into the second row of foliage and disappeared into the darkness, headed north along the west edge of Long Lake.

Butch and Brad loped across a field, the grass swishing against their bellies. In the distance, a dog howled. Butch turned toward a distant housing development. When they got close, Butch loped toward a yellow house surrounded by a chain link fence. He jumped the fence and angled across the back yard. He thought of the occupants sleeping inside. If they knew of the danger passing by, they would never sleep again without their lights on.

A while later, Butch stopped in a back yard of a house filled with decorative shrubs and hybrid roses. Hundreds of odors inundated his mind as he sniffed the air. He ignored the everyday background odors, but a few, like those from the roses and aromatic shrubs were pleasantly accepted. Butch snorted and shook his head with disappointment. The one odor he was hoping to detect was not there. Butch trotted out of the yard and turned upwind from the houses.

They were careful not to travel downwind and give the other werewolves a chance to pick up their scents. If they got a whiff of them, they would be the hunted. Butch came to the north end of the Long Lake, where County Road 11 intersected Long Lake Road. He stopped and waited for Brad to catch up. Brad stopped and sniffed the night air, searching for the elusive foreign werewolf scent. Butch knew it would only take a few molecules of the 'were scent' to give the enemy away.

Butch glanced at Brad and mind spoke, "I hope the other teams are having better luck than we are."

"Yeah, we won't know until we get back to the car."

"It is funny that in all our searching, no one has found them."

"We will."

Butch said, "I've got a feeling tonight is the night." Butch recalled what grandfather said earlier tonight. He could see him in his mind, standing before the teams saying, "I'm confident, that if we persist and do not falter, we will find their lair. It is only a matter of time and then we will destroy them."

Butch told his grandfather, he was not going to stop searching until they found the killers of Marsha and then. . . .

Butch grunted and Brad followed him in their dash across a street and down into the ditch. They circled southward back toward Pike Lake and their car.

Two hours later, Butch and Brad finished the full circle. The two werewolves stood in the bushes at the back of the Park and Ride lot. They reversed the change and retrieved the clothes they had stored under the bushes. Butch walked through the bushes to the car and reached down along the driver's seat for the trunk release. He walked to the rear of the car and removed two beers from an Igloo cooler. He threw a can to Brad and then leaned against the fender of the Cadillac.

Brad joined him and let out a big, dejected sigh. "Shit."

Butch downed half the can in one gulp. "Ah, that hits the spot." He turned and slammed the cooler lid, closed the trunk and boosted himself up on the back of the trunk. Leaning back against the curve of the rear window, he said, "Well, Brad, at least we know they are not in the New Brighton area."

"Yeah, but I was hoping we would be the ones to find them," Brad said, shrugging his shoulders. "Ah hell, let's go home."

They finished off their beers and threw the cans behind a clump of bushes. Butch climbed into the passenger's seat. Brad started the engine just as the cellular phone buzzed.

Butch looked at Brad and then at the cell phone. He picked it up as if it was a hot coal. "Hello," he said, grabbing the dash with his left hand.

The elated voice of Jerrold said in his ear, "We have located the prize. Come home."

The phone went dead.

"They found them," Butch said, no longer tired. He reached over and messed Brad's hair. "Come on lets go. Grandfather wants us home."

Brad grinned and jammed the accelerator to the floor. The car shot toward the exit of the Park & Ride lot.

"Slow down, Brad," Butch cried, balancing himself with both hands on the dash, as the car skidded around a corner. "We don't want to kill ourselves, do we?"

"You're right, Butch," Brad said, with a trembling voice, as he eased his foot from the accelerator.

Chapter 24
Blow Them Out Of The Hilton

Two nights later, at 1:30 a.m., Richard, Brad and Butch ran along the Minnesota River Bottoms, their pawed feet splashing through the water-soaked swamp. High on a bluff to the north, Butch caught a glimpse of the outline of old Fort Snelling still guarding the Minnesota River. Below the limestone cliffs, streams of cars moved on Highway 5 toward St. Paul or the International Airport.

Butch's fur-covered legs carried him through shoulder high grasses, while his thick padded feet kept him from sinking into the spongy ground. His head moved back and forth, dodging twigs sticking out from low branches, trying to pluck his eyes out.

"I never tire of being in werewolf form," Butch thought. An inner excitement grew in him when he thought about their assignment tonight. He was proud they picked him as a member of the attack team. He threw his head back and forth, feeling a peak of excitement mushroom through his brain.

His eye caught a bit of light streaming through the overhead branches and he knew right away, what pushed his excitement to such a high level. A quarter moon hung in the sky like a beacon, bright and golden. Butch growled and lowered his head a fraction to let a branch brush over the top of his head.

Uncle Richard led the attack team toward the hotel strip located south of the International Airport, along Freeway 494. It was Richard and Fred who located the Morsching werewolf hideout in the Hilton Hotel.

Richard surged out ahead of the other two as they approached the hotel area. Richard carried an ATW (Anti-Tank Weapon) strapped to his back. He claimed it was more comfortable to carry it in that position while running on all fours; it did not bang his legs as much. Brad carried three high explosive missiles in pockets of a special vest, made for guide dogs to carry objects for their master. The missiles did not interfere with his movements, as he ran without effort behind his dad. Butch carried a set of binoculars strapped tight against his body to prevent them from flopping around. They still irritated him by rubbing against his fur, producing a sensitive spot on his chest.

A rabbit scurried in front of Brad and then froze statue-like; hoping the strange animals running through his woods would ignore him. Butch sensed the rabbit's fear, which sent a flash of exhilaration shooting through his mind. He ran on savoring the moment. There would be another time to chase rabbits. Butch glanced at the sky and watched wispy clouds sail across a star filled sky. He thought, "God, being alive is great."

The werewolves were shadowy blurs, invisible because of the darkness and the speed at which they traveled. Butch stopped at the top of a small knoll of land and looked at lights flashing from the tops of buildings.

The hotel area was just ahead. Butch followed Richard and Brad up a steep bank, which brought them out of the bottoms area. They crested a small, grass-covered hill, which overlooked the Hilton Hotel parking lot and stopped. The three werewolves dropped to their bellies in the grass and looked for signs of humans in the parking lot.

Brad's Adams apple convulsed, as he gulped air loudly. He looked back and forth between his father and Butch. Butch suspected Brad was afraid, not knowing what to expect and was even more nervous than he was. He wondered why Richard volunteered Brad, when everyone knew him as a young, inexperienced and easily frightened werewolf.

Earlier that afternoon, Brad admitted to Butch, he was scared. Butch caught Brad's furtive glance and he winked.

Brad's mouth gaped open in surprise. "Butch," Brad said to him, "how can you be so cool? Aren't you afraid?"

Butch shook his head no and turned to stare at a flat-roofed utility building standing alone in the middle of the parking lot. He said to Richard, "What now?"

Richard nodded his muzzle in the direction of the utility building. "Let's head for the building in the middle of the parking lot and get on its roof."

Butch looked at Brad and noticed his eyes tightly closed, "Are you all right," he asked.

"Yeah, I guess," Brad said, blinking his eyes.

Richard started to sneak forward, "Okay then come on." Richard signaled with his paw. "Once on top of the building we should be safe, no one should be able to see us up there."

Brad ran across the parking lot behind his father. All you could hear was the footpads softly scuffing the tar and the scratch of their claws. Richard cut behind some cars and zigzagged between several more, before reaching the building. Richard slowed down and then increased his speed. As he neared the side of the building, he launched himself eight feet to the rooftop.

Butch passed Brad and jumped toward the top of the building. His front paws hit the edge; he skidded on the rock-covered roof and almost lost his footing. Butch heard Brad growl and turned to see Brad's front legs slipping back over the edge.

"Help me, I'm gonna fall," Brad mind spoke. Brad's front paws hooked over the edge of the roof, while his back ones scratched against the side of the building in an effort to lift himself. Butch reached down and hooked his paw under Brad's foreleg. With his teeth, he grabbed the nape of Brad's neck and pulled.

Brad tumbled to the rooftop with a yelp and then jumped up, "Christ, you damn near broke my neck," he cried.

Butch looked at Brad with a disgusted scowl, the sides of his mouth pulled back in a threatening shape. "You are welcome," he said and turned away.

Richard bumped both of them with his shoulder. "Keep quiet. Someone might hear us."

They made the transformation back to their human forms. All three lay on the flat roof, naked and shivering.

Butch lay in the dark shadows next to Richard. He scanned the parking lot to see if anyone saw or heard them jump to the rooftop. He did not see anyone, but listened, half expecting someone to scream and give their position away. The surrounding area remained quiet, except for the sound of hard rock music coming from a side entrance to the hotel and traffic from Freeway 494.

After a few minutes, Richard sent mentally, "Okay, Butch," the words reverberated in the chamber of his mind from which he could hear and understand them, "locate their rooms."

Butch picked up the binoculars from the ledge in front of him and located the windows on the tenth floor. The windows popped right into his eyes, even though the room lights were out. Butch scanned the side of the building and came to rest on the third window from the south end. According to the hotel clerk, the 'Johnson family' occupied the three end rooms on the tenth floor. The clerk told Butch there were six people in the Johnson party, four men and two women.

Butch lowered the binoculars. "All the rooms are dark," he said.

"Maybe they are sleeping," Richard said, and then said, "What should we do?"

Butch shrugged. This was his first attack, his first real action against other werewolves. What did he know? He looked to Richard for leadership, but doubts flashed through his mind over Richard's indecisiveness.

"They are probably up there, smelling us right now," Brad said with a nervous catch in his voice, "let's blow up the rooms and get out of here."

Butch turned to Brad and noticed he was shivering. "Cripes, that cannot all be from the cool air. He is scared shitless," Butch thought.

Richard sat up and positioned the ATW on his shoulder. Brad jumped up and pulled one of the missiles from his vest. The shell slipped from his hands.

Brad let out a weak squeak. He caught the shell with his hand and pinned it against his leg. He grabbed the missile with both hands, lifted it up, and shoved it into the ATW tube.

Butch shook his head in disbelief. They are going to shoot. "Hold it," Butch said. "We don't even know if they are in the rooms."

Richard looked at Butch, a bewildered frown on his white face. At least he did not shoot, Butch sighed.

Butch said, "We can't afford to waste this opportunity, to just blow up some empty rooms. We won't get another chance to kill them this easy again," he finished.

"We can't stay here all night," Brad exclaimed.

"He did not even hear what I said," Butch said under his breath. Butch knew Brad was afraid and near panic. He was expressing his fear, fear of being exposed, and fear of attack by the other werewolves. Butch knew Brad was worried over the fact the hunted could fight back.

"Don't worry, Brad," Butch said. "We are safe. No one knows we're here."

Brad gathered courage from Butch's assurance and relaxed.

"Butch is right," Richard said, lowering the ATW. "We will wait, but not too long."

They settled down on the roof to wait for some sign the enemy was in the rooms. Butch rolled to his side and brushed at some pebbles that stuck to his skin. He lowered himself below the edge of the roof sheltering his body from the cool breeze coming up from the river bottoms. Brad picked up the binoculars and scanned the rooms every five minutes for some sign of life.

A half hour later, Brad stuttered. "Hey, the lights just went on in two of the rooms."

Richard and Butch jumped to a crouch.

"Shhh," Richard cautioned, his voice quivering. "Do you see anyone?"

"There are four people in the middle room," Brad said between clenched teeth.

"Here," Butch said, "Let me see." Brad handed him the binoculars. In the binocular view, he saw a dignified looking man walk to the balcony door and push it open.

Brad watched the man on the balcony and thought he could hear him moving. Butch became nervous. He said, "Shit, that guy looks dangerous."

Butch watched Ralph, the leader of the Morsching pack. He walked out on the balcony and leaned against the railing. Through the binoculars, Ralph's image was clear. Butch's eyes widened. It looked like Ralph was sniffing the night air.

Brad must have cranked up his vision, because he hissed, "Christ, he, he smells us. Shoot, Shoot."

Richard brought the ATW to rest on his shoulder and froze, waiting for Brad to double check the missile.

What are you waiting for?" Brad cried, "You are still loaded."

"Okay Uncle, shoot," Butch said. Some of Brad's fear fueled his excitement. Brad's fear was intoxicating.

Butch watched the laser beam come to rest on the second group of window from the corner of the tenth floor. Richard squeezed the trigger.

"WHOOSH"

The missile left the tube trailing a red tail of light all the way to the window.

Butch yanked a second missile from Brad's vest and slammed it home in the ATW. Richard sighted on the other lighted room and squeezed the trigger.

"WHOOSH," screamed the second rocket.

The side of the hotel lit up with a bright, white flash of fire, as the exploding missiles demolished the whole corner of the building. The roof crashed down on the three rooms. Bricks and chunks of cement dropped through the air to the tarmac below, smashing several cars.

"Come on," Richard said, "change and let's get the hell out of here."

Butch strapped the ATW to Richard's hairy back, gathered up the spent shells and shoved them back into the pockets on Brad's vest, put the binoculars back in its case and tightened the straps holding it in place, and then started his change.

Richard leapt over the edge of the roof to the parking lot and streaked across the exposed tarmac, dodging behind and between cars. Butch raced behind Richard. They both stopped on the grassy knoll at the edge of the parking lot and looked back for Brad. Brad was still on the roof of the utility building, half way through his change.

Butch threw out a mind probe, "Come on Brad, we got to get out of here."

Brad finished his change, leapt from the roof, and flashed between the cars. When he hit the knoll, he did not even slow down.

Fear drove all three of them to seek the safety of the bushes at the bottom of the slope.

Butch did not stop there; he kept running until he was in the protective shelter of the Minnesota River Bottoms, a good half-mile from the hotel. He slowed down when he was deep in the trees. Richard and Brad caught up to him, but ran right by him without even seeing him.

"Hey guys," Butch said from his mind, "slow down." Neither of them slowed. Butch ran after them and drew alongside Brad. "Hey, slow down," he said, as he dodged around a tree.

"THWACK," A noise like a watermelon hitting cement sounded next to Butch's head. Frightened he shied away. He stopped and glanced back to see what made the noise. He saw Brad lying on the ground. "Oh shit," Butch said, letting out a bark that sounded like a laugh.

Brad ran head on into an oak tree.

Butch let out a barking laugh, as a picture of Brad hitting the tree appeared in his mind. He swung around and loped back toward Brad's prone body.

Richard skidded to a stop and trotted over to crouch beside his unconscious son. "Brad wake up," he said. His eyes darted around, as though he expected someone to charge them from the trees. He turned to Butch. "Hurry, we have to get out of here. Come on, we will carry him."

"Uncle, he's too heavy," Butch said, trying to hold back his laughter. Caught up in the humor of what happened, he forgot the fear that sent him scurrying away from the explosion. "We'll have to wait for him to wake up."

"Uh, okay," was all Richard said, "but, not too long."

Butch could not hold back any longer. A series of barks came from deep in his chest. He laughed until weakness over came him and he plopped over on his side and lay on the ground shaking.

Richard failed to see the humor of the situation. "Damn it, Butch, this isn't funny."

Butch laughed all the harder.

A few minutes later, Brad stirred. Butch stifled his laughter and nudged him to his feet. Richard and Butch supported Brad, one on each side of his body. They needed to assist him all the way back to the car.

Chapter 25
How Close To Failure?

The next morning, the entire Guhl pack gathered in the basement of Jerrold's mansion in Wedgwood. The room was one big area with a twenty-four foot conference table occupying the center. On the wall behind the head of the table hung a plaque dedicated to grandson Fred, who died in a 'motorcycle accident', the day after the Longville massacre.

Jerrold stood at the head of the table with a big smile plastered on his face. He was talking with Richard and Bruce, his two eldest sons.

Butch knew they were waiting for George and Barbara Buchannan to arrive before starting the family meeting. Five minutes later, Francis and his son, Carey, escorted George and Barbara followed by their children, Elliot, Sue and Amy into the basement.

"That's it, Grandpa," Carey said, "Everyone is here."

"Okay, Okay," Jerrold said, irritated at the delay. "If everyone would take a seat, we'll get started."

The family members hurried to find a place to sit. The adult members of the pack occupied the chairs around the table, while older grandchildren filled the second row with the rest spilling over on to the floor.

"The first piece of good news comes from Elliot." Jerrold waved him to his feet.

Elliot stood up and glued his eyes on the paper he was holding. "Carey and I talked to the receptionist at the Hilton yesterday and got the license number of the car the other werewolves came in," he blushed. "Well, they did not come in werewolf form; ah you know what I mean. Anyway, we now know they came from Madison, Wisconsin."

Everyone cheered.

"The second bit of good new comes from our raid last night. Richard," Jerrold said turning to him, "Will you give a report of the raid last night on the Hilton Hotel, where the Madison werewolves were staying?"

Richard stood up with an air of importance. "Father assigned Brad, Butch and I as the team to attack and kill the foreign werewolves in their hotel. Last night, we left the Fort Snelling parking lot about midnight and followed the Minnesota River bottoms until we arrived at the Hotel strip across from the airport maintenance area. We waited on top of a utility building in the middle of Hilton Hotel's parking lot for them to return to their rooms. When they showed up, we blew up the rooms with an ATW.

"According to the news this morning, we accomplished part of our goal. The explosion killed three of the six, two women and a young man. Three others survived. Two of the survivors were in the elevators on their way up to their rooms at the time of the explosions and the third one; we assume is the pack leader somehow survived the explosion."

"Why didn't you wait until they were all in the room?" Bruce said.

Brad answered from the second row of chairs, "Because, the big one came out on the balcony. I saw him sniffing the air. I knew he smelled us and I told dad to shoot."

"That's right," Richard said, "Brad said one of them was sniffing the wind, I shot before they could smell us and get out of the room."

"Richard, tell them what Butch did," Jerrold said.

"Well," Richard blushed and hesitated before going on. "If it hadn't been for Butch," Richard started to explain, reluctant to talk of Butch's part in the attack. He knew it did not shed a positive light on his leadership. "We would have destroyed the rooms earlier in the evening and missed them. Brad and I thought they were sleeping," he said.

"Explain," Jerrold said.

"Richard cringed. "When we first got there, the rooms were dark. Brad and I assumed they were sleeping, but Butch disagreed and convinced us to wait. They weren't in the room, but showed up later and we killed three of the bastards." Richard finished and sat down.

Jerrold clapped. "Good job Richard, Brad and Butch," he said, looking at each of them. "Next time be sure you don't waste an opportunity," he looked at Richard. 'Wait and kill them all."

Butch sat watching Richard's bungling of the story. He jumped up red faced and said, "We will Grandfather," before Richard could offer any more excuses. The tone and emotion of Butch's words surprised several members of the pack, who leaned forward and stared over at him. Butch's voice carried as much authority and promise as if it came from the Alpha. A few felt the power in Butch's statement and could not prevent themselves from reacting to it.

After the meeting broke up, most of the family members left. Butch and Jerrold worked together in the office. Butch loaded information on the computer, while Jerrold sat at his desk working on new assignments for the pack.

Jerrold put the tip of his ballpoint pen in his lips and concentrated on finishing one of the assignments. He shrugged his shoulders; it felt like eyes staring at his back. The hair at the base of his neck sprang erect. He swiveled his head and looked over the top of the desk lamp. Butch was not staring at him, but off into space. Jerrold swung back to the computer screen, a worried look creasing his forehead.

A few moments later Butch said, as much to himself as to his Grandfather, "You know, if I would have been in charge last night, six enemy werewolves would be dead right now, instead of only three."

Jerrold turned and looked at Butch. He knew by the tone of his voice, Butch was not bragging, but stating what would have happened if he had been in charge.

"Explain what you mean," Jerrold demanded.

"For one thing, Uncle Richard was too impatient. He would have blown up empty rooms, until I convinced him to wait."

"Did the man on the balcony smell you?"

"No, I was watching with the binoculars and saw the guy sniffing, but that doesn't mean he smelled us," Butch said, shaking his head. "Everything happened fast. According to Brad, the man was sniffing the air. The funny thing was, we were downwind and I could not smell him, so I don‘t think he could smell us."

Jerrold's head shot up. "Oh, Richard neglected to tell me that."

"Unless he has better powers than we do, I don't think he could smell us," Butch went on. "But, just before Richard's first shot, someone was trying to probe my mind." Butch hesitated. "Even then I would've waited for all of them to show up. If any of those in the room tried to leave, then I would've blown the rooms up."

Jerrold stared at the picture of his father, James, on the wall over Butch's head. "You know," he spoke in a low whisper. "I never noticed before how much you look like my father." His gaze studied Butch. "Butch, I want you to forget what happened last night. I do not want any internal trouble coming from this. Richard did the best he could. I know Brad gets too excited and acts before he thinks. I probably should have replaced him with someone else. With more experience, Brad will do better. The important thing is you did a fine job. I have a feeling it will be just a matter of time until we get the rest of the Madison group. I promise you we will get them," Jerrold said raising his voice.

Chapter 26
The Conflict Widens

Parked in the third row of cars in the Woodbury Mall parking lot was a dark, blue Chevy Suburban. The Suburban occupied the same spot for the last three days. Today it was Pete and Will's turn on surveillance. They sat huddled in the Suburban, watching the activities going on in the Dry Cleaning Store in front of them, watching and waiting. They tracked the coming and going of the people inside the store.

Will sat up, snapping the reclining seat erect. "Uncle Pete, how much longer are we going to sit here?" he grumbled.

"Until we learn all we can," Pete yawned, not at all intimidated by Will's impatient tone.

Will turned in his seat and looked at his uncle. "Cripes, I have learned all I need to know. I am tired of waiting. Let's just walk in and kill them."

Pete rolled his eyes toward the top of the Suburban and rotated his head toward Will. He smiled when he noticed Will's jaw muscles expand and contract, betraying his anger and impatience. "No, we will not do that until Ralph tells us to," Pete said. The words came out slow and easy, in a fake southern drawl. "Ralph said not to do anything until we scoped everything out. Just sit back, relax, and keep your eyes open."

Will released his seat and it banged back into a reclining position.

The snow started to fall around 6 o'clock, big, slow falling flakes. Pete thought it was about time. The ground was usually snow covered by early November, but here it was the second week in December and this was the first snowfall. Maybe there was something to this global warming crap.

A movement inside the Dry Cleaning Store caught Pete's eye. He saw the woman, identified as Diana, walk to the front door and flip the open sign so it now read "closed". Then he saw Andy appear from the back room carrying some packages. Two teenage kids followed him. Pete recognized the kids, as the ones who were in and out of the shop all day. They were making deliveries, he thought.

In a few minutes, the lights went out and the store grew dark. Four people came out the front door and waited while Andy locked the door. The four then walked two rows into the parking lot and got into a gray Dodge Caravan.

Pete nudged Will. “Okay action man,” he drawled, “time to go to work. Let’s follow them.”

Will grabbed the steering wheel and pulled himself to a sitting position. He straightened the seat and started the Suburban. He was relieved doing something rather than sitting around. He recognized Andy and Diana Groschen sitting in the front seat as the Caravan passed in front of him. He waited until two more cars got between them before he pulled out to follow. The Dodge Caravan turned right on Valley Creek Road and swung over to the left lane. At Woodlane Drive, the van made the tail end of the green arrow, as it turned left.

Will skidded to a stop and said, “Shit.” He hit the steering wheel. “Now we’ve got to wait for a green arrow. We’re gonna lose them.”

Pete laid his hand on Will’s arm. “Take it easy. They do not have any reason to try to lose us. They don’t know we are following them.”

When Will got a green arrow, he accelerated onto Woodlane Drive and sped south faster than the posted limit. He felt the need to catch up. At the nursing home on the corner of Lake Street and Woodlane Drive, the light ahead was red. “There they are,” Will said, seeing the gray van waiting in the left turn lane.

He pulled behind the van and when the light turned, followed it onto Lake Drive. Will dropped back and stayed in the left lane as the gray van moved over to the right. In a couple of blocks, the van signaled for a right turn. Will moved to the right, put his signals on and followed the Dodge around the corner. When Will finished the turn, he saw the van was a block ahead. Will hit Pete on the arm and said, “Hey, they are turning in to that driveway.”

“I can see,” Pete said, rubbing his arm. “Take it easy. Just drive by.” Pete turned as they drove by and watched the gray Caravan pull into the garage. "Ah, 8-5-46," he said, repeating the number he read from the side of the door, "8546."

At the intersection, he picked up the street name from the white on green sign, "Stratford Road, let me write it down," he said.

8:30 that night found the Suburban once more parked in the Woodbury Mall lot. This time, three men were sitting in the vehicle, waiting.

Ralph opened the car door and slid out on the snow packed parking lot. "Okay," he said, "We are just going in to have a look around. We don't want to cause a scene or draw attention to ourselves, but if an opportunity comes up, we'll take advantage of it." He looked in the back seat. "Pete, take the timer and the C4 with you, just in case."

Pete reached under the front seat and grabbed a small black box with two wires dangling from it, "Got it."

Will led the way toward the mall entrance, snow crunched under his feet. The three men walked through the main doors and turned right down the first hallway. Two-thirds of the way down the hall, Ralph saw a sign, 'Groschen's Dry Cleaners'.

Ralph stopped at a maintenance door, twenty-five feet beyond the Dry Cleaners entrance. He backed against the door and leaned back with his legs crossed in front of him. Pete stopped next to him and Will stood in front of them. Ralph glanced self-consciously up and down the hall.

An old couple was moving up the hall towards them. The old man stopped in front of one of the display windows. He put out an arm and stopped the old woman. They both stared at the display. A kid screamed and Ralph riveted his head around in the opposite direction, to see a woman pushing a stroller, with a howling kid jumping up and down in it.

When the hallway cleared, Ralph nudged Pete and said, "Pete, open the door."

Pete glanced at Ralph for a second and then understanding flooded his face. He reached behind his back, as hair threaded out from the follicles of his hands. He grabbed the doorknob and twisted with werewolf strength.

Ralph heard tearing of metal come from inside the door.

Pete smiled and looked at Ralph, “Done,” he said.

Ralph pushed the door inward and followed it into a storage room. Pete and Will scurried in behind him. Will closed the door, remembering not to slam it.

A night light over the door leading into the Dry Cleaning store dimly illuminated the storeroom. Ralph walked over to three rows of boxes stacked against the wall. His eyes swept to the rear corner, where five metal barrels sat huddled.

“Ralph,” Pete said, pointing to the barrels. “We found a way to annihilate some more of the bastards.”

The barrels were marked, ‘Caution Dry Cleaning Fluid Extremely Flammable’.

“Excellent,” Ralph said, with a catch in his voice. “Hook up the C4 and timer on the back of the middle barrel.”

Pete walked over to the barrels and grabbed the rim of the second one. He tried to move it, but it would not budge. “Will, give me a hand,” he grunted.

Together the two wrestled the barrel forward about a foot. Pete reached over the top of the barrel and half way down attached the explosives to the backside with a piece of duct tape. Five minutes later, the three ‘shoppers’ walked out of the mall.

They met light traffic on Highway 10 and 61, as Will drove toward their new hideout in downtown St. Paul. He looked at Ralph. “Grandpa, when are we going to set off the bomb?”

“We’ll wait and see if they discover the broken door knob tomorrow. If they find the bomb, we will know; the police will be all over the place. At any rate, we need to stake out the dry cleaners and get a look at how many of them are inside tomorrow. It would be nice to catch at least four of them in there, then boom.”

“BOOM,” Pete echoed from his place behind Will’s head.

Will jumped and then looked at Pete through the rear view mirror.

Pete's face took on a crazed expression. "We'll send their asses to hell," he nodded. A gurgle escaped from his mouth.

The next day, Will and Pete sat in the Suburban outside the Groschen Dry Cleaners. Will shivered as the minus twenty-degree cold, seeped in to the Suburban through the metal doors. He reached for the ignition and started the Suburban. In a few minutes the heater was putting out warm air

They took turns watching customers enter and leave the store. By last count, Pete figured there were four members of the Guhl pack inside. There were never more than four 'targets' in the store at any given time and most of the time there were two.

"When should we blow the bastards up?" Will said, looking at Pete. "I'm getting tired of sitting out here doing nothing. If we wait too long they might discover the explosives. We're never gonna get more than four in the store at any one time."

It was almost dark and Will knew they would be closing the store soon.

"I suppose you are right, kid," Pete said, nodding his head toward the storefront.

"Here's what we are gonna do. We will wait until the two customers leave and then do it. How does that grab you?"

Surprised, Will said, "Do you mean it?"

"Yeah," Pete said.

Inside the store Judy, Francis Guhl's sixteen-year-old daughter, was busy waiting on two customers, while Diana, Andy and Cheryl Groschen were busy hurrying around the store, turning off equipment and cleaning up. All of them were oblivious to the presence of enemy werewolves outside and the threat they offered for them inside.

Finally, the two customers walked out of the store carrying several hangers of clothing draped in plastic.

Will waited, watching the people walk to their car. His hands held the detonator on his lap. He turned to Pete, who stared into the storefront. Pete nodded and Will pushed the silver lever up, on the side of the small black box. A red light blinked on.

Will placed his thumb on the red blinking button and pushed down. A tremendous muffled explosion erupted within the Dry cleaners store. The glass windows ballooned outward and shattered into a million pieces. A fiery ball crashed through two adjacent shop walls, sending merchandise out into the parking lot.

Will watched the top of the building erupt into the air. A dense mushroom of fire and smoke lifted the cement slab roof into the air like chunks of Styrofoam. Pieces of concrete and twisted steel girders rained down on the parking lot.

Will jumped when the car next to him disappear under a large piece of concrete. Small pieces of concrete rained down on the Suburban, causing three dents to appear in the hood. Will's eyes and mouth opened wide as he put the Suburban in gear and drove out of the parking lot.

Chapter 27
Wild Challenge

Francis pleaded, "Father, we have to put more effort into finding them." Tears of anger and helplessness coursed down his cheeks. He was Jerrold's fourth child. He lost his daughter, Judy Guhl, in the Dry Cleaner Store explosion.

Jerrold and Francis faced each other from opposite sides of the archway in the living room of Jerrold's mansion. A group of family members returning from the funeral home entered through the front door. They froze when they heard Jerrold and Francis arguing.

"We are looking everywhere for them Francis," Jerrold said, his back arching into a shrug. Tears ran down his cheeks. As leader of the pack, father and grandfather to those killed, Jerrold felt the loss of his daughter, Diana, son-in-law, Andy and his two nieces, as much, if not more than anyone else did. He needed to remain strong for everyone.

"That's not good enough," Francis said.

A frightened look spread across Jerrold's face. Francis was becoming hysterical. "He is going to lose control if I do not do something," Jerrold thought.

"Everyone should be out looking for those bastards," Francis screamed, with his face pointed toward the ceiling. Francis's head dropped to his chest and he shook his closed fist in Jerrold's face. "All you do is sit in your office hiding, while our pack is being destroyed."

Jerrold backed up a step, shocked by the intensity of Francis's anger.

Francis's face turned red; he trembled and released a mournful growl. His body started to shake. He was losing his usual steel grip on his emotions.

The pack leader could not tolerate any challenge to his authority. A space in Jerrold's brain sizzled the moment Francis tumbled over the edge. He knew when one of his pack lost control. Jerrold watched speechless as hair sprouted from Francis's hands and face. His head distorted, as skull bones began to melt and reshape. His face grew a long shaggy muzzle with fangs hanging over the sides of his jaws.

Jerrold shook himself out of his inactivity. Why did he hesitate? He spoke to Francis mind to mind. "Francis, stop the change NOW, or I will be forced to hurt you."

Francis ignored the warning. Jerrold could not postpone his change any longer. If Francis became a werewolf before him, in his present frame of mind, he would attack Jerrold and kill him.

Jerrold's temple veins popped out. He hunched his back and initiated the change. Jerrold enjoyed the familiar feeling, allowing the change to flood through him. Blood raced through his veins carrying the chemicals of change, bringing about the painful, yet welcome conversion of his body. His bones melted and remolded into the thicker, larger, werewolf-shaped forms. His body grew and contorted into a fur covered, muscular, werewolf. Jerrold made the complete transition in forty-five seconds, catching Francis just reaching the end of his change.

During all of this, Butch was sitting in the downstairs office, staring at the phone. He had raced back from the funeral home, not wanting to talk with anyone. He, like many of the pack, was upset with grandfather for the passive way in which he was dealing with the Morsching Pack. Ever since the dry cleaning explosion, too much inactivity on the part of Jerrold created a lot of frustration within the pack.

Butch and everyone else knew how the pack should be responding and it was very different from the way grandfather was handling things. Butch wanted revenge for the recent deaths of Uncle Andy, Diana and his two cousins.

Butch jumped when he heard running footsteps in the hall outside of the office. With a loud crash, Brad burst into the room and plopped down into the chair on the other side of the desk from Butch. "How did you get home so fast," Brad asked.

Butch said, "Shit, Brad can't you ever walk into a room?" Butch sat down and added, "I left early." He twisted the phone cord in his fingers. "I could not stay. I did not feel like talking to anyone."

An uncomfortable stillness fell over the room. Butch dropped the phone cord, looked at Brad, and said, "Is everyone back?"

"Yeah, most of them are upstairs, but two groups decided to take the long way home, if you understand what I mean."

Butch fidgeted and bit down on the inside of his cheek, drawing blood. "Oh-Oh, they went off hunting on their own. I do not suppose they cleared it with Grandpa. He's going to be mad."

"No, they did not ask him. They knew what his answer would be," Brad said.

"Shit, things are falling apart around here," Butch said in a whisper. For some reason, he felt nervous; a tight knot grew in his stomach. He did not know why he felt so jittery. Maybe it was because family members were striking out and hunting on their own. He was upset over the deaths of four of his pack members, but knew the family had to work as a unit. The feeling that some big shit was about to hit the fan worried him.

He stared at the phone. Maybe one of the teams was about to call and tell him they found the enemies new hideout. Butch slapped the table. The inactivity was upsetting everyone. If they did not find the Morsching pack members soon the family was going to fall apart.

Brad turned and looked at Butch. "Maybe the other werewolves left the Twin Cities?"

"No, they are still here," Butch said. His mind was on something else. "With their recent success, they will want to finish the job. No, they are still hunting us."

A loud crash sounded through the ceiling. Butch froze and his face paled. A scream tore through his mind. He heard the forceful mind message that Jerrold sent to Francis. It exploded in his head. Frightened, he leaped to his feet and rushed out of the office and up the stairs.

A bewildered Brad followed behind at a slower pace.

Butch rushed into the living room and skidded to a stop. Several members of the pack were in the room with their backs against the wall.

Butch turned and saw Jerrold and Francis facing each other in werewolf form. They stood fang to fang. Blood dripped in a steady stream from several cuts on Francis's shoulder and neck.

Francis shook, like a dog shaking water off his fur after a swim. His lips curled back and he screamed, "Kill, Kill." Frothy strings of saliva hung from his fangs and splattered to the floor.

Butch turned to those standing wide-eyed against the walls and said, "What happened? Somebody do something."

No one answered or moved. Francis was out of control and Jerrold was trying to shock him back to normal.

With no forewarning, Francis leapt at Jerrold and sank his teeth into his father's left shoulder. Francis shook his head back and forth, ripping out a chunk of flesh. Jerrold stumbled back with a howl of pain, blood spurting from the wound.

Jerrold feinted toward Francis's left side. When Francis moved to meet his thrust, Jerrold changed directions in mid-air and dove under him.

Butch watched Jerrold reach up with his muzzle and clamp down on Francis's throat. The two bounced and rolled on the floor. Francis had struggled, trying to throw Jerrold off, but he did not have the strength to break the hold on his neck. Francis's trachea collapsed shutting off his air supply. He struggled for a moment and then went limp.

Jerrold maintained a firm grip until he was sure Francis lapsed into unconsciousness. Then, he released the pressure.

Jerrold staggered back against the desk. He was dizzy from loss of blood. Blood covered the floor, desk and several pieces of furniture. Jerrold wobbled on his four legs and then sagged to his knees. He tottered there for a few moments and then toppled to his side, banging his head on the floor. His mouth opened and closed, like a fish out of water. He was trying to say something, but no words came out of his mouth.

Butch glanced at Brad, whose face was white as chalk. Butch disturbed by what he witnessed, still felt an excitement and pride for the way Grandfather handled Francis.

Butch marveled at Jerrold's strength and power. I do not know if I could have stopped from killing Francis. As leader of this pack, it will be necessary for me to consider my actions carefully and then act, just as grandfather did.

Butch watched Francis's unconscious body transform back into his human form. Brad walked over to Francis and tended his wounds.

"How bad is he?" Butch said.

Brad probed one of the bloodier wounds. "None of his wounds are very deep," he said. "The self-healing process will take care of his cuts in a couple of hours."

Jerrold passed out from loss of blood. With each breath, his chest quivered. Slowly, his body transformed back to its human form. Little puffs of breath wheezed from his mouth. Butch walked over to Jerrold and knelt over his body. He stuck his thumb against the artery that was squirting blood. Using his other hand, he applied pressure on another bleeder in grandfather's groin area. Grandfather's shoulder wound, where Francis tore a piece of flesh away, was oozing blood. Butch knew the missing chunk of flesh would replace itself, if grandfather did not die from all the blood he lost. Butch saw another wound on grandfather's side leaking blood. Butch looked at Elliot standing glued to the wall, with a dazed look on his face.

"Elliot, I could use your help," Butch said, motioning with his head for him to come over.

Elliot shook his head and looked like he was coming out of shock. "Yah, coming," Elliot said and walked forward. He dropped to his knees next to grandfather and Butch.

"Here, hold your hand on this cut," Butch said, as he released the pressure on the groin wound. Elliot pushed down with his big hand. "Not so hard," Butch said, pulling up on Elliot's arm. Butch then shifted his hand to the side wound and applied pressure. The flow of blood stopped.

Fifteen minutes later grandfather rolled his head from side to side, as he regained consciousness. He moved his good arm up and felt his wounded shoulder. The wound was already beginning to heal over, but it would take a couple of weeks before new flesh completely refilled the jagged hole. Scabs covered the small vessels, but tissue fluid still seeped from the damaged tissue.

"Just lay there and rest grandfather," Butch said.

He turned and walked over to Francis, who was still lying on the floor, his eyes staring up at the ceiling. Butch knelt down next to Francis and their eyes locked. Butch stared deep into Francis's eyes. Butch's nostrils flared. "You stupid jerk." he said. "Your self pity and lack of control almost killed grandfather. If you ever do something like that again, I will kill you myself."

Francis's face turned white. Something deep within Butch's eyes terrified him. He whimpered and with difficulty tore his eyes away from Butch's hard cold stare. Francis shivered; he knew that if he responded incorrectly at this moment, Butch would kill him. He believed that with certainty.

Francis turned and looked at his father. Sane once again, he knew his behavior was wrong. He attacked and tried to kill his father, "Father, forgive me," he cried. "It was my grief over the death of Judy. I lost control. Do you understand?"

Jerrold looked at him with contempt and said, "I will forgive you this time, my son." Jerrold could not keep a menacing growl from escaping from deep in his throat. Jerrold locked eyes with Francis and said, "This time only."

Francis knew the next time he committed a serious mistake he would die.

"Remember, you are not the only one who has suffered a loss, Jerrold said.

Chapter 28
Butch Gets His Chance

A few days later, Jerrold sat at his desk, with a contemplative look on his face. He rotated his shoulder and winced from the pain. New flesh restored the deep shoulder wound to its original form, but the pain remained and reminded him it would take more time to heal.

Jerrold's thoughts wandered to the conflict they were having with the other pack. He scolded himself over his feelings of uncertainty in how to end the war. He reminded himself, he was getting too old to lead the Guhl Pack. Maybe it was time to give up his Alpha position.

In the basement, Butch sat in front of the phone bank logging reports from the teams. Four teams were out scouring the next suburbs on the list. Each team's goal was to locate the Morsching's new hideout. Butch came in at six o'clock in the morning to cover the phones and by noon was already bored. He would rather be in the field searching for the other werewolves. He leaned back in his chair and threw his feet on top of the desk. He popped the top of a Sprite and took a big swallow.

The red phone rang. Startled, Butch jerked his feet off the desk. The front legs of his chair slammed to the floor. He felt apprehensive as he picked up the receiver. He knew even before anyone spoke it was not one of the teams reporting in. "Yeah," he said. Butch listened. His eyes grew round and glassy. He laid the receiver on the desk and ran upstairs.

"Grandfather," Butch said, as he slammed into the office door. The door banged back against the doorstop and swung half way closed again. "Aunt Barbara is on line two," Butch said.

Jerrold stared at Butch, his face ashen and his left eye twitched. Beads of sweat popped out on his forehead and upper lip. His heart fluttered in his chest.

Butch suspected his grandfather knew the news was not good. "She's at United Hospital," Butch blurted out.

Jerrold's mouth opened and closed like a fish sucking water. "What is wrong now?"

"She told me Sue and Amy were killed in a hit and run accident and Elliot was injured, but still alive."

"Oh God, when did it happen?" Jerrold said, as a frightened, vacant look crept across his ash colored face.

Butch glanced at his watch. "One o'clock, just an hour ago."

Jerrold did not move.

"Grandfather, Pick up the phone," Butch said, pointing at the telephone. "Barbara's waiting."

Jerrold still did not move. He stared at the telephone for a few more seconds, appearing to Butch, as if he did not want to hear the bad news from Barbara.

"Grandfather," Butch said again, "She's on the phone."

Jerrold extended his arm, picked up the receiver, and put it to his ear. "Hello, Barbara. Butch told me what happened. I am sorry. Give me the details."

"This was no accident," Barbara cried. She was unable to continue.

Jerrold felt the loss in her voice. Jerrold interrupted her sobbing. "Their deaths will be avenged by the pack," he promised.

Barbara started to babble between sobs.

"Easy, don't cry," Jerrold pleaded.

For a moment, Butch thought Jerrold was going to break down, but instead he sat up straighter in his chair. Color rushed back into his face. He looked angry, but in control of himself once again. "Barbara stay at the hospital, I will be there in half an hour." Jerrold hung up the phone, then his shoulders slumped and he lost it. He dropped his tear stained face into his hands and his shoulders shook.

Butch did not know what to do. It embarrassed him to see his grandfather like this. He said in a hushed voice, "Grandfather, this is a senseless loss for the pack."

Jerrold looked up. "I don't understand how this could have happened. I thought I set up enough steps to safeguard our pack from any more deaths. I did not have the heart to ask Barbara why she did not attack the killers. Butch, do you know what happened? She did not tell me how the girls were killed."

Butch frowned, "Just what Barbara told me. She said a semi-truck rear-ended them, on purpose. It happened on Interstate 94, a block east of Snelling Avenue. Both girls ended up on the pavement. The bastard stopped the truck and then backed up over them, making sure they were dead."

As Butch repeated his conversation with Barbara, course dark hair started to sprout on his face and hands. He glanced at his hands and stopped the change.

"Oh, God," Jerrold said, when Butch finished. "When is this going to end? Why are they trying to kill us? What did we do to cause them to invade our territory? It must end before anymore of my pack is killed." He looked at Butch. "I don't know what to do anymore."

"Be strong grandfather. You are the pack leader." Butch said a serious note in his voice. "We have not been aggressive enough in pursuing the other werewolves. We have been reactionary, when we should have taken the offense. We need to take the fight to them. We've been sitting back letting them kill us off at their leisure."

"What would you have me do?" Grandfather said, throwing his hands into the air.

"I am not telling you what to do," Butch said, "but it might be a good idea to have the more vulnerable members of the pack stay in a secure area. Allow them to go out with an escort of two or three pack members." Butch picked up a pencil from the desk and clicked it against his fingers.

Jerrold shook his head and said, "Butch, thanks for your advice, but I'm too tired and distraught to decide what to do right now. Stay on the phone bank. I need to get to the hospital."

Butch jumped in front of Jerrold. He felt it was now or never. "Let me finish," he persisted. "I want you to listen to what I am going to ask you. I know this may not be the best time grandfather, but please, listen."

Jerrold looked surprised and nodded.

"I want you to let me form my own team, one that would work independently from the rest of the pack." Butch spoke quickly. "I promise you I will find the rest of the werewolves and kill them."

Jerrold's face broke into a wide smile colored with sadness. "You are too young and inexperienced, Butch," grandfather said. "I am touched by your sincerity and determination, but if anyone is going to lead a team as you suggest, it should be someone like Richard."

Butch's face contorted in anger. "But, I won't fail as the others have," he said. "You've got to trust me. I know I can do it. No one else in our pack has been able to show any results."

Grandfather hesitated. He thought of the ramifications of allowing Butch to strike out on his own. It was crazy, but then he remembered Butch was not an ordinary pack member.

The number of family members who already died flashed through his mind. He needed to do something different.

He weighed the pros and cons of Butch's request. Butch handled the hotel attack well and he has shown the kind of abilities needed for leadership.

"Okay Butch," Grandfather said, "I will let you set up your own strike force under three conditions. First, you have to see if anyone will follow you. In the second place, the team must be limited to five members and the third requirement; you must clear any action you take with me before you carry it out. Do you agree to abide by these rules?"

"Yes grandfather, I agree," Butch said, not believing his ears. "You won't be sorry."

Jerrold smiled weakly at Butch and gave him a shove on the shoulder. "Now get out of here," sadness washed over his face. "I have got to go to the hospital."

Butch hurried out of the office before grandfather could change his mind.

Chapter 29
Butch Shows What He Can Do

George Groschen stood next to the kitchen sink, flexing the biceps on his left arm, then his right. At fifteen years old, he was big for his age, husky and athletic. He stared out the window, losing his gaze in the clouds, as his mind pondered the death of his parents, Andy and Diana, in the dry cleaning explosion.

He was angry and felt a deep loss. He did not know how to grieve, anger always got in the way. Feelings of guilt plagued him, because he felt he should have been in the store with them when it exploded. He survived and they did not, it was not fair. His whole being seethed with hatred for the Morsching werewolves. They caused the deaths of his parents. There was a score to settle with them, but his grandfather would not let him hunt on his own, and for that, he seethed.

Coreen, George's thirteen-year-old sister sat at the kitchen table, staring at a puzzle the two halfheartedly worked on. Her parents, brother and sister spoiled Coreen. Coreen was well developed and George tried to protect her from older boys, who were hitting on her. Her golden hair held in place by a red banana clip allowed several stray strands to swing free over her left eye.

A yellow T-shirt overlapped the blue Jean shorts she wore. She missed her parents very much. Especially at this moment, because no one was there to get her breakfast or clean up after her. Diana and Andy spoiled her and now they were dead. George made her get her own breakfast and she did not like that. Thing would change when their Aunt arrived to care for them.

George turned from the sink and walked back to the kitchen table. He looked down at the pile of puzzle pieces and pushed some of the pieces back from the edge of the table. He sat down on the kitchen chair and rested his elbows on the table, holding up his chin. Piles of pieces arranged by color patterns lay around the skeleton of the puzzle. He picked up a piece and began to search for where it fit.

Coreen wiped the tears from her face and looked at the puzzle. "I don't want to do this anymore," she whined.

George heard a noise at the kitchen door. It sounded like a growl. He dropped the puzzle piece he was holding and froze. Oh, Shit. "Shhh, they are coming for us," he said, looking at his sister.

Since the explosion that killed his parents, warnings in the back of George's mind kept surfacing, telling him that the foreign werewolf pack would be coming for him, to finish the job. He growled and jumped up putting a protective arm around Coreen.

She screamed, more at George's quick movement than the apparent threat George voiced. She did not know why she was frightened, but she was.

There was a knock on the kitchen door. George put his hand over Coreen's mouth and stood with his eyes wide open, afraid to answer.

A voice called from the porch. "George, are you in there? Come on, I know you are in there. Open up. I need to talk to you. George, this is Butch, open up."

"Butch," George said, relief flooded from his tense body. "Is that really you?" His hand dropped from Coreen's mouth and slid down to grab her by the elbow.

"Yeah, it is me," Butch banged on the door again. "Open up." As he waited, he reached over to the side of the door and flicked a piece of peeling paint from the siding.

George hurried to the kitchen door and pulled back the deadbolt. When the door swung open, he was relieved to see Butch standing on the back porch. He shoved the storm door open and grabbed Butch by the arm, pulling him into the kitchen. "Boy am I glad it is you."

Butch's face turned ashen, when he realized why George was happy to see him. "I did not understand. It could have been the Morsching werewolves at the door. I am sorry if I alarmed you." He banged his fist on the kitchen cabinet. "Grandfather should have thought of this possibility and insisted you stay at his house. I have tried to convince him that everyone should be brought together for safety reasons, but he won't listen."

"Well, anyway I'm relieved it was you." George sighed, patting Butch on the back.

Butch sat down at the kitchen table. Coreen walked over and sat on his lap. She put her arm around his neck and laid her head on his shoulder. A shudder went through her body.

"We have to get grandfather to plan ahead and take more precautions," Butch said. A frown creased his forehead. He put his arms around Coreen and gave her a hug. "You are safe now," he said with a smile.

Butch watched George fight back tears. He looked out the kitchen window to avoid embarrassing him. Butch experienced the sadness George was feeling and his eyes became moist.

George wiped his eyes and said, "I'm mad at grandfather for not letting me hunt those bastards. They killed my mom and dad." George bit the inside of his cheek, drawing blood. "I wish there was something I could do," he cried throwing his arms up in frustration.

Butch smiled and nodded. He knew how George felt, for he was experiencing those same feelings. He thought, "If I were in George's shoes, I would be out hunting the other werewolves, no matter what grandfather said.

"George, that's why I am here, I know you want revenge for your parents' death." He shifted Coreen to his right knee and leaned forward over the kitchen table. "Let me get right to the point. Grandfather has given me permission to put together an independent group to hunt the Morsching werewolves. I want you on my team."

George looked puzzled.

"Are you interested?" Butch said rubbing Coreen's back.

"You bet I am," George said.

"Great," Butch said, feeling relieved. One team member was a start. "You have to follow my orders, without question. If you can do that, you are in."

George sat up straight and looked at Butch with a serious look on his face. "Butch," he said, through red, moist eyes, "I promise to follow your orders as long as we track them down and kill them."

"Good," Butch said, happy with his first recruit, "Welcome to the team. Now, shall we take Coreen over to my parents' house? She can stay with them." George nodded his agreement. Butch said, "She will be safer there." Butch pushed Coreen forward, to see her face. "Coreen, is that okay with you?"

Coreen's lips grew into a pout and then spread into a smile. "Yes, I will be happy to get out of this house. As long as I am here, all I do is sit around and cry. It is so hard to believe that mom and dad are never coming back," she sniffled, and looked into Butch's blue eyes. "What I would like to do, is go with you and help kill those werewolves too," she said, her face brightened at the thought. "But, I don't suppose you would let me do that, would you?"

"No, I am afraid not," Butch said with a shrug. "You will have to let George do the killing for you. Grandfather limited me to five members on my team." He put his arm around Coreen's shoulder and gave her a hug.

"Yeah Sis, I will get them for you," George promised. He turned to Butch with a big smile. "What are we waiting for? Let's go."

After dropping Coreen at his parent' home, Butch drove with George to Midway Hospital, where Elliot Buchannan was still a patient. He made a miraculous recovery from the hit and run 'accident' in which his two sisters were killed. Elliot was twenty-five years old and stood six feet five inches tall. He weighed two hundred eighty-five pounds, all solid muscle.

When Butch and George walked into Elliot's hospital room, he appeared to be sleeping. A book lay open on his stomach. Elliot was not sleeping, he was thinking of his dead sisters. A low rumbling growl echoed from deep in his chest. The frustration he experienced motivated the growl. Elliot struggled to maintain control and not let his anger push his change.

The covers hung over the side of the bed. Butch saw that Elliot wore one of those asinine hospital gowns, split in the back and just covering his boxer shorts. A picture of Elliot walking down the hallway with his butt hanging out flashed through Butch's mind. He smiled.

Elliot felt a presence in his room. A momentary bolt of fear flashed across his face and his eyes snapped open, the book slid to the floor. It took him a moment to recognize his two cousins standing in the doorway.

"Whooo, hey guys, am I glad to see you," Elliot managed to blurt out. He sat up and swung his legs over the side of the bed. Self-conscious, he pulled the front of his gown down to cover his shorts. "What are you doing here?"

Butch smiled.

George wrinkled his nose. He did not like the smell of hospitals. He grinned at Elliot and said, "Visiting an injured cousin. How are you feeling?" He plopped down in a stuffed chair near the window.

"I'm okay and ready to get out of here." Elliot picked up the fallen book and set it on to the table next to his bed.

Butch lifted the book and gazed at it before speaking. "Elliot," he said, paging through the book. "How would you like to get revenge for the death of your sisters?"

Elliot cocked his head and stared at Butch before answering, "I'm willing to do anything grandfather asks," Elliot said, not quite knowing what Butch meant by the question.

"Are you willing to do anything I ask?"

"What do you mean anything you ask?" A frown creased Elliot's forehead. He looked towards the door before adding, "Grandfather is the pack leader."

Butch put his hands on the back of the chair in front of him and then made direct eye contact with Elliot. "Grandfather has given me permission to form my own hunting team and I want you to be one it. If you decide to join the team, you will have to follow my orders. Can you do that?"

Elliot thought for a moment and then said, "I won't have any trouble following your orders, but you have to promise me that I get to kill one of those bastards with my bare hands."

Butch's face broke out in a broad, wide smile, "If that is all you want, you have my promise," Butch said and then added, "You will get your wish." Butch walked around the chair and sat down on the edge of the bed next to Elliot. He touched his arm. "Now, we have to pick two more for the team. Do you have any ideas who should be included?"

"Maybe Brad?" George said.

"I don't know," Butch said. "I have worked with him a couple of times and he seems to get overly excited," Butch smiled remembering the time Brad knocked himself out running into a tree. "But he is a good fighter," he said

"He can change faster than any pack member, except for grandfather and maybe you," Elliot said looking at Butch.

"I think Brad would be a good addition to the group," George said.

Butch shrugged his shoulders, "Okay, if you guys say he is okay, he is in. Now, who else should we consider?"

George thought a moment and then said, "Maybe we should include Jake."

Elliot's eyebrow rose as he looked at George and said, "He is only fourteen years old."

"I know, but he can read people's minds and he is big for his age," George countered.

Butch looked surprised. "He can? It might be a good trait to have on our team," he said. He looked at the other two. They both shook their heads. "Okay, if they accept, that'll complete our team."

Butch spent the rest of the day tracking Jake and Brad down. Both agreed to join his team. He was elated. Now his real hunt could begin.

Chapter 30
Butch Makes A Point

The next day, Butch reported the completion of his team and the members to Grandfather for his approval.

"Congratulations," Grandfather said after Butch explained his success in rounding up his team. "It surprises me that you were able to get four members to follow you."

Butch's goal for his team was to locate the Morsching pack's hideout and kill them. He knew from the hotel registration there were six members in the original group. Two women and a man died in the ATW bombing, which means three of them are still alive.

Of course, that number would not mean anything now. More of their pack might have come to the Twin Cities. Butch cringed at that thought. If their whole pack were here that would spell big trouble for his team and their pack.

On the other hand, he believed those from the hotel were still in the Twin Cities. It would be easier to find them on our turf and even the score.

Five days later, an unknown assailant robbed and clubbed Richard's daughter, Sharrie to death. The police said it was a homicide committed when she resisted the robber. The pack knew it was more than that. A purse-snatcher would not beat someone to death, just to steal a purse.

The anger and frustration of the Guhl pack was approaching wild abandon and the threat of individual action. Many of them wanted to forgo the Alpha's decision to take out the Morsching's in human form. Jerrold was able to maintain control by making one concession; Butch's team could kill in werewolf form.

One o'clock in the morning found Butch and his strike team starting another search for the Morsching werewolves. Butch leaned against the workbench at the back of Jerrold's garage, the others gathered around him. There was a hint of cedar smell in the air from a pile of wood chips beneath the wood lathe at the other end of the workbench.

"Remember," Butch said, "to carry your cell phones with you at all times. If you locate them, call me. When all five of us are there, I will decide how best to carry out the attack. Does everyone understand?" He scowled, waiting for everyone to acknowledge his order.

George turned away with an angry look on his face.

"George, there will be no attack on the other werewolves until the whole team is present. Do you understand?"

"Okay, but remember, you said I could get revenge," George said.

"I remember, but if you cannot follow orders, you will be off the team," Butch threatened.

"That is not necessary. I understand your orders and agree to follow them," George said, afraid Butch might not include him.

Butch looked at the others. They nodded their agreement.

The team drove into downtown St. Paul to begin their search. If the surrounding suburbs did not hold the Morsching Pack, maybe they were in one of the downtown areas. Tonight they would search St. Paul, around the Capitol.

Elliot drove north on Wabasha Street. The city was quiet. Streetlights showed a scattering of people still on the streets at two o'clock in the morning. Elliot hit the next three stoplights green and came to the corner where the old Dayton's Department Store stood. He drove the length of the building and turned left down a narrow, dark alleyway. He followed the paved area marked deliveries and emerged in the loading area behind the building.

Butch looked around. He noticed a dim light coming from a bulb in a clear glass globe, over a steel-jacketed door at the far corner of the building. Elliot coasted the van in behind a parked delivery truck and stopped. The van in the shadows of the truck would be hard to see. Unless someone drove around the truck, no one would know it was there.

Butch stepped out of the van. A cold breeze blew loose strands of hair into his face. He brushed the hair back in place and glanced up at the overcast night sky. It felt like it was going to snow. Butch leaned over the hood of the van and opened up a map of St. Paul. "Does everyone remember their assignments?" Butch asked, shining a small flashlight on the map.

The others gathered around Butch, looking at the map. "Jake and Elliot are you okay with your assignment?"

"Yeah, we know where we are going," Elliot spoke by mind thought.

"We do too," Brad said.

"Okay," Butch said, "Make sure you cover your areas carefully. I will be cruising around in the van. Remember to call me if you get a whiff of them."

The four-team members shed their clothes. Jake and Elliot were the first to complete their change. Fur bearing, four-legged beasts of the night replaced the human forms. They twirled around and raced away along the side of the building toward Wabasha Street. A few minutes later, Brad and George followed them.

The pairs of werewolves raced north on Wabasha at speeds over fifty miles per hour, stopping in dark shadowy areas whenever a car passed by. Three people came around a corner and caught Brad and George out in the open. Surprised, the two werewolves accelerated by the humans, who felt the breeze of their passing, but did not see them. With only a few hours to search the city north of Interstate 94, they did not have time to waste.

Butch waited a half hour before leaving the safety of the loading dock. It was three o'clock in the morning, when he passed by the State Capitol building. He found a secluded side street, north of University Avenue, where he parked between two other cars and waited for a call from his team.

He stared at his cell phone, willing it to ring; hoping one of his team would call and say they found the other werewolves. He grunted and leaned back in his seat, willing the patience required to wait for some word from his team. If this search turned out like all the others, this call would tell Butch they finished checking their assigned area and found nothing.

At four a. m., Butch's phone rang.

"Butch," Elliot's voice said in a harsh whisper. "We found them."

Butch swallowed, choking on his saliva, but managed to say, "Where?"

"I'm at the corner of Lexington and St. Clair. There is an open garage in the back of a blue house on the corner. Meet me and Jake there."

"Okay, give me fifteen minutes. I will call Brad and George. Depending on where they are, they might reach you before I do. Make sure you wait for me."

"I would suggest you park down the block," Elliot said. "They are in an old two story white house on St. Clair Street, 7699. Hurry, Butch and remember your promise."

Fifteen minutes later, Butch turned off Lexington onto St. Clair. Half way between the corner streetlights, he coasted to a stop. He shut off the motor under a big, leafless, snow-crusted, Elm tree.

Butch looked around. A dark, rusted out Buick was parked two car lengths in front of his van. Across the street, light from the peak of the garage, reflected on the snow creating a field of sparkling diamonds.

Butch removed his clothes in the back of the van and made the change into his werewolf form. He jumped out of the van, cursing when the dome light illuminated him in a circle of light. He quietly closed the door and crouched beside the van shaking. Slowly he relaxed.

With a silent growl, he ran through the snow to the shadow of the nearest house. He stopped in the dark and surveyed his surroundings. The neighborhood was quiet. He loped across two yards and followed the side of a stucco house back toward the alley.

He spotted the blue house on the corner and the old garage Elliot mentioned behind it. He ran to the side of the garage and peeked around the open garage door. The four members of his team were inside. Butch stepped into the darkness of the garage.

"Okay," Butch said in greeting. "What is the set up?" He tried to appear calmer than he felt. He leaned back against the two by four wall to steady himself. The others stood around the front of an old rusted Ford Taurus.

Elliot hunched his back forward and with eyes sparkling in the dark, his long muzzle opened showing his large canine teeth. He laid a sheet of paper on the hood of the Ford and cupped his furry paw around the big end of a flashlight. A narrow beam of light illuminated the paper. Butch moved closer and looked at the hand drawn map.

Elliot explained the situation. "The house they are in is just two doors west of here. It has a front and a back door, four windows on the east and four on the west side," he pointed at the drawing of the house with his other front paw. "Two upstairs windows are open a crack."

George shrugged, bumping Jake's shoulder on one side and Butch on the other, as he said, "I suppose they like fresh air," he said.

Elliot snarled at him and said, "We need to stay downwind as we make our approach or they might smell us," Elliot cautioned.

"How many do you figure are in there?" Brad said, images of his dead parents flashed through his mind.

"I don't know," Elliot said, flexing his muscles.

Butch watched the fur along Elliot's arm ripple.

"Ah, there are two Morsching men upstairs in separate bedrooms," Jake said.

Butch glanced at Jake and noticed his red eyes were staring at the side of the garage, as though fixed on the white house.

"How do you know?" Brad said, with a puzzled look on his werewolf face.

"I can see them," Jake said.

"Ah, bullshit," Elliot cursed. "Nobody can see through buildings."

"If Jake says there are two, that is what we will find," George said.

Butch moved away from the hood of the Ford and leaned against the stud wall. "Okay, Elliot, Brad, I want you to cover the outside, in case they try to escape from us."

Elliot looked disappointed, but nodded his willingness to follow orders.

"The rest of us will go in the front door and decide what to do once we get inside," Butch said, "Any questions?" Hearing none he said, "Let's go."

Brad and Elliot scampered out of the garage and loped to the shadows near the back porch of the white house. The others followed Butch across the back yard toward the front of the house. Butch stopped at the corner of the house and then crept to the front door. He pointed to George and then at the doorknob. George nodded and twisted the doorknob until something broke inside and the door popped open with a squeak.

The three werewolves froze for a moment listening to see if anyone stirred inside. When nothing happened, they crept into the entryway and closed the door behind them. An archway led into the living room, while a short hall led to the kitchen at the back of the house. Next to the archway, stairs led to the second floor. Butch took the stairs two at a time, his toenails clicking on the wooden steps. The steps squeaked once, when Jake put his weight on the middle of a step, instead of at the sides. Butch froze and waited a few seconds before continuing up the steps again.

At the top of the landing, light from a streetlight entered through a small circular window and dimly lit the hallway. There were four doors along the hallway. Butch shrugged his shoulders, not knowing behind which doors the two Morsching men' slept.

Jake tapped Butch on the shoulder. When Butch turned, Jake pointed to the closest door and held up one finger and then pointed to the third door down the hall and held up one finger.

Butch sent a mind message. "I will take the third door. George and Jake, take care of whoever is behind the first one."

Butch tiptoed past the first two doors, unable to keep his claws from clicking on the hardwood floor. He heard George let out a low gasp when Butch brushed against a strip of wallpaper producing a loud tearing sound. Butch stopped and pushed the strip back in place, but it just curled away from the wall again.

Butch glanced at George and Jake. He was surprised at the massive shadows they cast on the hallway wall. Jake's eyes glowed bright red.

"Ready? Here I go," Butch said mentally. With a snarl, Butch hurled his bulk against the door. The door ripped from its frame and crashed into the room. It bounced off the dresser and fell to the floor. Butch's werewolf vision allowed him to see a pale image of a man's face, sitting up in the bed.

The man's eyes were bulged wide open. He looked the same age as Butch. The sudden invasion caught him off guard. He was still in human form. Butch leapt on the bed, driving the man to the mattress. He squirmed beneath the covers. "If you attempt to change," Butch said, "I will tear your throat out."

Will cried out, "I won't, just don't hurt me." Will ceased his struggles under Butch's weight.

Butch sensed how terrified the man was and kept his urge to kill him in check. Beneath the covers, Will struggled to sit up. Butch pulled the covers back and grabbed Will by an arm. Butch heard scuffling sounds coming from the first bedroom and turned his head turned toward the noise. "Oh, shit," he said to himself. "They are in trouble."

Glass shattered as something hit the window at the end of the hall. The glass rained down on the roof of the back porch. Someone jumped through the broken window and landed on the porch roof, with a loud crunching sound. Whoever it was ran a few steps and then jumped. Butch heard the crunch of snow and a grunt, as the person hit the ground. Someone else hit the porch roof and jumped to the ground.

Shit, Butch thought, the other Morsching werewolf must have escaped. As much as he wanted to give chase, he knew he could not leave his own prisoner. He growled in frustration.

Butch thrust a paw at Will's arm, pushing him toward the door. From outside, Butch heard a loud, cracking sound followed by a muffled scream. The cry came from the backyard, where Elliot and Brad were on guard.

Jake burst into Butch's room with a frightened look on his face. "He got away. George went after him."

Butch shoved Will toward Jake. "Bring him," he said, and then Butch ran from the room and down the stairs.

Butch smashed through the back door and did not stop to open the screen door. He landed on the frozen snow in the backyard. He did not know what to expect. He was afraid he would find either Elliot or Brad dead and the Morsching werewolf gone.

A movement at the corner of the porch caught him by surprise and Butch swung his clawed fist towards the outline of a werewolf. Millimeters from slashing the werewolf's neck, Butch recognized George and pulled back just in time.

"God, Butch," George squealed, "You could have killed me."

"Sorry buddy, I did not recognize you right away."

Elliot and Jake were standing over the limp form of a heavy-set man, still part werewolf. From the contorted angle at which the body lay, Butch could easily see that his back was broken.

"I stopped him," Elliot said, matter-of-factly. "He came through the window in werewolf form. As soon as he hit the ground, I grabbed him. He was no match for me. I broke his back, twice." Elliot pantomimed how he bent the body over his leg and then moved his two arms down.

"You have avenged your sisters," Butch said. To himself he thought I am sure glad he is on my side.

Elliot said. "Yes, but I am still not satisfied. I won't be until all of them are dead." He turned toward Will, who stood between George and Jake.

Will was afraid Elliot was going to grab him and break his back, the same way he broke Uncle Pete's and he involuntarily took a step backwards. He looked at the dead body of his Uncle, "You killed Uncle Pete," he said.

"Just like I am gonna kill you," Elliot said, walking toward Will. "Your uncle's death does not make up for my two sisters and the others your pack have killed," Elliot said, spitting saliva at Will. "I will take pleasure in killing you."

Will shuddered; he shuffled backwards under the intensity of Elliot's glare. He tripped over Brad's extended leg. Elliot moved towards the prone enemy.

Butch said, "Wait." Elliot stopped. "Take him with us," he said turning to Brad and George. "We need to question him. We need to learn as much as we can about the other pack." Then he turned back to Elliot. "Elliot, drag the other body closer to the house and cover it with snow. Hopefully they won't find the body soon."

Will was frightened. He thought he was courageous, but in the presence of five angry werewolves, he did not like this game any longer. No one spoke to him and he could not read any of their thoughts.

"God, I wish Ralph were back from Madison," he thought. Will enjoyed killing the woman in the parking ramp and wondered if they would find out, he was the one that killed her. The Morsching's are not cowards, he thought, as he worked up his courage. "Just wait until Uncle Ralph gets back. He'll kill all of you."

Elliot lunged at Will.

Will let out a scream and turned white, his breath coming in gasps. He realized this war was all about dying, on both sides.

Butch said, "Come on, let's get to the van and change. We need to get out of here before someone wakes up and sees us."

Chapter 31
Butch Issues A Challenge

Drops of condensed moisture ran to the lower corner of the basement window. In the droplets, Butch imagined he saw an outline of a wolf crouching at the top of a hill, staring down at a deer. Butch's eyes stared at the images, not seeing beyond the glass.

New beads of moisture slipped down the glass, washing away the wolf and deer. Brad cleared his throat and Butch turned back to the prisoner sitting on the sofa. Brad sat on one side of Will, George on the other, each holding an arm.

Brad looked like he was ready to reach over and take a bite out of Will. Elliot with a broad scowl on his face sat on wooden chair facing the intimidated prisoner.

Butch thought, Elliot is not helping the interrogation by frightening the prisoner.

Jake leaned against the wall, his feet crossed at his ankles. A pensive look grew on his face, as he studied the prisoner.

Butch let his gaze travel over Will. He is not that different from us. I am sure he loves his parents and his pack, as much as any of us do. He must know the thrill of the hunt and the joy of the kill, as we do. If he is like me, then at this moment he is afraid of dying.

Jake shoved off from the wall. "Did you hear that," he said, shaking his head, while looking at Will. "They have a chemical called Al. . .Aldropamine. It eliminates the killing urge for a long time."

Will looked up at Jake, a startled expression on his face. "How do you know that?"

Jake ignored the interruption, "My God, when they hunt, they only have to kill one human. That satisfies the entire pack."

Butch moved away from the window. "Good work Jake," he said. "I'm going upstairs and tell Grandfather." He smiled. "This is gonna make him happy."

Jerrold was coming out of the kitchen and motioned Butch to follow him. They walked down the hall to his office.

"Grandfather," Butch said, settling down in the stuffed chair against the wall. "Jake's extracted some interesting information from our prisoner."

Jerrold turned and threw Butch a chunk of bologna he had taken from the refrigerator. "Good, I could use some good news. Out with it," Jerrold said as he smiled, walked around the desk and plopped down in his swivel chair.

"This other pack has a chemical that represses the need to kill humans."

Jerrold rocked forward placing his elbows on the desk and stared at Butch. "What? How does it work?"

"Jake says the chemical is called Aldropamine. It blocks the urge to kill humans. He says their pack only has to kill one human to satisfy the craving for the whole pack."

Jerrold swiveled his chair to the bar and poured himself a drink from a cut glass decanter. "My God, that is something we could use."

"We'll see if we can get the formula out of Will."

Jerrold rubbed his hands together. "Good . . .Good, this will eliminate our need to kill so many humans every five years. What else did you find out?"

Butch laid his head back and threw his right leg over the padded arm of the chair. He closed his eyes and said. "We know where all of the Morsching werewolves live."

The bushy eyebrow over Jerrold's left eye raised producing wrinkles on his forehead.

Butch opened his eyes and stared at Jerrold. "If it is okay with you, my team will be paying a visit to Madison, Wisconsin. We'll give them some of their own medicine, but this time in their own territory."

Jerrold slammed the glass in his hand on the desk; it exploded spilling the contents. He jumped erect in the swivel chair and said. "Aren't you forgetting something? I am the Alpha. I make all decisions that pertain to my pack and you need my permission for such a venture."

Caught off guard by the vehemence of Jerrold's outburst, Butch's eyes flashed with anger. What had he done to deserve such a violent reaction? All Butch wanted to do was carry the battle to the other werewolf pack and instead of praise his grandfather went ballistic. "I did ask. I said if it is okay with you."

"Our agreement pertained to local hunts," Jerrold said. "You have enough glory to last you for a while." Jerrold punctuated each word by stabbing his forefinger on the desktop. His face was beet red and his eyes bulged. He leaned back in his chair. "We are not going to do anything more to upset them for a while. We'll sit back and see what they do."

Butch could not believe what he was hearing. He was hurt and angry. He sat up and stared at his Grandfather through slitted eyes. "Grandfather," he said in a low, controlled whisper. Each word echoed with crispness and challenge. "I did ask your permission to carry the fight to them. Why does glory enter into the situation? I have not done any of this for glory or recognition. My team has carried the fight to them because you have not. I have done everything I promised you I would do. I resent your attitude. My team has done a good job and now you want us to sit back and do nothing. That is not the way to win this war. We need to act now, while we have the initiative."

Vessels popped out and pulsed in Butch's neck. "That has been the problem with your leadership; you always want to wait for them to take the offense." Butch's voice grew loud and raspy. Jaw muscled bulged and his face flushed. "We cannot let them always make the first move. You are out of touch with what is happening. They kill more of our pack and then we react too late.

Jerrold's chest puffed out as he said, "As pack leader, I will make those decisions and I have made up my mind."

Butch jumped to his feet and slammed his fists down on the front of the desk.

The sudden move startled Jerrold and sent him sliding back in his chair. He thought Butch was attacking him and threw his hands up to protect his face.

Butch pounded a fist on the desk and said, "No, I will not accept that. I do not agree with you and the pack does not agree with you either. From now on I will decide what the pack does." He could not believe he said that. He stood up straight and pointed at Jerrold, realizing there was no turning back. He had just challenged his grandfather. He was furious with his grandfather for taking a do nothing approach in the way he handled the fight with the Morsching Pack. "No more!"

Jerrold jumped to his feet, violently sending the swivel chair back against the table behind him. Bottles crashed to the floor. "You are forgetting your place," he screeched, pointing a finger at Butch.

Butch shoved the desk into Jerrold's legs and hunched his back, beginning his transformation into his werewolf form. "No, I am not forgetting myself. You have done a lousy job of protecting the pack. Your constant hesitation has allowed them to kill too many of us. You are no longer fit to lead us."

Jerrold lost control and screamed, "You ungrateful whelp. I see I need to teach you a lesson in humility." Jerrold hunched his back, rushing into his change.

Butch was already halfway through his change. Butch completed his change and leapt across the desk. He grabbed his Grandfather by the shoulder and bit down hard. His muscular jaws brought canine teeth together. Butch felt the humerus separate from the socket with a pop. He released his hold and jumped back.

Jerrold howled in pain, as he completed his change, "You have attacked the Alpha. For that you will pay with your life." Jerrold limped around the desk on three legs and faced Butch. Blood poured from the wound in his shoulder, matting his shaggy fur. Salivary foam leaked from his jaws leaving white streaks on his chest. His anger was so great; he did not feel the pain radiating from his shoulder.

"Grandfather, this is your last chance. You are no longer fit to lead the pack," Butch said. "Back down or I will make you."

"You, you are nothing but a mere pup," Jerrold screamed, not believing his ears. "How dare you challenge me? I will kill you." Jerrold launched himself through the air.

Butch knew what was coming and rolled to his side. Even anticipating the move, he was barely able to get out of the way in time. He felt the scrape of Jerrold's teeth just miss his throat. Butch scampered to his feet and wheeled to face the frustrated, snarling werewolf face of his Grandfather.

Jerrold looked puzzled. He could not understand how that move failed him. It always worked for him in the past. A few feet separated the two contestants. Butch feinted to the left and then sprang towards Jerrold, turning over in mid air. On his back, he slid under Jerrold. He used his front paws to force Grandfathers head into the air. He shoved his muzzle up between his paws and clamped his jaws around Jerrold's throat. He held on while his rear end swung around taking grandfather's feet out from under him.

The vice-like grip on Jerrold's throat cut off the flow of air to his lungs. Butch increased the pressure, stopping millimeters before the cartilage rings in Jerrold's trachea would snap.

With each jerk and twitch, Jerrold's windpipe closed even tighter. In a last attempt to escape, Jerrold brought his hind legs up and raked fur and flesh from Butch's stomach. Even though the pain was unbearable, Butch did not relinquish his hold on Jerrold's throat.

Colored lights flashed before Jerrold's eyes, as oxygen depletion rendered him unconscious. His hind legs ceased their clawing.

Butch relaxed his grip on Jerrold's throat. He did not release his grip, afraid Jerrold might be faking. After a few seconds, Butch opened his jaws and rose on weak legs. He stumbled back toward the desk. He shook his head. He could not believe he had defeated the pack leader. He raised his muzzle and howled. He was elated with his victory.

Butch jumped to the top of the desk, sat back on his haunches and released another blood-curdling howl.

"I am the new pack leader," he broadcast, "I now rule the Guhl pack. From this day forth, I will take care of mine."

Brad, Elliot, Jake and George heard the message in the basement, where they were still questioning Will. The strength of the message drove them to their knees. Elliot howled in pain and covered his ears. Brad and Jake dropped to their sides in pain. George just stood with his mouth wide open, not believing what he had heard.

Elliot fought his way to his feet, hands still covering his ears. "Jake, guard the prisoner. Brad and George follow me," he said. The three raced for the stairs and bound up them three at a time. They burst into the office and saw Butch in werewolf form sitting on the desk, bleeding from gashes on his stomach. They saw grandfather lying behind the desk on the floor, with slow growing red pools of blood seeping out beneath him.

Elliot said in disbelief, "Butch, what have you done?"

George ran to Grandfather's side and knelt next to him, as his body began to change back to its human form. He checked him over and said, "He's still breathing. Grandfather will live."

Elliot stared at Butch, still not believing what he saw with his own eyes.

Butch looked at his team members and knew that this was a crucial moment. Either they would kill him for attacking the Alpha or they would accept him as the new leader of the Guhl pack. "I challenged Grandfather for pack leadership. He has lost touch with reality. He has let too many of our pack be killed. He has not done a good job of protecting us against the Morsching Pack. I will be a better leader. From now on, we will be more aggressive in searching out and destroying our enemy. No more waiting for them to attack us first."

Grandfather blinked his eyes and sat up slowly.

"Are you okay Grandfather," Brad asked.

"I will live," Jerrold said. He moved his injured shoulder and moaned from the pain.

Rising up from his sitting position on the desk, Butch said, "Grandfather, I have defeated you in combat. Do you submit to my leadership?"

Jerrold made his way to his feet, holding his injured arm. He looked at Butch and then lowered his head. "I don't have any other choice. You have beaten me. I will submit to your leadership. I recognize you as the new Alpha of the Guhl pack."

George and Brad stepped forward and assisted Jerrold to the couch. They lowered him to a reclining position.

Now the true test, Butch thought and then said. "Elliot, George and Brad, I need your help. Will you recognize me as your new pack leader?" He was not sure what to expect from them. He stood and stared at them, waiting for their response. Elliot looked at his Grandfather and noticed his closed eyes. He looked like he was dead. Jerrold looked weak, vulnerable, and beaten.

The pain radiating from Jerrold's shoulder was so severe that he paid no attention to what went on around him. Butch was shell-shocked. Butch knew that each pack member would decide whether to accept Butch's leadership or to fight him on behalf of the Alpha.

Elliot looked at Butch and said, "I will follow you."

"I will too," George said, nodding toward Butch. "You have been a good team leader and will make a good pack leader."

Brad hesitated and then stepped forward. "I agree with Elliot and George. You were not afraid to take the fight to the Morsching Pack. I have been proud of our team. We did some good. I will follow you."

That evening the entire pack gathered in Jerrold's basement. By now, each family member heard what happened between Jerrold and Butch. They also knew that Butch's team supported him. Anyone that might have harbored thoughts of challenging Butch needed to consider his team's sworn allegiance to him. There was the distinct possibility the team members would fight to protect Butch's claim to the leadership position. No one wanted to assume responsibility for causing a schism within the pack, knowing it would destroy the family.

Taking all of these factors into consideration, the pack members accepted Butch as their new leader. Once leadership was decided, each family member stepped forward, pledged their continued support in the fight against the Morsching werewolf pack, and renewed their promise to lay down their lives for the pack.

The last one to step forward was Jerrold. Everyone turned as he walked into the basement. They watched him, wondering if he would challenge Butch. He walked down the full length of the table. Those sitting on the floor rolled out of his path. Jerrold stopped in front of Butch, head held high and shoulder squared.

In a deep voice, Jerrold said. "Butch, this was my pack. You defeated me and now the pack is yours. You beat me in a fair fight. I accept you as my pack leader. I want all of you to understand that this family can not afford dissension and for that reason I will follow Butch." He looked at Butch and said. "I pledge you my total allegiance." Jerrold removed the ring from his right ring finger and handed it to Butch. "As pack leader, this is yours," he said.

Butch looked at the ring, covered with ancient symbols and other inscriptions etched into the gold. In the center of the ring was a large, shining, green Emerald. This ring belonged to the first Alpha pack leader.

Butch took the ring and slipped in on his finger. "Grandfather, I thank you for your oath and for this ring." Then a broad smile crossed Butch's face.

Jerrold looked puzzled and thought, "Was he making fun of me?"

Butch noted the raised eyebrow on Jerrold's face and said, "But, the ring doesn't fit me, yet." He handed it back to Jerrold. "Will you hold it for me until I grow into it?"

Everyone laughed and the tension melted from the room.

Chapter 32
One Invasion Deserves Another

The middle of April should have meant nice weather was on the way, but Tuesday morning dawned cold and blustery with a hint of snow in the air. A blood red, sun rose over the edge of the eastern horizon, casting frigid, yellow-red rays through the kitchen window of Jerrold's home. A single black cloud floated slowly across the face of the sun, and like a blemish in the sky, grew larger.

The mansion still served as headquarters for the pack. Jerrold walked into the kitchen and saw Butch staring out the window, he said, "My father used to say a dark cloud over the sun was a sign of impending death."

Butch glanced at his Grandfather and wondered, a sign of death for whom. He looked apprehensively at the sun and the growing cloudbank before turning from the window.

He played over in his mind the dangers of what he was going to do. "Grandfather, I know we have talked about this many times and do not see eye to eye on how to deal with the Morsching Pack. I am not one to sit back, wait for the enemy to do attack and then react. I have decided to carry the battle to their backyard."

Jerrold's neck grew red. "Butch, it sounds like you have made up your mind. You are the pack leader. I do not have to agree with you, but I will do whatever you ask."

For over an hour, Butch's team hurried between the house and garage, packing, eating and joking with each other. Butch's mind raced, trying to think of anything he might have overlooked. He was anxious to leave. "Okay guys that is enough. Let's get going. We need to reach Madison before dark."

Fifteen minutes later, George walked into the kitchen and said to Butch, "The van is loaded, but Brad isn't here."

"He went home for the ATW," Butch said. "He will be here in a few minutes."

George shrugged, pulled out a chair and sat down at the kitchen table.

Elliot came in from outside rubbing his hands together and said, “Boy, this cold really seeps into my bones. When is it going to warm up?” He detoured to the counter and grabbed the coffee pot and three cups. He plunked the cups on the kitchen table and filled them. Butch and George nodded their thanks and grabbed a cup. Elliot pulled out a chair and sat down.

Silence grew in the room. George and Elliot stared into their cups, with blank unreadable expressions on their faces. Butch got up, walked to the sink and looked out the window. He stared into the red sun and wondered what the outcome of this expedition would be.

A few minutes later, Brad pulled into the driveway, honking the horn of his white Dodge. Jake ran to the Dodge and banged on the hood.

Brad jumped out, “Hey, don’t put any dents in the hood.” He grabbed the camouflaged ATW from the back seat. He carried it to the van and loaded it in the back.

Butch dumped the rest of his coffee down the sink and turned saying, “Brad’s here, let’s go.”

Elliot was the last to leave the house. He closed the kitchen door, then turned and cleared the four steps in one leap to join the others at the van.

George looked at Brad. “We thought you were not coming. We were going to leave without you.” He tried to cover the wide smile that broke out on his face.

An excitement ran through the whole team. They were nervous about taking the fight to Madison. It was a big step and the first major attack under the new Alpha. It was Butch’s idea to take the offense and keep the Morsching pack guessing. If anything went wrong with this mission, the blame would fall on him, but it was a risk he was willing to take.

Chapter 33
We Too Can Invade

It was Four o'clock in the afternoon when they arrived in Madison. Because Jake had read Will's thoughts, the Guhl team knew where all the Morsching's homes were located. The Morsching's would heavily guard their homes, so Butch decided to look for them at some of the storage facilities they owned. They drove up and down streets just to get a feel for the city, all the time trying to pick up the telltale scent of the werewolf. At six o'clock, they got lucky and picked up the distinct smell of werewolf on the easterly wind, a few blocks from one of their warehouses. Brad pulled the van to the curb.

Everyone piled out and stood with noses into the wind sniffing. They marveled at their luck, at locating the Morsching clan that fast. They had expected to spend several days trying to find some of them away from their homes.

The sun had dropped behind the surrounding buildings. The sky was gray-blue with dark cumulus clouds floating toward the southeast. At ground level, a thin haze floated and swirled over the streets, releasing a flurry of snowflakes.

Brad raised his head and cast around. "I can smell three of them just ahead of us," he said, pointing up the street.

The others drew air into their nostrils, trying to pick up the distinctive scent of the werewolf. For all their effort, they were not able to smell anything.

Butch kept sniffing. For a moment, he thought he smelled the familiar wet hair of a dog, tinged with a taste of rusting iron, but he was not sure.

"Where are they," Elliot said, showing his frustration, at not being able to smell them. His shoulders shook with irritation.

Brad glanced at him, "I can see them a block ahead. They are crossing the street, stepping up on the far curb." He pointed at the deep shadows alongside a tall building up ahead.

Butch squinted; probing the area Brad pointed at and thought he saw three faint, dark spots moving away from them.

"See there, just beyond the fire hydrant. Two guys have black leather jackets on and the other one in the middle is wearing a red Bulls jacket," Brad said.

"Aw, you are shitting me," George scoffed. "You cannot see that much better than the rest of us."

"No, he is telling the truth," Butch said, awe coloring his response. "If he says they are there you better believe him. You will have to take his word for what they are wearing. I thought I saw something move where he said they were. "Come on," Butch said starting across the street. He jogged, trying to close the gap between the three enemy werewolves and his team.

"I still can't see them," George scowled. He looked at Brad, disbelief still showing on his face. "How in the hell can you see what they are wearing?"

They closed the distance between the werewolves ahead. This was not a good place to attack them--they would wait. They were on one of Madison's downtown streets, three blocks off Main Street. Several cars with their lights on came down the street towards them. Even though foggy haze made it difficult to see very far, Butch knew there were other humans in the area and they would hear any fight that broke out on the street. The flashing light from a bar several blocks ahead was the only evidence any of the stores were open.

Jake hushed George and Brad, who were still arguing. "I'm reading one of them. They are going to turn right at the end of the next block. They are heading for one of their warehouses. It is a storage places for high tech supplies and weapons," Jake grew quiet and then said. "That fits with the information we got out of our prisoner, Will.

"Come on," George whined. "You guys are pulling my leg. Brad can see in the dark and we know Jake can read minds, but that far away?"

Butch looked at George and said, "Don't be a dumb ass, you know Jake saw into Will's mind and dug out the stuff regarding the

Aldropamine and other things. If he says he is reading the thoughts of one of those guys up ahead, I believe him."

Butch marveled at Jake's ability to read the other werewolf's thoughts and Brad's ability to see well in the dark, two powerful talents to have on his side.

Elliot put his arm around Jake's neck and gave him a squeeze. "Nice going kid. I don't know how you do it, but I am glad you can."

Brad put his arms out to the side and Butch and Elliot walked into them. "Wait," he said. "They are just going into the warehouse."

Chapter 34
Death In A Warehouse

Ralph Morsching followed by his nephew, Roger Jarvis and his son, Brandon pushed through a heavy metal door and disappeared into the warehouse.

"Okay, they went inside," Brad said.

Light fluffy snowflakes started to fall through the fog from the dark clouds overhead. The snowflakes stuck on the wool fibers of Butch's pullover, like dewdrops on morning grass.

Butch waited with the team for five minutes and then said, "Okay let's change." They quickly undressed and began their transformation into werewolves.

It was still a mystery to Butch how the change from human to werewolf and back was possible. What happened during the bone crushing changes that transformed him into a werewolf was scientifically impossible to explain. Nevertheless, he marveled at the efficiency of the process. In less than two minutes, he grew a foot taller, added four inches of hair over most of his body and redistributed muscle and bone into a new body pattern.

Butch gathered up his clothes and followed the side of the building towards the door. The others followed close behind. The click of claws and the footprints left behind betrayed their presence. They clustered around the metal door.

Butch leaned his weight against the door and found it locked. He nodded to Elliot. Elliot grasped the doorknob and twisted, his muscles bulged. The tearing of metal within the inner mechanism emitted a loud screech. Elliot leaned his weight on the door and it swung inward. Butch led four Guhl werewolves into the warehouse. They laid their clothes in a neat row next to the door, then swiveled their heads, sniffing, trying to locate their enemy.

Brad sniffed, "They are headed for the far end of the warehouse."

Wooden crates were stacked in rows, with aisles wide enough for the passage of a forklift between them. Cross aisles intersected the long rows allowing access to adjacent rows. Between the rows, circular lights hung suspended from the rafters every fifty feet. "Spread out and head towards them," Butch sent thoughts from his mind to the others.

Butch followed one of the aisles toward the other end of the warehouse. As he approached the far end, he heard voices. He walked with toenails lifted. At the end of the row, Butch peeked around a stack of crates and saw three men seated around a table.

A single bulb hung from the ceiling on a long cord, casting a circle of light over the table and men. A long workbench stacked with tools and boxes, stood against the end wall.

A lighted Coke machine illuminated one end of the workbench, pushing back the darkness, claiming a bit of territory in a dark corner. There were several rifles and shotguns propped against the wall next to the pop machine.

Butch cocked his head to the side and listened.

"We have not heard from Will since Pete was killed," he heard Ralph say. Ralph stood up, put his foot on the chair, and braced his upper body on his knee. "We'll have to assume he is either dead or captured. If he were still free, he would have contacted us by now. Tomorrow, I am going to take a team to the Twin Cities and find out what happened to him."

"That's just great," Roger said, with sarcasm. "You were wrong to take such a small group to the Twin Cities."

Ralph said, "Is that a challenge?"

"No," Roger said, "but, I still say it was a mistake on your part."

Ralph relaxed, realizing Roger was no threat to his leadership. He leaned back and crossed his arms over his chest. "Maybe you are right."

"What are we going to do now," Brandon asked. He was Rogers' twenty-five years old son. He made the human kill on their last hunt and already moved up the ladder of influence in the pack.

"If my instincts are right," Ralph said, "I have a feeling they will be coming for us. It wouldn't surprise me if they were already in

Madison." He slapped his fist down on the table and said. "As soon as Tom arrives we will figure out a way for you to ambush them when I am gone."

Ralph stood and dug his knuckles into his tense back muscles. He stretched and said, "Brandon, get three beers from the pop machine." He looked at him and said. "While you do that, I'm gonna walk down and get a couple of those machine guns that just came in. We need to take a look at them."

Ralph left the circle of light around the table and walked toward the far aisle, where he disappeared into the blackness. Brandon walked to the pop machine, opened the door, grabbed three bottles of Old Milwaukee and circled back to the table.

Roger picked up a pencil lying on the table. He concentrated, and then started to jot down some ideas for setting up an ambush. He jumped when Brandon banged two bottles of beer on the table.

Brandon smiled, "Hey, Dad, why are you so jumpy?" He plopped down on a chair.

"You heard Ralph. Those Guhl werewolves might be in town looking for us right now. It makes me nervous."

Brandon sat back and wondered how it would feel to kill another werewolf. Killing a helpless derelict was one thing, but another werewolf, capable of fighting back and killing him might be more than he would care to face.

Darkness was complete out in the aisles of crates, except for the few circles of light. If either Brandon or Roger would have looked down the aisles, they might have seen duel orbs of gold and red studying them. One pair of glowing eyes disappeared as Butch blinked.

Four werewolves waited for Butch's signal to attack. Butch was primed, his breath deep and rapid. He was ready to start the battle and kill the enemy.

Brad stood in the dark aisle, afraid. His heart fluttered, damn near on the verge of fibrillation.

In Elliot, the killing madness mounted until it was unbearable for him to wait any longer. He fought to maintain control.

George quivered, as he leaned against the edge of a crate. "Butch," he mind spoke. "We can't wait much longer."

It sounded like a plea to Butch. He worried that George or Elliot might attack prematurely. He sent out over his mind link, "We have to wait until the other one comes back and attack them while they are together."

Elliot said, "Why don't two of us go after the one that left?"

Butch thought a moment. "Not a bad idea," he projected, "but, wait a couple of minutes. He said he was going to return."

Butch was glad the other werewolves could not read their minds. It gave them a real advantage with Jake being able to read their minds. Butch's heart missed a beat as he thought, what if they do have someone like Jake? What if the one who left heard us communicating and went to call for help. Butch started to second-guess his thoughts. Should they take the two of them sitting at the table or wait for the other one to return? He hesitated, not knowing what he should do. He realized that command had its problems.

Meanwhile, Ralph walked out of the far aisle carrying two machine guns. He stopped and swiveled his head. A puzzled expression grew on his face as he listened to muffled words in his mind, like when a radio is out of tune and picking up a second station. At first, he thought his mind was playing tricks on him. He tried to understand the garbled words, but could not make them out. The worried expression on his face grew more exaggerated. He thought, "Maybe I am picking up secondary mental thoughts from Brandon and Roger." He projected from his mind, "Hey, guys, are you screwing around?

Roger looked up from his writing. "What do you mean?" he said by mind link. Roger's question popped into Ralph's head, loud and clear."

"Are you guys mumbling? Trying to scare me?" Ralph projected mentally.

"No, we are sitting here having a beer," Roger said. "Really Ralph."

"Okay." Ralph shook his head dismissing the problem for now and started walking back to the table. All of a sudden, a shiver ran down his spine. It dawned on him where he had heard muffled sounds like this before. His thoughts screamed, "I heard the same sounds the night of the attack at the Hilton Hotel in Minneapolis." He said via his mind link, "Roger, Brandon, some of the Guhl werewolves are in the warehouse. Run for it."

Jake intercepted the exchange. "Butch," he projected, "they know we are here."

"Oh, shit," Butch screamed over his mind link, "Elliot you and Jake go after the single one. The rest of us will attack the two at the table."

Roger and Brandon did not bother to change into their werewolf forms. They jumped from their chairs and raced toward the steel back door next to the pop machine.

George and Brad flew from the aisles in pursuit. In their werewolf form, they were on Roger and Brandon before they reached the back door. Roger attempted to change, but George leapt on his back and grabbed him by the throat. He yanked back tearing through carotid arteries and pulling rings of cartilage from Roger's trachea.

Butch flew past Brad and pounced on the back of Brandon, who screamed in a high-pitched feminine voice. The scream cut off when his neck vertebrae snapped. Two Morsching werewolves died in less than thirty seconds. Blood poured from the inert bodies onto the cement floor, pooling and trickling toward the wall.

"Thanks a lot," Brad said to Butch, as he looked down at the two dead men. "You could have let me kill him."

Jake's cry for help echoed through Butch's mind causing pain, he dropped to his knees. Jake was injured. Butch jumped to his feet and ran full speed down the second aisle, followed by George and Brad.

When Elliot and Jake ran toward Ralph, he dropped the machine guns, turned and ran back down the aisle. He heard the screams of Roger and Brandon and nearly turned back. He initiated his change and in werewolf form raced down the aisle. He knew the Guhl werewolves were coming for him. He surveyed the immediate area trying to figure out how to escape.

If he continued to run down the aisles, they would hear him and quickly find him. He looked up and a smile creased his face. He ran a short distance and jumped twenty feet to the top of the stacked boxes. He crouched in the darkness and gave a silent prayer for Brandon and Roger. He knew in his heart that they were dead.

Ralph heard the click of running claws and his heart skipped a beat. Two werewolves raced down the aisle toward him. His eyes followed the noise caused by their claws and spotted two shadows streaking below him. He knew it was not Roger or Brandon. He waited until the first shadow passed beneath his perch and then launched through the air at the back of the second one.

The weight of Ralph drove Jake to the floor. Air whooshed from his lungs and the crack of rib bones echoed between the boxes. Ralph lunged for Jake's neck, but missed as Jake pulled his head to the side. Ralph caught him high up on the front left leg and bit down hard. Bones cracked and Jake howled.

Elliot heard Jake cry out behind him and skidded to a stop. He grew enraged with himself for being stupid. He let out a blood-curdling growl and ran back up the aisle.

Ralph's sensitive ears heard the other one coming back towards him and released his hold on Jake. He would finish him after killing the one returning. He turned to meet the hurtling body of Elliot.

Ralph rose on his hind feet and met Elliot fang to fang. They dueled with their fang-encrusted muzzles. Teeth clashed against teeth, as they parried and thrust at each other.

The size and strength of the werewolf he fought surprised Elliot. He wondered for the first time in his life, if he had finally met his match. Elliot knew if he kept his opponent occupied the others would arrive to help him.

Ralph had never met a werewolf that came close to his size. No one in his clan dared challenge him because he was so much bigger than everyone else was. This was different; here was a werewolf that matched him in size and strength. Ralph grew alarmed when he was not able to dispatch Elliot quickly. He realized the others were coming. If he did not quickly kill or disable this foe, he would be the next to die.

Elliot was stronger than Ralph was, but not as fast. Elliot kicked out with his hind feet and bulled Ralph onto his back. Ralph's head bent to the side exposing his neck for a second; Elliot went for the vulnerable spot, but Ralph recovered and raked his hind legs across Elliot's exposed stomach.

Wicked, long claws ripped strips of flesh from Elliot's stomach. Elliot ignored the pain, and fastened his teeth on Ralph's skull. He bit down hard trying to crush the skull, but his teeth slid down the bone stopping at the cheek and ear. Elliot yanked his head back tearing pieces of flesh from the side of Ralph's face. Ralph lashed out in pain and sent Elliot skidding across the floor. Elliot slammed against a crate and turned over. He was growing weak and exhausted from the prolonged battle.

Ralph took the opportunity to leap to his feet and run down the aisle toward the front door. Elliot weakly raised his head and watched as the only opponent to best him disappeared into the safety of the darkness.

Charging down the aisle, Butch saw Ralph in 'were' form, running ahead of him. Two werewolves were lying on the floor. Butch told George and Brad to continue after the one running down the aisle. The two whooped and howled when they caught sight of Ralph.

Butch skidded to a stop next to Jake's thrashing body. Jake was still conscious and in a lot of pain. A pool of blood surrounded his shoulder. Butch ran his paw down Jake's crooked arm and felt the jagged end of broken bones sticking through the fur. Jake gasped for air and winced with every inhalation. Butch suspected Jake's ribs were broken. The broken arm and ribs would repair themselves once he changed back to his human form, if he could.

Butch took Jake's uninjured paw and placed it over the spurting blood coming from his shoulder. After a minute the blood stop flowing, Butch slid over to Elliot and checked the deep claw marks on his chest and abdomen. Elliot lay with both of his paws holding some of the strips of flesh in place. Blood oozed from around the edges of the strips. Butch looked for any streams of blood, but did not see any. Good, there was no damage to any major arteries.

"I'm sorry," Elliot moaned from between clenched teeth. "I am to blame for letting him get away."

"Don't worry Elliot," Butch said. "You did your best." He pawed Elliot's good shoulder, "Can you change back to your human form?"

"I will be able to, just give me a minute," Elliot moaned.

George and Brad trotted up the aisle.

"He got away," Brad said.

"Don't worry," Butch said. "We have other problems that need our attention." Butch trembled, but fought to control his emotions. "Brad, we need the van, Jake is in too much pain to change back right now. We need to get out of here before they come back."

Jake raced for the door, made his transformation to his human form, dressed and ran through the snow for the van.

"What do you want me to do?" George said.

"Help me get them to the front door."

In a few minutes, the van pulled up to the steel front door, a horn honked.

"Come on George, let's carry Jake out before we change back to our human form," Butch said.

"Elliot, try to change. You are too heavy to carry and it will be easier to get you in the van."

Elliot struggled to change. It took him longer than normal to complete the change, but when he finished; wicked, red welts remained on his stomach and chest. He stood on his own, shoulder hunched to lessen the strain on the tears in his stomach muscles.

George helped to dress Elliot. When they finished Elliot said, "Quit fussing, I'm okay."

Elliot walked over to where Jake lay. "Here, Brad," he said, "let me carry Jake."

"Are you sure," George said, putting a hand on Elliot's arm.

"Yeah," Elliot sighed.

Elliot lifted Jake, who was still in werewolf form. He carried him to the van and laid him on the floor in the back.

"Okay George and Brad, let's change back to our human forms and get dressed," Butch said.

The transition reversed itself as they changed from werewolf to human. Bones melted and reformed. Butch's body reabsorbed the coarse red hair and converted it into cellular protein. They dressed and jumped into the van. Brad accelerated and carried them away from the warehouse.

Butch turned from the front passenger seat with a big smile on his face. "Good job everyone. Even though we took a few licks, we did well for our first battle in Madison, not bad at all."

All night, the Morsching pack hunted for the Guhl werewolves. Ralph was frantic. Having outsiders in his city was a personal affront to his leadership. He pushed his pack hard. They scoured the black and Asian districts at night as werewolves.

Traveling at high speed up and down the streets and through the alleys, they spread out to cover half of the city. With dawn, they reverted to their human forms and used vehicles to crisscross the city. They could not find any evidence the foreign werewolves were still in Madison, not a single scent.

"Either the bastards are stashed away in one of the suburbs or they have gone back to the Twin Cities," Ralph howled in frustration. They will pay for disrespecting us and killing Roger and Brandon. We will get even with them."

Chapter 35
Vote For Truce?

Two days after the attack team returned from Madison, Jake was sitting in Jerrold's basement in front of the fireplace. His arm was still in a sling, but the rest of his injuries had healed. The rest of the pack was already sitting at the table or in a second row of chairs, waiting for the meeting to start. Several logs sent yellow-red flames up the chimney and heat radiating into the room.

Butch walked into the basement and patted Jake on the shoulder as he passed by toward his spot at the head of the table. A few late comers filed in behind Butch. Butch waited until everyone settled down before calling the meeting to order. He told the pack of his team's success in Madison.

The pack needed some positive news, but did not seem as excited as Butch thought they would be. The accolades and congratulations were lacking the enthusiasm Butch expected. Butch sensed an undercurrent of dissatisfaction and was puzzled at was causing it. He took a moment and scrutinized those in the room, wondering why anyone would be unhappy with what they accomplished in Madison.

Elliot stood up to address the group. He waited until everyone was quiet and then said, "In spite of injuries to Jake and myself, we were very successful in our first raid. We killed two werewolves from the Morsching pack. We should start planning for our next raid, before they recover and attack us again."

It did not take long for the discussion to send another expedition to Madison to end without a satisfactory conclusion. Elliot looked around the table with a confused expression on his face. He shook his head and sat down.

Richard swallowed. He was not happy being the spokesperson for the opposition. Richard rose, put his hands in his pockets and then took them out. From the corner of his eye, he saw a concerned expression flash across Butch's face. Richard spoke quickly, "Butch, a few of us are not happy with the direction you are taking the pack. Some have even considered you behavior irresponsible."

The corners of Butch's mouth curled upward as a growl escaped in Richard's direction.

"Easy Butch," Richard said, "Please, listen to what I say without getting angry. I am not challenging you or anything like that, but several of us want you to know how we feel and what our concerns are. I was selected as the spokesperson."

"Butch's face turned crimson and blood vessels popped out on his temples. "What do you mean? How am I being irresponsible?" he said, clenching his fists, trying to remain calm. "Haven't I carried the battle to them?"

Richard looked around and then said, "That is the problem. When you took your team to Madison, you left the rest of the pack undefended and without your leadership."

"Yeah, that's right." Richard's wife, Mary chimed in.

Butch saw the determined expression on her face, as if saying anyone who contradicted her or her husband had better be ready to fight.

Eleanor, Bruce's wife sat farther down the table. She said, "Just to carry out revenge against the Madison werewolf pack was no reason for you to leave us vulnerable."

Butch released his pent up energy and anger with a sigh. He knew what they were saying was right and yet he felt frustrated over their accusations.

Butch said, "First of all, I thought I left you with enough protection. I left behind most of the pack, enough werewolves to fend off any kind of attack the Madison pack may have launched. Apparently, some of you do not understand or appreciate what we accomplished by attacking the werewolves in their own territory. Christ, most of them will have to stay in Madison, because they do not know if we are still there or when we will attack them again. We have put them on the defensive for the first time, as I promised you I would do. Don't you realize that they will not be able to launch a concerted attack on us, for fear we will be doing the same?" He felt betrayed and let down by his own pack. "If you don't appreciate what

I have been trying to do for you, then someone needs to challenge me."

"Butch, no one wants to challenge you. We just want you to listen to our concerns," Grandfather said from across the table. "Attacking the Morsching pack in their territory was good, it did put them on notice, but Richard is right. You should have stayed behind. As leader of the pack, you were irresponsibly exposing yourself to possible injury or death. Your major duty is to give the pack the leadership it requires. You should have put someone else in charge of the mission and stayed behind with your pack."

Others mumbled their agreement. Jerrold looked at Butch, to see how he was taking the criticism.

Butch slid his chair back and stood up. He looked around the great hall, stopping at the face of each family member. He raised his right hand and then dropped it to his side. He did not know how to express what he felt. He started to speak and then stopped, only to start again and stop once more. Finally, he cleared his throat. "I understand that being pack leader requires some learning on my part," Butch said, "but you need to understand, my first priority is to destroy those responsible for killing my pack members." He brought his shoulders back and stood taller. "I can see where I should have stayed with the pack. I am the Alpha and I did not want to send someone else to do a job I felt I should do. I understand what you expect regarding the Alpha's leadership. I know my presence is critical to the survival of the pack. I did not lead the Madison expedition for personal revenge, but because I am your leader. Now that I realize how you feel, I apologize for leaving you. It will not happen again," he said.

"Well put, Butch," Grandfather said, smiling from across the table.

Butch nodded towards Jerrold and a smile worked its way across his face. "As long as everyone is speaking their mind, let me have my turn." Butch said, looking down at his shoes. He wondered how best to propose his idea. "Before the Madison attack I began searching my soul considering the future of our pack. I was going to bring this up later, but now is as good a time as any. I would like you to think about what I am going to propose. Do not take this as an order, decree, or anything like that. This is just an idea I want us to think about, discuss and decide what to do with it.

"What has plagued me ever since the Morsching Pack first attacked us and killed Marsha is this; what good does it do for werewolves to kill each other? If we keep on as we have been; them killing a few of us and then we killing a few of them, soon we will all be dead. Will the killing stop only when only one werewolf is still standing? What are we accomplishing by killing each other?" He noticed that many of the pack were nodding their heads in agreement with him and found the courage to continue, "Here is what I would like to do. I would like to offer the Morsching pack a truce."

Mixed gasps, groans and growls of both agreement and anger erupted in the room.

Butch spoke louder. "Hey, Listen, I know some of you agree with me and some of you do not. Here is your chance to express your feelings, but do it one at a time," he said and then he sat down.

George jumped up, his face was crimson and he trembled, "How can you suggest we beg for peace? Those bastards killed my parents," he sobbed. "I have not received my pound of flesh, yet. My body cries for their blood. We need to kill them until they are all dead."

Shouts of agreement and growls of vengeance accompanied George's stirring speech.

Jennifer, the wife of Francis, stood up holding on to the edge of the table. Tears welled in her eyes. "Listen to me," she pleaded.

Butch was surprised. This was the first time Jennifer spoke at any meeting he attended. Members of the group were yelling at each other. Arguments grew between individuals. The situation was getting out of hand.

"SILENCE," Butch's voice boomed into their minds.

Everyone froze.

Butch said, "You will show courtesy to those wanting to speak. Wait your turn."

The pack studied Butch. No one was willing to challenge him; those standing sat down, turned toward Jennifer and waited.

"Jennifer, please continue," Butch said.

Jennifer looked embarrassed, but spoke in a teary voice. "As you know, I have lost my daughter, Judy to the Morsching pack. She died at the same time George's parents did. Our pack has also killed many of the Morsching werewolves."

Jennifer stopped and took a couple of deep breaths before continuing, "In spite of what has happened between us, they are more like us than they are different. They are werewolf. Would it hurt us to try what Butch suggests? Can talking to them hurt? If we tried to understand them, maybe we could live in peace. I don't know--," Jennifer grew embarrassed and sat down; she leaned her head against her husbands shoulder. He put his arm around her and hugged her.

George Buchannan pushed his chair back and stood.

Butch was surprised, Big George was another quiet member of the family, who attended meetings, but very seldom said anything in front of the group. He was the husband of Barbara, Jerrold's oldest daughter. Smiling, he waited until everyone was quiet. "The butchers backed a truck over my two daughters, killing them, and for that we have killed many of them, but vengeance will not bring back my girls. If we must continue to fight, if we have no other choice," he said, "then that is what we will do," he said matter-of-fact. "But, I agree with Jennifer, it wouldn't weaken us to try to talk with the other wolf pack. At least, try to find out why they attacked us. If they will not listen then, we have lost nothing. We can always continue the war."

The room grew very quiet. No one else indicated a desire to speak. Butch played with a pen, twirling it through his fingers, as he waited for another minute to pass, then he rose. "Does anyone else wish to speak?" Butch said, looking around the room, giving anyone the last chance to talk.

When no one responded, Butch said, "I see two options open to us. One, we continue to fight and kill the Morsching werewolves and I am sure, some of us in turn will die, or two, we can contact them and ask if they are willing to sit down and discuss the situation. If they do not want to talk, our path is obvious. Let's vote."

Jerrold's head turned so fast, Butch thought it might become detached. Jerrold jumped to his feet with a stunned look on his face. "Butch, the pack does not vote," he said, shocked at the thought of letting everyone have a say in a decision reserved for the Alpha. "The leader, the Alpha always makes the final decision. We have never voted on anything. Starting with my Grandfa--."

Butch slapped his hand on the table before him, "Grandfather," Butch interrupted, "I agree there are some things that should not change, but I am the new leader and this is one change I will make. We will vote. Now, please sit down."

Jerrold's face flushed and slowly his eyes looked down at the table. He sputtered, "Yes, Yes, my leader."

Butch raised a hand. "Now, all those who want to continue the fight against the Morsching werewolves, raise your hand.

George, Elliot, Thomas, Aerial and two others raised their hands.

"Okay, all those willing to see if the Morsching pack is interested in sitting down and voicing joint concerns, raise your hands."

All the rest, except for Grandfather and Rob raised their hands.

"Okay," Butch said, "that's settled. I will contact the Morsching werewolf pack."

Several said at the same time, "How?"

I am going to release our captive, Will. He will take the offer back to Madison."

George jumped to his feet and wailed. "We cannot let our prisoner go."

"George," Butch screamed from his mind.

The mental blast caused George to sag and lose his balance. He grabbed the side of his head and dropped into his chair. He looked like someone hit him with a sledgehammer.

Butch looked at George and said, "George listen to what I am going to say. We will not always vote. I will still make decisions when I feel they are in the best interest of the pack. Let me explain my reason for releasing Will. By releasing the prisoner, I am hoping the Morsching Pack will take our offer as a sign of good faith. I say it will be done."

George raised his head with a look of defiance on his face.

Butch glared at George. "George, do you agree with my decision or do you wish to challenge me?"

George blanched "No, No I agree. I do not want to challenge you." George saw Butch in action. There was no way he wanted to fight him.

"Okay," Butch said, "If that is settled, as soon I get an answer, you will be informed. In the meantime, stay alert. They may already be in the Twin Cities looking for revenge."

Chapter 36
Parley

Butch was not surprised when Ralph Morsching agreed to attend a sit down meeting. He was surprised Ralph agreed to come to Woodbury for the meeting rather than insist on a neutral site.

Butch asked Richard to arrange the rental of a conference room at United Realty in Woodbury, just off Bielenberg Trail. Butch figured that was the most neutral a spot they could find and it did offer a degree of privacy. The meeting was scheduled for the following Tuesday, at ten o'clock in the morning.

Five members were to represent each pack at the table. Each pack would provide one guard for the doors.

Tuesday came. Butch was nervous when he walked into the meeting room followed by Grandfather Jerrold, Richard, Elliot Buchannan and Jake representing the Guhl Pack. The Morsching Pack had not arrived.

An ugly, brown, shag carpet covered the floor of the meeting room. Sterile, naked, white walls set the atmosphere for the meeting. An old oak conference table dominated the middle of the room. Five captain's chairs lined each side of the table.

Glasses, cups, coffee pots and pitchers of ice water occupied the center of the table. Picture windows on one wall flooded the room with sunlight and scenes of traffic moving by on Valley Creek Drive. Double glass doors were located at either end of the room. The south doors gave access to the outside, while the north doors opened into another meeting room and the stairs leading to the first floor.

Brad poked his head through the double doors, "Here they come," he said.

The Morsching representatives walked into the room with an air of confidence. They seated themselves on the other side of the table. The Morsching team consisted of Ralph, Tom Jarvis (Ralph's brother-in-law), Henry (Ralph's third son), Cheryl Franzen (Will's mother) and Will Franzen.

The two teams stared at each other across the table.

Ralph turned to Jerrold and said, "You called the meeting. Why don't you explain what you have in mind?"

Butch smiled; their leader made his first mistake by assuming the oldest member was the pack leader. His source of information must have been Will and Will did not know of Butch's challenge for leadership of the pack.

"Thank you, Mr. Morsching, I will," Butch said, holding back a smile when Ralph turned with a shocked look on his face to stare at Butch.

Henry hit the table with his fist. A hateful look painted across his face, he snarled, "We have killed six of your pack members."

Ralph snarled and Henry blanched and sat back in his chair.

Butch turned toward Henry and said, "Let's set the record straight. You have killed eight of ours. But then, we got a late start in the battle," Butch turned back to Ralph and said with a smile. "This meeting is not for the purpose of waving our flags in each others faces. We thought it might benefit both of our packs if we were to meet before any more killings occurred. Seeing that we both have 'the trait', it might be in our mutual interest to dispense with killing each other off. Of course, you might prefer to continue the killing until only one of us remains standing." Butch poured himself a cup of coffee and gazed across the table at Ralph, waiting for a reply.

Ralph stared at Butch. He listened carefully to everything this young leader said. He wondered if there was more meaning behind the words than he was picking up. Could asking for this meeting be a sign of weakness? Were they afraid we would destroy them? He let his eyes take in the row of Guhl men. They did not look weak or frightened, if anything, they looked angry and were having a difficult time controlling their emotions.

Ralph let his gaze settle on Butch once again before he said, "You really don't know why we attacked you, do you?"

"Now that you mention it, we don't. Why don't you explain?" Butch said pleasantly.

"Okay, your pack attacked the city of Longville and killed fifty-four people, then left incriminating evidence behind. Didn't you realize your carelessness put not only your pack at risk of being found out, but ours as well?"

Butch was shocked. He found it hard to believe what he was hearing. "Is that why you attacked us?" he said. He pointed a finger at Ralph, "Is that why you came into our territory and killed members of my pack?"

Jerrold opened his hands and slapped them down on the table. "Please, we need to remain calm. With your permission Butch, let me explain. Before we found out from Will that you have a chemical to curtail your madness, we had to satisfy our needs in the traditional way. Each individual needs to kill a human once every five years. I cannot believe it was any different for your pack before you found the chemical. Without human flesh, we lose our sanity and become nothing more than wild beasts. For ages, eating human flesh has been the only way to hold the wild side from overpowering us. Certainly you understand that."

The expression on Ralph's face was still one of disgust as he said. "We understand the need as well as you, but we have learned to control ours. We limit our entire kill for the pack to one human." Ralph frowned and then with an accusing glare said, "You were responsible for the Longville massacre, for the killing of fifty-four humans. To us that seemed a little excessive."

Butch answered, "Yes, you are right. We did kill more humans than was required, but they killed and wounded two of ours. I can assure you that will never happen again. Even so, what gave you the right to attack us?"

Ralph leaned forward, "We were afraid your actions would expose us as well as yourselves. We viewed your behavior as a direct threat to us. We thought you were already out of control."

"How could our attack on Longville have exposed your pack," Butch said. "Even if they would have traced the killings to us, how many humans would believe the killings were really done by werewolves? Even if they found out werewolves were responsible for the killing, why would they have any reason to suspect more than one pack existed in the United States?"

"The need to kill, to gather human flesh can not be ignored," Elliot said. "If you are a werewolf, then you understand that."

Ralph started to interrupt, but Butch sat up with a threatening growl. "We learned from our captive," nodding at Will, "that your pack has a drug which reduces the need to kill one human for each werewolf. We did not have your drug and did what we needed to do to retain our sanity. Our pack tried to control the hunt, in order to escape detection, but things got out of hand in Longville."

"We did not know there were other werewolves on the face of the earth," Richard said. "We lived as our ancestors taught us and will not make excuses for our behavior."

Butch leaned forward and said harshly, "Richard."

Richard closed his mouth, sat back, and remained quiet.

Ralph bowed his head; he did understand. "See the problem from our viewpoint. When we learned that the mass killings in Longville were done by werewolves," he said, "we assumed you were already over the edge. We felt obligated to hunt you down and eliminate you in order to protect ourselves."

"As you explain it, I understand why you thought we were out of control," Butch said. He looked into Ralph's eyes, "We do the same thing when one of ours is lost to the wild side. I can understand why you thought we were out of control, but you did not even try to make sure we were over the edge before you attacked us?"

"That is true. We believed you were already too far gone," Ralph said, trying to get Butch to see his point. "It has been so long since we needed to make individual kills, that we assumed you were already lost to the wild side."

Butch raised his hand into the air stopping Ralph from continuing, "Now that you know we are not insane, does that affect your perception of us?" he asked.

"With what you have told us and what I see of you I admit we made a mistake," Ralph said. His shoulders slumped. "There are so few of us left in the world, we would be wise too call off this war and pool our resources," Ralph breathed out an audible sigh, shocked by his own admission.

"I agree," Butch said. He looked across the table into Ralph's eyes, the eyes of his former adversary. Butch stood up and extended his hand across the table. "We have more to gain through cooperation than from killing each other," he said. "With your help and the drug, my pack will be less conspicuous in the future. We have no wish to be discovered by the humans and annihilated."

After several more hours of discussion, both sides accepted the peace terms. Both pack leaders realized that members from both sides would continue to harbor grudges for the killing of their loved ones. Enforcing the truce and stopping any further killing would be up to both of the leaders. Butch and Ralph agreed to meet monthly to discuss mutual problems.

Butch left the meeting feeling a sense of accomplishment. The future looked brighter for his pack and the continuation of the werewolf specie. Butch felt good, proud for establishing peace between the two packs. He could now concentrate on other problems affecting his pack.

One of the problems he wanted to change was the small size of his pack. He wanted to expand the pack to fifty werewolves. One way to gain new pack members was by infecting selected humans with the curse. Another way was to push for a selective breeding program within the family. Butch expected a great deal of opposition from the pack if he proposed a controlled breeding program. He knew it would take time to convince his members, but now there was time to work on them.

Chapter 37
Exposed At Last

As a rookie cop, Fredrick Brucker was handsome and dashing in his dress blues. Now fifteen years later, he was not so appealing, but his looks was not his problem. He was a Detective sergeant working out of the St. Paul Homicide Division. With his intelligence and police savvy, he should have been a top detective, but he was not. He was a brown nosing, backstabbing sneak. He rose up the ladder by doing or saying anything that pleased his superiors. He wanted respect, but no one liked him or wanted to work with him.

He was able to survive and advance because within the St. Paul Police Department there was room for all kinds of officers, even his kind. Fredrick Brucker was one to lick the boots of anyone necessary to rise to the top.

It was not that he did not work hard or put in as much time as anyone else, it was just that his methods were all too obvious. In a rugged sort of way, he was still handsome, with receding dark, wavy hair, a prominent, chiseled nose and hard athletic body. He still got his share of second looks from attractive women, but once they knew him, the relationship nosedived.

Kollecki was shocked when Lieutenant Brucker walked into his office. He watched as he closed his door.

"Captain, I have something I will share with you," Lieutenant Brucker said, "but only if I can be part of the team that investigates the matter."

"What can be so important that makes you think I want to work with you?"

"After you listen to this tape I have, you will."

Reluctantly Captain Bill Kollecki agreed. What bothered Kollecki about Brucker was not his spineless behavior, but his habit of smacking his lips. It was just too much for Bill Kollecki to handle.

Bill Kollecki listened to the tape. Afterwards, he sat in his office with his elbows propped on his desk, fingers tugging at his lower lip.

The Captain's red tie with white dye marks flowing and swirling across it, making his chest look like the vortex of a distant galaxy. The tie hung loose around his neck and dangled off the side of his stomach.

Captain Bill Kollecki was a large man, a former college athlete, but now at fifty-two, he carried a respectable potbelly. He possessed a brilliant analytical mind, which helped him solve some of the toughest cases in the Twin Cities over the past several years.

"Well Captain, that is some pretty damaging evidence isn't it?" Lt. Brucker said, smiling in an obsequious fashion.

A stale, cup of coffee sat on Bill Kollecki's desk, left over from an hour ago. "Unbelievable. . .weird," was all Bill Kollecki said. Stunned, the Captain shook his head. What he had just listened to shocked him as nothing else ever had. Werewolves were pretend, found only in science fiction stories, but the tape proved they were real. A far different story from what he believed two hours ago.

Later in the week, Captain Bill Kollecki played the tape before the Police Commissioners in a closed meeting. Afterwards, they appointed him to set up a task force to investigate the unusual number of homicides involving the well know Guhl family of Woodbury, Minnesota and the Morsching family of Madison, Wisconsin. The two families had apparently made peace after killing members of each other's families. Both families were werewolves and it was Kollecki's job to gather evidence and prevent them from continuing to carry out their attacks on humans.

Chief Robertson told Captain Bill Kollecki to handle the investigation with delicacy because both families had a lot of influence with powerful politicians and law enforcement officials.

Bill Kollecki met with Lieutenant Brucker to begin setting up the team to investigate the werewolf clans. They sat around a small table in Bill's office.

"Well, Lieutenant it looks like we will be working together," Bill said.

"Thank you for keeping your word," Brucker said.

"I am going to call our group the 'Fur Bearer Task Force'. What do you think of the name?"

"It sounds marvelous," Brucker said, smacking his lips together.

Bill frowned, "We need to involve the FBI. This problem is too big for us to handle alone. Besides the FBI, we need to include the Minneapolis Police Force, the Woodbury Police and the Washington County Sheriff's Department. Let's set up a meeting with those groups as soon as possible."

"Sir," Lieutenant Brucker said, anxious to get the action rolling on the biggest case of his career, "With your permission, I will contact all the groups and ask them to send a representative to our meeting. How does Wednesday sound for a time?"

Bill Kollecki checked his calendar. "Go ahead and set it up."

After the Lieutenant left, Bill sat alone thinking for a long time. Where did the werewolves come from? If they exist in the Twin Cities and Madison, how many more will we find in the United States or for that matter the world? It was still hard for him to accept that werewolves really existed. He heard them admit it on the tape, what more proof could he ask for. My God, they admitted to killing all of those people in Longville. How many more unsolved disappearances and deaths have they been responsible for over the years? He shook his head, unable to comprehend the depth of his own question.

The morning of the organizational meeting of the Metropolitan Fur Bearer Task Force started out on a dreary note. A dark, cloudbank rolled in from the west threatening rain. The sun tried to hold back the clouds by highlighting the leading edge of the rolling clouds with gold, but the clouds pushed over the city anyway and blotted out the sun.

Raindrops pelted FBI Agent, Jim Fillispie's Jacket, as he hurried across the street. A Ford mini van bore down on him and he jumped for the curb. He gave the driver a dirty look, but the driver did not even notice him.

Ahead wet, gray steps led up to the doors of the St. Paul Police Station. Stepping through the door, he glanced around the interior of the station. "Typical," he said, "sterile brick and wood, without a personality or a welcoming feeling in its entire structure."

To his left stood a worn pulpit from which the Day Sergeant directed activities within the station. A gray-haired Sergeant sat hunched over the pulpit, reading the sports section from the Pioneer Press, oblivious to what was happening around him.

"Hey, Sergeant," Agent Fillispie's voice boomed. "Where am I supposed to meet with Captain Bill Kollecki?"

"How should I know?" the Sergeant said, as he peered over the top of the paper. "No one tells me anything around here." He removed his wire-rimmed glasses and laid them in his open glass case. "Damn Timber wolves," he said, and then slapped the paper down.

"I'm Agent Jim Fillispie-FBI. I'm supposed to attend a meeting called by Captain Bill Kollecki, ah, for the Metropolitan Task Force. I believe that is the correct title."

"Oh, why didn't you say so?" The Sergeant shoved the newspaper aside and looked at a clipboard. "The meeting is on the second floor, room 214," he said. "You can't miss it. Just take the elevator." The Sergeant pointed to his left, then put his glasses back on and picked up the paper, ending the conversation.

"Thank you," Jim Fillispie said, as he turned and walked down the hall. Jim was a tall, thin man. He head carried a full flowing mane of red hair and a protruding nose. He looked like a geek, but in his case, looks were deceiving. Not only did he hold a black belt in Karate, during the Iraqi War, he was an assassin with Special Forces before joining the FBI.

As Jim stepped off the elevator on the second floor, he noticed a police officer in a dark blue uniform standing outside of room 214. Jim Fillispie angled across the hallway toward the officer.

"I need to see some identification," the officer said, placing his right hand on the handle of his revolver and taking a step forward.

"Hmm," Jim Fillispie thought, "security seems tight." He showed his badge and ID.

The officer peered at his name and then checked it against a list on the clipboard he was holding. He nodded and opened the door for Jim. Jim walked into the room and looked at the large group of officers milling around the room. They were talking and drinking coffee. Four men stood toward the other end of the room. Behind them was an old, wooden table holding a slide projector. Jim recognized Captain Kollecki talking with the three men. Jim knew two of the men. One was an officer from the Minneapolis Police Force; the other was the Sheriff of Washington County and the third man he did not know.

Captain Bill Kollecki looked up and saw Jim Fillispie, he smiled and called across the room, "Hi, Jim, come on over and join us. Coffee and rolls are on the table," he pointed.

Jim headed for the coffee first. He doctored the coffee with creamer and a bag of artificial sugar. He grabbed a frosting, covered Bismarck and wandered over to the Captain.

"Captain, good to see you again," Jim said, shaking Bill's hand, as he balanced the Bismarck on top of his coffee cup. Then he turned to the others. "Hi, Grant, how are things with the Minneapolis Police Force?"

"Having a hell of a time with gang killings, but that's nothing new for you. Glad you will be joining us, Jim."

"Hi Jim," Sheriff Bob Franklin said, wiping a gob of frosting from his hand, on his pants before grabbing the extended hand of Bill. "I never did get a chance to thank you for pulling my ass out of the fire on that killing of the restaurant owner in Stillwater. Thanks."

Jim nodded.

Bill Kollecki introduced Jim to Lieutenant Brucker, the third man in the group and then placed a hand on Jim's elbow, "Now that you're here, we'll get started."

Bill walked over to the coffee pot, refilled his cup and walked to stand in front of the screen at the front of the room. "Hey, everyone," he said. "I would like to get the show on the road. Take a seat, will you?"

There was twenty-five police officials from various Minnesota local, county, state agencies, plus three police officers from Madison and one FBI representative. Some of the officers were involved in the initial investigation of the Guhl and Morsching killings, but few were prepared for what they were going to learn today.

The Captain moved to the small wooden podium, as everyone found a seat. Jim sat down next to Grant and Sheriff Franklin.

Bill raised his hands and waved for everyone's attention. "A few of you know why we are here today, but for the other new Task Force members, I would like to bring you up to date."

He walked to the front of the room and turned some knobs, the lights dimmed. Bill pushed the button on the remote controlling the slide projector and the first slide splashed on the screen.

The picture showed the body of a man with his arms and head detached, lying next to his body. Underneath the picture, the sub-title said, "the worst of the Longville killings." The next slide showed several humans ripped apart. Arms and legs showed close ups of where pieces were missing and teeth marks were obvious.

Bill said to a silent and very sober group. "We have proof the Longville killings, together with a number of recent deaths throughout the Twin Cities of members from the Guhl family and the Morsching family, are all linked. These two families have been killing each other off in the Twin Cities and more recently in Madison. At first we thought the recent deaths were gang related, maybe involving drugs, but that isn't the case, at all."

"Just a minute," Agent Jim Fillispie interrupted. "Is this Morsching any relation to Federal Marshall Ralph Morsching, out of Madison?"

"The same," Sheriff Franklin said.

Captain Bill Kollecki took a drink of coffee and said. "Neither group has any affiliations with organized crime. Until Lieutenant Brucker tumbled across a meeting between the two families, we could not find any real ties between them. Officer Brucker taped a meeting the two families had in Woodbury a few weeks ago. I would like to play the tape for you at this time.

"Did you have a court order for the taping?" Jim Fillispie said.

"Only a bench warrant based on a lie," Bill said.

"Then, you know it is not admissible in court," Jim reminded the others.

"We don't intend to ever use the tape in court," Kollecki said, shaking his head. "Jim, you will understand why after you listen to the tape."

Bill turned to the others. "I would like you to hold your questions until after you listen to the tape. We have edited out the nonessential material, but the original tape is available for anyone wishing to listen to the unedited version. Go ahead Lieutenant."

The tape played to a silent audience for forty-five minutes. After it was finished, no one moved. Most of them were as shocked, as the Captain was when he first listened to it a week ago. FBI Agent Jim Fillispie stood up. He walked over to the coffee table, refilled his cup and then sat down again.

"Captain," Jim Fillispie finally said. "Other than this tape, do you have any other concrete evidence linking any of these individuals to the killings in Longville or in the Twin Cities?"

"No."

"Are there any witnesses who have seen either a Guhl or a Morsching as a werewolf?"

"No."

"You are basing your belief that they are werewolves solely on this tape?"

"Yes."

"We need more evidence than just the tape, some we can use in a court."

"Evidence, yes. Court, no."

Grant Johnson, the Minneapolis Police Officer, jumped from his seat, interrupting Bill and Jim's dialog. His eyes dilated, pupils the size of dimes, his arms moved in jerking motions in front of his body. "Bull shit," he said. "Werewolves don't exist. They are just in science fiction, you know, in movies and comic books. You people are nuts. I do not believe any of this crap. I will not."

Grant calmed down and his face broke into a weird smile. He stared at Bill. "I get it. This is just an elaborate joke."

Bill Kollecki did not smile.

Grant paled and said. "You are not kidding, right? What are you guys trying to do?"

Captain Bill Kollecki and Lieutenant Brucker grabbed Grant's swinging arms and led him back to his chair.

"Sit down, Grant," Kollecki said. "No one is trying to psyche you out. This is on the level and we need your help."

Grant gulped, took a deep breath and calmed down.

"Are you okay?" Captain Bill Kollecki asked, absently rubbing Grant's back.

Grant expelled a blast of air from his lungs and took in another deep breath before answering, "Yeah, I'm okay. . .now."

"What is our next step?" Agent Jim Fillispie said from his seat.

"Like you said, we need more evidence," Captain Bill Kollecki said, as he looked down into his coffee cup. For a moment, a startled expression jumped onto his face. He saw the shape of a wolf in the coffee grounds at the bottom of his cup.

Sheriff Franklin stood up and walked to the front of the room. "The Steering Committee agreed to conduct a raid on one of the families. It looks like that may be the only way we can get direct evidence; get one of them to change into a werewolf before our eyes."

Deputy Alan Baker shook his head. "You cannot do that without a search warrant or what we find cannot be used in court of law."

"Chances are whatever we find will never appear in court anyway," Sheriff Franklin said.

"You realize we will be acting outside of the law if we do that? We'll be nothing more that a bunch of vigilantes" Fillispie said.

"Do you have any doubt what we are facing after hearing the tape?" Bill Kollecki said.

Jim Fillispie shook his head. "No, I accept what you are telling me and what I have heard," he hesitated and then said, "and maybe a raid is the only way to find out for sure."

"We have tried putting them under surveillance, but they are cautious and we have not been able to catch them in werewolf form or for that matter, doing anything illegal," Lieutenant Brucker said.

"Okay," Bill Kollecki said, making eye contacts with each man present. "We will be working outside the law, but that is the only way I can see to handle this situation. There is no way we can convince a judge to issue us a search warrant. He would laugh us out of his chambers. You are right Jim, eliminating the werewolves, will make us nothing more than a vigilante committee." He stopped and grimaced, then said. "Are you with me or not?"

Each head nodded affirmatively.

Chapter 38
Report To The FBI Director

Jim Fillispie took the next flight to Washington D. C. and reported to the Director of the FBI what he had learned in Woodbury, Minnesota. The Director was flabbergasted. At first, he did not believe what Jim told him, but after reviewing the tape, he accepted the wild tale. He was paranoid that the information would leak to the press.

The Director told Jim, "If the public finds out werewolves exist, can you imagine the mass terror that would break out? It would send our nation into a total panic. People would end up shooting their neighbors. Thousands of innocent people would die. You must keep a lid on this. How sure are you this group you are working with will not let something leak to the press?"

"I believe everyone is on board. Tell me how you want it handled," Jim said.

"The Fur Bearer Task Force will have to act as an independent group. I will use my authority to request whatever you need from any law enforcement body you suggest. What your group does to rid our country of the werewolves is up to them. I imagine you will have to work outside the law. The FBI will give you all the resources and help we can. If you are caught breaking the law, the FBI will try to cover for you, but if what you do becomes public knowledge, the FBI will have to disclaim any knowledge of your actions. You will have to face the consequences. Do you understand my position?"

"Yes sir," Jim said. "I kind of figured that's how we would have to operate. I will keep you informed."

He returned to the Twin Cities on the next available flight.

Jim and Bill Kollecki began to gather the personnel they needed to wipe out the werewolves. They limited the group to those who attended the initial meeting in St. Paul and filled in the rest from recommendations of the core group. Because of the top-secret nature of the 'Fur Bearer File', no other governmental agencies would be involved or advised as to the function or purpose of this group. If any of the Task Force members were caught committing unlawful acts, they would have to suffer the consequences.

Chapter 39
The Beginning Of The End

Two weeks later, on June 21, the first day of summer, three unmarked cars sat in the darkness waiting for Captain Kollecki to arrive. One of the cars contained three men, the other two vehicles held two men each.

Heavy clouds pushed to the east. A few drops of rain splattered on the windshield of the Ford Explorer. The wind rocked the vehicle and then died, producing an eerie calm.

A couple of minutes before two o'clock A. M., a single car with its lights off coasted to a stop behind the others. Captain Bill Kollecki glanced at his watch before exiting the car. Agents and officers poured out of the other vehicles.

Lieutenant Brucker leaned into his unmarked vehicle and pulled out a shotgun. He walked back to the Captain's car. Bill pulled his Kevlar vest over his head and slipped on a nondescript black jacket.

Brucker said, "There are three people inside Richard Guhl's house, Richard, his wife, Mary and their son Brad."

This raid was critical. Captain Bill Kollecki realized that all future action tonight depended on what they found during this raid. If they found proof that any of Richard Guhl's family was werewolves, two other teams were standing by, ready to raid the homes of Jerrold Guhl and Tom Guhl.

Also waiting the outcome of the raid on Richard Guhl's home were teams in Madison, Wisconsin. The homes of Ralph Morsching, Tom and Francie Jarvis, and Herbert and Marian Morsching were under surveillance. The teams were waiting for the signal from Bill to attack and destroy the occupants.

Bothered by the flagrant disregard of people's rights during these raids, Bill Kollecki could only shake his head. He reasoned if they were right and the Guhls were werewolves, the saving of future human lives was worth violating their privacy. If by some chance, they were wrong and the Guhls were not werewolves, heads would roll all the way up to the Director of the FBI. The biggest lawsuit for violation of constitutional rights would set back law enforcement many years.

Seven members of his 'hit team' surrounded Captain Kollecki. "Okay, listen up," he said, "The other teams are in place and will commence their raids the moment I give them the go ahead. Remember, we do not kill until we have definite proof they are werewolves. We have to see one before we kill anyone. Once we have visual proof, we will terminate everyone in the house and for God's sake, do not leave any incriminating evidence behind. Okay, take your positions and wait for my signal."

Jim Fillispie stood next to Captain Bill Kollecki. He leaned over and said, "It still bothers me, what if we are wrong? If they aren't werewolves, we are in deep shit."

"Yeah, you're right," the Captain said. "But we have been over this many times. The wrong we might be committing is nothing if we end up doing the right thing." He studied Bill's face. "If you can't give the team your support, stay out of it."

"No, I'm okay."

Two officers used the hundred and fifty pound metal 'door buster' to break open the front door. Eight masked, black, clothed men rushed into the living room. No warning was given that it was the police invading the house. The lamps on their heads cast bright circles of light on the wall and furniture. Some of the light beams collided, as heads swung around the room making sure none of the occupants was present.

As a group, the eight officers rushed upstairs and started kicking open doors. Bill Kollecki, leading the charge entered the first bedroom and found Richard standing next to his bed, part way through his change into a werewolf.

Richard growled, "You dirty bastards. I thought there was a peace agreement?"

Bill choked when he swallowed a wad of saliva down his windpipe. He was shocked and frightened. He did not have time to cough. He stared at a red-coated werewolf, five feet in front of him.

His headlamp illuminated the upper body of the beast. Richard's mouth was wide-open, showing fangs and glistening yellow eyes.

Richard turned his elongated muzzle toward Bill, opened his mouth wide and howled. He snapped his fangs together and the clacking of teeth brought Bill out of his frozen condition.

Bill screamed, "They are werewolves. Kill everyone. "He brought his 9 mm up and emptied the clip into Richard's chest.

Bill was surprised to see red blood gush from the chest wounds of the werewolf. For reasons he could not explain, he expected a different color. He watched mesmerized, as Richard fell across the bed, critically wounded.

Sheriff Franklin stepped into the room behind Bill Kollecki. The flashlight attached to his head shined on the werewolf, he cried out, "God, help us."

Mary leapt from the corner of the room at Sheriff. Franklin. The Sheriff heard the click of her toenails on the wooden floor. He wheeled around and shot the black-haired beast three times. Mary's momentum carried her forward. She threw her paws around the Sheriff. They tumbled to the floor.

Mary was already dead, but Sheriff Franklin did not know that, as he lay beneath the shaggy animal in a dead faint.

Bill directed his beam of light on the Sheriff and the fur covered female beast. He was shocked when the werewolf changed before his eyes into a naked human female. Directing his attention back at the male werewolf on the bed, he watched as it also transformed into the naked body of Richard. All werewolf features disappeared. He gasped when the flesh around the bullet holes began to close and then stopped.

Lieutenant Brucker knelt on the bed next to the body of Richard and drew a hunting knife across Richard's throat. He kept sawing until the head rolled free. His light shined on Kollecki's face as he said, "I read this in a book and it's one way of making sure they stay dead. Now, let's see the bastard get up," he said. He walked over to the naked body of the woman and decapitated her.

In the next room, Brad was fighting for his life. He was able to complete his change into his werewolf form before the agents broke into his bedroom. As the masked men entered his bedroom, he attacked them from behind the door. Three of the men turned toward the deep growl and illuminated Brad in their headlamps. They screamed at the sight of a monster so close to them.

Brad grabbed the nearest agent and raked claws down the front of his body. Blood gushed from a torn carotid artery. Brad threw the body from him into the legs of a man raising his rifle. The man fell over backwards. The third agent leaned into the room and shot Brad several times with a 45 magnum.

Even though wounded, Brad jumped forward biting down on the agent's arm. Bones cracked. The agent screamed and dropped his gun. Brad grabbed the man by his head and threw him against the wall. The agent on the floor pulled his revolver and emptied it into Brad.

Brad collapsed to the floor and slowly transformed back to his human form. The agent with the injured arm got up. His arm dangled by white tendons below the elbow. As pain shot through his mind, he screamed, his face locked in a mask of fright. He was not screaming because of the pain, but from the mental strain of confronting a werewolf. That image pushed him over the edge.

"That was a costly raid," Agent Jim Fillispie said to Bill Kollecki as they walked out of Richard's house arm in arm. "One agent was ripped to shreds by the boy and another agent ended up with a separated forearm and a mental breakdown, but he will survive."

Jim was still concerned about the absence of search warrants and other disregards of individual freedoms. Nevertheless, he was grinning with satisfaction; it was as though he just scored the winning touchdown in his high school's championship game. "It bothers me that we killed a woman," Jim said.

The Sheriff joined them and said, "She wasn't a woman when I shot her."

You are right, she was a werewolf and to my way of thinking, no different than the others," Bill Kollecki stated.

"Yeah, I guess so," Jim sighed. "Did you okay the other raids?"

Bill said, "Yeah, I sent the order a few minutes ago."

"Good, let's go back to headquarters and wait for the other teams to report in", the Sheriff said.

Chapter 40
Werewolves At A Premium

The 'Fur Bearer' teams killed Jerrold Guhl, Tom Guhl, his wife Susan and their children, Jake and Nicole. No agents were injured.

Captain Bill Kollecki's team was sitting around the second floor of the Station House after their raid. They were waiting for the other teams to report in. Officer Rogers said from the other room. "Hey, Captain. Madison's on line two."

Bill picked up the phone on his desk and hit the button for line two. "Hello, who is this?" he said.

"Captain Perkins, code 15 Charlie Zulu."

"Okay, what have you got, John?"

"Two agents killed and three injured, but our first three missions were a success, considering how ferocious those bastards are. We processed Ralph Morsching and his wife, Adrian, their son Joe and his wife, Marian and their three children, Pete's wife, Mary was at Henry and Joan Franzen's home and they died along with offspring, Mary and Henry Jr. How'd you guys do?"

"We lost one man and another wounded, but we were successful in completing our first three targets. We will be leaving on our second excursion as soon as the other two teams get back to the station."

"We will be leaving ourselves. Good Luck Bill, I will call you when we finish up here."

The three task force teams split up to attack the last three Guhl families; Team one would take care of Rod, Elizabeth and their children Butch and Ann; Team two would take out George and Barbara Buchannan, and their son Elliot; Team three would exterminate Bruce and Eleanor Guhl and their children Tom, Cherrie and Carol.

In spite of the time spent gathering information of the various family habits, routines, and especially important, the layout of each the Guhl homes, Bill Kollecki still worried. He was afraid that if someone warned the Guhls of the first attacks, there would be hell to pay. If the werewolves were waiting for them, he believed the outcome would be very different from the first attack.

The raid on Bruce Guhl's home resulted in the death of everyone, except for Bruce's daughter Cherrie. She jumped out of her second story window and escaped into the night.

Butch woke out of a sound sleep. The digital clock said it was 5:10 A.M. He sat up; sweat beaded on his forehead, his T-shirt saturated with perspiration. He squinted, trying to recall the nightmare that woke him. He remembered seeing giant bears surrounding his pack and killing them one at a time.

He watched as werewolf heads separated from their bodies. The pictures in his mind were very vivid, but quickly blurred before he was able to identify who they were. All he remembered after that was a bunch of shadows.

Even though he was awake, Butch still felt apprehensive, as though something from his nightmare was waiting to come to life. He grabbed his pillow and smacked his fist into it trying to force himself to concentrate.

He growled frustrated that he could not pinpoint what roused him from a deep sleep. Was it just a nightmare or was there some deeper meaning to the anxiety he felt? Butch projected his hearing throughout the house and listened, first to his parents, Rod and Elizabeth, tossing restlessly in the next room and then he surveyed the rest of the house. . .nothing. He got out of bed and walked to the window.

He pushed the curtain aside and looked down on the ghost-gray sidewalk near the front door, then followed it out to meet the street. His red sports Mazda sat in the driveway.

No one was up at this ungodly hour, he assured himself. He relaxed, dismissing the feeling of doom that gripped him. As he turned back toward his bed, he caught a flash of car lights coming down the street from the north. The car was two blocks away. Most likely, someone is coming home from work or a late party.

His eyes grew larger when he saw two cars following the first one. He watched the first car, waiting for it to pull into a driveway, but it did not; it kept coming down the street toward his house, still followed by the other two cars. Butch jumped back from the window. Eye contact with the car sent shivers down his spine. The hair on the back of his neck stood erect. Did these cars hold the bears of his dream, coming to kill the wolves?

The cars slowed and as one glided to the curb three houses before they reached Butch's home. Apprehension grew in his mind. He watched four men get out of the first car, a car without any dome lights coming on when the doors opened.

More men piled out of the other cars and gathered in a group. The men started walking down the sidewalk towards his house. Butch ran into the hall and burst into his parent's bedroom. "Dad, Mom, wake up," he said.

Rod rolled to an upright position, rubbing his eyes. "Butch, what's the matter?"

His mother was sitting up with an alarmed expression on her face. She brought one of her fists up to her mouth.

"Dad," Butch said. "A bunch of men are coming for us."

"Who, the Morschings," Rod said.

"I don't know who. . . ."

Just then, the downstairs front door smashed in and Butch heard running footsteps downstairs. He instituted his change. "Mom, Dad, you hide. I will protect you," Butch said, and then ran out to meet the flood of men rushing up the stairs.

Butch ran along the railing toward the head of the stairs. The first man up the stairs was almost at the top. Butch reached over the railing and raked his claws across the man's throat. Blood spurted from his neck in two pencil-sized streams, followed by a hissing of air. The agent toppled back down the steps, and like the head pin in a bowling alley, took those agents lower on the steps down with him.

By now, all of the agents were shouting and screaming. Butch ran down the hall, just as his father came out of his bedroom. Rod ran to the head of the stairs. Butch saw the bullets rip across his father's chest and he howled.

Like a slow motion nightmare, he watched his mother run down the hall from her open bedroom door and drop to her knees over her husband's body. A hail of gunfire slammed into her and she slumped to the floor dead.

Several agents rushed up the stairs swinging Uzi machine guns over their heads. Butch vaulted over the railing and landed in the middle of them. A roar escaped through his fangs bringing screams of fear from the agents. Butch moved fast, as he ripped, bit and crushed any flesh he touched. More shots and a great deal of shouting warned him of additional men entering the house.

Butch left the dying remains of those around him and vaulted up over the railing. He raced down the hallway and into his room. He looked for a place to hide. It dawned on him there was no safe place; they would search the whole house until they found him. Footsteps raced down the hallway. Butch turned to meet his death, but vowed to take more of them with him.

He stopped as a scream tore through his mind, "Who will lead the pack?" Butch slumped in anguish. "AARRRRRooooooooooo", screamed from his fangs. He turned and ran for the window, putting his arms up just as he smashed through it. Once on the ground, he raced away, cutting across yards and down alleys, until his house was far behind him, but the visions of his dying parents was still with him.

The second team successfully annihilated Barbara and George Buchannan and their son Elliot.

At the Groschen house, an Aunt who had come to care for the children was sleeping in the master bedroom. Coreen was upstairs asleep. A bad dream woke George at five a. m. In his dream, people were hunting and killing werewolves. The nightmare was so realistic; he rolled out of bed and tried to call Butch, but got only a busy signal.

Alarmed, he dialed Grandfather's number and got a busy signal. He thought of waking Coreen and driving over to Grandfather's house, when the front door blew in off its hinges. He heard running feet coming up the stairs and started his transformation. The first agent to enter his bedroom lost his head. "Coreen," he mind screamed. "We are being attacked. Get out, run."

Two more agents rushed into George's room. The first agent through the door shot George in the chest. George ignored the sick feeling growing within and pounced on the man, ripping open his chest. The second agent screamed when he saw the fate of his partner. He turned and tried to escape, but George launched himself through the air and landed on his back, driving him to the hall floor.

George bit down on the man's neck crushing his cervical vertebrae. George's legs felt like they weighed a ton; he shook his head trying to clear his vision. Blood leaked from his chest bringing on overwhelming weakness. He struggled to breathe. He turned to look for the next victim. He saw a man standing down the hall with a twelve-gauge shotgun pointed at him. He managed to pull the dead man at his feet up with his mouth.

The dead agent absorbed the full blast from the shotgun and slammed back into George, knocking both of them to the floor. The agent with the shotgun swung the barrel at George and pulled the trigger. The lead pellets tore through George's back, breaking his right shoulder and puncturing his lung. George coughed and wobbled up to stand on three legs. In a mighty effort, George lunged at the man. As he fell, he caught the man by the upper thigh. Frothy blood streamed out of George's mouth as the corners curled in a wicked smile. George snapped his head to the side.

The man screamed in agony as his leg muscles tore loose. "Please don't kill me. Oh, oh, it hurts."

George managed to reach up with his left forepaw and rip up through the man's stomach, sending intestinal coils flying throughout the room. The man collapsed, whimpering as he died.

Another man raced up the stairs and pointed a pistol at George. George growled feebly, his limbs barely moved as he tried to respond to the threat. A stream of nine mm bullets pushed George's head into the floor. A vision of Coreen running through a wooded area was the last thing George saw. He smiled and died knowing Coreen escaped.

During George's stand, thirteen-year-old Coreen Groschen transformed herself into a werewolf and climbed out the second story window. She dropped to the ground and fled into the dark. The killing frenzy of George saved her life.

Out of the entire Guhl family, only three remained alive, Butch, Coreen and Cherrie. None of them aware the others were alive.

In Madison, the only werewolves to survive were Will and his sister, Ann Franzen. They had been at a late night party and arrived home after the police killed their parents and departed.

Captain Bill Kollecki felt like a failure. Five werewolves remained alive. If the Metropolitan Fur Bearer Task Force got their way, the last five werewolves would be dead, as soon as they tracked them down. They would not stop hunting them until they were all dead.

Chapter 41
Laying Low

Butch threw back the flap of the green Eureka tent. Prairie grasses gleamed golden in the morning sun for a half a mile around his tent. The heads of the grasses undulated as a gentle breeze blew across the field.

His campsite, hidden on the top of a plateau, overlooked the St. Croix River. Everything was so quiet; it created a false impression of peace. For the moment, Butch forgot what happened last night. Then memories flood his mind. He would never forget the killing of his family and all of his relatives.

Last night, after escaping from his invaded home, he ran through the ditches alongside Bailey Road until he reached County Road 19. From there, he cut across field and forest until he reached Afton State Park. He made his way to the plateau people hiked into from the Park Headquarters to camp. Even before he went to the campgrounds, he stopped at the main shelter at the park and used the pay phone to call all the families. No one answered any of his calls.

He finally registered to camp for five nights and then ran up t the campgrounds on the plateau.

At the edge of the prairie grass, Butch dug up the camping supplies the pack had buried months ago, just in case someone needed to seek shelter where no one would look for them.

He did not know where else to go or what to do. He needed time to think, to figure out what his next action should be. He figured he would be safe in the campground high above the St. Croix River for at least a few days. He did not know how many, if any of his pack survived. Chances were if they came after him last night, they knew who the other werewolves were and where they lived.

Several times during the night, he tried mind-calling members of his pack. He did not get any response. Did that mean all of his pack was dead?

"Oh God," his mind pictured his parents dying. . ."The bastards." Some they killed were not even werewolves."

The second morning after the assault found Butch lying in his tent planning what he was going to do. Sadness over the loss of his family kept disrupting his thoughts. At 10:00 in the morning, he heard a truck approaching his campsite. It bumped down the grassy trail. Butch lay in his tent alarmed over the approaching truck. His heart thumped in his chest, as fear paralyzed him. He finally shook himself free of the fear and began to change into his werewolf form.

Butch flinched. The truck stopped a few feet from his tent, casting a shadow over half of the tent. He would not give up without a fight.

The truck door slammed and Butch jumped. He was half way through his change. He rose on four legs, poised to tear through the tent and attack the intruder.

"Hello the tent," a voice from outside called. "I'm the park ranger. I just stopped by to see if everything is okay."

A growl escaped from the tent. Butch relaxed, reversing his change. After a long silence, he was able to say, "Everything is fine. I was sleeping."

"Oh, sorry, I didn't mean to wake you," the ranger said. "Say, be sure to keep your dog on a leash in the park.

"Okay," Butch said.

Butch heard the truck door open and then slam. The starter turned over and the shadow on the tent moved away. Butch fell back on his sleeping bag, trembling.

Later in the afternoon Butch walked down to the visitor's center and used the phone outside the bathrooms to call everyone's house one last time. He got a recording telling him again that the number he dialed was no longer in service. He decided to try the Morschings in Madison. Maybe they could give him some answers, as to what happened.

Butch dialed Ralph Morsching's home and let the phone ring; no one answered. Next, he tried Will Franzen's home phone. Butch let it ring ten times and was ready to hang up, when the phone stopped ringing. He heard someone breathing on the other end. "Hello, Hello, is anybody there?" Butch said. "This is Butch Guhl. Don't hang up."

Will cried into the mouthpiece, "You bastards."

Butch felt the frustration, hurt and anger pour forth in those two words.

"I thought there was a peace agreement between our packs," Will said. "I'm going to get even with you. We will. . . ."

"Listen to me Will," Butch pleaded, interrupting the voice on the other end. "We were not responsible for the attacks. My entire pack is dead. Some governmental group found out we were werewolves. I am not lying."

Sobs came from the other end of the line. Butch heard Will talking to a girl between sobs.

Finally, Will said, "Okay, I believe you are telling me the truth. What are we going to do?"

Butch said, "Our family has a safe hideout located on Little Sand Lake just north and west of the town of Remer; that is in north central Minnesota. If you look on a map of Minnesota, you will find it just southwest of Grand Rapids. Join me there as soon as you can. You will be able to find me by scent. Whatever you do, make sure you are not followed."

"Did any of your pack survive," Will said.

"Not as far as I know. Nobody has answered any of my mental calls and all of their phones have been disconnected," Butch said.

"What will we do when we get there?" Will said.

"I don't know," Butch said. "We'll talk about that when you get here. I have not thought that far ahead. I just know I have to get out of the Twin Cities."

There was a long silence, but the line was still open.

"Are you coming?" Butch asked.

After more silence, "Yeah, my sister and I will be there as soon as we can."

Chapter 42
Butch Heads for Remer

Butch arrived at the cabin on the north shore of Little Sand Lake seven days ago. He spent most of his time swimming and hiking through the surrounding forest. Twice he drove to Remer for groceries and newspapers.

There was one small paragraph in the St. Paul Pioneer Dispatch newspaper regarding a burglary of the Jerrold Guhl home in Woodbury, which resulted in the death of the occupant. The perpetrator of the crime was unknown at this time. There was no mention of the deaths of his other relatives. How could they keep all of the deaths from the press? Some very powerful forces were at work in ridding the country of the werewolves.

Three days passed. Butch grew impatient and nervous waiting for Will and his sister to show up. Many unimaginable things could happen to them as they journeyed to Remer. Butch could not leave without giving them ample time to reach Remer. Anyway, he did not have any idea where he would go. That was his dilemma, where to go and what to do when he got there. One thing he knew, he could not stay in the Remer area much longer. He knew “they” were looking for him and he was afraid "they" would eventually find him.

Butch was sitting on the porch swing, feeling the loss of his family and his isolation. He stared out through the porch screen at the shimmering lake a hundred feet away. Birds sang and chirped cheerfully in the surrounding trees. Their cheerfulness only added to Butch’s depression. How can they be happy when I am so sad,” he asked himself.

A red squirrel chattered somewhere in the pines nearby and his animal instincts clicked in. His head swiveled to the right and he spotted the critter sitting on a branch, ten feet up in a large Red Pine tree. Butch growled and the squirrel raced for the top of the tree.

Before leaving Woodbury, Butch went to the Wells Fargo Bank and withdrew eighty thousand dollars. He contacted a man at a pawnshop his grandfather took him to once and arranged for forged identification papers to help him change his identity.

The station wagon Butch used to get to Remer, sat in the driveway. The car formerly belonged to a senile old woman, now a resident in the Woodbury Nursing Home. The car registration was still in her name. Butch was sure no one remembered the transaction. Jerrold purchased the auto from the old woman's nephew two months ago and the car sat hidden in a rented garage until Butch took it. There was no way anyone would trace his whereabouts through the car.

When Butch left Afton State Park, he made his way to the garage where the car was stored. From there he drove to Grand Rapids, where he slept in the front seat until morning and then purchased a large supply of groceries. He drove around the countryside all day to see if anyone was following him and then made a dash for the cabin on Little Sand Lake in the dark of the night. Other than his immediate neighbor and Will, no one knew he was here.

Butch decided to give Will seven more days to show up. If he did not show up by then, he would leave. One of the options he was considering was to head for Montana and lose himself in the mountains for a few years.

He gave up hope any of his own pack was still alive. They all knew of this safe house. He figured survivors would have already shown up by now.

Chapter 43
Unanticipated Company

It was two o'clock in the morning. Butch bolted upright in bed. Sweat covered his body and wet pajamas stuck to his chest and arms. "Oh, shit, another dream," he moaned. He swung his legs over the edge of the bed and sat up holding his head. The dream was bad, but he could not remember the details.

He sat for a few minutes until the terror of the dream subsided. He started to lay back down when he felt a calling in his head. A pleading female voice cried out, "I can smell you. Who is in the cabin? Please answer me."

A second female voice blended with the other, "Grandfather, Daddy, are you there?"

Butch was shocked to hear a mental attempt to communicate with him. He could not answer for a few moments. Finally, he found his voice. "This is Butch. Who is out there?" When there was not an immediate answer, he sent with greater force, "Who are you?"

"Oh Butch, thank God. This is Cherrie and I have Coreen with me."

Butch heard muffled sobs.

"Oh, Butch, we are tired. Can we come in?"

Butch tasted the fear emanating from Cherrie, but took no pleasure from the pain telegraphed to him. She sounded very frightened. He said. "Yes, you are safe. Stay where you are and change to your human forms I am coming out to get you."

Butch pulled the blankets off his bed and ran for the front door; Cherrie was already running up the steps in her naked human form. Butch pulled a blanket around her, as she threw herself into his arms and sobbed uncontrollably. Butch hugged her, as tears bunched in the corners of his eyes.

He looked up and saw Coreen appear out of the darkness, standing timidly several feet away. Her eyes were large, reminding him of a deer. She looked as though she would melt back into the bushes at the slightest wrong movement from him. She needed the assurance of the pack leader and safety he was supposed to provide.

"Come here Coreen," Butch whispered.

Butch held out his arm and Coreen raced to him, hugging his waist. She began to sob, her body jerking with pent up grief. A lump grew in Butch's throat, as he fought back his own tears. Now was the time to show his strength. He was still the pack leader. He wrapped her in a sheet.

"Come on, let's go in," Butch said, leading the two girls through the porch and into the living room of the cabin. They would not let go of him. "You guys look like you have had a tough time getting here."

"Oh Butch, it was bad," Coreen said, holding on to his arm with no intention of letting him go and losing him as she lost the rest of her family.

"We are so tired," Cherrie said her voice filled with weariness.

"How did you get here?" Butch said.

Coreen said, "We ran the whole way."

"We traveled in the woods as werewolves," Cherrie said. "We thought it would be dangerous to take one of our cars. We thought whoever killed our parents would still be looking for us."

"You are right," Butch nodded, pulling them toward the kitchen. "Say, I bet you are hungry. Sit down and I will make something for you to eat."

The two girls attacked everything Butch set on the table. After eating for half an hour, the girls slowed down and pushed their chairs back from the table.

Cherrie looked up with sadness, her big brown eyes red from crying. "Is there anyone else alive?" she asked, in a tearful voice.

"Cherrie if anyone from our pack was alive they would have been here by now," Butch sighed. "I was shocked to hear you. I'd given up on the idea that anyone else was alive."

Cherrie carried her dishes over to the sink and then turned, asking, "What are we going to do, Butch? Everyone else is dead and I'm afraid whoever killed them is still looking for us."

Coreen started to cry. "What if they find us?"

"Hey, they are not going to find us. Everything will be all right," Butch said, trying to console them. "I won't let anything happen to you."

Butch got up and took Coreen's hand. "Come on let's go sit by the fireplace," he said, as he led them into the living room.

Butch sat on the sofa with Coreen, holding her close. Cherrie threw a pillow in front of the fireplace and curled up under the blanket Butch had wrapped around her.

The girls poured out their experiences, Cherrie telling Butch how her parents died, and Coreen telling how her brother, George had woke her and told her to get out of the house. He died allowing her time to escape. They went on to tell how they made the hundred and seventy miles trek to Remer, hiding in the forest and eating squirrels and rabbits.

Butch finally shared some of his thoughts for their future. He was concerned how they would survive the search that was taking place for them right now.

Cherrie's eyes were half closed, as a big yawn spread across her face. Butch looked down at Coreen and smiled protectively. She fell asleep on the sofa. "You two need to get some sleep, Butch said. "We'll talk more in the morning."

Butch carried Coreen in a bedroom and tucked her in. He showed Cherrie which room to take and left her with a hug. The digital clock on his nightstand said it was ten minutes after five in the morning.

Butch woke with a start. It was eight o'clock. Scraping noises were coming from the kitchen. Jumping out of bed with a pounding heart, he stopped his movement toward the noises. He remembered the girls were here. One of them was probably up and cleaning his messy kitchen. He stretched his hands over his head, running his fingers through his hair. He put on an old stripped robe that someone had left in the cabin. The odor of toast mingled with the smell of eggs, bacon and butter started his stomach rumbling. He blinked in disbelief as he walked into the kitchen. The table was set and Cherrie was busy standing over the stove.

Cherrie looked up when she heard Butch come into the kitchen. "I couldn't sleep," she said, looking embarrassed.

Halfway through breakfast Coreen stumbled into the kitchen, rubbing sleep from her eyes. "Hey, I'm hungry too."

Cherrie teased. "Too late, Butch ate everything."

"You are teasing me," Coreen said. "I can still smell the food."

After breakfast, everyone got dressed, went out to the screen porch, and sat on the swing. The girls felt the need to talk some more of what happened to them and the rest of the family. Butch listened and seethed, feeling the hatred growing within his mind. He knew nothing would ever be the same again.

Butch tried not to laugh as he listened to Coreen's humorous recollections of journeying through the forest on her way to Remer. It took a few moments before a humming noise penetrated Butch's subconscious mind. He cocked his ears toward the road and focused on a car motor. Butch twitched as he jumped up and stood on tiptoes, ready for action.

He looked out through the porch screen, straining his eyes to see over the top of the bushes out toward the driveway. He spotted a red Ford Escort coming up the driveway. His hearing was sensitive and he heard the tires crunching on the dried pine needles littering the driveway.

Butch grew alarmed. He grabbed Cherrie by her elbow and caught up Coreen's hand, ready to run through the house and out the back door. He squinted and sniffed the air, trying to see or smell who was in the car. His heart pounded in his chest, as he prepared for the change.

"Oh, God, they have found us already," Coreen cried and grabbed onto Butch's arm, fingernails biting into his flesh.

Butch saw two people in the front seat of the car, but they were still too far down the driveway for him to recognize who they were. Light reflecting from the windshield further hampered his vision. Butch pushed the girls into the living room and waited in the doorway. The car pulled to a stop next to his station wagon.

Butch saw the faces of the people in the car. His shoulders relaxed and air rushed from his lungs. It was Will Franzen and his sister. Both stepped out of the car.

"Will," Butch sent mentally. He turned to Cherrie and Coreen, "its okay," he said, before he raced out the screen door and down the steps toward the newcomers.

He ran around the back of his station wagon and threw his arms around Will saying, "Boy am I glad you made it."

A month ago, they were mortal enemies plotting to kill each other, but the truce and recent killings of their packs somehow made Butch consider Will as a brother. The blond female walked over to Will and slipped her arm through his.

"Butch," Will said, "this is my sister, Ann"

Butch turned to the girl and said, "Hi, Ann." He gave her a hug and she returned it with a big sigh. "I was worried you ran into some trouble."

"No, we got out of Madison okay," Ann said, looking into Butch's eyes. "I hope we have left all the killing behind us."

"This is not the end of killing," Butch said, convinced that was a true assessment of the situation. He grabbed Will and Ann by an arm and started to lead them toward the cabin. "Come on, I want you to meet two of my cousins."

"Just a minute," Will said, as he pulled his arm free and walked back to the car. He leaned in the open window and grabbed two bags from the back seat. He jogged to catch up to Butch and Ann. As they mounted the steps leading into the screen porch, Cherrie and Coreen inched out of the living room.

Butch introduced Will and Ann to his cousins.

The five remaining werewolves sat in the living room well into the afternoon, talking of the recent slaughter of their family members. The shedding of a flood of tears and the use of many Kleenex happened before hunger distracted them.

Chapter 44
A Quiet Interlude

Meanwhile, back in St. Paul, Captain Bill Kollecki, Task Force leader of the 'Fur Bearer Squad' was mounting an intensive manhunt. The Task Force knew there were five surviving werewolf member, but had no idea where they might be.

Going through all the data, Bill knew that three Guhl werewolves from Woodbury and two Morsching werewolves from Madison had escaped. The 'Fur Bearer' team from Madison convinced Bill that the two Morsching survivors were no longer in the city. Bill suspected they might have joined forces with the three from Minnesota.

When they first came up with the name of their squad, the Captain thought the name 'Fur Bearer' was appropriate. Now, he was not so sure. If someone outside of the team saw the Task Force's title, how would he explain what it meant?

Bill was afraid the media was digging into the killings and would start to ask the wrong questions. The press accepted the initial report that the killings were drug related.

Bill already sidetracked two reporters who were questioning the drug story. They could find no evidence that Jerrold Guhl, a pillar of Woodbury society and leader of many charities was a drug lord.

Reporters linked the explosion of the Dry Cleaners store owned by Andy & Diana Groschen, in which four people died, to the death of Jerrold Guhl. The St. Paul Pioneer Press was calling for a more intensive investigation. The mayor of Woodbury expressed his concern over the deaths of the Guhl family members. The Guhl families were solid members of his community, and for all of them to die violent deaths deserved a much deeper investigation.

Until now, the Task Force was able to cover up any suggestion that the law enforcement community was involved in any of the deaths, but the media was asking specific questions. All it would take is for one small piece of evidence to point to a police officer and the public would soon learn the secret Kollecki was trying to hide.

All of the Fur Bearer Task Force's efforts were devoted to finding the five survivors. Once they were disposed of, things would quiet down and in a few months, anything about the Guhl and Morsching families would be old news. Bill was hampered in his search by the fact his Task Force could not use the normal police channels to track down the fugitives.

He knew if he asked for help from other agencies, someone would learn of the existence of werewolves. Getting other agencies involved would elicit questions he would rather not have to answer. Members of the Task Force begin to visit town after town, showing a few pictures around and asking if anyone saw the fugitives. They knew who was still alive. It was just a matter of time before they would find them.

Bill's search teams were frustrated. It was as though the five remaining werewolves vanished, at least from Minnesota and Wisconsin. In spite of the difficulty his teams were experiencing, Captain Kollecki was a patient man. He knew the five werewolves were out there, somewhere. He knew eventually that a break would come his way. When it did, he would gather the Task Force and end the chapter on werewolves in the United States for good.

"I'm getting tired of sitting around this stupid cabin," Coreen grumbled. She threw the remains of a glass of water back into the sink, some of the water splashed up the side and on the counter top.

"Well," Butch said, "what do you want to do?" He was tired of listening to an immature, thirteen year old pout. He was ready to close his mind to any further whining. She had complained constantly for the last three days.

"I wanna go home," Coreen cried. "I want to hang out with my friends and do fun things again." She plopped down on the sofa in a sprawl.

"I'm sick of your constant complaining. Why don't you just go ahead and go home," Butch said, throwing his hands into the air. He was tired of explaining why she could not go back to the Twin Cities.

"Can I really?" Coreen said.

"Sure, why not," Butch said, "If that is what you want to do. I will even give the police a call and let them know you are coming. That way, it won't take them as long to find you and do to you what they did to your family."

"Coreen started to cry. "You don't care what happens to me," she sobbed. Tears rolled down her round cheeks and her eyes got all puffy.

Cherrie glared at Butch, "That's cruel, Butch. " She walked over to Coreen, and put her arms around her shoulders.

Butch relented, letting his anger go. "Coreen, I'm sorry. I care what happens to you, really I do," he tried to explain. "But, I'm tired of listening to your whining all the time, about going home. You know darn well we cannot ever do that, ever."

"Ah, Butch," Cherrie said, patting Coreen on the back. "She knows we cannot go home, but that doesn't stop her from missing her friends and all the things she used to do."

Cherrie sat on the edge of the couch holding Coreen in her arms. She rubbed Coreen's back and rocked her back and forth, like a baby. "Coreen," Cherrie said. "You need to stop talking about things that can never be. You need to work with Butch and the rest of us, that way we can all stay alive. Remember, those government people killed our parents and relatives. And you know they are still out there searching for us."

Butch grinned sheepishly and walked over to the couch. "I'm sorry Coreen." He gave her a pat on the back and then walked out on the porch.

Butch looked through the screen at the sunbeams lighting up the green grass beneath the trees. He felt the outdoors tugging at him and decided to take a walk. With hands in his pockets and head down, watching the ground in front of his feet, he followed the worn trail down to the edge of the lake.

Stepping up on the weathered dock, he walked to the end of the L-shaped section and gazed across the water at the row of brown cabins on the far shore. Little Sand Resort, people were swimming, screaming and splashing around, seemingly without a care in the world. His eyes telescoped on two shapely women throwing a beach ball back and forth in front of the cabins.

Under different circumstances, he would have gone over to check them out, but now, he merely turned and looked down the lake. On the far end, he spotted two fishing boats. From this distance, the people looked like stick mannequins, perched on the edge of their boats holding matchsticks over the water.

Butch wondered if he would ever be able to live a normal life again. "Where would he and his pack eventually end up? For all that, would he even survive to see next summer," he asked himself.

The next morning, Ann and Butch were sitting together on the porch swing, while Will and Cherrie finished the dishes.

Coreen bounced out to the porch and said in her high-pitched voice, "Butch, I'm going to go for a walk."

Butch nodded with a smile. He watched her skip cheerfully down the steps onto the driveway and head toward the old abandoned cabin near the county road. The old cabin kept people from seeing Butch's cabin behind it. Driving in off the county road, the driveway appeared to end at the old cabin, but it did not. A grassy track continued around the old cabin and ended at Butch's safe house.

Butch glanced at Ann, who was looking at the lake. Lately, exciting thoughts about her went through his mind. She was beautiful, mature for her age and when she walked by, Butch could not help but watch. Butch did not know how to let her know he was interested in her.

He shook his head. Maybe this was not the time to start a romance. Next year Ann would have been a high school junior. Now she would not get that chance. He rationalized she might appreciate having something else on her mind besides death and fear.

Butch wanted to ask Ann to go to a movie with him. He squirmed on the porch swing, trying to screw up enough courage to ask her. Finally, he just blurted it out. "Ann, would you go to a movie with me tonight?"

Ann turned to look at Butch with a shy smile on her face and a faint blush colored her cheeks. "Yes, I would like that very much."

She stood saying, “I will tell the others we are going to the movies tonight.”

“No, don’t do that. I meant, just the two of us . . . to go,” Butch blushed and could not look at her. Boy, he thought, I am a pack leader. I should not be afraid to talk to her.

“Oh, I thought. . . ”, was all Ann could say, as her face colored even a deeper crimson.

Suddenly, Butch’s face switched from a smile to a look of sheer agony. He slapped his hands over his ears and jumped up from the swing. His mind filled with a scream from Coreen.

Chapter 45
Opposition Destroyed

"BUTCH, BUTCH, a car just turned into our driveway and it's going around the old cabin. There are five men in the car, they smell angry and afraid."

"Where are you?" Butch thought, frightened for her welfare.

"I'm okay. I am hiding in the bushes by the side of the road. They did not see me. Those men smell bad, Butch. Watch out."

"Good job Coreen," Butch sent to her. He was proud of how calmly Coreen sounded and how responsibly she acted.

Ann grabbed Butch's arm when he suddenly jumped up. The frightened look on his face alarmed her. "Butch, what's the matter?" she said.

Cherrie heard Coreen's mind message and came running onto the porch, followed by a bewildered looking Will. Cherrie fist flew to her mouth as she said, "Butch, what should we do?"

Butch raised a hand for Cherrie to stop. He realized by the look on Will and Ann's faces that they did not hear Coreen's warning and didn't know what was going on. He turned to Will and Ann. "A car full of men just turned into our driveway. Coreen spotted them and sent me a mental message," Butch explained.

"Who are they?" Will said, with a puzzled look on his face, but already knowing the answer to his question.

Butch looked at Will with a weird smile on his face. "Killers are coming, but they do not realize they are about to become victims," and then his face turned serious. "Will and Cherrie I want you to change and get into the woods above the garage. Ann and I will head for the woods by the lake."

Butch dashed out of the porch and sprinted behind some bushes, followed closely by Ann. They both initiated their changes. Butch felt a satisfying, pleasurable crunch and ripple pass through his body. In a matter of minutes, two werewolves stood among a clump of hazel bushes. One was big with a reddish tint highlighting his brown fur.

The other was two-thirds the size of the bigger one, possessing light brown fur. Their mouths hung partially open exposing long upper and lower canine teeth.

Ann growled, freeing herself of any last restraints. Butch answered. The killing urge was equally strong in both of them. Butch was angry these men dared to invade his territory and yet, happy at last to shed the feeling of being afraid they might find them. They were here and he was glad.

Ann could see how agitated Butch was. "Butch control yourself," she said.

Butch instantly brought the animal side under control. He crouched down and watched a dark blue Jeep through a screen of trees and bushes. The Jeep stopped fifty feet from the garage. He watched them carefully study the cabin. Finally, the car doors opened and the five men piled out. They hurried to the back of the Jeep and one of them opened the hatch door. One of the men passed shotguns to the others.

Next, a man with red hair handed each man a bandoleer of shotgun shells.

"They are well armed, Cherrie," Butch mentally broadcast to her. "Coreen, I want you to change into your werewolf form after we leave. Then move up next to the garage. Hide in the bushes. If any of them return to the Jeep, kill them. Can you do that?"

"You bet I can, after what they did to my parents and the rest of the pack," she said in Butch's mind.

"Watch out, Cherrie," Butch said. "They are coming around the garage towards you and Will."

"We see them," Cherrie said. "How do you want to handle this?"

"Our best chance is to lure them deeper into the woods," Butch said. "I want you and Will to make some noise, let them see you, then head north through the woods. They will follow you. Ann and I will follow behind them. Coreen are you still there?"

"Yes, but I'm scared."

Butch knew by the quivering in her mental message she was frightened. He was sorry he could not go to her, but they needed to destroy the men first, "Don't take any chances," he told her. "Keep a close lookout and let me know if anyone else shows up. Stay alert. We are going to lure the men deep into the woods and kill them. Will you be okay?"

"Yes, I will be okay." After a moments hesitation she said, "Butch, will you hurt them bad for me. Hurt them for killing my parents."

"Yeah, we'll hurt them," Butch promised. A growl low in his throat reinforced his words. "We will hurt them real bad."

Three of the agents circled toward the back of the house, making enough noise to put a pack of elephants to shame. One of them stepped on a brittle oak branch, which cracked with a resounding snap.

Another agent pushed through a clump of hazel brush, setting up a rattling of leaves and twigs slapping against each other. They did a good job of announcing their presence.

Will waited until he saw two of the agents thirty yards from him, then he ran through a circle of hazel brush, making as much noise as he could. Cherrie swung to Will's left and ran parallel to him. She deliberately stepped on any twigs or branches lying in her path.

Three agents heard and then saw the two werewolves running away. The werewolves appeared and disappeared through openings in the undergrowth. One of the men raised his shotgun, pointed in the general direction of Will and pulled the trigger. The buckshot whistled five feet behind Will, mowing a path through the brush.

Another agent yelled excitedly into his radio. "Hey Rob and Hal, get your asses up here. We just spotted two of the werewolves. They are heading north. We are fifty yards behind the cabin."

Agent Mike Fallon ran at an angle away from the lake. He saw a flash of a single werewolf at the same time as the Chief was yelling for Rob and Hal to come toward him. Mike flicked the button on his walkie-talkie, "Christ Chief, the bastard is running on his hind legs. He is just ahead of me. My God, he sure is big," Mike stopped, looked around and listened.

A wave of panic spread through his body. A shocked expression crawled across his face when he did not see or hear any of his team.

"Where are you guys?" he screamed into his mike. "I'm not moving until I know where you are," he cried.

Hal saw Mike fifty feet ahead of him and crashed through the brush toward him shouting, "Don't be such a coward, Mike."

Mike swore and said, "You wouldn't be so brave if you saw one of them running toward you."

Hal flashed by Mike saying, "Come on, let's get em."

A few moments later the Chief held his walkie-talkie to his flushed lips and panted," "Hurry up, I have got a couple of them just ahead of me."

"Chief this is Rick. Where the hell are you?"

"I'm a hundred and fifty yards from the lake and maybe a half mile north of the cabin," the Chief said into his mike, between breaths. Hurry up, we need to stick together."

Rick shrugged his shoulders. "Chief that doesn't do me a lot of good," he said. "I'm not very good at this boy scout stuff. I do not know if I am ahead of you or behind you. Yell a few times and then I will head for your voice. That's the only way I will find you."

The Chief sputtered and swore to himself and then finally realized it really was not such a bad idea. "Over here. I'm over here," he yelled.

It took a minute before Rick followed by Rob and Mike came crashing through the brush and stopped next to the Chief. Hal stumbled in from the opposite direction and dropped to his knees, blowing like a floundering horse. Rick and Mike looked at Hal and laughed. Rob grabbed Hal under the arm and lifted him to his feet.

The Chief shook his head. "We have to stay in sight of each other or someone is going to get lost or worse," he said. "I want you guys to fan out on each side of me, forty yards apart. Stay even with me and we will push them along the lake. If you see them yell out."

Hal and Rob quickly took the lakeside, that way they would not be as apt to get lost. Mike and Rick took off deeper into the woods. The Chief was in the middle.

Hal walked within thirty yards of the lake and felt sure he could find his way back to the county road if he needed to. He looked away from the lake and spotted Rob bending and dodging the brush. A minute later, he caught a glimpse of the Chief. Hal thought he was doing a good job of staying in a straight line. Hal picked up his pace when he notice Rob was getting ahead of him.

"Okay. Butch," Cherrie mind spoke. "Will and I have them spread out and following us. Where are you?"

"We are fifty yards behind them, Butch said. "Listen; if I remember right, you should be coming to a bunch of evergreen trees soon. When you see them, veer off to the northeast. Let them get a glimpse of you, that should entice them to keep following you," he said.

The woods around Butch were a mix of dark-green Spruce, Birch and Trembling Aspen. He inhaled deeply, smelling the resinous pitch from the evergreens, mixed with the smell of dying algae from the lake. He ran swiftly on all four legs, followed closely by Ann. Butch increased his speed and closed the distance with the agents. When they were thirty yards behind them, Butch slowed.

The agents made a lot of noise, making it easy to follow them. Occasionally he saw one of them and then a different one. At least he did not have to worry that a couple of them would drop back and ambush him.

"Cherrie, are you close to the open field," Butch mind communicated.

"Yes, I see an opening just ahead," she telegraphed.

"Good, this is it," Butch snickered. "Cross to the other side of the field. Make sure they get a glimpse of you before you disappear through the spruces. Then I want you to double back and get ready to ambush them. Be prepared to attack them when they get half way across the field. Ann and I will attack from their backside. Wait for my signal."

"Message understood," Cherrie said. "I will tell Will. We'll wait for your signal."

Will and Cherrie ran swiftly across the short grassy field. Under different circumstances, Cherrie would have stopped to enjoy the yellow coneflowers with their dark brown buttons surrounded by yellow petals. They grew in bunches among the tall stalks of grass.

She cut around a Jack Pine growing alone in the center of the field. Just as Will and Cherrie reached the far side, the Chief stumbled into the clearing.

"Hey, there they are," the Chief yelled. He raised the shotgun to his shoulder and squeezed off two rounds at the loping, shaggy beasts. He knew he missed them, as they disappeared into the trees on the far side of the clearing.

Rick and Mike burst out of the bushes behind the Chief in time to catch a fleeting glimpse of the werewolves before they disappeared.

Hal and Rob crashed out into the field puffing like a couple of locomotives and saw nothing. Hal bent over with his shotgun across his knees, puffing hard, trying to catch his breath. Rob dropped to his knees and raised his head to catch as much air as possible.

Hal looked over at the Chief and said, "Where are they?"

The Chief gave him a disgusted look before replying, "They just disappeared on the other side of the field. Come on, let's go."

Hal just lifted his head and wheezed.

The Chief took off across the field yelling back, "We are gaining on them,"

The other agents followed the Chief. Hal looked around. The silence was too much for him; he jumped up and raced after the others. He jogged across the open field holding his left side.

As soon as Will and Cherrie made it through the evergreens, they cut sharply to the left, dropped to all fours and crept back toward the edge of the open field. They lay down underneath a spruce tree and belly crawled up behind a thin shield of flowers and tall grass overlooking the field. They watched the agents run across the field towards them and waited.

The five agents spread out as they ran across the field. They hopped into the air to clear the tall grasses that caught their feet and slowed them down.

Cherrie grew nervous with anticipation. The agents were only fifty feet from the spruce tree where they were hiding. "Butch they are getting kind of close," she thought.

"We see them," Butch said. "We have reached the field.

Get them, now," Butch screamed.

All five agents in front of Butch heard him yell. The agents skidded to a stop and swiveled around.

Will's muscles bunched, as he leapt forward following Cherrie, who charged out ahead of him. He surged to catch up and they flashed across the timothy grass and flowers, eating up the fifty feet between the two closest agents in a matter of a few seconds.

Butch took the lead, bursting into the open field. Ann sleek and graceful easily pulled up alongside of him. They rapidly closed with the agents. Butch launched his body through the air with a blood-curdling howl coming from his open mouth.

At the same time, Will and Cherrie hit the agents from the other side. All of the agents were facing Butch when he entered the open field. At the last second, Chief and Rick heard a noise behind them and whirled back with surprised looks on their faces, aware too late; they had walked into an ambush.

Nevertheless, they brought their shotguns up quickly and fired. They did not have time to aim or adjust for the speed the werewolves were traveling and the buckshot went over the heads of the two beasts.

Butch's front legs slammed into Hal's chest, driving him backwards through the air. Hal landed on the ground with Butch on top of him. Butch reached down with his fangs and surgically ripped out Hal's carotid arteries and windpipe. Hal's eyes froze, large and glassy. He tried to scream, but he no longer possessed a voice box. His eyes merely blinked shut and glazed over.

To Butch's right, Ann slammed into Rob, sending him flying through the air. He hit the ground on his back; air whooshed out of his lungs. He lost his grip on the shotgun, which tumbled harmlessly through the grass. Rob gasped for air. Ann jumped on his stomach and shoved her muzzle towards his throat. Rob used his arms like swords, as he tried to fend off her darting, sharp fangs. She was in such a killing frenzy, moving with superhuman speed and strength. She pushed his arms out of the way and clamped her jaws down on his exposed throat.

The flesh in Rob's neck ripped like the sound of tearing fabric. The tender flesh pulled loose in one chunk. Blood spurted from his carotid arteries, shooting several feet through the air. Drops of blood splashed into Ann's face. She stood sprawled over his convulsing body and calmly licked the fresh blood from her muzzle.

Will reached Rick and rose up on his hind legs. He grabbed the agent by his shoulder and yanked. The shoulder joint separated with a bone crunching pop. Rick screamed. Rick and Will's intertwined bodies landed with a thud on the field's grassy carpet. Will raked his hind feet along the stomach of the agent, shredding clothes and flesh with each kick. Rick started to scream and never stopped.

His eyes rolled up so only the whites were showing. With his last conscious thought and effort, Rick brought his 45 automatic up. Even with the spasmodic jerking of his body, Rick was able to place the barrel against Will's back and pull the trigger repeatedly. The bullets tore through Will's spine and continued inward to shatter his heart. Rick and Will died together.

Cherrie threw her body at the feet of the Chief causing him to crash over like a bowling pin. She spun and thrust her muzzle into his groin. She clamped down and jerked her head violently to the side. Fabric and flesh parted, joined by a high-pitched scream.

"OH God, help me," the Chief yelled. The pain was so excruciating he lost consciousness, but that did not stop Cherrie from ripping his testicles free and then reaching up and tearing out his heart.

Special Agent Mike Cottley stood unmoving, surrounded by three werewolves, his gun hanging lifelessly at his side. It did not cross Mike's mind to resist, he knew he was already dead.

"Please don't kill me," Mike pleaded. "I won't tell anyone you killed the other agents. Let me go, please." The fear within him was so great, that Butch whined with ecstasy. The man lost control of his bladder and a wet flow of urine ran down his right leg.

Butch said, "Cherrie, kill him for what they did to your parents."

A week later, Captain Bill Kollecki, received information that one of his agent's cars turned up in Longville, Minnesota. Police

Chief, Dan Robertson wanted Bill to explain this to him. Captain Kollecki told him, “Very likely they are dead.”

The Chief's face paled, “Make sure you cover this up. People in Longville cannot handle anymore killing.”

Captain Bill Kollecki was not surprised the car showed up in Longville, after all, this was where it all began last October. The way his brain worked, it all made sense now. Bill believed the werewolves were in a hideout in the Longville area. As discreetly as possible, he concentrated the rest of his agents in the Longville area. Instructions were to search the surrounding country for the werewolf lair and not to come back until they found it.

Chapter 46
Sanctuary

Butch, Cherrie, Coreen and Ann, buried Will and the dead agents in the field where they died. Butch knew Ann was depressed over her brother's death even though she tried to hide her sorrow. Butch was especially attentive to her, which was not very hard to do. He was very fond of her and thought she felt the same way about him.

One night, a week after Will's death, the four remaining werewolves sat in the living room around the fireplace. A fire sent yellow-blue flames up the chimney and heat into the room. It was quiet. They stared at the flickering flames each lost in thoughts of their own. Some thought of those who died. Others wondered what was going to happen to them. They knew they would have to leave this sanctuary and find a better one. If one group of agents found them, others could do the same.

Butch and Ann moved to the sofa. He looked into her eyes and then took her hand in his. "It is time to make plans for our future and the future of our kind," he said.

Cherrie and Coreen turned from the flickering flames with quizzical expressions on their faces. The flames represented what happened to their packs. They were born, flourished and died. What saddened Butch most was the thought that this might be the end of their kind. Would the remaining four of them end up like the ashes in a dead fireplace?

"What kind of plans?" Coreen face lit up with an idea and she said, "Are we going home?"

"No, I am afraid not Coreen," Cherrie said, biting her lip, her fist pushing it into her mouth. "We cannot ever go home, honey."

"I know, but I still miss everything I used to have."

"We cannot stay in the cabin any longer," Butch said. "They'll just keep coming for us. Next time enough agents will come and they'll be better prepared."

Cherrie's face started to glow, the edges of her eyes crinkled. One of her dreams was to live free in the beautiful Rocky Mountains. "Why don't we go live in the mountains, maybe in Wyoming or Montana," she said.

"We could do that," Butch said. "We have more than enough money hidden away in secret accounts to do anything we want. The only problem I see with doing that now is we will attract too much attention. If we try to buy land, a house or a car, at our ages, people will question where four teenagers got all that money. I do not want to have to explain anything to anyone. When they start asking question, they are going to want to know where our parents are, what do we say then? Another problem with Montana, it is too far. Maybe when we are older we can go there."

"Well, then let's just go live in the woods," Coreen suggested angrily, her lips sticking out in a pout. She was still angry with Butch for knocking her idea of going back to the Twin Cities.

"I agree with Coreen," Butch said. "We could easily live deep in the forest. We would not draw attention to ourselves and no one would be able to find us. Food would not be a problem with all the wildlife that lives there. The place I am thinking of is so isolated no one should bother us. We. . . ."

"Butch, I was just kidding. I don't want to live in the woods," Coreen cried. "We won't have any television or ice cream. I don't like my idea at all."

"No, Coreen," Ann said thoughtfully. She moved from the sofa and stood in front of the fireplace. "That is the only option we have. Like Butch said, at least until we are older, then we can move somewhere else and begin a new life among the humans again."

Cherrie thought about what they said. "I guess you guys are right. Where will we go?"

"I know of a real isolated spot not far from here, where we will be safe. Four years ago, I canoed up in the Boundary Waters Canoe Area. The place is isolated and has several packs of wolves to cover our tracks and activities. We could blend in." He grinned and then looked playfully at Coreen. "Coreen, you have always wanted me to take you to the Boundary Waters. Well here is your chance. What do you say?"

"Yippee," Coreen said.

Ann frowned, "We could do the same in Montana, couldn't we?"

"Sure we could, Ann, Butch said, "but the B. W. C. A. is much closer."

Ann nodded, "Yah, you are right."

Epilogue

Hard crusty patches of snow lay on the north-facing slope of a secluded cliff, deep in the Boundary Waters Canoe Area. Rocky crags jutted high over the trees, looking down on Rose Lake far below. Half way up the inner curve of the cliff, a rocky ledge slanted into the air blocking the cave entrance from view.

Swirling air currents carried the smell of spring to the cave. It would not be long before the buds on the Aspens below would break out of their dormant state and the white of winter disappear for a short warm interlude.

The sun's rays played on patches of water below, sending splashes of light reflecting back against the rocks and into the cave. Behind the curved uplifted rock blocking the cave entrance, a yelping noise made its way to the opening. Inside, three female werewolves were playfully communicating with each other. Fresh dried grass littered the floor of the cave insulating it from the cold rock beneath.

The blond werewolf playfully nipped the ear of the younger dark black female, who in turn poked the hazel colored female with a sharp-pointed claw. Cherrie's reflex action caused her to jump with a yip. Finally, the three females settled down, lying quietly on the grass.

Two of them rolled over to lie on their sides. The larger female werewolf displayed a large extended stomach. Within the week, she would each bear a litter of 'pups'.

Restlessly, Ann the blonder of the three female werewolves rose clumsily on four legs and waddled slowly toward Butch sitting on his haunches at the mouth of the cave. Butch's ears perked up and his head swiveled toward her movement as she approached. Most of his attention was on the forest below. Intrigued by the movement of three deer along a trail at the base of the cliff, Butch watched them until they disappeared.

Ann nudged him, affectionately with her muzzle. Butch's mouth dropped open, showing his canine teeth. He leaned over to lick the silken fur on the side of her face. He projected his thoughts to her, “This isn’t such a bad life, is it Ann?”

“I have enjoyed my time here,” she said.

Butch thought, “With the birth of our pup, our pack will survive.”

Printed in the United States
141422LV00001B/4/P